A CAINE & FERRARO MYSTERY ROMANCE

DISARMING CAINE

JANET OPPEDISANO

Disarming Caine

ISBN Digital: 978-1-7778856-4-9
ISBN Paperback: 978-1-7778856-5-6

For everyone who's gone out on a limb
and spoken what was in their heart

FREE NOVELLA

To instantly receive the free romantic suspense novella *The Phoenix Heist*, with cameos by Samantha and Antonio and introducing the Reynolds Recoveries heist crew, claim your copy at

https://janetoppedisano.com/ThePhoenixHeist

CHAPTER 1

SAMANTHA

A GUST of frigid air bit at my cheeks and ears, sending me deeper into my thick jacket. The Midwest was damn cold in December. That or six winters in Texas and southern California had made me soft.

Probably both.

I heaved open the heavy glass door of Mason's Gallery and hauled it shut behind me, grateful to be out of the wind.

The door chime sounded my arrival, and a sharp female voice responded from the back room, "Is that you, Samantha?"

"It is."

The floors and walls were all painted white, providing a perfect canvas for the vibrant paintings and the sculptures on their simple stands. The artwork in the front room differed from the last time I'd visited. Still all abstract pieces with vivid colors and whimsical imagery, but only one I recognized.

Number Vee—a color field work of three stripes, light, medium, and dark blue—stood out from all the others, but more for the memories it evoked than its artistry. It had been my first art claim since contracting as a claims adjuster with Foster Mutual Insurance, I'd gone on the worst date of my life with its clueless artist, Cam-ron Parker, and it was the first repair Dr. Antonio Ferraro worked on for me.

The heels of my tall boots clicked as I strode across the gallery's main room, gravitating toward *Number Vee*. In the intense sunlight streaming through the floor to ceiling windows, I inspected the painting from the front and either side. Antonio's repair was as invisible under this light as it had been at the Ferraro's studio four months ago.

My boyfriend was so talented. So brilliant. So stunningly handsome.

And so, so far away.

"I'm in the office," came the voice. "Were you planning on joining me or were you just going to stare at paintings all day?"

I bit back a chuckle and cast a glance at the security camera embedded in the ceiling Rhonda was likely watching me from. Rhonda Wells, the gallery's owner, was a no-nonsense middle-aged woman who had a past beyond the borders of small-town Brenton, Michigan. I didn't know what it was, but there was a story there.

All she'd say when she called was that she had something *up my alley*. Her tone had me rushing over with a couple of hours to spare before my first Saturday site visit.

I'd met her in August when I was investigating an insur-ance claim for a burned painting which was purportedly by Marc Chagall. In the end, I—with both some help and hindrance from Antonio—determined it was a fake and that the fire was an arson covering up a murder. We'd also visited her to discuss a stolen painting he and I discovered at a charity gala that month.

Hopefully, that was the alley she was talking about.

"Be right there." I gave one last glance at *Number Vee*, searching for a sign of where Antonio had patched up the tear. Even knowing where it was, I couldn't see it.

As if on cue, my phone buzzed in the distinctive notification pattern I set for his texts. I slipped it out of my pocket to see what he had to say.

Are you free?

Warmth pooled in my belly from the near-contact with him. He'd been in Naples for the last three months, leading a small conservation team on a project at the Pompeii Archaeological Park.

Not breaking my stride, I texted, *Sorry, working.*

Before the phone was back in my pocket, it buzzed again. *I need to talk to you.*

I'm working. I'll call when I'm done. So my words didn't seem too harsh, I sent a kissing face emoji, which was greeted by the same. I stuffed the phone into my pocket. We'd spent an hour on a video chat first thing that morning. What was so urgent?

Rounding a corner into the second room of the small local art gallery, I trailed my eyes over the realist paintings. These were more my style, even the one I also knew was Camron's.

Rhonda's office door at the back was painted white to match the walls. When it was closed, patrons would barely notice, but it was wide open and tugging at my curiosity.

She sat in front of a computer at a small desk in the cramped space. A slight woman who spiked her short white hair and always dressed in head-to-toe black, the only color I ever saw on her was the pop of red from her glasses. She gestured to the coatrack by the door, then the chair across from her. "Thank you for coming so quickly."

"Your call certainly piqued my interest." I hung up my things and we shook hands before I sat. "What can I do for you?"

Her gaze returned to her computer monitor. "My daughter's in the market for a new house."

Not the start I was expecting. Maybe she was looking for my opinion as an insurance adjuster?

"I was doing some early scouting of listings which open soon and got a little carried away in the search." Rhonda swiveled her monitor to show me the realty listing for a fairly expensive residence in Brenton. My phone buzzed with a link she'd sent me to the realty site. "But what really interested me was a photo of the master bedroom, where I glimpsed a rather fascinating painting. Loose brushwork, soft visuals, English countryside, late 18th century. The photo didn't capture the entire piece, but I zoomed in. From what I could see of the signature, I'm sure it was a John Constable."

I tapped the link on my phone and scrolled through photos until I was on the master bedroom.

"One of my high-end sales art clients had expressed interest in purchasing a Constable. I dropped by the house yesterday to ask if I could see it. If I was right, I'd test the waters in case they might want to sell. But they claimed I was mistaken. No such painting in the house, they said."

Flipping through the bedroom photos, nothing stood out. I leaned toward her monitor. "Why are you telling me all this?"

"It was hanging behind their bedroom door. Not in a place of prominence, but in the shadows."

I scanned the room in the realty photo. King-size bed, simple frame, chair by a large window, and a dresser with mirrors on top. The mirrors reflected the photographer standing in the doorway and a foot-wide slice of a painting peeking out from behind the door. Odd place to hang something as prestigious as a Constable.

"I'm not new to the art business, Samantha. I know what this is."

"So why call me?"

"As much as I suspect things aren't on the up-and-up based on their reaction, I have nothing concrete. The police wouldn't listen to me. But after your performance at the auction and with the fake Chagall this summer, you can do something about it."

"Possibly." More like 'Damn right.' My stomach was already doing cartwheels while my brain ran through possibilities. Why would they chase her off instead of just clearing things up? Forgery? Stolen property? If there was one illicit painting, were there others?

I hadn't had a good art crime to sink my teeth into since I visited Antonio in Naples three months ago. We'd caught a trio responsible for stealing relics from Pompeii. But with only two of the four items recovered, we were left with more questions than answers afterward. Where did the other pieces disappear to? Who transported the pieces out of the city? With no solid leads, it hadn't amounted to anything.

"They didn't let you in at all?"

She shook her head.

I'd have to look at it myself. Get some photos. Compare it against the stolen artwork databases. I returned my focus to the listing on my phone, holding it up in front of me, and took a few screenshots. Zoomed in and took more.

Rhonda hummed quietly. "Should I be offering congratulations?"

I lowered the phone to look at her. "For what?"

"You certainly did not have that ring when you were here in August."

I turned over my left hand, which held the phone, and the diamonds in the white gold band sparkled, diving over and under the other white gold and black ceramic bands of the trinity ring. "No congratulations. It's just a promise ring."

The memory of Antonio surprising me with a ring exchange before I left Naples returned warmth into my chest. But I was working. Not focusing on him or his rare show of insecurity when he opened the box with a ring for each of us. 'Hopeless romantic,' he'd called himself.

"Quite the promise." She leaned closer, peering over her red glasses. "Let me guess... If I recall, Dr. Ferraro the younger seemed to have his eye—"

"Do you have a name?" The ring had started a lot of conversations since I got home—not to mention the blow up from my sister and family—but I put an end to every one of them. My private life was private, no matter who I chose to be with, nor how blatantly he liked to wear his heart on his sleeve.

"For?"

"The house owner."

She sat up straighter, a grin spreading across her face, likely accepting that I wasn't about to spill romantic stories. "No. The woman was polite, but her boyfriend was a jackass, even when I told him they could be sitting on a gold mine."

"The house sale doesn't open until January third." I put

my phone away and drummed my fingers on the chair's armrest. "I'll see what I can find out."

"I had a feeling." She stood and held out a hand to shake. "Let me know if I'm right."

"Definitely." I collected my things and walked out through the gallery with her.

She pointed out a few new paintings as we went and I nodded politely at each. We rounded the dividing wall into the front room and one caught my eye.

I paused, taking it in. A broad sweep of black paint swirling around the top, flecked with pastel drops which reminded me of stars. Below, a field of dark blue sliced through with pale green like the crest of a wave. It brought back memories of Naples—of the view of Vesuvius at night above the bay from the restaurant balcony where Antonio and I had...

A car slowed on the street outside the tall front windows. Not pulling over, just slowing.

Window rolling down.

The hairs on my neck stood up as trained instincts took over.

Step one: Observe.

Rhonda continued walking through the gallery room, not noticing I'd stopped.

The driver's arm stretched out of the window.

Step two: Orient.

The driver wore a balaclava over their face. Common in winter in these parts, but not when driving.

The shape and size were male.

In his hand. A gun.

The car moved slowly. Gun pointed inside the gallery.

Maybe at Rhonda, maybe not.

Step three: Decide.

The front room of the gallery was a large, open space. There was a sculpture stand ten feet beyond Rhonda. Too far.

She was still moving. No way to grab her and reverse course to get behind the dividing wall.

He aimed slightly upward. The floor was the safest bet.

Step four: React.

"Rhonda!" I yelled and propelled myself toward her.

She turned, eyes and mouth wide.

At the same moment I tackled her, the first crack sounded. It was dampened by the thick pane of glass. A whiz of air passed us. And a dull thud.

We crashed to the floor, me on top of her. I tried rolling us toward the stand.

I barely heard the next crack over her scream in my ear, accompanied by shattering glass. The weight of the front window collapsing in hit us like a wave of sound. But I kept her pinned and covered, wrapping arms around my head.

I looked up. A puff of dust floated in front of the wall where she'd been standing, five feet from the floor. I'd rolled us almost to the statue.

The gunshots continued. The second window blew in. The freezing air struck me.

Restart the cycle.

One: Observe.

I tipped my head, looking through my braced arm.

The gun was back in the car, window going up. The car picked up speed.

I launched off the floor and flew out the empty window frame, glass crunching underfoot. I ripped my phone out of my pocket and charged into the middle of the street, taking a video of the car that was already a block away. Zoomed in as much as I could.

A woman grabbed me, asking if I was alright, pulling me to the sidewalk. "Did you see what happened?" she yelled.

My attention snapped to her, and a gust of cold air traveled straight down my jacket, along my spine.

"Call 9-1-1!" I raced back inside, through the small crowd already forming.

CHAPTER 2
SAMANTHA

RHONDA AND I STOOD SIDE-BY-SIDE, next to the large table at the back of her office.

Staring.

Number Vee lay on the table, a perfectly circular hole through the medium blue stripe.

"You know, Samantha," said Rhonda through a clenched jaw. "I came to Brenton ten years ago, looking for a slower life than the one I lived in New York. No more Fashion Weeks, magazine spreads, or people with more money than actual taste. No sirens at three in the morning. Peace and quiet."

I nodded.

"This town's changed over the last year."

I'd moved back in the summer after being gone for six years, and I'd heard many times about the uptick in crime. Little things like shoplifting, graffiti, and break-ins for the most part. But things like this and Bobby Scott's murder were a whole other level. They were not the Brenton I knew.

"Sammy!" came an urgent voice behind me. I didn't have to recognize Brenton Police Officer Jimmy Slater's voice to know it was him. My old friend from college was the only one who ever called me Sammy.

I turned toward the door of Rhonda's office, and he came to an abrupt halt. His normally happy-go-lucky face was ashen, and his hat was crooked.

Panic etched his features, quickly softening when our eyes met. "You're alright?"

"We're both alright." I cast a backward glance at Rhonda, who hadn't turned from the painting. Voices floated in from the front of the gallery and a whizzing noise started, like the sound of a drill. "Forensics arrived?"

He nodded. "I would have gotten here sooner, but I was working a—never mind, that's not important. I'm just glad no one got hurt."

"An officer already interviewed us." I had another appointment to get to. Had to call Antonio back. Had to file the First Notice of Loss for *Number Vee* with Foster Mutual Insurance. Had to schedule an appointment with Ferraro's Fine Art Restoration and Conservation to get it repaired.

Had to...

I blew out a slow breath, steadying myself. "Can we go?"

Jimmy straightened his hat and pushed it back on his forehead, framing the early gray at his temples. "Yeah, I can take you out."

"I'm staying," said Rhonda.

"You sure? The forensics team will be here for a while and it's awfully loud."

"No one scares me off my property." She shifted her gaze away from *Number Vee*, a steel showing through her delicate features. "Besides, I have to make some calls about repairs, apparently. And to my other insurance companies."

"I'll come pick up the painting once the police are done with it."

She nodded and squeezed my arm, whispering, "Thank you."

I patted her hand and left with Jimmy.

"This town's going to hell in a handbasket, I tell ya." He rolled his shoulders as we walked, some of the usual spring returning to his step. "Good thing we got the Brenton PD around."

"Any hits on the video I sent?" I asked as we rounded the corner into the front room. It was even more crowded than when I'd left it with Rhonda and the painting, and definitely colder. The glass of the two huge windows carpeted the floor and one of the sculptures and its pedestals had toppled over. Officers milled about inside, discussing, taking notes and photographs, while a couple others maintained a perimeter outside.

A car rolled along the street, waved on by a police officer when it slowed too much. My stomach clenched and I scanned the driver. Just a blond woman with two kids in the back.

Jimmy continued, "I talked to one of the guys on my way here who said the video was shaky and the car was a ways off, but they're pretty sure they'll be able to grab the license plate."

"Good." I shoved my hands into my jacket pockets and balled them into fists. Rhonda could have died. Hell, I could have been shot grabbing her.

"I hear you kept Rhonda calm through the interviews, so thanks for that."

"I just distracted her." I withdrew a hand from my pocket to point where a hole had been bored out of the wall. Noting the shake in my hand, I stuffed it away again. "The first bullet impacted here."

Nearby, a pair of Tyvek-suited officers discussed a grouping of five holes, all within six inches of each other. One held the cutting tool they'd use to remove a segment of the wall around each bullet.

"Given how tightly grouped the other bullets were, I expect the glass deflected the first one," I said. The first bullet went straight through *Number Vee*. Rhonda had been closer to the tight grouping than the painting. If that first bullet had been with the others, one of us likely would have been hit. "It cracked the window, then the second bullet blew it out. After that, they kept firing as they continued along the street. Couldn't have been more than ten miles an hour, but still impressive aim considering the brick framing between the two panes."

One of the forensics officers gave me a once over, taking in my long dress jacket, tall boots, and tied-back hair. She pulled her mask and goggles out of the way. "Sorry, Detective. I didn't know you were here."

"These two are from the forensics lab in Lansing, so they don't know our personnel," Jimmy said to me before turning to them. "This is one of our witnesses."

"And the insurance adjuster who'll take the damaged painting when you're done with it." I stepped closer to the hole and stared at Cam-ron's name plate where *Number Vee* had hung.

The officer with the cutting tool removed his goggles. "Wait a minute. You're that insurance adjuster from the Scott murder case, aren't you?"

Before I could respond, Jimmy chimed in. "That she is."

The female officer's demeanor changed, her lips tightening. She wasn't the first to react to me that way. I could almost hear the professional challenge: How dare an insurance adjuster think she could do a police officer's job? How dare I prove an open-and-shut house fire investigation was the work of an arsonist covering up conspiracy to commit murder and fraud? And how dare I prove it all just so I could deny a claim for a million dollar painting, which was actually a forgery?

But this was work, not a popularity contest. I brushed it all aside. "What's the timeline for bullet analysis these days?"

She pulled her protection in place. "One day if we're lucky, more likely two or three. We'll need to get these wall fragments to the lab and free the bullets before we can send them off to NIBIN for ballistics imaging and cross-reference against other crimes."

"Thanks." I nodded, motioning to Jimmy I was done.

"I'll give ya a call when the painting's ready to go." Jimmy held the door open for me, eyes crinkled at their corners. "I'm just happy you're okay, Sammy. Things like this shouldn't be happening here."

I nodded, giving him the most reassuring smile I could. But the words stuck in my throat. What could I say? Rhonda was right—Brenton was a quiet town on the outskirts of Lansing, Michigan. Not even two hours away from Detroit, it was close enough to the big cities to have everything we needed but it never had the everyone-knows-everything vibe. It was small enough that people were safe, neighbors were trustworthy.

Then again, Bobby and Olivia Scott had lived in Brenton. And she'd had him killed.

I nodded at Jimmy and ducked out into the wind. As cold

as it had grown inside the gallery without the front windows, it had at least provided some protection from the gusts.

Before I was at the small crowd gathered on the sidewalk, my phone rang. Antonio again. I declined the call, not prepared to talk to him. Every fiber of my body wanted to sink into his arms, but he was five thousand miles away. If I started talking with him about what happened, he'd know I was about to start shaking and crying and wouldn't be able to stop. All it would take would be one sweet, kind word from him, thinking he was making it better, and instead it would all spill over.

Not in public.

He called right back. Maybe I shouldn't have programmed his number to bypass my Do Not Disturb. I declined and he called again. He wasn't taking no for an answer.

I sucked in a deep breath as I reached the crowd, coughing some of the frigid air out. An officer I didn't know pulled up the police tape for me to leave, and I scooted sideways to get between people, nudging them out of my way. Where had they all come from?

I clenched my jaw and held the phone to my ear. I would *not* tell him what happened yet. "What's up?"

Antonio spoke quickly. "You said you'd call me when you were done."

"I..." The two hours before my upcoming site visit had turned into twenty minutes. I had to get going. A work distraction was what I needed. "I lost track of time. I'm busy."

"Busy." His tone was flat. Irritated or disappointed, I couldn't tell. "When will you finish? I need to speak with you."

Something was off. He was normally charming and oozing

with compliments. His speech was relaxed, languid, the thick Italian accent dancing through my brain like the drag of his fingers over my skin. By this time, he should have called me beautiful or wonderful and told me he loved me or missed me. At least twice. This urgency was unlike him.

"Antonio, I have another appointment, so I need to wrap this one up and get over there. My day's fully booked, right up to dinner at my sister's. That's why we had a chat this morning."

"But this is Saturday!"

"So?" The pricking started behind my eyes as I pushed through the last of the crowd, and I ducked my head down to focus on the sidewalk. "You know I work odd hours. What's so important?"

He huffed loudly, likely running fingers through his hair. "I need to see your face. I have news."

"That you can't tell me by voice?"

"Can I call you at your sister's?"

"Of course. I'll be there around six."

"Marone. I'll be at La Fiamma at that hour."

Rhonda or I could have just been killed, but his big stress was clubbing? "Fine. We can talk tomor—"

Something pressed down on my shoulder. I jumped and spun, ready to strike.

The first thing I saw were the shocking blue eyes. Then the weak smile and perfectly styled blond hair. I smacked his chest as he withdrew the hand he'd used to get my attention.

"Nathan! Christ, you scared me half to death."

He spread his arms to hug me, but I put out my hand to stop him. His breath hung in a plume in front of him, until another gust blew it away. Hugging him would be as bad as telling Antonio what happened.

I had to get back to work.

"Samantha?" said Antonio on the phone, his voice raised.

I turned around and softened my tone. "Antonio, I have to go. We can talk tomorrow, okay?"

"Alright." He took a deep breath. "I love you, bella."

"Good." I paused. If only those three words were as easy for me as they were for him. Something held me back. Probably stubbornness. *Be honest with yourself, Sam. It's nothing but fear.* "I'll call you in the morning."

Once the phone was in my pocket, I turned to Nathan who wore an impeccably tailored navy suit and overcoat. I offered a hand to shake.

He looked at it, furrowing his brow. "What's this?"

"No hugs while I'm working, Nathan. What are you even doing here?"

"Prosecutor's office sent me to oversee some evidence collection and I heard you were involved." He shoved his hands into the pockets of his long coat and shrugged. "You okay?"

"Fine."

"How's the Italian doing?"

"I have an appointment." As the closest thing I had to a big brother, I gave him some latitude. But he pushed it where Antonio was concerned. "See you at Cass's tonight?"

He stepped closer, like he was going to try to hug me again. Likely wanting to break down the wall I'd put up between me and what happened. "Do I get two hugs when I see you there?"

"At this rate, I'm guessing none." I nudged him and frowned before heading for my truck.

CHAPTER 3

ANTONIO

THE BASS THUNDERED INSIDE ME, my vision swimming with each chest-pounding pulse. Any other night, being at the club with so many friends would be the perfect evening, but this night was torture. Everything around me was a reminder of the insurmountable void which had ripped through my stomach.

I dragged both hands through my hair, resting my elbows on my knees and stared at my shoes, which drifted side to side. No, perhaps that was my head drifting. How many drinks had I had? Too many, whatever it was. Coming here had been a poor choice.

Raising my eyes, I scanned the crowd. Samantha had come to this club with me once. We drank, danced, and made love in the VIP bathroom. Perhaps *made love* was not the right term. It had been carnal and desperate, full of overwhelming need. But it had followed an explosion of honesty and I'd seen the love in her eyes that night.

My jaw relaxed for a moment as her face came back to me. She'd been an absolute vision in the little dress she wore that night, with its Medusa-head medallions on the straps. I held tight to the black ceramic ring on my left ring finger. It was only a promise ring, but my whole heart was tied to it, despite my other half being an ocean away.

"What's wrong with you?" Thomas appeared next to me on the large red couch overlooking the dance floor. I had not seen him in an hour or more.

Tall and handsome, seven years my senior, he was working for me on a conservation project in Pompeii, on loan from the British Museum in London. He'd been Samantha's boss as an intern a decade ago, and possibly more than her boss, but I'd never gotten a straight answer from either of them on that. Not that it was my business. She had a life before me. It was alright that she'd been with other men. Men like Thomas Grange. And Nathan Miller.

"What's that face? You look bloody furious." Thomas bumped my shoulder with his, more forcefully than he should have. He'd also had too much to drink.

Swiveling slowly to look at him, I focused on keeping my balance. Once he became clear, I hollered over the music. "Mario took my phone!"

Thomas laughed loudly and slapped my thigh. "Take it back!"

"I'm far too drunk to do that." I leaned back on the couch, but the lights flared in my vision and I had to close my eyes.

He patted my knee and vanished into the crowd again. I flagged down a scantily clad club employee and asked for water.

Before she returned, Thomas slid onto the couch, waving a phone at me. "Ask and thou shalt receive!"

I took it from him, appreciating my lock screen for a moment—a selfie of Samantha and me at the airport before she flew home in September. I unlocked it, opening the video chat app. My finger hovered over her face. It was two in the morning in Napoli. Only eight in the evening in Brenton.

"What did you do, Thomas?" My cousin Mario landed on my other side, raising his voice. He reached for my phone, but I pushed him away. "He's not supposed to call her until tomorrow!"

After two failed attempts to reach into my pocket, I withdrew my earbuds and made the call. I couldn't wait another day. She'd be so upset from my news, I had to see her when I told her.

It rang and rang until the screen lit up. Her smile was broad, and she looked giddy with excitement. This was so much better than our call earlier in the day. I couldn't see her eyes clearly, though. The phone drifted to the side, as my feet had done.

"Hey, stranger! You still up?" Her voice was like a quiet song, soothing the ache inside me. I turned the volume up so I could hear her over the music, catching the tail end of a sniffle. "I'm so happy to see you."

"Samantha!" yelled Mario, leaning toward the microphone on my earbuds. She startled at his volume. "Come va, bellisima?"

Thomas joined from the other side. "Evening, Sam!"

She laughed, waving into the camera. I shoved both of them aside. Taking the hint, they left. To dance, to drink more, to get food in the courtyard outside. I didn't care.

I ran my hand through my hair, breathing out slowly. Why

had I called her without preparing something? How was I going to say this?

"You at La Fiamma?" she asked.

"We're having a celebration party." I needed her strength, but she kept moving and I couldn't lock my eyes on hers.

"You've been drinking." Her voice grew progressively flatter. Her subtle moods were normally easy for me to read, but the alcohol made it difficult.

"Sì, I have." I shook my head, leaning my elbows onto my knees again. "Too much."

"That's not like you."

I squeezed my eyes shut and breathed her name out as if it were a prayer. "Samantha. Oh, Samantha."

Her voice quavered. "Is everything alright?"

"I miss you, bella. So much."

"Yeah, we had this conversation this morning. What's going on? You said earlier you had to talk to me."

The waitress returned with my water, and I guzzled it.

"Antonio?" She was so quiet I could barely hear her.

I placed a hand over one ear, attempting to press more of the sound out. Noise canceling features could only do so much against the decibels in the club.

"What are you celebrating that you couldn't tell me about this morning or on the phone this afternoon?"

I didn't recognize the room she was in. The light was faint. It looked like a bedroom, but was not in the hotel she lived in. She'd shown me those rooms before. We'd lay on our beds earlier that day, heads and laptops on pillows, chatting for an hour, as though we'd woken up together. I knew her bedroom, and this was not it.

"Where are you, bella?"

"At Cass's place. I told you that. We're playing poker—" Her straight face fell to a frown. "—which I suck at."

"You should play a different game, then."

She shrugged. "Guest's choice."

That made no sense. "If not your choice, who's the guest? Is Lucy there?"

Something in her face caused my heart to lurch, nudging the haze of the alcohol aside. Our eyes met at last, but hers fell and she chewed on her bottom lip. What was she not saying?

"Samantha?"

"What's going on, Antonio?" The frown hardened and she raised her chin. "You said you needed to talk to me. Now you're drunk at some celebration I don't know anything about. Just tell me."

I groaned and forced the words out. "We'll be finishing the project early. Next week."

She furrowed her brows and spoke slowly. "But that's a good thing? You'll be coming home sooner?"

"I pushed them, bella. Made the team work hard, put in my own overtime. But it was such a success, they renewed the contract until April—"

She sucked in air and her eyes shot wide open. "What?"

"There were rumors it may happen, but Mario got the call this afternoon. We'll be doing the same conservation on the garden walls, with modifications more suitable for a new excavation."

"And you agreed to that?" Her pitch rose dramatically.

"What was I supposed to do?" My head fell forward, and I blew out a deep breath. "This is a tremendous honor. It's going to be published."

"You'll miss my birthday." The pain in her voice broke my heart all the more.

Her birthday didn't matter. I was not so drunk I couldn't understand that part. She worried I wouldn't come home. That my return in January was now April and would somehow become later and later until we never saw each other again. Some other Italian man had done that to her, and she thought I would do the same.

The room tumbled and bile rose in my throat. Mario was right. I should have waited until I was sober and had time to get past the sorrow consuming me. I should have been back in Brenton with her in early January. No more long distance. I could have seen her every day, held her, made love to her. I would have woken up next to her, not next to a laptop.

I lifted my head to see her. "You planned to take leave in January when I was scheduled to return. Come and visit me? Per favore? I can't go another four months without you."

She shook her head and looked up at the ceiling, blinking rapidly. "It's not that easy. I promised Cass. I can't miss her treatments."

"I know, bella." A burning sensation built behind my eyes, and I let out a long sigh. "I know."

Her sister had made it through chemotherapy, her mastectomy, and was in the midst of radiation. The prognosis was more positive than it had been in the fall, but Samantha was a good woman. An even better sister.

We stared at each other, so many words left to say, but none coming. The gentle sway returned, and I shook my head to clear it, making it worse. How was I going to fix this if I was stuck in Napoli and she was stuck in Brenton?

The door behind her burst open suddenly, light from the hallway spilling in to illuminate more of the room.

"Sam! Kevin just opened the Scotch!" Nathan Miller came into the room. Nathan Miller! The pretty, polished Assistant Prosecutor with the blue eyes who she called her big brother stand-in. The man who had threatened me, sucker punched me, and who looked at her with more lust than a big brother should. What was he doing there?

Her head fell forward, not looking at either of us. "So?"

He stepped further into the room, looking at me rather than her. With a smirk. "Can you give me a ride home?"

"Yeah, sure."

"Thanks, Sam." He kissed the top of her head, still focused on me. Cazzo Madre di Dio, the stronzo kissed her. "Don't know what I'd do without you."

My breath kicked up, the alcohol-induced haze lifting like a curtain. The door clicked closed behind her and she looked up at me again. Guilt etched on her face. This had been the lip biting information. She'd intentionally hidden him from me.

My jaw tightened. "What was that?"

"He's Kevin's best friend, Antonio. I told you, he's like a big—"

"Did you spend all day with him?" I shot off the couch and put a hand on the back to steady myself. He'd been with her when we spoke earlier. And he kissed her. He thought he could steal her from me while I was away. "You will *not* see him again!"

Her head jerked back, lip curling. "As if my day couldn't get any worse. You did *not* just say that."

"I did!"

"That's not your decision, Antonio! He's been my friend for almost twenty years!"

That was it. That was the last straw. She and I had been apart too long. Damn this contract. I squeezed my eyes shut to regain my center before scanning the crowd for Mario. He was on another couch, speaking with a woman with dark hair. I marched up to him and leaned toward his ear.

"I am leaving! I'm done!"

He grabbed me as I straightened. "What are you talking about?"

I held the phone up to point at him and realized Samantha was still there. The look of defiance remained on her face, but she was not angry enough to hang up on me or give up. That was something, at least.

Looking at her tense face, I bit back on the rage bubbling inside me. "I love you, Samantha. Don't forget that."

Before she could give me her absurd *Good* response, I hung up, and turned back to Mario. "You can tell the Board I'll be back after New Year's!"

He stood next to me, raising his voice so I could hear him. "You're not making any sense!"

"I'm flying home for Christmas."

"You are not."

"She's with Nathan Miller—"

"What?"

"They're at her sister's house together. He wants her, Mario, I know it. I can't give him four more months—"

He grabbed my arm, leaning in. "She'd never cheat on you, cugino!"

"What do you know?" I jerked out of his grip, throwing

the club into another spin around me. "I didn't think Faith would, either—"

"You should have listened to me then, too!"

I shoved him away. Five years ago, I'd come home early from a research trip to Napoli to find Faith—my fiancée at the time—in bed with another man. And Mario had warned me about her months before it happened. Samantha would never do that. Would she? Was she capable of doing that to me?

How long would it be until video calls and texts were not enough? Before her bed was too cold and those blue eyes too warm?

"What's going on here?" Thomas appeared next to me, arm falling around my shoulders. "You two look awfully serious!"

Did I honestly just tell her she couldn't see Miller again? That would only help him get closer to her. "I'm going home for Christmas."

Thomas jostled me, smacking my chest. "A holiday break from the taskmaster?"

Running fingers through my hair to clasp my neck, I nodded. "We'll work tomorrow to shut things down until January."

Mario laughed. "That will be a rough day. But I'll take one of those to earn two weeks off!"

I sighed, the memory of Samantha's raised chin battling with her smiling face and with Nathan Miller's kiss. "I only hope two weeks is enough."

CHAPTER 4
SAMANTHA

I CALLED Antonio back five times. No answer.

Smothering my face in a pillow, I let out a scream.

How dare he tell me I can't see Nathan? How was I going to last another four months without him? He was so upset. Was he alright?

Fuck him.

God, I missed him.

The emotions surged through me so fast, I couldn't hold on to a single one long enough to suppress it. All I wanted in the world was his arms around me, so I could get the whole shooting out of my system. But that wouldn't happen until April now.

I stormed back to the dining room, to our poker game, and dropped into my chair. Cass and her husband, Kevin, frowned at me. I'd left in a flurry, thinking I'd get a little comfort after my shitty day, and returned covered in frost.

"Sorry about that." Nathan toasted me with his Scotch and downed a shot. He didn't seem sorry at all. The conversation with Antonio had been difficult, but once Nathan had come and gone, it all changed. Jealous-Antonio came out. Jealous and drunk.

Good thing I couldn't reach him. We'd sort it all out once he sobered up. Maybe in the morning.

"Does the Italian always yell at you like that?" Cass frowned at me. My sister liked Antonio about as well as Nathan did. When I didn't respond, she shifted tack, softening her voice. "Did you tell him about the shooting?"

"No," I ground out. "I was too busy being interrupted by someone kissing my head." I shoved Nathan hard enough his chair tipped. "What the hell were you thinking?"

Righting himself, Nathan shrugged. "Habit?"

"Foul ball, man," said Kevin, downing his own shot.

Four more months. It was supposed to be three weeks. How could I handle four more months without him? I grabbed the cards and shuffled, dropping a few when I couldn't stop the shaking in my heads. I clenched my jaw against the anger, the sadness, the... the what?

I missed him so much.

An unsafe-for-my-heart amount.

Part of me relied on that smiling face on the other end of our calls, and it failed me the day I needed it the most.

"Sorry, Sam. I wasn't thinking." Nathan put a hand on mine to stop my shuffling. He leaned his head down to get in my line of sight. "Let me do that for you."

Fighting the lump growing in my throat, I sniffled. I dragged my palms across my face to wipe off the few tears that escaped. "He'll be in Naples until April now."

Putting an arm around me, Nathan pulled me close. "It'll be alright, Sam. April's not that far away and we're all still here for you."

~

"THAT'S IT." I threw my cards down, sending Nathan's pile of poker chips skittering across the table. "I'm done."

Kevin had passed out on the couch a half hour ago, and somehow Nathan cleaned house.

Cass and I stood and started tidying up, until she winced when picking up a glass. I shooed her hand away and took care of the mess myself. She'd started her post-mastectomy radiation treatments a week and a half ago and was dealing with pain and blistering, on top of healing from her surgery. She glowered at me but didn't reach for more.

Before I finished, she nudged me and pointed at Nathan, whose head lolled to the side. "You should probably get him home before he passes out, too."

"Good idea." I gave her a quick hug, happy to feel her weight coming back on.

"Or we can leave him on the other couch and you can crash here, if you... you know."

If I didn't feel safe. If I couldn't go back to my hotel room and not worry about the shooting. "Thanks, but I'm good. My place is plenty safe."

"If you insist." She forced a smile, telling me she was more worried about what happened than she was letting on.

"In case I didn't mention it yet, I love the new hairstyle."

"Thanks." She ruffled the pixie cut with her fingers. She'd always had stick-straight medium brown hair like our mother. Post-chemo, it was wavy like mine, the same light brown with red and gold highlights. "Kevin says it's sexy. Maybe I'll leave it short."

After another hug for my sister, I collected Nathan and

helped him to my truck, having to get behind him and shove him into the passenger seat.

"If you vomit in my truck, I'm going to kill you."

"No, you won't." He gave me that disarming smile of his, the one that made it hard to be angry with him, or made you tell him all your secrets. Any time I complained about it, he bragged it was why he was so good at his job.

"I know twenty-three ways to murder you with that pen in the cup holder. Plus I've got all the tools in back to bury you where no one will ever find you."

He laughed and closed his eyes. "I had too much."

"Yeah, no kidding."

His breaths grew deeper as I drove until he slumped to the side. Passed out.

That was probably the same thing Antonio was doing. Unless his overactive emotions were keeping him awake. I gripped the steering wheel and stretched out my jaw.

Four more months.

I swore to Cass I'd stay in town until her treatments were done. There was no time to go back to Naples until March, at the earliest.

How could he agree to the extension?

This was Vincenzo all over again. *My Visa wasn't approved. My mother's sick. A friend needs my help. The job offer fell through.* Delays became excuses until I flew to Italy to see him for—what turned out to be—the last time.

Antonio swore that wouldn't happen. Said all he wanted was to come home and be with me.

I was being selfish. He was right. In his circles, this project was a big deal—being published. But what did that matter when he worked as an art conservator for a small shop in Brenton, Michigan?

Lots.

Their work came in based on his family's rather considerable reputation, so his conservation project in Pompeii doing well was significant. Supporting the other person's career was important in a relationship.

But if that career kept you apart, how could the relationship work?

We'd already done three months and we'd become closer over that time. But, oh my god, I missed him. Missed his body. His lips. His smell. His touch.

And no matter what I told anyone—even myself—I wasn't alright. I'd been on edge all day since the shooting, no distraction enough to keep my brain off the sound of that glass and Rhonda's scream.

But what terrified me was that I kept thinking about Antonio. He was the one I wanted. Not my friends and family, but him.

I hit the call link on the truck. "Call Antonio Ferr—" Stupid. "Cancel."

It was midnight. Six in the morning in Naples. No chance he'd still be awake. And with my luck, that would be the moment Nathan would wake up and shout something that would piss Antonio off even more.

I glanced at Nathan, trying to hold on to my anger over his intrusion into the call, but I couldn't do it. He meant too much to me. We met when I was twelve. Soon after Cass and Kevin grew serious enough that she started bringing him home, Nathan started coming with them. My sister and the two men who became my big brothers. The three of them helped me through the end of my friendship with my best friend in college, through our mother's death, my divorce, and everything else.

But he didn't like Antonio and wasn't afraid to point that out. That was going to be a problem.

When I pulled up in front of his house, he didn't budge. Great.

I rounded to his side and opened the truck door, nudging him until he woke up.

He blinked, rolling his head slowly to me. "How did we get here so fast?"

"We teleported."

"Huh?"

"Never mind." I guided his feet to the running boards and caught him as he slid out. After negotiating his arm over my shoulder and mine around his waist, we made slow progress to the front door.

He swiveled his head quickly, and I narrowly avoided the headbutt. "You're the best, Sam."

His house was a light gray two-story in an exclusive neighborhood. Double garage, wrap-around porch, and lots of windows. We'd had game nights here, and I'd been over for movies and dinners, so I knew the place well. A beautiful house, but too big. He and his wife had planned for a few kids, but their separation eight months ago put an end to that. Three empty bedrooms were a waste.

Mind you, I lived in a hotel.

After six years of living in an RV.

He fumbled for his keys, which I snagged before he dropped them. As soon as we were in, the security alarm began whining.

"What's your code?"

He narrowed his eyes at the alarm panel.

"Nathan!" I smacked his cheek a couple of times and his eyes popped open. His hand lurched toward the panel. Three tries before he hit the right combination, which I committed to memory for the next time this happened. The divorce had been harder on him than he'd admit.

"My room's upstairs."

"Not a chance. You're sleeping down here." Where I could drag his sorry ass to a couch and not risk him falling more than a few feet.

We made our way past the stairs and his office to the family room. It was dominated by a propane fireplace with brick facing and a seating area with a structured gray couch, two stuffed chairs, and a glass table.

I navigated him to the couch, where he collapsed like a doll. He sat there, slouched, trying to lock his eyes on me. I grabbed the remote for the fireplace and turned it on for him.

"Thanks," he mumbled and snatched my hand. He tugged on it so suddenly and with enough strength that I lost my balance and narrowly missed falling on him. I landed next to him, and he chuckled, throwing an arm around me. "What happened, Sam?"

"You mean when you had way too much to drink, when I drove you home, or when you hauled me down on the couch?"

He looked in my general direction, unable to focus properly. "I love you."

"Yeah, I love you, too, Nathan. Now, you need some sleep." I patted him on the thigh and pushed him over. He didn't fight it and his legs came up onto my lap so I removed his shoes.

"What do you see in him?" His speech slowed and his eyelids fluttered.

I picked up his legs and squeezed out from under them. "Who?"

"Ferraro. I mean, I know what you *see* in him. He's so fucking handsome and rich and that stupid accent. But you need someone who's better for you."

"Thanks for your concern." Stooping, I dug in his pocket and removed his phone, placing it safely on the table in front of him. I pulled the throw blanket from the back of the couch to cover him.

He grabbed my hand again, pulling me down.

I knelt, putting our faces close to each other.

"He's dangerous, Sam, and I don't want you to get hurt."

My jaw tightened. Why stop at one drunk conversation tonight? *Let's make it two.* Both with stubborn men who didn't like each other. "Antonio's not dangerous, Nathan. And even if he was, I'm a big girl."

"If I told you half the things I know, you'd run as fast as you could." He let go of my hand and cupped my cheek. "I couldn't live with myself if you got caught in the middle of his shit and got hurt."

That sounded specific, more than a vague warning of danger that could mean anything from having my heart broken to being killed. "Is this more crap about that random family outside of Rome? The one that shares a last name with forty thousand other Ferraros in Italy?"

My voice rose as I spoke, too tired to control myself or push my doubts aside. It wasn't just a random family, but I wouldn't tell Nathan that. When I'd been in Naples with Antonio, there'd been clues about him being involved with the wrong sorts of people. Secrets, implications from a police officer, and a burner phone leading to someone who had information I didn't get to hear.

Antonio and I promised to spend our time apart getting to know each other, but there was a lot to learn. And so much I couldn't ask until he was here with me.

Nathan stared, his breath shallow and tentative, his hand still resting on my cheek. "Can't you just trust me?"

"Nathan, you're drunk."

"I know," he whined quietly. "I shouldn't be talking to you right now."

"If you've got details, give them to me." I took his hand away from my face and held it. Maybe the gesture would make him open up and tell me more.

"I shouldn't have had so much." He stared at our joined hands and began rubbing my knuckles with his thumb. His head rolled back and he whipped his hand up to the ceiling. "Oh, shit. I filed a claim earlier today."

I turned around to see a large water spot on the ceiling.

"Would you be my adjuster?" He giggled as his head fell to the cushion.

Christ, don't lose focus, Nathan. "We were talking about Antonio."

"Exactly."

What the hell did that mean? "Tell me what makes him so dangerous. What would I get caught in the middle of?"

"He's not coming home until April, you said?"

"Yeah."

"Good to know," he yawned.

I took his hand again and squeezed. Nothing. I tapped his cheek, trying to keep him with me. "Tell me!"

His eyes fluttered open. "I just want to protect you, Sam."

Hanging my head, I sighed. He was too drunk. His grip went slack, and I placed his hand on his chest. The kitchen was open to the family room, all dark wood and stainless steel. I rummaged through a few cupboards until I found a big bowl and returned to him, putting it on the floor below his head. Hopefully, if he woke up to vomit in the middle of the night, he'd have the forethought to aim for the bowl.

After that, I took a quick peek at the water damage. Didn't look complicated from downstairs, and I knew his ensuite was above the family room, but I'd check that out later. I logged into the Foster Mutual claims system on my phone and assigned his claim to myself. Wednesday evening appointment. His phone buzzed on the table from the automated notification.

On my way out, I straightened the sailboat paintings on the wall he'd run into and righted a small baseball trophy in an alcove. I found a spare house key hanging in the closet at the front door, enabled the security system, and locked up behind me.

I tumbled his words over in my brain as I drove home. Nathan had been feeding me warnings since July. He was working on a case with the FBI which involved a Ferraro family outside of Rome. I'd dismissed it originally because it was all conjecture and there was no link to Antonio.

But I knew more since my visit to Naples in September. Had Nathan learned something about Antonio that I deserved to know?

Or was it more overprotective macho bullshit?

CHAPTER 5
ANTONIO

EARLY THE NEXT AFTERNOON, I sat on a small bench in the Casa di Marte's triclinium, the formal dining room my team had conserved over the last three months. We'd spent the time cleaning, repairing, and stabilizing it so it would not require additional work for decades, if not longer.

Each pump from my heart stabbed through my brain. I guzzled water, as I'd been doing since I woke, hoping the headache would eventually pass. Minerva's painted face glowered down at me from across the room, as though lecturing me for my behavior. Every fiber of my being echoed that look, screaming at me to go back to my dark bedroom and stay there for hours.

Mario sat next to me on the bench. "Have you called her?"

Checking my watch, I shook my head. "She goes for a run when she wakes up, then weights, breakfast, and shower. It's only eight in the morning there. She was up late, so probably slept in and wouldn't be done yet."

"You mean you're avoiding her?"

I scowled at him, but he retrieved my phone from the

conservation desk where the laptops sat in the middle of our outdoor workspace.

He forced the phone into my hand. "Because she's been trying to reach you."

Five calls and three texts in the last hour. I should have been paying closer attention instead of nursing this hangover. "What do I say?"

"Start with an apology?"

"She must be furious with me." I put the phone face down on the bench and stared at my promise ring, remembering the words we said. We vowed to trust each other and to wait until I was home before making any decisions. Bile rose from my stomach, but it was beyond empty, other than water. "I can't believe I forbid her from seeing Miller. What kind of stupid—"

"Drunk and jealous, not stupid." He put the phone back in my hand. "Call her. You and your sad face are bringing everyone down. We'll never finish today unless you're helping, and we won't let you go to the airport until we're done."

I chuckled, looking at my team wrapping up our work on the Cupid wall. The three walls of the room were remarkably well-preserved excavations from Regio V in the ancient city. One wall focused on Mars—the Roman god of war, who the house was named for—and Venus, one on Cupid at the hunt, and my favorite wall, with Perseus presenting the head of Medusa to Minerva.

If I accomplished nothing else in my life, the work we did here would be my legacy—one I was proud of.

"Thank you, Mario. I think the pills are finally kicking in." I stood, walking away from the group, out from underneath the temporary structure overhead. As I reached the center of the open garden area, the sun beamed like a laser directly into my skull. The frescoes on these walls would hold Samantha and me apart longer than expected, but we'd make the best of it.

I let out a long breath and steeled myself. She was not with Miller. She was waiting for me, just as we'd agreed.

When she appeared on the screen, my heart leapt into my throat. There was no fury, but her smile was more tempered than usual. Her luxurious hair was tied back, still wet. And she was in her hotel again.

"Ciao, bella."

Her eyes moved past me. "You're at the Casa?"

"Before I say anything else, Samantha, I want to apologize."

"You don't need—"

"Sì, I do. I was *very* drunk last night, upset, and I said things I shouldn't have. You're right. Nathan Miller has been your friend for a long time, and I trust you." It was *him* I didn't trust. "It's not my place to choose your friends."

Her face softened, the smile reaching her eyes. "Thanks."

Mario was right. An apology was the best start.

"And I'm sorry I didn't return your calls earlier." I swiveled the phone to show the team and returned focus to me. "Sometimes I work odd hours, as well. I'll be here almost all day."

Her eyes fell. "No time to talk, I understand."

"Mi scusi, bella. That was not a dig."

Lips tight, she looked up again. Those furtive glances meant so much from her, and when I was sober, I understood it. She felt bad for pushing me off yesterday, and there was something else weighing on her.

"But this is the only time I can talk today. I have a few minutes, if you can chat?"

"How are you feeling? You were *really* drunk last night."

I removed my sunglasses. Another wave of nausea pulsed through me and I swallowed hard.

She gasped. "You look terrible! Your eyes are so bloodshot!"

"You should have seen me this morning." I gave an exaggerated shudder and she laughed. "Mario took over the taskmaster duties and it's been rough. Fortunately, I'm not the only one. Thomas is also quite hung over. What about you? Any news?"

"I was just checking my email." She shrugged one shoulder. "Two more offers."

"You're a popular woman."

"You know how small the art world can be. A gallery in Boston wants me to review their insurance policies, which I may do, because that's just a short contract. I could do it mostly online and take one or two day trips. And an art specialty carrier based in New York wants me to interview."

"New York?"

She continued speaking past that point, signaling she was not giving it any thought. "And I got a long email from Elliot."

Samantha had interned for Special Agent Elliot Skinner with the FBI Art Crimes Team straight out of college. He'd shown up in Napoli when she was visiting me in September, working with the Carabinieri TPC—the Italian art crimes squad—to investigate a theft from my Casa di Marte.

He was still pursuing her professionally, asking her to return to the FBI. Indeed, my girlfriend was *very* popular in certain circles.

"He danced around the painting from the auction." Her discovery of a stolen painting among the art up for auction at the hospital gala we attended in August had brought Skinner back into her life. "The last concrete lead he told me about was eight weeks ago, so either they've hit a brick wall or they've had a breakthrough he won't tell me about."

"Do you think he'd give you the details?"

"Not sure, to be honest. Sometimes he shares a lot more than he should, other times he's tight-lipped." She let out a long yawn. "If they found out who stole it originally, he'd at least tell me that they had. He also mentioned the Carabinieri haven't had any additional leads on the flower fresco or the pigment pots."

She paused, giving me an opportunity to tell her what I knew about the thefts which we investigated together in September. Samantha suspected I'd learned more than I told her, but didn't pressure me on it. Just continued on as though she trusted me completely, which was no doubt difficult for a woman as suspicious as she was.

When I did nothing but nod, she continued. "He also suggested submitting a paper on the Scott case to an art crimes symposium in California this summer. I may attend but presenting seems like a bit much."

"Any word on David and Olivia Scott?"

She turned from the camera, eyes scanning something beside her, likely her second monitor. "Let's see... last week's sightings include LA, Montreal, Boston, London, and—" She looked at me with an exaggerated frown. "—Bangladesh. So basically, the two of them got away with Bobby's murder plus a million dollars in fraudulent insurance settlements and the

FBI is no further ahead in tracking them down than they were in August."

"And how was last night?" I walked through the garden and the remains of the storage room where the Casa met with Via di Nola. Each room was little more than crumbled walls and newly excavated dirt—all the contents removed for cataloguing and research—but we referred to each based on their original purpose.

She picked up her laptop and walked to the bedroom, placing it on the pillow next to her. Lying down, she propped her head on an elbow. "What do you think? Shitty."

Exiting to the roadway through a break in the storage room's wall, I sat on the dusty sidewalk. I leaned back against the gray lava stone walls of the Casa, finding what little shade I could. December was cool enough that the crowds were thinner than the warmer seasons, so there was plenty of privacy. "From my news or my outburst?"

"Both." She rolled onto her back with a frown, looking at the ceiling. "We've already done three months. I know we can do four more, but only if we both want to. Otherwise, we're just wasting each other's time."

Heartfelt words were never her strong suit. She must have thought about this a great deal if she was talking instead of simply staring at me.

"This is not the first in a string of laters, bella. I still want this."

"So do I." Her jaw flexed and released, then she inhaled as though to speak but said nothing.

"Antonio!" came Mario's voice. We were running out of time, but I couldn't rush her. I stood, extending on my tiptoes to wave to him over the wall. I held up five fingers once I had his attention.

When she began speaking, her voice was unsteady. "Nathan's part of my package deal, just like Cass, Kevin, and their kids. It's a small package, but they're my family. He's been with me through a lot of highs and lows, and I've counted on him more than once."

Samantha Caine expressed herself through action, not through words. My plan had been to surprise her when I arrived home on Tuesday. Would she be happy to see me, or would there be a hint of panic in her reaction? That would tell me whether I could trust her fully.

But today, with her talking to me about this, I had no question she was still mine.

"Bella—"

"No, let me finish." She rolled to face me, determination etched on her lovely face. "You sure you want to wait another four months? There isn't someone else there who might be a better choice for you? Mario knows lots of beautiful women, or maybe someone you work with?"

Her husband had left her for someone else, someone he was better suited to be with. This was part of what held her back from me—a fear that she was not enough. As though I would someday make a similar choice.

Her face was rehearsed neutrality, holding the door wide open to let me walk away if I wanted to. She still didn't believe she'd been my North Star for longer than we'd known each other.

"There is no doubt in my mind, Samantha. You are the *only* one for me."

She nodded, eyes darting to me and away and back again,

letting the door close and the emotion peek through. "I feel something for you that's completely different from what I feel for Nathan. I've known him for eighteen years, and I would trust him with my life. But I've never—never—thought about him first when I woke up or last when I went to sleep. My heart's never skipped a beat when I heard his voice. And I've never clutched a pillow at night, wishing it was him."

Tears glistened in her eyes, and I clenched my jaw to stave off my own. I needed to hold her, feel her warm skin against mine, and show her everything was alright. I should tell her I was coming home. "Bella, I—"

Mario appeared on the sidewalk next to me, and I cut short, waving him away.

She ran a knuckle across her eyes. "I was perfectly happy with my solitary, nomadic life the last six years. I didn't want to set down roots again. Until I met you. Nathan wasn't what changed my mind. You were. And you still are. But you need to trust me." She dropped her voice to a whisper. "I'm not Faith. Stop painting me with her brush."

My shoulders sagged. How could I have doubted her? "I know."

"You keep saying you trust me, but last night was proof you don't." Her eyes finally locked on me. "There's still something inside you that thinks I'm going to cheat on you. The logical side of my brain understands that, but it breaks my heart every time I see it."

She lifted her left hand to the camera, showing the ring I'd given her the day she left Napoli. "I'm still wearing this promise ring, and I'm still waiting. And I'll continue waiting if it's what you truly want."

I swallowed hard, the lump in my throat difficult to speak

around. She was leaving me the out, as though it were even a possibility for me. "I love you, Samantha, and I'd wait for you until the end of time."

"Good." She nodded, wiping a palm across her face.

"Antonio!" Mario appeared again. "You need to come back to the room if we're going to do this."

I waved him away, more urgently. The day began with a plan to surprise her and figure out the truth. But I had the answer in front of me, clearer than I'd expected it to be, even at home. "I have to go, bella. Do you have Tuesday night free?"

She spluttered with laughter. "That's a strange shift in conversation."

"I'll be busy until then. Can we have a video chat? Maybe date night?"

"I'm work—" A brilliant smile lit up her face. "No. You know what? I can move my schedule around to clear it. Six o'clock, like usual?"

I nodded as I stood, barely able to contain my excitement. "Wear the dress you wore to my parents' house?"

She sat up with the laptop. "Wear your black suit?"

"I will. And I'll see you Tuesday."

My flight would arrive at five o'clock Tuesday. She'd be at her hotel at six, and I would show up at her door with dinner. It would be the best date night we'd ever had.

After hanging up, I threw on my sunglasses and raced back to the team. "Andiamo!"

Everyone turned to see me, surprise on their faces. Half an hour ago, I was moaning about everything being too loud and too bright. My conversation with Samantha had energized me, and I couldn't get out of Italia fast enough.

Two more days, and she'd be in my arms again.

CHAPTER 6
SAMANTHA

SLAMMING my truck's door shut, I glowered at the apartment building and punched the ignition.

"You are the pickiest woman in the world!" Lucy Chapman—my best friend and official pain in my ass—paired her phone to my truck's audio system and scrolled through her music.

I pulled out of the apartment complex's parking lot, resisting the overwhelming desire to squeal the tires. "I seem to recall you once taking twenty minutes to pick a flavor of ice cream."

"Doesn't count!" She started "Satisfaction" by the Rolling Stones.

"Are you kidding me?" I paused the music.

She blew a gum bubble at me and returned to picking a song.

"Their gym doesn't open until ten. Who doesn't let their tenants in at any hour they want?"

"And last week, you were complaining about a squeaky floorboard—"

"That wouldn't have driven you crazy?"

"And what was it the week before that? Oh, right—" She held her phone up, showing she'd chosen "Creep" by Radiohead and pressed play. "You didn't like the building manager."

Huffing, I focused on the road ahead of us.

"I still say you should move in with me." She popped another bubble, nose glued to her phone. "I know it's just a one bedroom, but we could find somewhere bigger—"

"You think I could find a two bedroom more quickly than I can find a one bedroom? I've been looking for three months!"

She nudged my arm. "I could pick it for us!"

I ran a hand over my face, jostling my sunglasses. "The whole point of moving out of the Brenton Arms is to set down roots. Make a commitment to stay in this town. If I move in with you, you're still the one with the lease and I can still leave."

"What about—"

I put up a finger to cut her off. She was trying to help, but after yesterday and this morning, my fuse was barely existent. Antonio didn't trust me. How could he say he loved me and wanted a future with me, but still think I'd screw around on him? Without trust, what kind of relationship could anyone have?

He was plagued with irrational fears I'd cheat on him. I hadn't met Faith, but I'd never had such an overwhelming desire to punch someone square in the face my whole life. Here I was, bending over backward to find a new home so he'd believe I wanted to be with him.

The hotel was a great place to live. Housekeeping, gym, pool, complimentary breakfast...

I blew out a deep breath.

A hotel was a great place to live in the short term, like when I'd planned to leave Brenton in the spring. He wasn't the only one looking for a future between us. So why couldn't I find an apartment I liked?

"Geez, you're in a pissy mood today, Sam."

I scowled at her, pulling to the side of the road in front of a two-story red brick Colonial with a concrete walkway leading to large double-doors. She looked at the house with its real estate agent's sign and 'Coming Soon' rider at the top.

"So, you'll buy a house instead?" She launched the realtor's website and started reading.

"I was talking to Rhonda Wells at Mason's yesterday—"

"Did you say hi for me?" She didn't stop scrolling through the listing.

"—and she said there's a suspicious painting in this house."

"Ooh!" Lucy wiggled her hips in her seat, forcing me to crack a smile.

"The sale opens in a couple of weeks, so I can't get inside to look before that. I was thinking—"

Her head snapped toward me, eyes glowing with excitement. "Digital snooping!"

"It sounds creepy when you say it that way." Scrolling through the images on her phone, I stopped on the one of the bedroom. "The master bedroom has a photo with a sliver of the painting in it."

She zoomed in. "Where?"

"It's reflected in the—" I leaned over to point to it, but it was the wrong photo. There was no reflection of the painting in the mirror. I flipped back and forth through the photos, eventually taking her phone to look closer.

"What do we do when we're done? Call Officer Williams?"

Janelle Williams of the Brenton Police Department had been my best friend growing up until we had a falling out in college. We'd patched up some of that damage since I'd moved home, but she wasn't the person for the job. "I have a contact with FBI Art Crimes. I'll call him if it looks like Rhonda's right."

She popped a bubble at me. "You ever going to tell me about that FBI thing?"

"I was in, I left, and that's the entire boring story." After cycling through the listing three times, I pulled out my own phone and showed her the screenshot I'd taken at the gallery. "This photo—the one Rhonda called me about—is gone."

"Even better! I've so got this." She dropped her phone into her bag and hauled a laptop out of her backpack. "Lemme get started."

"Why do you have your laptop with you?"

"You don't take yours everywhere you go?" She hooked a thumb over her shoulder to the back seat office of my F-150 Raptor, where I had a mobile desk, printer, and all the supplies I needed for doing my work on the road.

"Valid point." I pulled the truck out. "But let's go do this at my place before they think we're doing more than snooping on an upcoming listing."

～

"Yes!" Lucy's arms shot up into the air, startling me. She'd been talking in a constant low hum while she typed and clicked, so much that I'd blocked out both her and the program she had streaming through the television.

We sat next to each other on one of the couches in my hotel room, the junior suite I'd lived in since I moved back to Brenton last summer. Sitting room, bedrooms branching off either side, and a kitchenette which saw very little use.

I stuffed my fork into the heap of noodles in my takeout container and hit mute on the television remote. "I assume that means you found something?"

Lucy picked up her laptop from the coffee table in front of us and showed me a zoomed-in copy of the painting peeking out from behind the master bedroom's door. "I. Am. A genius."

"Clearly." I took the laptop and scrutinized the photo. It was far clearer than on my phone and sharper than it had been at Rhonda's. "How'd you find it?"

"Most real estate sites are pretty secure with their back-ends, but this one's rudimentary. I ran through some details on the console and some code inspections." She picked up her lunch, the scents of garlic and ginger wafting over me as she moved, and inhaled a forkful. She pointed at the browser's address bar. "The last part of the URL is the filename: *house-_25_large.jpg*. But if you look at the gallery—the master listing of all the photos—it jumps from twenty-four to twenty-six."

"So, you... guessed?"

"Sort of. Numbers just sort of jump out at me. The first five sites I found were hashed values, but—"

"Hashed?"

"Secure." She shook her head and took another bite,

covering her mouth as she spoke. "Do you really care about the details?"

I zoomed in on the dark photo and nudged her with my foot. "I guess I'll have to keep you around longer unless I want to learn all your tricks."

"Guess so!"

"Don't suppose you have any magic tool to make the door blocking out half the painting disappear?"

"No, but I can brighten it so you can see it better. Blow it up and look at that signature." She shoveled another mass of food into her mouth, dropped her empty container to the table, and took the laptop back.

Programs opened and closed. She typed and scrolled around, muttering about a Belgian photographer's studio her parents took her to once. Sure the story was more for herself than me, I set about cleaning up our lunch.

Butterflies danced in my stomach as her speech grew faster and faster. That usually indicated things were going well.

John Constable painted small and large pieces. Based on the photo, this one was roughly two feet high, but we didn't know if it was landscape or portrait, so it could be wider or narrower than two feet.

If Lucy could sharpen the image enough, I might be able to do a visual search through a stolen art database or possibly submit it for an AI comparison. As excited as I was, it was still possible it was a print or a copy. But why would they chase Rhonda away, then take the photo down from the real estate listing if that was the case?

No, there was something going on here, and we were getting to the bottom of it. Then I could call Elliot and show him what I could do. He wanted me to come back to the FBI and work for him, but that would mean leaving Brenton—and Antonio.

I didn't want that. I wanted both.

Solving the thefts from Pompeii should have been my opportunity to negotiate an agreement which could keep me in Brenton while working remotely as an FBI contractor. But I hadn't achieved enough there.

Maybe if we could add this Constable theft—if it really was a Constable and it really was a theft—to my list of accomplishments, I could use it as a bargaining chip.

I disposed of the last of our meal and brought the plastic dessert container and two forks over to the couch. "Any progress?"

"Boom!" She exchanged the laptop for the sweets. "This pie is all mine."

"Amazing." I took her laptop to the dining table and placed it next to mine. Dark trees covered most of the visible canvas, a cloudy sky hanging above.

"Meh." She dug into the cherry pie we'd picked up and moaned with her first bite. "Oh my god, Sam, this is awesome."

"You can have my slice." A river cut up from the bottom, disappearing behind the bedroom door. One figure next to... I zoomed in closer. Next to part of a wooden structure. A flash of red for the figure's shirt, one of Constable's hallmarks. Above his head, a bit of white? And some light brown? "It's a windmill!"

She bounced from the couch to my side. "What's a windmill?"

"Here." I pointed to the base and then the blade, little more than slivers in the digital image. "The rest of it's behind that door, but it gives me data for my search."

"Sweet. You sure you don't want this pie? The crust is beyond flaky. And there's sugar crystals on the edges."

I nodded, opening the FBI's Stolen Art Database.

"Do you think they made this crust with butter, shortening, or lard?"

Two Constables in their database, one mentioning a windmill, but sadly no photograph of the paintings. Next: Interpol's database.

"I read you should always use lard. A lot of people avoid it these days because, you know, lard, but it produces a better crust."

I sifted through potential matches while Lucy babbled about proper ways to sift flour. How was this master-of-trivia, plugged-in maven, my best friend? I wouldn't have believed it four months ago.

Interpol had three hits—two with a windmill and one without. The two with windmills didn't quite match the one we were looking at, but it could have been a trick of the light or some damage. "Shit."

"Sorry, did you actually want your piece?"

"No clear matches. Either I need to get into that house to get a look at the real thing or I need to submit the image for a visual comparison."

"As much as I love the digital snooping, not sure I'm up for breaking and entering."

I snatched the container from her and moved back to the couch and my fork. "I should call Elliot and get his thoughts."

"Elliot's that FBI agent from the press conference you were in about the Scotts?"

I nodded and shoveled a giant piece of pie in my mouth. This was a minor setback. The paintings from the FBI database could be duplicates of those in the Interpol database—I'd check when I finished the pie. And if they were, I could still research how and when each had gone missing. Maybe that would lead me somewhere.

"He's the FBI Art Crimes contact?"

"Mm-hmm," I indicated around a mouthful. It barely registered on my tongue before I swallowed it. "I'm going to keep digging a little more before I call in reinforcements."

"Hey! I'm reinforcements!"

"You know what I mean."

"I know, I know. Not super secret won't tell my friends about it kinda reinforcements." Lucy'd been my secret weapon in more than one investigation already, but even she didn't have all the resources I needed.

"Ha ha." My phone buzzed with a reminder, and I shot off the couch. "Dammit—we need to hurry up! Our slot at The Ridge is in fifteen minutes and we still need to get changed into our rock climbing gear."

"I'd move faster if you let me eat the rest of that pie."

I handed the container to her so she could scarf down the last bites. "I'm pretty sure extra pie will make you slower."

After tossing the container into the sink to clean when I got home, I threw my backpack over my shoulder and waited at the door for her.

"I was thinking about hitting the bouldering wall."

"Not a chance." I locked up behind her and grinned over my shoulder. "That five-point-six route is calling your name. I refuse to continue teaching you anything else until you conquer it."

CHAPTER 7

SAMANTHA

Two days later, I put the truck into park in front of Ferraro's Fine Art Restoration and Conservation. Black lamp-posts lined the two-lane street, decorated with little Italian flags and flower baskets overflowing with pine boughs and red bulbs. This section of Calabria Street—where the street signs read Via Calabria, as it would have been called in Italy—was the heart of Brenton's Italian business community. It was dotted with small shops like Ferraro's, including my favorite cafe down the road.

The front of the white-washed building had large glass windows, providing a view of the reception area with its black couches and Sofia's two-tiered desk.

"Any news on that painting?" Lucy asked from the passenger seat, while she scrolled through some message feed.

"Based on what I found in the FBI and Interpol databases, I'm thinking it's either one that was stolen from Los Angeles in 2013 or Vancouver in 2012. But I need to get a closer look and check out the back of it to be sure. They're having an invite-only showing just after New Year's I'm going to wrangle an invite to—did you want to come with me?"

"In-person snooping?"

"Isn't that what you do during a showing? I was also planning on canvassing the neighborhood to find out about the owners."

She looked up from her phone. "Do you know who they are?"

"Yeah, the Homeowners insurance is through Foster. It's an older couple and I couldn't find anything on them that would indicate they were art thieves. I've heard about worse, though."

"Like the retired bus driver that stole that Duke of Wellington painting?"

I grinned at her. "Well done, my young padawan."

Her eyes lowered under the compliment and she turned to look through the tall front windows of Ferraro's. Her gaze snapped back to me immediately and she popped a gum bubble. "Who. Is that?"

I leaned forward to see around her. Sofia, Antonio's older sister, sat behind her giant desk, talking to a slender man in a blue suit. Lucy's head swiveled to the office and returned to me again. I recognized her look. It was the same one she gave Antonio and Nathan every time she saw them. "That's Antonio's younger brother, Lorenzo."

"Tell me he's single?"

I'd only met him once, at an ill-fated dinner at Antonio's parents' house. He was a copy of his older brother in many ways; handsome, with killer cheekbones, tousled dark hair, and a flirtatious streak. Not quite a clone, though. He was a couple inches shorter, twenty or thirty pounds lighter, and had a smile that was slightly less dazzling. Although I may have been biased.

Without waiting for a response, Lucy hefted open the door and slid out. I snatched *Number Vee*'s case from the back seat and hustled to catch up to her. The police had released it much faster than I'd expected. No leads about the shooting, though, so I'd scheduled time tomorrow with Foster's top investigators to talk it over.

As we stepped into the studio, I inhaled deeply, centering myself in the room. The scents and sounds were the same as always—spicy irises and Vivaldi—and Sofia stood from her chair.

"Samantha! Lucy!" She wore a tight cobalt blue dress, accentuating her impressive curves. Her full black hair danced around her face, like she was walking down a runway. With kisses to each of our cheeks, she put her hands to her hips, feigning a glare. "You didn't tell me Lucy was coming with you."

Before I could respond, Lucy stepped around Sofia and threw out her hand toward Lorenzo. "Hi. I'm Lucy Chapman, Sam's best friend."

"It's a pleasure to meet you." He smiled warmly at her, shook her hand slowly, then nodded to me. "Samantha, it's been too long."

"Is that my Samantha?" boomed Dominico's voice as he rounded the reception wall, which divided the entry space from the large studio behind. Antonio's father was my height, with salt-and-pepper hair, deep olive skin, and the broadest smile of anyone I'd ever met. He elbowed his way past Lorenzo to get to me. As he grabbed me by the shoulders, I offered my cheeks and he made exaggerated kissing noises before grabbing my free hand.

Since Antonio had left, I'd been to Ferraro's once for a painting and a few times to visit Sofia. And Dominico had called me 'my Samantha' every time.

"Dr. Dominico, this is—"

"I told you already. It's Dom." He patted my held hand, turning his smile to Lucy. "Now, who's this vision?"

I nudged Lucy, who was chatting with Lorenzo. "This is Lucy Chapman, a friend of mine."

Dom inserted himself between Lucy and his son, taking her by the shoulders to kiss more air than he had with me. Keeping a grip on her and retrieving my hand, he shook his head slowly. "So much beauty in one room. How can I survive this day?"

"Papa, if you'll excuse us." Lorenzo's accent was as thick as Antonio's. Dom had moved the family from Brenton to Rome when Antonio was five, so the boys grew up with Italian as their primary language. "Lucy was going to tell me about her last trip to Roma."

Lucy beamed and they drifted to the reception couches. That girl worked fast. He'd better be single and not just flirting with her or we'd have words. And then some.

I slipped my hand from Dom's and put the case on the top tier of Sofia's desk. "We're just here to drop off this painting, then we'll be out of your hair."

Dom patted my back gently. "Let's take it to my work-space. I can look at it now."

"That's alright. I can leave it with Sofia. I imagine you're very busy with Antonio away."

"Have you heard his news?" asked Sofia absently,

returning to her position behind the desk. Her focus was on Lucy and Lorenzo, a glimmer of mischief in her smirk.

"That the project's been extended into April? Yeah, he told me Saturday night."

"Right." She shook her head quickly before turning to me, like she'd forgotten what she was doing. "I'm glad he told you. He was upset."

"I don't understand why. It's fantastic news!" Dom took the case from the desk and headed around the reception wall to the studio. "Come with me, my love."

I eyed Sofia, but she avoided my gaze. Intentionally. It was clearly intentional. A prickling sensation traveled up my fingers, accompanying the knot twisting in my stomach. What was she hiding from me? "Sofia?"

"Papa's waiting for you." She shooed me away and sat behind her desk.

I gave her a moment more, but she was very good at ignoring me. Work or personal—what was my priority? Work, it had to be work. I turned slowly, rubbing my fingers together to get the blood flowing, and followed Dom.

As I entered the studio area, I saw three familiar faces. Alice, the blond restorer; Frank, Antonio's cousin and Alice's boyfriend; and Zander, the heavy metal fanatic with his over-sized headphones. Alice and Frank sat at ten-foot long white tables, open underneath where they stored many tools of their trade. She wore a headband with a magnification visor over her eyes, studying something on a small painting at her table. He was rolling a handmade swab across a large painting on his desk. Zander sat at an easel in the back of the room, with the morning sun shining in on him from the windows behind.

Alice gave me a smile and a wave. "You going to ID this painting for me today?"

Frank looked up expectantly.

"Italian Baroque, 16th century?" I meant it as a joke, but she nodded. When I was first introduced to Alice, I'd identified a painting from that period and style she was working on. It had obviously impressed her. I smiled, Sofia's avoidance continuing to hang over me, preventing a laugh.

"Samantha, you're mine this morning." Dom waved me over to him. He'd opened the case and had withdrawn the paperwork.

After donning the pair of nitrile gloves he handed me, I lifted the painting and placed it on his desk.

"What is this?"

I pointed to the hole in the middle of the medium blue stripe. "Bullet hole."

"I haven't dealt with one of those in a while," he sighed.

"But, you have before?"

"A few times, yes." He put up a hand for silence and any further questions died on my lips. Had he seen bullet holes in paintings because when you restore thousands of paintings, you'll see a bit of everything? I'd been to the studio many times before, but this was only the second time I'd met with Dominico professionally. I couldn't ask him for details like that, could I?

Donning his headband and flipping down the magnification visor, he closed in on the painting to examine how the fibers had been impacted. He moved this way and that, taking the damage in, and flipped the painting over to inspect the back.

I smiled and pointed out the backing Antonio had applied. "Antonio fixed a tear in it in August."

He stepped back from his close review and flipped it over to look at the front again. He lifted it on an angle and looked at the back, the front, then the back and front again.

"It was exceptional work." I smiled, thinking of the day he'd called me in to pick it up. He'd gifted me a pastry and a copy of his doctoral dissertation. He'd been so charming, working hard to impress me. *I should text him about that. That would make him happy.*

Dom straightened, nodding slowly. "Yes, outstanding work. Maybe we should leave it for him to do."

"I don't think they want to wait until April."

"No, when he's home for—" He cut off abruptly, his face dropping. His eyes flicked toward the reception area and back to me. Frank and Alice did the same. "Ah, yes, good point."

The knot tightened in my stomach. They were hiding something about Antonio. All of them. When I turned around to follow their eyes, Sofia was standing at the dividing wall between the studio and the reception area. Her face was tight, likely a mirror of my own, her arms folded.

Suddenly, Sofia threw her hands out, rushing toward me. "Oh, I can't stand it! He's coming home for Christmas! He arrives at five!"

I gaped. *He what?*

She flung her arms around me and everyone else laughed.

"That's why he was working all weekend?" The knot exploded into an army of butterflies in my chest. I was going to see him. Today! Get that hug and tell him what happened Saturday and finally have him tell me everything was alright. I had to shower and get changed. Tidy my hotel room. Pick up my dress from the dry— "And why he scheduled date night tonight?"

She released me, nodding vigorously. "He's such a troublemaker! Promised me not to tell, but I told everyone—" She looked past me to her father. "—and warned them all to keep quiet when you were here."

My heart did a cartwheel. He'd be home for Christmas! "I'll pick him up! Gimme the details."

"Perfect!" She grinned wickedly; she loved messing with her brother. "Turn the surprise on him!"

MY FOOT HIT the accelerator and I made my way onto the street, heart hammering the whole time, and the smile not leaving my lips. "I'm sorry, Luce. We'll do lunch later."

Lucy's eyes were plastered to her phone. "Is it too soon to text Lorenzo?"

Antonio was such a troublemaker. He'd planned date night so he could surprise me. My schedule was already clear for the evening, but I could reschedule one other appointment and get ready. I had to shave my legs. No time to pick up the dress, though. Swap out the cotton underwear, for sure.

I hadn't asked how long he'd be home, but Sofia said Christmas. "Oh my god, I'm calling Cass! She'll have to make space for Christmas dinner."

Lucy popped a gum bubble. "I'm still invited, though, right?"

"Of cour—" I smacked her thigh. "Shit! The Constable!"

She tore her eyes away from her texting app.

I'd picked up extra appointments for the holidays to get

me through the last weeks of waiting for Antonio to come home. People were on vacation this week, so I couldn't shift them back. Next week, maybe. "Luce, think you can canvass that neighborhood for me? Sounds like I won't have the free time I thought I would."

"You got it, boss!"

CHAPTER 8

ANTONIO

I STRODE through the Lansing airport, moving with the crowd from my flight, phone pressed to my ear. "Are you here yet, Sofia?"

"No, soon."

"When you say soon, do you mean five minutes or one hour? Will you be inside or waiting outside the airport? I don't have a winter jacket with me."

She huffed. "Just wait for me at Arrivals."

Shooting a look heavenward, I returned the phone to my pocket.

"Do you need a ride?" Kayla, a pretty woman with blond hair and freckles, had sat next to me on the flight from Detroit, and we'd spoken the whole way. Granted, I did most of the talking.

Laughing, I shook my head. "My sister knows how important this is. She won't be late, no matter how she teases."

"Why isn't your girlfriend picking you up?"

My chest swelled at the thought of Samantha. Despite what I'd seen on our call Saturday night, she was still mine, and she was so close. "It's a surprise. She doesn't know I'm coming home for Christmas."

"When will you see her?"

I adjusted the leather duffel on my shoulder with the few things I brought with me. No checked bags to slow me down. "I'm heading home first to clean up."

She looked me up and down, raising an eyebrow. I did the same. White linen button-front shirt, sleeves rolled up, brown pants, and cognac dress shoes. Good clothes for travel, but not enough to see Samantha for the first time in three months.

"I need a suit. Perhaps a tuxedo. Do you think that's too much?"

She laughed, covering her mouth with a hand. "Are you proposing to her?"

I swung my bag down and rummaged in an interior pocket, withdrew a small blue leather box, and eased it open to show her the ring.

Kayla sucked in a deep breath. "Wow."

The band was platinum with channel-set diamonds, simple and straight-forward like my Samantha. The center stone was a brilliant-cut show stopper, barely two carats. Convincing her to say yes would be enough of a battle without having to argue about the weight of a piece of compressed carbon.

"I had it custom made for her a month ago." It glittered as we walked, its fire reminding me of Samantha's ferocity, over-whelming and yet breathtaking. I tucked it back into its zippered compartment, my heart fluttering. "I doubt it will be today. It may not even be this visit, but eventually, yes."

"Well, if it's not today, then a tux is too much. But to be

honest, with a ring like that, it won't matter what you're wearing." She laughed, shaking her head. "What about flowers?"

"No, she's not a flowers type of woman." That was a mistake I only made once. Samantha thought they were a distraction. Perhaps someday she wouldn't doubt the sincerity behind them, but not today. "There's a cafe in Brenton that makes her favorite pastries. I was going to pick up some chocolate hazelnut cornetti. We have a plan for a date by video chat at six, so I'll show up at her door with food just in time."

Kayla put her hand on my arm. "Antonio, you really give me hope there are good men left out there."

I smiled back at her as we arrived at the top of the escalator. "I'm so excited to see her, I can hardly stand it." My hand flared out in front of me, unable to express myself with words alone.

As we stepped onto the escalator, heading down to security and the Arrivals area, I'd planned to search out my sister. But my gaze immediately settled upon the most wondrous sight in all the world. Samantha. I didn't have to scan the crowd—her soul tugged at mine, pulling my eyes to her.

"There she is," I breathed, my hand frozen in mid-air. "Look at how beautiful she is."

She wore a long navy jacket over a skirt and white blouse, with tall boots. And her long hair captured in that damnable bun. Draped over her arm, the coat I'd asked Sofia to bring to the airport.

Samantha's eyes were wide. What was the matter? Was there danger somewhere? No, danger would cause Samantha to run toward it, not freeze in place. Then her brows pulled down.

Kayla said something, but the words were lost to the air.

Samantha's eyes were not on me. They were on Kayla. I leaned in front of her and waved at Samantha, blowing her a kiss as I straightened.

She rolled her eyes. *Cheesy*, she'd be thinking. But the corner of her mouth had quirked up.

I checked the woman on the step below me and slipped between the edge of the escalator and her bag. Jostled with a suitcase on the next step. Excused myself to a man on the next. Bracing my hands on either handrail, I launched over the next bag, almost losing my duffel in the process.

I looked up, and Samantha was biting back a smile.

Weaving my way between people, apologizing over and over, I ignored the turn to baggage claim and hurried out of the secure area to meet her.

I stopped directly in front of her, dropping my bag without a care. Her beautiful eyes, blue-green and shining like the waters of the Aegean Sea, her luscious lips, the strong body hidden under her coat. The growing smile.

She stared up at me, the few inches I stood taller than her, her eyes not quite focusing. "Welco—"

I grabbed her face between my hands and took her mouth with mine. Her lips parted, but her tongue didn't move, her whole body rigid. She hated public displays of affection. Any other day, I'd only tease. But today? After being apart for so long? Wrapping one arm around her, I pulled her close. I had my love back in my arms and that was all that mattered in the world.

She gradually softened, responding to my touch, and her tongue swept across mine. Running her fingers through the short hair above my ear, she sighed, sending shock waves through every inch of my body.

Throwing the other arm around her, I leaned back, pulling her into the air. She broke from the kiss to laugh. As I put her down, we rested our foreheads together, our smiles beyond control.

I kissed her nose quickly. "My arms are complete again with you inside them, bella."

She chuckled, rolling her eyes. "You're so cheesy."

"And yet so wonderful, sì?" I breathed in deeply, taking in her lovely citrus scent. "Would you believe I feel nervous?"

"Hardly."

I touched my lips to hers. So soft, so perfect. "Only one thing's wrong."

"What's that?"

Brushing my hand along the side of her head, my fingers paused at her bun. I smirked. "May I?"

She continued smiling in return, and I pulled a couple of pins out before her luxurious hair fell loose in graceful waves. A blush crept up her cheeks. It was so intimate, in such a public place, it surprised me she'd agreed.

"You're so much more beautiful in person." I ran my fingers through her hair and kissed her deeply. The kiss grew more urgent as she squeezed the back of my neck, and a guttural noise erupted in my chest. I switched to a hug before my body reacted in ways it shouldn't in the middle of Arrivals. "I almost forgot how good you taste."

Her lips brushed my neck as she whispered, "And how good you smell."

I leaned away from her. "Sofia spoiled my surprise, sì?"

"Your father, actually."

"When did you see him?"

"I picked up *Number Vee* on Saturday for some repairs."

I arched an eyebrow.

"Long story. Not important. How long have you been planning this?"

Another kiss. "I called my travel agent when I got home from the club. It took some work and a few layovers to get here so close to Christmas, but I couldn't wait four more months to see you again."

"And the date night thing?"

"I had to be sure you'd be available." I stroked one lovely cheek and kissed the opposite one. "It's been too long, bella."

"Say my name," she said, biting her lip.

"Samantha," I breathed out, slowly. Under her jacket, there would be goosebumps.

"God, I love the way you say that. Sa-mahn-tha," she said, mimicking my Italian accent and brushing my lips with a thumb.

The touch sent another jolt through my body, every fiber begging to have her naked underneath me. Or atop me or next to me or anywhere near me. "We should be going. I need you somewhere private."

Her eyes widened briefly and she separated to hold up the coat she carried. "Sofia sent me with this. It's cold out."

As I shrugged it on, I whispered, "I'd hoped to be removing clothing when I saw you, not putting more on." I leaned closer, bringing my mouth to her ear, and brushing it lightly with my lips. "Your place is closer than mine."

She wrapped her arms around me, under my long coat before I could do it up, and her hands trailed down the curve of my ass. She pushed her groin hard against mine and I groaned.

We kissed one more time and I pulled away, picking up my duffel. "Andiamo, bella."

"What about your bags?"

"I only brought this one. My winter clothes are still here."

She grabbed my hand and yanked me toward the exit at a near-run.

IN THE PRIVACY of her truck, I turned her face to mine, kissing her again, our tongues reacquainting themselves. She moaned into my mouth and cupped my cheek while I snuck a hand under her jacket, popping one button of her blouse. Just enough space to access a firm breast. She withdrew the hand and moved it to her thigh, hitching her skirt up a few inches.

"Bare legs." I sank my hand to the inside of her thigh and rode it up to her crotch, to her silky underwear. "You must be cold."

"I am, but I thought you might like it."

I rubbed my fingers against her panties, finding her hot and wet.

She sucked in a quick breath. Despite feeling even more ready than I was, she grabbed my forearm and separated me from her. "You know, the more you do that, the longer it'll take for us to get to my hotel."

"I'll sit in the back if needed." I inclined my head to the back seat with a wink. "Care to join me?"

She laughed, continuing to hold my arm at bay. "Just relax and enjoy the ride."

"Oh, I intend to, Samantha. All night." Sì, I needed her flesh against mine.

She squeezed her eyes shut and blew out a long breath before putting the truck into drive.

Once we were on our way, her hands were occupied, so mine took residence on her thigh. She snapped her legs together and swatted me away, but I was persistent.

"Oh, bella, just here?" I pouted, pointing at her mid-thigh. "Per favore?"

She rolled her eyes, which I took as permission.

My hand nestled between her legs, falling into a rhythmic stroke just under the hem of her skirt. Her legs were long, lithe, like the rest of her athletic body. Undoubtedly able to snap a man in half. "And I should ask now, in case we need to stop somewhere—"

A small noise rumbled from her chest as my hand climbed a few more inches.

"—I know we agreed when our test results came in—" When I reached her underwear, she tamped down on the accelerator.

She pushed the hand away again, rolling her hips in her seat. "You can't do that while I'm driving."

"—but we're done with the condoms, sì?"

She flicked me a glance from the corner of her eyes, a delicious smile spreading across her lips. "Yeah, just you, me, and my IUD."

"And if it fails, and you do become pregnant, we'll get married and—"

The smile rapidly switched to a frown and she smacked my chest. "That was not part of the discussion!"

"It was in the discussion in *my* head." I pinched her leg and she knocked the hand away, but I snuck it back. To the spot she had allowed and no higher.

Perhaps an inch higher.

Shaking her head, she said no more on the subject, but she didn't say no. She was so guarded emotionally, but I found this worked. Bring up an idea she was uncomfortable with, laugh it off, and let her mull it over until she realized she was comfortable with it after all. It had taken many such nudges for her to go on a date with me in the first place and there would be a great deal more in our future.

This visit would undoubtedly be full of them.

CHAPTER 9

SAMANTHA

ONCE WE WERE past the front desk in the Brenton Arms, our pace increased exponentially. The closer to my room, the faster we got. When I stopped at my door, at the end of the hall, he swept my jacket to the side and grabbed my hips from behind. He pressed against me, already hard.

This was going to be a long night.

"Open the door." His voice was muffled as he ran his mouth along my neck.

My inner muscles clenched and released, whining for him, and I braced a hand against the wall, blood thundering in my ears. "I can't while you're doing that."

He hauled my skirt hem up at the side, thrusting a hand underneath to stroke the outside of my underwear. "Shut up and open it before I tear your clothes off right here."

I fumbled in my purse for the keycard, shuddering to a halt as he dragged his teeth along my earlobe and slipped a finger inside my panties. With a deep breath, I snatched the card, swiped it across the lock, and it clicked. He spun me to face him, pinning me against the door, and his mouth captured mine. It was a demanding kiss, all tongue and teeth. He turned the handle and we stumbled in.

Before the door swung shut, my purse hit the floor. Our jackets somewhere near the closet. Another step in. He pulled at a button on my blouse, unable to undo it. With a quick tug, buttons went flying, and he ripped it off me.

"I'll buy you a new one." His breath came in bursts, his touch rough and urgent.

My hands clutched in his hair, across his back, on his face, and my tongue couldn't get enough of his. Pulling his shirt out of his pants, I dragged my nails along the powerful muscles lining his spine. God, I'd missed his body. I hoisted my skirt and grabbed his neck. He caught me when I leaped, wrapping my legs around his waist. I squeezed tight, unable to get close enough to him. Not getting enough friction.

"Marone, you're strong," he murmured into my mouth as we slammed against the wall of the entryway.

"Ow!" The light over the sitting room flickered on, and my back arched away from the switch. He grinned wickedly and carried me past the kitchenette to a couch, where we collapsed as one. I pushed him off, far enough I could unbuckle his belt. Before I could progress to his pants, he leaned one arm on the back of the couch, his broad shoulders flexing as he dipped down, making a trail with his hungry tongue along the edge of my bra.

"I've studied the most beautiful art ever created." He eased the fabric of one bra cup down, rolling my nipple between his lips and sucking it into his mouth.

I gulped in air, surrounded by his delicious vanilla and amber scent. The button on his pants was too far away.

"But your body—" His gaze rose to meet mine, jaw flexed

and nostrils flared. The need in those eyes stabbed into my core, heightening the throbbing inside me. "—is the most breathtaking canvas in all the world."

I curled my fists in his shirt, forcing his face to mine. My body was craving his touch. Not his words. "Shut up and take me to the bed. I hate this fucking couch."

I latched on with my legs and he wrapped one arm around my lower back, straightening without effort. Our mouths locked together, and I clutched a handful of his hair. We rounded the couch, past the dim light shining through the balcony door, and turned to the bedroom. He grunted as he ran into a side table next to the second couch and took a step backward to regain his balance.

A deafening crack echoed through the evening—a gush of air whooshed behind me—an instant before the overhead light went out.

We were plunged into near darkness.

CHAPTER 10

ANTONIO

"Cazzo!" That was a bullet! I dropped us to the floor, rotating my body to cushion her descent. But she crashed onto the table anyway, crying out as she did. Frantic voices erupted from the hotel rooms around us.

Ice flowed through my veins. Was her reaction from hitting the table or had the bullet grazed her on the way past?

She was on hands and knees, and her head snapped up, long hair streaming about her. Her head swiveled back and forth, impassive eyes touching every surface, and one hand pressed me down as though to use me as leverage to get up. She checked her watch.

I reached for her, to pull her closer to the floor and safety, ensuring I was between her and the balcony door, where the shot had come from. "Were you hit? Are you—"

Another peal rang through the room, as the balcony door exploded inward and a wave of frigid air hit us.

With it, daggers shredded across my back. I clamped my eyes shut, biting back the pain. Not a direct hit of a bullet, but a searing sensation spreading out from my right shoulder. Something had struck me. Possibly glass.

But I was fine. *Focus on Samantha.*

I pulled her closer, shielding her.

She pushed me away from her and pointed to the bedroom we'd been aiming for. "Keep your head down! Go that way!"

As I rose, she pressed on my head to keep it lower and encourage me forward. I grabbed her arm and propelled her ahead of me, crouching over her as we dashed to safety.

We landed behind the bed, and she asked, "Do you have your phone?"

I winced, contact with the bed slicing into my back. "In my jacket."

"Dammit, mine's in my purse." She grabbed a laptop from the bedside table.

"Why the laptop?"

"Only option for 9-1-1 we have."

The bedroom's window was far smaller than the balcony door, plus the bed provided significantly more cover. We were safe here. I sealed my eyes shut, breathing through the agony in my back, while she typed furiously on the keyboard.

I cracked an eye open to see the laptop screen. Two direct message windows, one with her friend Janelle and the other with a man named Jimmy. Both included her address, an urgent request for officers, and advising them shots had been fired.

One reply from Janelle, *Dispatching officers. Hold tight.*

Samantha just finished typing. *Shots originated south side of building. Came through 3rd floor balcony door at chest height. Hit ceiling 15 feet inside. Shooter's at ground level.*

How many shooters? was the response.

Samantha dropped the laptop and crawled into the adjoining bathroom.

"What are you doing?"

She darted up to grab the vanity mirror and snapped it off its extending arm. Staying low, she dashed toward the window.

"You are not—" I rolled to my side and grabbed her leg, bringing her to a skidding halt and she hit the floor. Pain exploded up my arm, through my head, and a wave of nausea overcame me.

"Let me do my job," she hissed and kicked out of my grasp, back up on her feet and at the window before my brain cleared.

"This is not your job, Samantha!" I ground out.

"The best chance the police have is accurate intel."

Another gunshot burst through the balcony doors, the thud of it hitting the ceiling just loud enough for me to hear over the blood pounding in my ears.

Samantha rose next to the window, flat against the wall, and angled the mirror to see out. "The hotel backs onto a wooded trail by a stream. Kids drink down there sometimes and do stupid shit."

I'd seen glimpses of this side of her, the side passionate about chasing down thieves, but this was different. Someone was shooting at us and she was trying to get closer, not further away.

"This is not stupid kids." Dampness spread across my back, hopefully sweat, but likely blood. I pushed through it and crawled to her feet, reaching for a hand. "This recklessness almost got you killed in Napoli."

She swatted in my direction, focused on the mirror. "Gimme a minute."

Another loud crack and a dull thump behind Samantha. This one was not in the living room. It was on the other side of the wall from her.

One more crack and the bedroom window shattered, the mirror flying out of her hand.

She yelped, and with the distraction, I was able to yank her to the floor. Another bullet flew into the bedroom, the whizzing noise sending a fresh wave of panic through me. She was not getting away from me this time.

I pushed her toward the bathroom and snatched the laptop so she wouldn't come back for it. As firm as possible, I said, "Now stay down!"

She didn't argue, just grabbed the laptop and typed out a message to Janelle. *I only see one shooter. In the woods, by the trail behind the building. Far end.*

Another gunshot. Screams from inside the hotel almost drowned out the sound of the bullet impacting the ceiling in the bedroom.

Samantha checked her watch. "Goddamnit! It's only been five fucking minutes!"

I landed against the wall, fire licking through my back, but I grit my teeth against it and pulled her onto my lap. Two walls, a bed, and my body between her and the shooter. She tried to escape; to take the laptop, to check the window again, who knew?

"Stop fighting me," I whispered, and pressed my lips to the top of her head. "I won't let you go, bella."

Her body gradually eased, and her face dug into my neck, letting me wrap my arms more fully around her. We huddled together for what felt like half an hour, until the sirens approached.

The laptop pinged.

I woke the screen and read the message. "Janelle says the police are here and she wants to know when the last shot was."

Samantha made a move as if to push away from me, but I had her with my better arm, and she wouldn't escape. "Tell her 6:32. What time is it now?"

"6:42."

I typed the response, not letting her head go. Another message appeared. "She says Jimmy's with them and she'll be here as soon as she can."

Was she right about it being drunk kids down on the trail? Surely not. One or two random gunshots or even a peppering all at once would make sense for that, but not the slow and intentional aim from one window to the next as we switched rooms.

A crew of thieves had threatened Samantha's life when she was in Napoli with me. One of them had put his hands on her and paid the price. A man working for my cousin Cristian—the one who'd saved her life—assured me the thieves were not an ongoing issue, but was he wrong?

Visions of the apartment in Napoli swallowed me. Walking in to see her gashed forehead, the beaten man on the floor, blood covering so many surfaces. The way she could barely stand the next day. At least this time, I was here to protect her. "Everything will be alright, bella. I'm here."

Her body grew soft and her hands slid against my chest. Nestling closer, she let out a ragged whisper, "Good."

I kissed the top of her head and leaned into her. The way

she said it that time, full of gratitude and peace, relief and comfort. Perhaps *Good* had meant *I love you* all along.

The screams and yells in the other rooms continued, doors opening and closing, people knocking to check on others. Hurrying feet in the hallway. While Samantha and I just breathed together, our hearts trying to find each other's rhythms.

We startled when fists pounded on her door. "Brenton PD! Sammy, it's Jimmy! Everything's clear! Open up!"

Rushing to the door, we straightened our clothes as best we could. She smoothed her skirt, I buckled my pants, and we searched for her torn shirt. I threw mine over her in the rush, and she did one strategic button.

The pounding came again. "Sammy! Answer me, or we're coming in whatever way we can!"

"I'm here, Jimmy!" She swung the door open.

The officer's gun was out of its holster before I could blink, trained on me. "Who's this?"

"My boyfriend," said Samantha, hands raised. "He's not a threat."

Jimmy assessed the scene, glancing from me to Samantha and sweeping every surface. Apparently finding no immediate risk, he holstered his sidearm as quickly as he'd drawn it and sauntered into the room. "That explains a lot."

"Explains what?" I narrowed my eyes, the light from the hallway exceedingly bright after the dark bathroom.

He was a couple of inches shorter than me, a lanky man who likely looked imposing only because of his vest and duty belt, which provided an illusion of breadth and size.

"Jimmy Slater. I'm an old friend of Sammy's." He

extended a hand, giving me a blatant once-over. "You must spend a lot of time at the gym."

I didn't like this man, but he was a friend of Samantha's who didn't touch her the way Miller did, so I smiled and shook his hand. "Antonio Ferraro. You worked on the Scott case, sì?"

"I did." A muscle in Jimmy's jaw ticked, but the easygoing manner didn't falter. From what Samantha told me of the case, it had been closed early, until she and Janelle had it reopened when they uncovered the arson and murder. I vaguely remembered speaking with Jimmy outside of the Scott house after the fire. He must have been the officer who did the poor original job. "Got any lights in this place?"

"Yeah." Samantha turned on the lamp we almost knocked over before the first gunshot. Two feet away from where the broken glass littered the floor.

Energy tumbled through my stomach. That table saved her life. She could have been killed. Then where would I be? We should have stayed on the couch she hated so much.

Jimmy said, "We didn't find a shooter, but—holy shit, you're bleeding, Sammy!"

CHAPTER 11

SAMANTHA

"I'M FINE." Other than the bruises and strain from the mirror being shot out of my hands, I didn't feel any pain. When I turned to face them, they spun me away, Antonio prodding my upper back, where the shirt was still damp.

Another male officer joined us. "Slater, it's him, not her."

I stepped behind Antonio, goosebumps crawling up and down my arms. My hand clamped over my mouth, and I practically screamed, "Where's the ambulance?"

Antonio's right shoulder was covered in blood, the lamplight glinting off pieces of glass embedded in his back. When he put the shirt on me, I'd assumed it was damp from sweat. But the glass from the balcony door had hit him. Every wince, every clench of his teeth, he was hiding pain and I made it worse fighting him off.

Jimmy waved the other officer to the door, and he hustled out of the room.

Antonio turned to me, grasping my forearms as I began to tremble. He kissed my forehead. "It's just a scratch, bella. I've had much worse on the football pitch."

"Liar," I snapped.

He pulled me close, wrapping his arms around me.

Keeping my hands on his bare chest, I pushed away. I didn't protect him. I'd failed.

An EMT arrived, the officer with her pointing to Antonio. She inclined her head to the bathroom. "Let's get you in there and take a look."

Antonio kissed my cheek and left with her. My eyes stuck with their retreating forms. What if he hadn't run into the table?

Jimmy clapped his hands, and my focus snapped to him. "Sammy, I need you present." He stood by the balcony door, glass crunching under his feet. "I've got two officers outside and a K-9 unit on the way. Whaddaya think happened?"

I dragged my brain away from the bathroom. Antonio was fine. Just cuts and scrapes, maybe some bruises, but fine. I was fine.

Deep breath in. Deep breath out.

What if he hadn't run into that table?

"What was that, Jimmy?"

He waved me over, and I joined him and the other officer by the balcony door. Three flashlights swept back and forth at the end of the parking lot, dipping behind trees and branches along the edge of the trail.

"Janelle said you knew where the shooter was. They looking in the right spot?"

I nodded, pulling Antonio's bloody shirt closed and wrapping my arms around myself. "Yeah, it was right along there, hidden in the trees."

"And what's your opinion? Any chance it was intentional?"

Seven bullets. I'd seen the muzzle flare in the mirror and it had been steady, not wavering like in a drunk's hands. Surely not, though. Why would someone be aiming at my room? "Kids go drinking down there sometimes. The officers will probably find a bunch of broken bottles."

What about Nathan's warnings? Or the threat against my life in Naples and the man who could have killed me when I found the stolen relics? My hand rose to my forehead, to the smooth skin of the scar he'd left me with. Elliot would have warned me if that guy was out of jail, right?

It was only three days after the shooting at Mason's.

No. It was all a coincidence, linked to the rising crime rate in Brenton. Had to be. Even though the first shot came when we were passing by the balcony doors. The others kept coming after we'd left the room. And why shoot into the bedroom wall or through the window?

Unless the light reflected off the mirror and gave me away.

Jimmy nodded slowly. "My thoughts exactly."

Stop acting like a scared little girl. Be honest. "It's always possible, though."

He nodded again. "Think you two can compile a list of anyone who might want to hurt you?"

"Will do." My hair danced as a gust blew in, sending another shiver through me. "Your team talk to witnesses yet?"

Jimmy and the officer who'd brought in the EMT shared a nod and the officer left. Jimmy and I stared out the broken balcony door, watching the flashlights move. He tapped a button on the radio on his shoulder. "Find anything?"

"Sam?" The familiar voice choked out my name, and I spun to see Nathan. He rushed to wrap me in his arms, holding me so tight I could barely breathe. "They called me in to—I didn't know it was—Are you alright? All that blood on your shirt!"

"It's not mine." I leaned my face away so I could see him, but he didn't let go. After my calls with Antonio over the weekend, the last thing I wanted was for Antonio to see me hugging Nathan.

No. I already told Antonio there was nothing to worry about. He needed to trust me.

The bathroom door clicked open and a low growl told me it was too late.

"Get your hands off my woman." Antonio stalked out, bare-chested and ready for a fight.

"We're not done!" The EMT trailed behind him, carrying a thread attached to his back. Her voice was demanding, but his focus went no further than Nathan.

"Ferraro." Nathan let go of me and squared up with Antonio. "I thought you were still in Italy."

They bumped their puffed chests, jaws set, and my stomach lurched.

"Gentlemen." Jimmy approached them, his demeanor soothing.

"Go ahead. Want to take another shot?" Antonio pointed to his left cheek, where Nathan had sucker-punched him after we broke up in August. "I'll give you a free one before I make you regret touching her."

Nathan's finger rose to Antonio's face. "This is on you! You and your goddamn family—"

"Stronzo!" Antonio shoved him suddenly, knocking him onto the couch. Nathan shot back up, but I got between them.

"Stop!" I put my hands on Antonio's chest while he glowered over my shoulder at Nathan. I lowered my voice. "We talked about this."

"What the fuck is going on here?" Every face snapped to the doorway, to the sharp and commanding voice. Janelle. Thank god. She was in plain clothes, jeans, and a red sweater under her long black jacket. Huge gold hoop earrings brushed her shoulders, highlighting her ebony skin and buzz cut hair.

Antonio looked back at me, breath slowing. Our relationship was still so new, I couldn't read his features. His brows furrowed and relaxed, jaw flexed, eyes flicked between me and Nathan. Angry? Upset? Jealous? Stressed?

"Sir. Ma'am." The EMT floundered under Janelle's glare. She picked up the loose thread she'd dropped when it got physical. "I need to finish sewing him up."

"You!" She pointed at Antonio, then at a chair. "Sit. You —" She pointed to Nathan. "Over with Slater." Finally to Jimmy. "Sit rep!"

Antonio pulled out a chair at the dining table, his eyes following Nathan like a predator waiting to pounce.

Jimmy rattled off details as Janelle strode through the room. Where he needed equipment to look threatening, that was just her nature. It always had been. She carried herself like she was taller than him and she could have beaten him arm wrestling any day.

I held Antonio's hand while the EMT worked on him and Jimmy talked. This was certainly not what I was expecting for our first night back together.

Antonio winced as the EMT removed a chunk of glass from his shoulder. He looked up at me, responding to something in my face. "I'm fine, bella."

I needed to get out of this room, away from these people.

The walls were getting closer. But I couldn't leave him alone. Couldn't abandon him. "That's my line."

He squeezed my hand. "But I actually am."

Jimmy's radio squawked. He answered it and updated the room. "K-9 found a track but lost it. They've collected some bullet casings where Sammy spotted the shooter."

While he was talking, Janelle's phone rang. She headed into the spare bedroom to take the call.

He continued, "Nothing from any of the neighbors. We'll see if we can find anything else when the sun comes up."

Not what I was hoping to hear.

The paramedic applied a gauze bandage across Antonio's right shoulder to cover the stitches and other cuts she'd cleaned up. After a small lecture on keeping the area dry for a day and watching for signs of infection, she asked if I needed any attention. I declined, but Antonio insisted. She checked my pupils, prodded at my elbow, and declared I was alright before she left.

Janelle returned to the main room, slipping her phone into a pocket. "Forensics is on their way. Where are you staying tonight, Sam? I'm going to have a patrol car posted outside."

I nodded. "I'll talk to the staff and book a different room here."

"No!" Antonio and Nathan said at the same time. At least they could agree on something.

"What if they were coming after you and decide to finish the job later?" asked Nathan. "You can't be alone. You'll be safer at my place."

He stared at me, those big, earnest blue eyes imploring. Bad idea, Nathan.

Antonio stepped around me, closing in on him. He spoke clearly through bared teeth. It was quiet, but his words carried. "She's mine, not yours. Don't forget that. She's staying with me."

Janelle inserted herself between them before it could escalate. Her voice was flat, as though this was routine police work. But she wasn't in uniform, so she wasn't actually working. "We need statements. I'll take Sam's while she's packing. Dr. Ferraro, you can do the same with Slater in the spare bedroom."

Antonio's lip curled and released, then he nodded and planted a kiss on my temple before sequestering with Jimmy. Once inside my room, Janelle closed the doors to the sitting room and the bathroom. I pulled out an overnight bag and crossed to the closet.

"Sam, stop." She placed a hand on my back, and I froze.

My hands drifted to my face, hoping to scour the evening from my brain.

She wrapped an arm around my shoulders. "I'm off duty. You can come home with me."

"No." The adrenaline high was fading fast and a tremor shot through my hands. The noise of the gunshot, the feel of the bullet behind my head, and falling to the floor. It looped in my memory, over and over. "I need to be with Antonio."

"Are you safe if you go with him?"

"Yeah. I—What?"

She turned me so we were eye-to-eye. "You know exactly what I'm asking. He appears to have a short fuse."

My hand headed back for my face, but she restrained it, not letting me hide from her. "It's Nathan. He and Nathan have a—I don't know. Nathan's been an ass this week, like he's trying to piss Antonio off. They really don't like each other."

"He's usually a good judge of character."

"Usually, but..." *Shake it off. Get control.* I looked at the closet and she released me so I could retrieve enough clothes for an overnight stay and work tomorrow. Stuffing them in the bag, I paused and dropped onto the edge of the bed.

Janelle sank down next to me. I'd missed our friendship over the years. We had a long way to go back to where we were, but it didn't matter tonight. Somewhere inside of us was a bond we couldn't break. My head fell to her shoulder and she put her arm around me again. Like we used to do as kids, when someone was mean and she'd stood up for me. Being two years younger than everyone else in our classes made me a target. She'd been my protector until I learned how to do it myself.

"I'm going to catch whoever did this, Sam. Both shootings. I promise."

"It was a really close call, Janelle." I swallowed hard, pushing past the lump stuck in my throat, but I still heard how shaky the words were. "If he hadn't been here, I'd be in a body bag."

"I understand. No one will think less of you if—"

"I would." I sat up straight and resisted rubbing my elbow or my hip, which throbbed from hitting the table as we fell. "Jimmy and the other officers would. I've apparently got a reputation."

She grinned, squeezing me. "You would've been a better cop than Slater, that's for damn sure."

A spluttering laugh escaped my lips, snapping me out of

my mood. "Seriously, though, Antonio would never hurt me. He spent this whole incident trying to protect me."

"Trying to?"

I gave an innocent shrug.

She frowned and cocked an eyebrow. "You were jumping into the line of fire?"

"Yeah, something like that."

"Stubborn as always." She gave me one last squeeze and stood. "Alright, I'll trust you. But if he lays a hand on you, my door's open."

"Thanks."

"After you kick his ass, that is." With a wink, she swung open the door to holler at Jimmy. She apparently had a reputation to uphold, as well. "Slater! I need to go. Come and finish Sam's statement."

CHAPTER 12

ANTONIO

THE DRIVE to my building was a quiet one. I stared out the window, unsure what I could say to Samantha, while she fumed. Likely over my fight with Miller. But she was coming home with me, and I could make it up to her. How, though?

The focus and calm inside her through the ordeal would have impressed me, were it not for the risks she took.

"Welcome home." Her voice cracked as she pulled her truck into a parking space, not looking at me. "Can you gimme a minute to call Cass? She should hear it from me before she sees it on social."

"Sì." I grabbed my duffel from the back and slid out, making my way to the front door with its glass awning. The building was red brick, ten stories high, tall for Brenton. I looked up as I walked, to my penthouse with its reflective windows. We should have come here instead of going to her hotel. This building was the safest in town.

When I arrived at the door, I turned. She remained in the truck, hand over her face, rubbing up and down. There were enough lights around the parking lot, I could see her put her phone to her ear. She was agitated, her free hand flailing, then returning to her face. She nodded, shook her head, leaned toward the center console and sat up again. Five minutes I stood there, waiting, until she hung up, leaned over again, punched the steering wheel, and let her head fall forward onto it.

Everything I'd said since the shooting was wrong. She had to give me a chance to fix that, but watching her in the truck, it was not even clear she'd be joining me.

The two officers dispatched to watch the building for the night pulled up next to Samantha's truck and got out. One knocked on her window and her head shot up. She put up a hand, nodding vigorously, and got out to join them with her overnight bag.

I opened the door for all three as they arrived, entering the vestibule. Producing a key, I unlocked the door, and we entered the cavernous three-story foyer with its patterned marble floor, chandeliers, and seating areas. The foyer always smelled like lilies and cedar, fresh and inviting, with classical music playing quietly in the background. It was good to be home, even under the circumstances.

Samantha's hand found mine as I entered behind her and the officers, although she still didn't look at me. She scanned the room, from wall to wall, floor to ceiling. She told me once she measured things in her head and scouted exits, as a way of becoming familiar with unknown places. Once she finished, she'd discover its beauty.

Marcus, with his short gray hair and impeccable black suit, stood behind the concierge desk. In his sixties, he managed the building and all its staff. Clear-eyed, never missing a beat, he inspected each person with me. "Welcome home, Dr. Ferraro.

We weren't expecting you back so soon. Do you need a hand with anything?"

I gave him a curt nod, understanding his implied question. "These officers will check my condo before we go in and then watch the building overnight."

"Will you be home long, sir?"

"Eleven nights."

"Would you like one of your vehicles brought out of storage?" He was excellent at his job. Discreet, professional, and knew the tenants well.

"Sì, the Levante, per favore." I inclined my head toward Samantha. "And this is Ms. Caine. Extend her every courtesy. She'll be staying with me."

"Tonight only," she said.

My stomach sank at her words. Tonight only? I opened my mouth to debate, but she shot a glare at me, then to the officers. *Not in public*, that look said.

We took the last elevator, using a separate key to access the penthouse floor.

One of the officers positioned himself directly in front of the doors as we rode, hand resting on his gun. "Does the elevator open directly into the residence?"

"No. There are two penthouses, and each has a separate door."

At the top, we stepped out of the elevator, facing a towering mirror with a gold leaf frame. I gestured to the right, to my door, bracketed by two six-foot-tall paintings. Fire and ice, reds and oranges to the bottom, blues and silver to the top. Heaven and hell.

Samantha's gaze drifted to the ceiling and she drew in a deep breath. I let go of her hand and unlocked the door with the last key. The officers moved in ahead of me with hands on their sidearms, while I deactivated the alarm from my phone.

Not that there was any need. I'd called a private security firm while Samantha was packing; they'd already swept the place and would also watch the building overnight.

I returned to the space between the two penthouse doors. Samantha's eyes, wide and full of awe, scanned the high ceiling. My chest swelled and the last couple of hours faded into the background.

"Did you do that?" Her voice was breathy, and she didn't look away from the painting that decorated the ceiling.

"Sì, I did." I stood next to her, taking her hand again, and looked up with her. It was a copy of *The Creation of Adam*, by Michaelangelo, one of the most well-known frescoes of the Cappella Sistina, with Adam reaching his hand out to God's. I'd painted it the year I moved in, the same year I bought the gilt mirror and the potted plants framing the other penthouse door.

"It's beautiful." She squeezed my hand, interlacing her fingers with mine, her agitation diminished.

ONCE THE OFFICERS had cleared my condo and left in the elevator, I held the door open for Samantha, and she entered ahead of me. She stopped where the marble floor of the foyer transitioned to the dark oak hardwood, casting her gaze around the expansive common room. It was the first time she'd been here, but the tour would wait.

Before anything else, now that we had privacy, we had to speak of what happened.

I turned to lock the door and dropped my duffel next to me. A man's job is to protect his family and provide for them. I couldn't protect her fool self from the shooter. She kicked me away, waved me off, fought me when I tried to hold her in the bathroom. I was as useless as I was in Napoli when some other man saved her.

And she wanted none of my money.

What did I have to offer her?

Samantha would say I was overreacting, roll her eyes, and laugh it off; but she didn't understand. She'd filled the man's role in her life for so long, she couldn't drop her barriers and let me take over something. Anything.

Staring at the ground, leaning against the door, I took a deep breath.

"Antonio? Are you alright?"

The stress of my project being extended, the exhaustion of my trip home, the hole in my heart for the last three months. The horror at her hotel.

And the anger. Seeing Nathan Miller with his arms around her had fueled a fire in my belly, so hot I could barely think straight. When he kissed her during our call Saturday night, I could have launched my fist through the phone. He was always there, waiting for her.

"Do not—" I kept my voice as steady as I could, but it trembled. "—ever do that again."

"Do what?" Her boots clicked on the marble as she approached me, her hand sliding across my back.

I splayed my fingers on the door and tried to unclench my jaw. "Protect me."

"What?" Her voice was quiet and her face neared mine, the scent of citrus wafting over me.

My vision blurred as the first tears built against my lids. I turned to her, taking in her beautiful face, her striking pale-green eyes, her brows drawn down in confusion.

Someone tried to take her from me. Not just from me, but from the entire world. My fist landed against the wall by the door, pain screaming up my arm into my shoulder from the impact. My voice rose too many decibels. "Hand on my head to keep it down, like I'm a child!"

Her lip curled, and she stepped back. "It was an instinct."

"I'm supposed to be your hero!" I vibrated, the fire erupting, consuming all my best intentions. I closed the distance between us. "Not the other way around!"

"Why? Because you're a big tough guy?" Her face hardened, and she shoved me away from her. "And I'm what? Just a little girl?"

I stared, blinking away the tears. Her chin raised, ready for a fight. This was my Samantha, fierce and defiant. And what was I doing? What kind of man was I being now?

I had to speak honestly, not use words borne out of shame or jealousy. That was all they were.

Let it go.

My breath came in a ragged spurt, the tears falling. "Your hair moved."

Her chin dropped. "My what?"

I returned to her, reaching for the caramel-colored hair draped over her shoulders, not daring to touch a single strand. "The first bullet. I saw your hair move. It was so—" My throat closed over, catching the rest of the words. It was so close to her head.

Samantha nodded slowly, picking up speed as her eyes

began to glisten. When her jaw quivered, she moved in to me, her head falling against my neck. "Yeah—I felt—in the air."

I threw my arms around her, holding tight while she shook. "I'm so sorry, bella."

She took a stuttering breath as her brave, stubborn facade crumbled. When the first gunshot rang out, a switch flicked inside her. Intense, focused, with her emotions tucked even further away than usual. She broke for only a minute, when she saw the blood on my back, until the switch righted itself, and she shut it all down again.

Now, she finally let go, and allowed me to see her most precious secret. That she was not invulnerable.

"This wasn't the first one." Her voice was so quiet I could barely hear it. "Saturday at the gallery... I wanted to tell you, but..."

I clutched her tighter. She'd said something Saturday night when I talked to her from the club—about her day being terrible—but I was so caught up in my own problems, my own anger, that she said nothing more than that. "Let it out, amore. I'm here."

"All I've been thinking about since then was this." She sniffled. "Your arms."

What if she'd been at her hotel alone tonight, walking past the table she knew was there instead of stumbling into it? Would things be different? Would I be coming home for her funeral?

"Cuore mio," I whispered.

And what happened Saturday? What other risks lurked in this town?

She pulled closer, shuddering as her tears fell, and we

remained locked together for long minutes. Holding her tight, I absorbed all I could. All her pain, her fear, her sorrow.

This was what I had to offer her.

Once her sobs slowed, I put a hand to her face, kissing her salty cheek. "There was nothing I could do."

She straightened enough to look at me, and I wiped her tears away. "You didn't have to—"

"No, but I should have."

"I can take care—"

Placing a finger against her lips, I shook my head. The finger drifted across her mouth, down her chin, and her chest heaved. I was her man, and I could provide more comfort than a simple hug. I could show her how much she meant to me, even when my words failed.

I pressed her against the wall, combing my fingers through her silky hair. Her powerful leg wrapped around my hips and she pulled me closer. She wanted the same comfort I did. The same reminder of how much we meant to each other.

Her skirt rode up, allowing me to grind myself against her exposed underwear, hardening against her hidden softness.

She tilted her head back, lips parting and lids fluttering closed. I captured her mouth with mine, my tongue seeking penance. We moaned in unison, our hearts pounding against each other. I dug my fingers into her leg, the sleek muscle of her thigh flexing possessively. Her arms wrapped around my neck, sending a jolt through my body as she hit the stitches. I winced, the pain a reminder I had protected her. I had not completely failed.

I broke from the kiss, taking my finger in my mouth, then slid it under her panties to explore her swollen sex. The heat in my cock intensified as she writhed under my touch, groaning into my mouth.

Her hands moved to my waist, undoing my belt, the buttons, the zipper, gaining speed as she progressed. When her hand wrapped around me, her tiny inner muscles clamped on my finger, and a guttural vibration echoed through my chest. She stroked my length to match the rhythm of my finger inside her, but only for a moment, before she nudged my arm out of the way with an elbow.

"Make me forget what happened." She guided me to her entrance, and I moved her underwear aside to sink into her. We sighed as one as I pushed in slowly. Her walls stretched around my bare cock, and she tightened, sending a course of energy straight into my heart.

Heaven.

Her hands slipped under my jacket, raking up my sides. She *had* been scared, but true to who she was, she kept it buried.

"We're safe now, bella. We're together." I pulled back slowly—excruciatingly slowly—stroking her emotions as much as her body.

She squeezed her eyes shut and our foreheads met, her voice dropping to a whisper. "I was so afraid he'd kill you."

I moved gently inside her. "I'm alright."

"I can't lose you again." She choked the words out, latching tighter with her leg and arms.

"Never, amore." I kissed her, softly.

But her leg pulled me to her harder, and I picked up speed, burying myself deeper, trying to purge the evening's terror from her mind. We moved as one, her hips meeting me, the ecstasy growing rapidly.

I drove into her, her gasps fueling my grunts. It was primal, full of urgent need. Every thrust one more *I love you* and *I missed you* and *I'm so sorry*. I needed her, and she needed me.

"Oh god, Antonio! Please!"

Tightening my fist in her hair and digging my fingertips into the flesh of her luscious ass, I launched her over the edge. She rocked her head back in a silent wail of climax as I exploded inside her, her body spasming around me. Rapture rolled from me into her and an aftershock hit her, bringing her to a second rapid orgasm.

I continued moving until she finished, reveling in every moment with her. We breathed the same air, our bodies calming from their peak.

"I missed you." Her words flowed out on a long exhale, so quiet I almost didn't hear them over the blood still pounding in my ears. She held so much back, but her love was there, no matter how afraid she was of giving her heart to me.

All these years, dating a long string of women, looking for one who'd love me for me, not for my body or my bank account. I was a hypocrite, upset Samantha wanted me for exactly the things I hoped for. I had to stop worrying about her rejecting me, about Nathan Miller, about all the scars in my past, or I would simply push her away.

"I love you, Samantha." The words tripped off my tongue as though my mouth was designed for them. I straightened enough to see her clearly, her heavy lids and soft smile causing my heart to beat faster. "I've dreamed of this moment for one hundred and four days."

When I tried to withdraw, her leg wouldn't release me. She cupped my face and stroked my cheeks with her thumbs.

Staring and blinking, the sign she was thinking of important things, unsure what she felt secure enough to say. "Don't leave me."

"Never." I held myself inside her, basking in her tenderness, at the look in her eyes when the walls around her heart dropped for just a moment. In those eyes, I saw my love for her returned. If only I could leap over those walls before they went back up and live in that world with her.

Instead, I bit her bottom lip.

"Take me to bed," she breathed through a suppressed chuckle. "My leg's getting tired."

"I didn't think your legs ever got tired." With a smirk, I pulled out of her and zipped my fly. "Time for the teasing to begin, sì?"

She laughed. "Uh oh, I'm in trouble now!"

"The best kind of trouble." I winked and leaned down, grabbing around her thighs, and threw her over my good shoulder. Pain tore through my back, but it was worth it—she squealed and smacked my ass when I straightened. On our way to the bedroom, I flung her long jacket over her head, hoisted up her skirt, and sank my teeth playfully into one luscious cheek.

Another smack to my ass. "You're gonna pay for that, Ferraro!"

"I'm counting on it, Caine."

She was feeling better, and I'd done that for her. Now I had eleven more nights to show her how much I loved her, how there would never be another woman so perfect for me.

But more importantly, I had eleven nights to help her realize she loved me as well.

CHAPTER 13

ANTONIO

THE FLAMES from the gas fireplace danced around the quiet bedroom the next morning, the only noise Samantha's steady breath. She claimed to always wake at five, but it was almost six and she lay sprawled on her front on the far side of the oversized bed. I'd been awake for an hour already, despite us not getting to sleep until two.

I'd designed the room like a cocoon, all grays and creams with cherrywood furniture. Three of my paintings hung on the walls, green and blue pieces, which evoked memories of foggy mornings on the shores of Napoli.

From the reading nook window, I scanned the dark town, the street and vehicle lights nothing but a blur. The shooter was lurking out there somewhere. Two shootings in the past week. Had her investigation in Napoli caught up with us again? Or was it merely a coincidence?

I moved to the edge of the bed to watch her sleep, hung my things up in the half-empty closet, considered running a bath. Flipped through three books. Stared at the fire. Nothing settled me.

Finally, I sank into the plush chaise longue between the curtained balcony doors, watching her continue to breathe. Continue to live.

Thank everything in the entire universe I ran into that table.

A pinging noise startled me, and her hand flung to the bedside table, to her phone. She groaned quietly, looked at it, and put it back down. With a yawn, she stretched and reached behind her, to the bare spot where I'd slept. She rolled over slowly, likely taking in all the details of the room.

"Painting over a fireplace is a fire hazard," she mumbled, before ending on her side, facing me with a lazy smile and another yawn. "You're up early."

"No, bella. You're sleeping in. It's noon in Napoli already."

I crossed to the bed and slipped under the covers. She turned away from me, and I didn't stop until my body met hers, sliding easily in my silk lounge pants. Nestling back, she removed all the space between us, stretching through her spine, and burrowing her legs underneath mine.

"When I woke this morning, I saw you lying there, so beautiful." I pressed my lips against her and inhaled her fragrance, pushing one arm under her head. "I couldn't go back to sleep, for fear it was another dream."

She shook with quiet laughter, kissing the arm under her head. "So cheesy."

I caressed her side, circling my hand to the front of the sleep tank she'd worn to bed, ending over her heart.

She sank deeper against me, interlacing her fingers with mine, rubbing her cheek along my bicep. "I missed you."

"All days are nights to see till I see thee," I whispered into her hair.

Gripping my hand tightly, she finished for me. "And nights bright days when dreams do show thee to me."

I laughed softly, locking my legs around hers. One more thing we had in common, our love of Shakespeare.

"Which sonnet is that?"

"Forty-three. I read it many times while I was away." Stroking her chest with my thumb, I relaxed into the embrace, my lids becoming heavy. Perhaps more sleep would come after all.

She twisted around, pressing her head against my bare chest, moving an arm and a leg to drape over me.

This was paradise. "I think we should stay here all day, bella."

"That sounds wonderful, but I have to go to work."

The encroaching tiredness vanished in an instant, and my heart skipped too many beats. Less than twelve hours ago, she'd nearly been killed. She couldn't leave. "Call in sick."

"I can't." She brushed her fingertips along my skin, far calmer than I was. "I volunteered to pick up extra time over the holidays, so a few of the other adjusters could go on vacation."

"No, you can't go to work today." While failing to release my tensed muscles, I did my best to maintain a playful and flirtatious tone. I trailed a hand to the small of her back and pulled her closer to me in a further attempt to prevent myself from slipping into ridiculous commandments.

She pushed back from my chest to see my face, her lips tight. "Antonio, I have responsibilities."

"As do I. I need to keep you safe." The words came out

sharper than intended, but she didn't get angry this time. Instead, she became serious.

"I'll be fine." She placed a hand over my heart, bringing my attention to how fast it beat. Before I could speak, she moved the hand to my lips and sat up. "Listen. Best-case scenario, last night was a one-off. Worst case, someone's after one of us."

"Like the man Eva sent after you?"

"Elliot would have told me if he was out of jail." She shook her head when I opened my mouth, silencing me. "Your visit was a surprise and no one would have expected you at my place, so it isn't you. My schedule's erratic. There are very few things I do the same every day but heading back to my hotel is one of them. If someone was waiting for me, they'd know to watch there at night. I won't be doing anything standard today, I swear. Plus, I know how to spot a tail and how to lose one."

Her hands waved as she spoke, and I grabbed one to kiss it.

"Call the police if that happens."

"Now, what about you? This is a really secure building. Are you going to stay here all day?"

"No, I need to go out."

"Then you need to be careful, too."

"We could go together?"

She clasped my hand and frowned. "I'm going to work. I'll be careful. You'll be careful."

There was no point in arguing with this woman. I forced a smile and changed the subject. "Last night, you said you'd only spend one night here. But that was hardly a full night's sleep. Can I interest you in another?"

She grinned, nudging me before sliding out of the bed. "Hard to argue that point."

"So, this is a yes?" I followed her out of the bed, wrapping myself around her.

"This is a yes," she said in her silly pretend accent. She kissed my cheek and escaped my grasp. "But right now, I need to clean up and get ready for work."

"What time should I expect you?"

"My last appointment's at six, but it's in Brenton, so probably around seven?"

"Why so late?"

"I have a full calendar this week. It was supposed to be a distraction until you got back." She shrugged. "Nothing interesting, either. Paperwork, calls, and emails first thing. Couple hours with SIU after that. Site visits for the afternoon."

"SIU?"

"Special Investigations Unit." She took my hand, leading me to the ensuite. "Don't worry. It's just fraud and stuff."

I followed her into the bathroom, with its bright marble-tiled floor and walls, a long vanity table with cushioned stool, and tall windows lining the outer wall. "That sounds more like the sort of thing you should normally be doing."

She nodded, a flash in her eye making it clear I was right.

"I've got five minutes before I need to be out the door!" Samantha hollered from the bedroom.

"Perhaps showering together would be wiser in the evening?" I called back after the front door closed behind me. I'd ordered food and strong coffee, which had been waiting outside my door. It was likely all cold given our distraction in the shower, but providing her with another orgasm had been a higher priority.

She stumbled down the hall, hauling her cargo pants on, wet hair trapped in a braid, carrying a mass of clothes and her winter boots. It was impressive how fast she dressed, given I'd only managed to wrap a towel around myself. "That bathroom is as ridiculous as you are."

"Wait until we have a bubble bath in the whirlpool tub." I waggled my eyebrows, unwrapping a breakfast sandwich for her.

"I'm so hungry!" She dropped everything and took a huge bite.

"Your hair will freeze outside."

She nodded quickly, tucking her shirt in, then pulled on a sweater with the Foster Mutual logo on it. When she stopped chewing, she opened her mouth again, and I provided another bite. Flipping her wrist, she checked her watch and covered her mouth. "I hate being late."

"Sì, I know. Perhaps I should have a clock added into the shower."

She rolled her eyes, but after a deep swallow, they shot open. "Shit! I almost forgot! Jimmy wants us to write a list of anyone who might want to hurt us or something. For his investigation. I'll text you his contact info."

"That will be a long list."

She smacked my chest, took another bite, and threw on her jacket. "I've got the trio from Naples already. Oh, and I also forgot—Cass invited you over for Christmas dinner when I talked to her last night."

"I would love that."

"Word of warning... your arch-nemesis will be there." Her

words were light, but the way she paused gave her true feelings away.

"I *am* sorry about how I reacted last night." I held the sandwich out for her, but she didn't take another bite.

Instead, she fixed her gaze on me and, for once, the honesty flowed immediately. "Listen, either you trust me or you don't. And if you can't figure out a way to get past this jealousy thing, we may as well just call it quits."

A fist tightened around my heart at the prospect of losing her over this. "Bella, I—"

"I don't have time to debate this right now." She knelt to tie her boots, too easily avoiding me.

"I'll make you a deal." I knelt next to her. Two could play at this honesty game. "I'll trust you about that. And you'll trust me when I say you're the one for me. No more doubts."

She finished a double-knot and frowned, scanning the common room. "This place is way bigger than you need. What is it? Fifty feet by thirty? Twelve-foot ceilings, for sure. I mean, what do you do in here?"

"So, back to my deal?"

She blew out a deep breath and turned to me, nodding. "I'm working on it."

"That's all either of us can do." I kissed her nose and we stood as one. When I offered her another bite of food, she accepted. "And it's big because I host big parties."

The room included a sitting area with television and gaming systems, a reading corner, and the dining room. Open concept with pale walls, two trimmed weight-bearing columns, and rugs over the dark hardwood. A balcony followed the length of the room, outside the floor-to-ceiling windows.

Off the end with the dining room, the kitchen was separated from the great room by a granite-topped breakfast bar with five bar chairs. Between the foyer and the kitchen, the circular metal staircase climbed to my studio upstairs. Her gaze had lingered on it last night when we broke for a snack, but we were too busy for a tour.

"Big parties?"

"Sometimes, sì." I shrugged as she took another bite and cocked an eyebrow at me. "I have a lot of friends."

She covered her mouth, eyes tracing along my body, pausing where I'd tucked the towel. The corner of her mouth twitched, telling me I would soon be naked. "That's something we definitely don't have in common."

"Does this bother you?"

She grinned, her gaze finally coming back to mine. "Any chance you'll still be dressed like this when I get back?"

I exaggerated a roll of my eyes, which caused her to laugh as I packed her breakfast in a bag. "Not a chance, bella."

"Want me to pick up dinner?"

"No need. I'll have something ready when you get here." I grinned, kissing her one more time before she left. "Be careful."

"You, too." She accepted the bag and opened the door, winking at me as she yanked the towel off and snuck out.

ONCE SAMANTHA WAS GONE, I dropped my food on the dining table and made my way to the bedroom. I sat on the edge of the bed, draped the towel over my lap, and stared at my phone.

My cousin Cristian had once been my idol. Strong, confident, and always in control.

Then I grew up and found out what he and my uncle did for a living. I barely wanted to speak with either of them, but there was no denying how much Cristian helped in September. Had it not been for one of his men, Samantha would have been killed over the Pompeii thefts.

Would calling him make it better or worse? Was he involved? Did he know who was? Only one thing was clear: Neither Cristian nor any of his associates would go on any list for Officer Slater, regardless of the answer to those questions.

I hit his number and waited.

"Antonio!" came his loud voice when he picked up. "Tell me you're calling about a Christmas visit! Papa will be so excited to see you!"

They lived just outside of Roma on a grand estate by the sea. Since I arrived in Napoli, they'd asked over and over when I'd visit. My response was always *later*.

"No, Cristian, I'm in the States."

"I thought you were in Napoli until April?"

He'd already heard about the extension. Of course. As my cousin liked to tell me, he did two things well: hear things and make things happen. "I'm only visiting."

He chuckled. "The girlfriend?"

"Sì, the girlfriend." I leaned forward on my knees and took a deep breath. "There was an incident last night..."

"You're alright?"

"Shaken only. But I need to know who's behind it. In September, you warned me of someone looking to step in when your father—"

"Antonio." His voice was sharp and commanding, as it always was.

"I know. Not over the phone."

"Someone tried to hurt you?"

"We were shot at. Several times. Pinned down in her hotel room." I ran a hand over the pillow where she'd slept. "She's trying to pass it off as an accident, but I don't believe her. This was not the first shooting in town this week."

"The three are still in custody."

My shoulders relaxed. Then it was not those who threatened her in Napoli—the fresco thief, his conniving girlfriend, or her thug brother. "But the one who paid them is not."

"Don't assume you know things you don't."

As Samantha suspected—but never asked outright—I knew who was behind the thefts from Pompeii. She'd guessed their powerful backer was a man named Pasquale Fiori, whose yacht we'd visited. But I was told secrecy was the price for her life, and it was a price I gladly paid. "If it's not them, then who?"

"I'll make some inquiries."

Picking up the pillow, I inhaled her scent from it. Was Nathan Miller right? Were my family and the poor choices of my youth coming back to haunt the woman I loved? "I've not worked for your father in—"

"Antonio!"

I stood, grimacing, nerves still as frayed as last night. She'd be gone for eleven hours, and all I wanted to do was follow her the entire time, to be certain she was safe. But she could take care of herself—she was trained, as she liked to remind me—and I had a great deal of work to do. "I'll never forgive myself if she's hurt because of me."

"I'll let you know if I hear anything."

CHAPTER 14

SAMANTHA

I HIT a button on my laptop, broadcasting the security feed from inside Mason's Gallery to the eighty-inch screen on the wall. The Oaks conference room, with its table large enough for twenty, had the best television at the Foster Mutual Insurance office.

I was joined by Harry Bell and Tonya Quinn, Foster's Special Investigations Unit. Insurance fraud was a thirty-plus-billion-dollar-a-year problem, and no insurance company, regardless of size, was immune. SIU's role was to help combat that by investigating suspicious claims.

"Tell me again why we're doing this?" asked Harry.

As usual, Quinn picked up where he left off, as though they shared a brain. "You don't think this is a fraudulent claim, do you?"

They were both on second careers; he'd been a police officer, while she'd been a private investigator. Both were in their early sixties, with well-grayed light brown hair and intelligent eyes that missed little.

I was a contractor, working for a large independent adjusting company, who'd negotiated a daily contract with Foster to provide additional claims management bandwidth. Winter was slow, but rather than releasing my contract until storm season in the spring, I was re-deployed part-time to work with SIU and improve my investigative skills.

Since starting with Foster in the summer, I'd identified eighteen instances of fraud. The most significant was the million-dollar fraudulent artwork claim. Then there was the discovery that the company's president—Roger Foster, my former father-in-law—was taking bribes to push phony claims through.

"I just wanted to talk over the incident," I said.

Quinn flipped her laptop open while I cued up the video, and she gasped. "Mother of pearl, Samantha! You're a witness on this claim. One, you cannot be working a claim you're listed on—"

"I know, I wasn't thinking."

"And two, what happened?"

"Watch." I hit play.

The camera hung high on the rear wall, giving a near-complete image of the front showroom, including Rhonda and the street outside. I was far enough away at the time to be out of view.

The car entered the frame from the right side, well below the speed limit. The driver's window was down and a person wearing a balaclava held a gun out of the window, letting off several shots. I came sprinting into the frame just before the noise started—Quinn shot out of her chair and Harry grumbled something—and tackled Rhonda to the ground. One windowpane shattered, then the second. As the car sped off, I launched from my position and ran out of the frame.

Quinn hit pause on my laptop and held my hand back when I tried to play it again. "You doing alright, hun?"

"Fine." I stared at the laptop. I'd already watched the video at least a dozen times before they arrived. In the moment, tackling Rhonda seemed like the only choice, but watching it again, I realized I put myself into more danger by running across the room than Rhonda had actually been in.

What did I want out of this meeting? What were they going to glean from this video that the police hadn't been able to? Maybe I was hoping they'd tell me I did the right thing, because no one else in my life would.

"Brave," said Harry. "Foolish, but brave."

"You want to talk it out?" Quinn sat, turning off the compassion and shifting into business mode. *That* was what I needed. "Let's watch it. Fast, slow, sound on or off, whatever you want."

I played it again in slow motion. We turned the volume up but couldn't hear much beyond the gunshots and yelling.

A separate exterior video gave us a closer view of the shooter and better sound.

"You got the license plate?" Harry scribbled on the notepad in front of him when Quinn read the details from the claim file. He pulled out his phone, fingers flying over the keyboard.

Quinn stood and approached the television. "Zoom in on the shooter."

The face was concealed, other than a slit for vision. The video feed was black and white, but it was clearly someone with light skin and dark eyes.

Harry finished typing and looked at the screen. "Not much to see, is there?"

I switched back to the interior security feed, pausing on a zoomed-in view of the shooter, gun muzzle lit up.

I joined Quinn at the display, tapping the gun. "We can see he was alone—I'm going with *he* based on size and shape. The gun came out after he was in front of the gallery and disappeared before he sped up. This was an intentional shooting at the gallery. There was literally nothing else he could have been aiming at. Regardless of that first bullet almost hitting us, I saw the bullet pattern inside, and I'm not sure Rhonda was the target. It definitely wasn't me—I was halfway across the room."

Harry hit play, on slow motion.

"First shot hits the painting," I said. "I tackle Rhonda to the floor. Two, three, four, fi—Harry, stop!"

I hurried to my seat and dragged the video back to where the gun first appeared. "Count the muzzle flares."

We all focused on the screen, counting.

"I got six," said Quinn.

"I got seven," said Harry.

I reset the video and played again with the sound off before we had a consensus. "Definitely seven."

Quinn sat at her computer, pouring through details. "Preliminary police report is attached to the claim. It said six bullet holes inside the gallery."

"Yeah. One through the painting and five clustered together." I tapped my screen. "What does this mean?"

Harry and Quinn's eyes met, and he said, "I need to go talk to Rhonda, anyway. Let's take a look in person."

∾

WHILE I DROVE the three of us to Mason's Gallery, Harry received a call from a friend of his at the Brenton PD.

"No big surprise," he said as he hung up. "Stolen vehicle."

Quinn nodded from the back seat. "And I checked before we left—it's not covered by Foster."

I pulled into a parking spot down the road from the gallery. "What do we do with that information?"

"Nothing." Harry hauled on a thick pair of gloves, tucking them under his parka sleeves. "Given the shooting at the Brenton Arms last night, I expect the police will make both shootings their top priority."

My stomach dropped and my hands froze on the steering wheel. Last night was an accident. It had to be an accident. *Calm down, Sam.*

"Sam?" Quinn touched my arm.

"Yeah?"

"You've got white as a sheet, hun."

I took in a deep breath and turned to Harry. "You think they're connected?"

He raised an eyebrow. "Do you believe in coincidences?"

"I try to?" I released my hands from the wheel, one finger at a time.

"Seriously?" He raised the eyebrow higher and frowned. "After Roger and all those fraudulent claims you uncovered this summer?"

I focused back on the steering wheel. "No, not really."

"How many shootings do you think there are each year in Brenton?"

"Not a lot?"

"Close enough." He put a hand on the door, ready to leave. "Two in the same week is a pretty big coincidence."

"Harry, stop." Quinn squeezed my arm. "Sometimes events like that can trigger anxiety, especially since we're coming back to Mason's."

"It's not Mason's that's bothering me. It's—I'm staying at the Brenton Arms." I closed my eyes and covered my cheeks, breathing deeply to calm my heart. "The shots were fired into *my* room."

"I hadn't heard that." Harry swiveled in his seat, looking back at Quinn. "My contacts would only say the presumed targets—"

My hand shot to Harry's arm. "Presumed targets?"

"—were an unidentified couple—"

Quinn put a hand in front of Harry to cut him off. "What do you have in common with Mason's Gallery or Rhonda?"

"Nothing." I paused, while they both stared at me with the 'Think harder, Sam' faces they gave me at least once a week. "I've handled a few claims for her, that's all."

Quinn shook her head. "There's more. Why were you at the gallery on Saturday? And don't tell me it was to look at the art."

"She had a favor to ask."

"But you have nothing to do with her?"

"She called me that morning because she found a painting she suspects is stolen. I was there to get the information and maybe start a little digging."

Harry took over. "Why you?"

"Do you have any idea how much publicity I got off that Chagall case?" I huffed and rolled my eyes. "I'm still getting contract offers four months later."

"And you're still with Foster?" said Quinn.

There had been a lot of amazing offers. Job positions, contracts, investigations, insurance consulting. But I wasn't leaving Brenton until after Antonio was home for good and we had a chance to build something. "Don't even go there."

Quinn rubbed my arm. "Ahh, this is where the *unidentified couple* comes into play?"

Time to change the subject. "Let's go see Rhonda."

"You're worried about him, aren't you?"

"Terrified." I swallowed hard and flicked my gaze back to her. It wasn't her business, but the words came anyway. "I've been on edge since Saturday, jumping at every loud noise. But today, I've been fighting my need to call him and make sure he's alright."

Harry patted my arm. "Until you get the all clear from the police, are you carrying?"

How to answer? Tell them I'd considered it at least three times last night while sitting in the truck outside Antonio's place?

He lifted the center console to reveal my gun safe. "Because I know you've got at least one weapon in there."

"How did you know that?"

Quinn nudged my shoulder. "You dance around what you did before becoming an insurance adjuster, but we do all the background checks. We know you were a federal agent, even if it was short-lived, and we know you have a concealed carry permit."

"To be honest—" I closed the console. "—I thought about it. I figured it would put me more on edge, so I just have my stun gun in my bag."

"Good." Harry put a hand on the door again. "Just be

aware of your surroundings. In our line of work, we end up in a lot of strangers' homes, and you have to put faith into those strangers being good people. Sometimes they're not."

ONLY FOUR DAYS after the shooting, the broken window at the front of the gallery had already been replaced. Two days before Christmas, at that. Rhonda must have had contacts.

Harry pushed open the door. The chime rang and he leaned his head in. "Rhonda! You here? It's Harry Bell!"

She came around the corner, dressed all in black as usual, her red glasses hanging from a chain at her neck. "What are you doing here, Bell?"

He barked a laugh as she folded her arms. "You asked me to come by."

Rhonda turned her frown on Quinn and me but cracked a smile and waved. "I told you to get my window fixed, not visit."

"And miss out on your sterling personality?"

She shooed him away. "Get out."

Quinn leaned closer to whisper, "Rhonda and Harry go way back."

"Harry goes way back with everyone in town, it seems." A frigid breeze circled us and crept up my neck, so I pulled my collar up.

Harry stopped next to me and chuckled. "She'll be out in a minute."

If this were about the painting, we'd be inside. "What's going on?"

"Rhonda called me this morning." He shoved his hands

into the warming pockets of his huge navy parka. "She was complaining about the repair to the front windows, like I have some say in it."

"It was your nephew!" snapped Rhonda as she stepped outside, bundled up in a long black wrap jacket.

"Niece's ex-husband," he muttered.

She glowered at him over the red rims of her glasses, then turned the look on me. "Good to see you again, Samantha. Did you consider what we talked about?"

I nodded. "It's a work in-progress, but I think you were right."

Her lips twisted into a sly grin. She seemed to be handling the shooting far better than I was. "Of course I was."

The two large gallery windows were separated from each other by a foot-wide section of wall, faced in brick. Rhonda marched up to it and jabbed a finger at the spot where the frame met the wall. "Look at this!"

The frame was dented, and a chunk of the brick was missing.

"I agree. Not well done." Harry's focus returned to me. "What's our job, Sam?"

"It's not to repair this. Foster covered the painting, not the gallery."

He nodded. "Put that aside. Our actual job."

I pulled up my hood to keep the cold air off my neck. "There was damage to something Foster covers and our goal is to find if it's a fraudulent claim."

"And do you think Rhonda would do that?"

"Harry Bell!" Rhonda smacked his shoulder.

He looked at her from the corner of his eye. "I'll talk to him, don't worry."

"Good. And make it fast." She glared at him, which turned rapidly to a smile for Quinn. On her way inside, she said to me, "Let me know if you find anything interesting. I need all the distractions I can get right about now."

"Will do." I turned to Harry. "No, I don't think she would."

Quinn added, "You're responding based on your interactions with and assumptions about Rhonda. Do we have all the details we need to make an objective assessment?"

"No." That answer was easy. If it was yes, she wouldn't have asked. But *what* were we missing? "I did the initial interview with Rhonda—even though I probably shouldn't have. We have the video and preliminary report from the police. Ferraro's estimate is in for the repair. One red flag on the claim for it being the second loss within a year."

"And we're missing..." Harry's brows rose, expectant.

"Well, we don't have the final report from the police, and we're pretty sure one bullet is unaccounted for."

"Which means..."

It meant the police were screwing this up like they had the Scott fire case. They were missing things or hurrying. Or just didn't care. "It means we can't rely on the police report, can we?"

"Exactly." Harry nodded. "As far as Foster Mutual is concerned, I don't suspect anything fraudulent on this claim. I wanted to go over this more to keep you alert going forward. We've been having issues with sub-par investigations for going on a year now. It's hard to tell with many claims if it's some failing in the police department or if it's related to what Roger did. We don't know yet how many people he paid off or lied to, which makes our job harder than usual."

"Like with the Scott case, which was closed as accidental."

"You have good instincts," he said. "You were in motion before the shots started, so you must have realized something was happening before the gun was even out of the window. Focus on those instincts and never be afraid to verify the evidence that's presented or redo an interview."

"But no recruiting, right?" said Quinn, who received a frown from Harry.

I stared at the spot on the frame Rhonda had complained about. It was shoddy work, like she said. Granted, the wall was old enough the brick and mortar had crumbled in areas, leaving several holes and gaps. Without redoing the entire facing, it would be hard to make a perfect repair.

The sun glinted off something in one hole, around five feet up from the sidewalk. *Was that brass?* My heartrate picked up. I closed in on the wall, casting a shadow over it, losing sight of what had caught my attention.

"Find something?" Quinn's face came even with mine.

"Possibly." I pulled out my phone and directed the light into a hole in the mortar, then pulled off my gloves to pick at some loose pieces around it. The cold bit at my fingers and one of my already chipped nails tore off. It had to be the missing bullet. "I don't suppose either of you have pliers on you? I have some in my truck, but—"

A pair of pliers appeared from one of Harry's pockets.

Whatever brass-colored thing was stuck in there was in deep and didn't want to come out. I dug the pliers into the hole, using them to break up some of the loose material until I could get a proper grip. Leaning against the wall for leverage, I heaved on it until it flung out. It was so sudden, I lost my grasp on the pliers, and the bullet went skittering across the sidewalk. "Shit!"

Harry and Quinn leaped after it with me, but my reflexes were the fastest. I was down on my hands and knees, scrambling before it dropped into a storm drain.

"Thank god it didn't go down the—" In a crevice left by the concrete eroding around the edge of the drain, another flash of metal. A bullet casing. And it looked fresh. Not worn down by months sitting here, being run over, trampled, and pummeled by rain or snow.

I stood, holding the bullet from the wall and the fresh casing. Harry produced a clear bag from one of his pockets, and I dumped them in.

"Interesting." Quinn took the bag, examining the two items. "I was going to say, if the police found seven bullet casings, they would have been looking for a seventh bullet. They obviously missed both of these."

"Not standard procedure." Harry joined Quinn, inspecting the bag. "We've contaminated the evidence—"

Quinn interrupted, holding the bag toward me. "But the police already have everything they need."

I reached for it, but hesitated.

Harry took the bag and stood beside me, folding the plastic around the casing. "You destroyed the bullet, so no evidence is coming off it the police don't already have. But the casing has some key markings."

Nodding, I accepted the bag and rotated the casing. "Not as accurate for tracing as a good bullet, but there are still distinct marks, including at the back from the firing pin."

"Good job." He clapped me on the shoulder and headed for the truck. "Keep it as a souvenir."

This bullet could have been the one to pierce the second window. It could have deflected like the first one and landed somewhere unpredictable. This bullet could have landed in me.

But just like the table saved my life last night, the brick post may have saved my life Saturday. I was definitely keeping the damn bullet.

CHAPTER 15
SAMANTHA

I HUSTLED through the sliding front doors of the Brenton Arms hotel. Twenty minutes to arrange for a new room, grab my things for another night at Antonio's, and be out the door for Nathan's water damage claim.

The lobby was full of chairs and tables, the bistro to the left busy with patrons enjoying food and drinks. I headed to the front desk at the right, welcomed by the day manager, Geoff.

"Got any mail for me?" I snagged a cookie and water bottle from the tray they always had ready for guests, and he gave me a forced smile. Something was wrong. Other than the shooting last night?

He held up a finger and slipped through the door at the back. The long desk was rich dark wood, matching the wall behind. A glass panel with an etching of the hotel's name graced the rear wall.

I called after him with my priority request. "And I need to switch rooms if mine won't be fixed within the next few days. I know Christmas is in two—"

When he emerged, the forced smile had transformed into a grimace. "The top one's from management."

"Management?" I took the three envelopes from him.

"Sorry, Sam. Nothing I can do."

I opened the back flap of the top letter.

"Basically, you have to vacate the hotel."

I paused before the letter was all the way out. "Vacate?"

"By Saturday."

"Hardly." I pulled the letter out and shook it open. Scanning the text, I hit the high points: Vacate, Saturday, multiple noise complaints, danger to the other guests. "You're kidding me! Is this about last night? That's not my fault!"

He put up his hands, scanning the lobby and other patrons, as though worried I was making a scene. "I told them you've been here for months without a single complaint, but—"

"But the long-term discount means I'm not paying enough?"

His brows pinched as his hands fell to the desk. "I'm sorry."

Geoff had always been pleasant and helpful, and he wasn't responsible. Taking a deep breath and straightening from the aggressive stance I'd fallen into, I nodded.

And took another two cookies.

I hit the stairs beyond the lobby two at a time to the third floor and walked to my room. The apartment hunt suddenly became much more urgent. Three days to leave. Where was I going to go? Lucy offered her place, but it wasn't big enough. Probably Cass's.

Or Antonio's until he left again. Last night, he assumed I'd stay with him the whole visit. That would buy me until

New Year's. But I'd said it was a one-night deal. Why? Stressed, scared, upset over him fighting with Nathan. But he'd done everything else right. Tried to protect me—while I fought him off—comforted me, distracted me.

The door to my room was the same one as last night, when Antonio's hands had been all over me. But instead of my thighs clenching, it was my grip on the handle. We could have died. I'd sworn to him I wouldn't follow my routine, but here I was, at my hotel again, at almost the same time as yesterday.

All I could do was stare at the door and try to ignore the sound of blood pulsing in my ears.

Get it together, Sam.

A door opened and closed down the hall and I startled, my heart leaping into my throat. Just another guest. I watched her as she walked to the elevator, not even looking back at me. I was safe. Definitely overreacting. No one was waiting outside my windows.

When my phone rang, my whole body jolted. I ripped it out of my pocket and snapped, "What?"

"You alright?" Janelle's voice was sharp, sounding more like duty than empathy.

I exhaled, leaning my head against the door. "Fine. What's up?"

"I've got good news."

The elevator dinged and a tall man in a thick black jacket headed toward me. Hands in his pockets, head up, looking straight at me. Did I enter the room or not? *Keep an eye on him.* Should have grabbed my gun. He smiled and nodded in greeting.

"Sam? You there?"

"Yes, *Officer*, good to hear from you."

"Where are you?"

The man stopped two doors down from me, produced a keycard, and disappeared into the room.

"Fuck." I filled my lungs and held them still again.

"Sam!"

"Sorry, Janelle. I'm standing outside my hotel room, freaking myself out."

"Go into your room. It's okay. We caught him."

"You what?"

"Slater put the screws to some guys he knows."

I swiped the card by the lock and opened the door.

"He pulled a double shift on this one, just brought the guy in. Said no one treats his friends that way." She chuckled. "Maybe he's not a half-bad cop after all."

"Have you interviewed the suspect yet?" I put my bag and mail down on the kitchenette counter, leaving my jacket and boots on. One step beyond the counter and I froze. The blood smeared across the carpet practically screamed at me. I hadn't even noticed when the shattering glass hit Antonio; I'd been too focused on getting us to safety.

"Yes and no. He's not talking until a defender shows up, but he was carrying concealed without a license and resisted arrest, so we're holding him on those. Nathan charged in as soon as he heard and threatened the guy with at least fifty years behind bars."

I swallowed the panic down and headed into the bedroom. Avoided looking at the side of the bed in case the blanket was stained, too. I threw enough fresh clothes into a backpack for tonight and tomorrow.

"Anyway, the statement we got from Slater's guy sounds solid. Said he was with the shooter yesterday. Drunk and high, he pulls out his gun, bragging about what great aim he's got. 'Third floor, balcony door, watch this,' he says."

Zippering the bag, my gaze drifted to the ceiling, where forensics had removed three bullets. "Real funny, asshole."

"Informant tries to stop him. He fires the rest of the rounds, then they take off when they hear the sirens."

I sank onto the bed, suddenly aware of how fast my heart was beating and the tremor in my hands. "Thanks for letting me know."

"We're waiting on Lansing forensics to release the evidence, but we've got this guy's handgun, so we can match them up. I'll let you know if something goes sideways here and it turns out he's the wrong guy. Keep your guard up but try to stay calm."

"I'm working on it."

"Before you go..." She paused, sucking in a couple breaths as if to start talking before eventually continuing. "Everything alright with the boyfriend?"

"Really good, actually."

"I'm glad. I'll call when I know more."

I hung up and stared at the phone for a few minutes. What a couple of days. I needed a friendly voice. Janelle's was good, and Cass was my go-to. But what I needed was Antonio.

He answered before the first ring finished. "Ciao, bella!"

My nerves unknotted at his deep voice, every word like music. "Hi."

"It's wonderful to hear your voice."

"Yours, too." More than I'd thought it would be. A lot more. For three months, we'd talked on the phone, knowing we wouldn't see each other in person for a long while. But hearing him, knowing he was only ten minutes away, was different. It was comforting. If I really needed him, he was right there.

"What's the matter? You sound—"

"You're not going to believe this."

"Hmm?"

"I'm at the hotel."

"Are you safe? Do you need me?" Ready to protect me again.

"I'm fine." I stood and walked to the main room. "Good news is they caught the shooter from last night."

"Fantastico! This is marvelous news!"

"Yeah, it is. I'll give you the details tonight." My gaze fell to the boarded-up balcony door.

"Why don't you sound happy? There's bad news?"

I scrubbed at my forehead, as if it would fix something. "Yeah, they're kicking me out."

"They're what?"

"I got a letter. I have to vacate by Saturday."

He was silent, other than a quiet hum of acknowledgment. No invitation to stay with him. I screwed things up last night. I'd have to call Cass.

"I swear, Antonio! I've been looking for an apartment since the end of August! What am I going to—"

"Samantha." He said it softly, like wrapping me up in his arms, soothing my every nerve. "You're staying here tonight. Worry about the rest later."

I rolled my neck. *Calm down.* This news, being in the hotel room, Harry talking about the shootings being linked. "I'm only working in the morning tomorrow, so I'll pack up when I finish."

"Would you like company for that? I can carry boxes."

"You're supposed to be taking care of your injured shoulder. No box carrying." And no me carrying, but he'd done that and soaked his stitches in the shower this morning, too. That shoulder was going to take forever to heal.

"I'm an excellent packer. I can do color-coding or by theme or—"

"Nah, I can handle it my—"

"Bella, let me reword. Can we spend that time together? I promise not to get in your way."

I stared down at my feet, smiling, warmth pooling in my chest. "Yeah, I'd like that."

"It's settled! Are you done work?"

"No, just picking up some things for tonight. Then I have one more appointment."

"Alright. Well, I must go. I'm quite busy."

"Oh! Sorry for interrupting!"

"Never too busy for you. See you at seven."

As I hung up, I blew out a long breath, head falling back. Forensics had dug three holes out of the ceiling over the kitchenette. There was more work to do in here than just cleaning bloodstains and replacing the balcony door.

Wait.

Three bullet holes here, three in the bedroom. As the shooter switched from the balcony door to the bedroom window, I'd heard another bullet impact the outer wall and seen debris fly away in the mirror's reflection.

Just like the extra bullet in the pillar between the two windowpanes at Mason's.

I stared at the balcony door. The board wasn't across the entire space, just the door itself. I could still open it. Go out and see if they missed a seventh bullet here, too. Walk out onto the balcony because the guy who tried to kill us was locked up. Show that bastard who's boss. Show him I wasn't afraid.

Maybe even find another souvenir.

The walk to the door took longer than it should have. Small steps around the blood. Brushed my fingers across the top of the side table which saved our lives. *I should take that table with me when I leave.* A lump lodged in my throat.

But I was stronger than this fear. I had control over my body.

My heart would slow down. Any minute now.

My hand gripped the door handle and I eased it open, stepping out into the cold. The parking lot lights were on, but the trees beyond were dark. If they had the wrong guy and someone else was down there, it was too late for me.

But no bullets flew. Cars came and went, people walked to and from their vehicles.

The balcony was ten feet long, a concrete slab with thick metal railings, and it didn't reach the bedroom window. I leaned over the edge, scanning the brick and mortar facing, like I had at Mason's.

And there it was. A hole in the mortar, two feet away from the edge of the balcony, at chest height.

What to do now? The front desk could put me in touch with hotel maintenance... but I dug my hand into my pocket and pulled out Harry's pliers. I'd forgotten to return them.

Stretching out, I repeated my actions from Mason's. Dig out the loose bits, widen the hole, grab on, and pull. I leaned over, hooking one thick boot into the railing to my side, and heaved on the bullet until my entire arm swung out. This time, I held tight to the pliers and to the bullet.

I hurried inside, locked the door behind me, and pulled

the bag from Mason's out of my pocket. The bullet was so damaged from piercing the brick, other than being the same caliber, there was no use in comparing them. But the search at Mason's had also yielded a casing. If the police had collected six bullets, they'd have a maximum of six casings.

Stuffing it all into the zippered security pocket inside my jacket, I grabbed my bags and mail, then tore downstairs to the edge of the parking lot. There was a casing down there some-where, and I was going to get my souvenir.

CHAPTER 16

SAMANTHA

NATHAN SWUNG his front door open, surging forward to grab me in a bear hug. "Did you hear the news?"

"They caught the shooter from last night?"

"Damn straight!" He released me and ushered me in. "I'm going to put that asshole away for a long time over this."

"Janelle told me you were a little intense."

He laughed, taking my jacket and hanging it up while I kicked off my boots. "She tossed me out! Good thing, or I would have missed our appointment."

As we walked down the hall toward the living room, the scent of fried mushrooms and garlic washed over me. I'd interrupted his dinner. "Need to reschedule? I don't mind."

He waved it off. "I just had it delivered. It'll keep."

"Speaking of keeping things..." I dug into my pocket and produced his spare key.

With a groan, he accepted it. "I have to apologize for Saturday. That was... I don't remember anything past you pushing me into your truck."

I careened into him, almost knocking him into the wall. "What are friends for?"

"And then last night." He put an arm around my shoulders and squeezed. "I'm sorry about flying off the handle like that. You know I just—"

"—want to keep me safe. I know." It felt more like he was trying to drive a wedge between me and Antonio.

There was a step ladder set up under the water spot on the ceiling. Nathan let go of me and crossed to the kitchen. "Listen, they messed up my order and sent me two meals. I don't suppose you want to eat before you get down to business?"

"No, thanks, but you go ahead."

"Glass of wine?"

I laughed as I climbed the ladder to take a closer look. "No, I'm working. But again, you go ahead."

He uncorked a bottle of white and poured.

"When did you first notice it?" There was discoloration on the ceiling, only three inches across, but close enough to the wall, there could be hidden damage.

"Thursday evening."

I pressed my finger to it. Solid, not squishy, so it could have been a one-off event, rather than standing water or continued flow. "Your ensuite's above here. Have there been any leaks?"

His gaze went to the ceiling. "Maybe?"

"I'll head up and look."

"Sounds good." He joined me, two glasses of wine in hand. "You want?"

I shook my head. "Remember how I'm working?"

"Yeah, yeah." He returned both glasses to the island in the kitchen and we headed up the stairs. The second floor was all pale hardwood and cream-colored walls, covered in sailing photos.

"This—" I tapped a photo of Nathan, Cass, Kevin, and I aboard the USS Constitution in Boston, the summer after I graduated from high school. "—was always one of my favorite summer vacations."

"How many hours did you force me to spend in the Gardner Museum?" He flipped on the light in his bedroom and went in.

"Not enough."

Contrasting with the hallway, his bedroom had deep plum walls and dark wood. A king-size sleigh bed dominated the space, facing a big screen television, which hung above a long bookcase. Stacks of books were piled on every surface.

As an insurance adjuster, I walked through many people's private spaces and thought nothing of it. Sometimes they were nice, sometimes they were so filthy I didn't want to touch anything. Still, they were just rooms which could contain damage and it was work.

But this was Nathan's bedroom. It felt like an intrusion. I'd been in his house several times but had only seen the bedroom on my first visit, when he was still living with Tina.

A book on top of the bedside table caught my attention, pulling me to it. Like gravity.

He turned at the bathroom door when I didn't follow him. "Sam?"

"Complain all you want, but..." I lifted the book, running a hand over the textured cover, admiring the Rembrandt self-portrait at its center. I flashed it toward him before flipping through the pages. It was *Stolen*, the only book the Isabella Stewart Gardner Museum had authorized about the theft of thirteen priceless works of art from their museum. The largest property theft of all time, let alone the most prominent art crime, which was still unsolved.

Once upon a time, I'd believed that case was my destiny—I was even born on its anniversary. The FBI had originally assigned me to Boston to help with the case, putting it within my grasp. But then I left.

Stolen had been on top of a museum guidebook and a few others about the heist. "What's with all this?"

Laughing, he returned from the bathroom and plopped down on the edge of the bed. "I wasn't exactly expecting you to come up here."

"So?" I sat next to him.

He reached around me to take the guidebook and absently flipped through it. "Do you remember I told you this summer I was working on a case with the FBI?"

"Of course." How could I not? It had been Nathan's first warning about Antonio and his family. I'd brushed it off as ridiculous, but the time I spent in Naples with Antonio made me question how valid the warning was. "A smuggling..."

My hands slowly raised to cover my gaping mouth, and he nodded. There was no way he was working on my dream case.

I said, "Elliot Skinner told me you were working with him."

Nathan closed the guidebook, tapping it against his forehead. "He mentioned that. Told me to stop telling you things because you'll put more than two and two together."

I stifled a laugh and nudged him with my shoulder. "Failed that test, didn't you?"

"Always had a weak spot for you."

My phone buzzed in the telltale pattern I'd set for Antonio. The one that passed my Do Not Disturb. "One sec."

He opened the guidebook again while I read the text.

When can I expect you? Checking so dinner's ready on time.

I'd told him seven, but it was almost seven already. We still had to do Nathan's statement after I looked at the bathroom. I replied, *Looks like closer to 8.*

He responded with a sad emoji, and my heart sank. He'd flown so far to see me and all I was doing was working. The rest of the week would be better.

I'll be as fast as I can.

That earned me a kissing face emoji. I laughed, tucking the phone back in my pocket.

"Always jump when he says to?"

I swiped the book from him and hit his shoulder with it. "My boyfriend's been away for three months. I've missed him and I'm excited to see him. This isn't about me jumping."

He opened his mouth to speak, but I hit him again.

"Time for you to spill, Nathan. What's your problem with him? If there's something real—not conjecture—that I should know about, tell me now."

"I don't know what you mean." He swiped the guidebook from me and tossed it on the pile.

"Bullshit." I turned on the bed, folding a leg up so I could look at him straight-on. "Saturday night, you told me he's dangerous. Said I'd run as fast as I could if you told me half the things you know."

"I was drunk Saturday. Just ignore everything I said."

"Is this related to the smuggling case? You told me this summer there was a Ferraro family involved. Did you learn something?"

"I—" His mouth clamped shut, no more words coming.

"Fuck, Nathan, c'mon!" I shoved him and stood. "You can't say you're trying to keep me safe and not tell me why!"

He sagged, elbows on knees. "It's his uncle. I can't tell you more than that."

When I was in Naples, a police officer intimated that Antonio might have been behind the theft of a fresco from Pompeii. That officer had just transferred from Rome and had said he was familiar with Antonio's family.

Dominico's brother Andrea ran the conservation studio in Rome. He had another brother somewhere in that area, whose son was Cristian, whom Antonio said he hated and wanted nothing to do with. Antonio's other uncles were on his mother's side, so it wasn't them.

"Which one?" I asked but was met with silence. Antonio had hidden a burner phone from me in Naples, connected to some sort of *family business*. My stomach lurched and I slid back onto the bed. Did I want to ask the next question? The answer could have significant consequences. I couldn't look Antonio in the face if I didn't. "Is... Antonio... involved?"

"No." Nathan's head stayed down. "I suspected he was, but they intercepted a call confirming he isn't."

"Why did you suspect him?"

"Sam, I can't tell you more." He craned his neck around to see me. "Call Elliot if you want details. I really can't."

"You know, Cass is basing her opinion of him on what you've told her. If things have changed, I need you to fix that."

"Promise me you'll be careful." He held out his arms, and I leaned into his embrace. "I still don't trust him."

"You don't know him." Pulling away, I chewed on my bottom lip, my heart beating hard enough I could feel it in my neck. "He'll be at Christmas dinner, so I expect you to give him a shot."

He nodded, but then made a vomiting face and grinned.

"Alright, now that that's all done." I stood, working up to my best smile under the circumstances. "I need to check out that bathroom, so why don't you eat dinner and I'll be down soon."

He squeezed my arm and left.

I hauled out my phone and sent a text to Elliot, *Want to talk about smuggling ring.*

Before I could slip it back into my pocket, he texted back. *I'll be at Brenton PD Tues morning. 10am work for you?*

I responded in the affirmative and got back to my claim.

How could I make time speed up to Tuesday, but still have it slow down so I had more time with Antonio? And how was I going to focus on him when I had so many unanswered questions?

CHAPTER 17
ANTONIO

SEVEN O'CLOCK HAD TURNED to eight. I leaned on the railing of my long balcony, watching the traffic ten stories below. It had been dark for hours, streetlamps and twinkling Christmas lights providing a magical glow to the evening.

The woman who was never late was late for me. Was this how life would be with her? Was her man lower priority than everything else?

No. On Sunday, I'd asked for a date night on short notice and she rearranged her plans. I'd showed up unexpectedly yesterday, disturbing her well-organized and busy schedule. But Christmas was in two days, then the weekend. We would have those days together, at least.

A humongous truck—and she made fun of how large my condo was?—pulled into the parking lot in front of my building and the smile crept up my cheeks. Late, but here.

I remained still, the crisp winter air biting through my tuxedo shirt and the stringed melodies of Vivaldi carrying through the balcony door. Samantha exited the vehicle, retrieved a bag from the backseat, and looked up. Her face was in shadow, but I could feel her smile in my heart. She stood next to the truck, staring up at me, and pulled out her phone.

Mine rang, and I plucked it from my pocket. "Who is this?"

She chuckled. "A homeless woman in need of lodging for the evening."

"My girlfriend should be arriving at any moment. I don't think she would take kindly to that."

She hummed. "Maybe I should check with my sister."

I tsked at her and was greeted by another quiet laugh. "That would be a shame. I have a great deal of wine and some delicious food up here. We may need help finishing it all."

"Maybe I'll come up for a nibble, then I'll leave."

"I warn you. The nibbling may not be limited to the food."

"Ooh!" She threw the bag over her shoulder and walked toward the door. "That's piqued my interest."

I headed inside, closing the balcony door behind me. White pillar candles flickered from every surface, our only light other than the pot lights in the kitchen. I'd pushed the living room furniture toward the walls, creating a large dance space. Two thick bouquets of white roses and hydrangea adorned the ends of the dining table. "There may be a surprise or two, as well."

"I hate surprises." A whoosh of air sounded through the phone as she entered the building.

"Really?" I put my phone on speaker and opened my security app, showing the front door, lobby, and outside of my apartment. When I pressed a button to unlock the door for her, she laughed again.

"That was easy. How do I call the private elevator?"

"Just walk to it." I straightened the wine glasses and cutlery at her table setting, the small white jewelry box hidden behind her first glass. Surely, she would notice it right away, but how long until she acknowledged it? Another glance at the video feed, and I crossed toward the kitchen, smoothing the tuxedo jacket hanging from the breakfast bar chair. "So, what was that about hating surprises? Are we talking big surprises or small ones?"

She dropped her voice while she waved to Marcus at the concierge desk. "Well, I did get a big surprise last night and it was fantastic."

I placed the phone on the counter and rolled up my sleeves. As she approached the elevator, I tapped another button and sent it down to her. "And another big surprise in the shower this morning, I believe?"

She spluttered and put a hand over her eyes as she stopped. The bell dinged, the door opened, and she got in. "This is what I call service!"

"Only the best for the homeless woman crashing on my couch this evening." I threw an apron over my dress clothes, tucked the undone bow tie under my shirt, and turned up the flame on two burners on the cooktop. One to boil water for the tortellini, one to warm the truffle sauce.

"Couch? I don't even warrant one of the spare bedrooms?"

Opening the warming drawer, the scents of rosemary and oregano from the tagliata steak flowed over me. It would be perfect once she was ready. "Perhaps if you're nice enough to me, I may let you stay in a bed."

She exited the elevator and paused, so I glanced at the phone. She frowned at herself in the mirror, looking exhausted. Such a long day and so little sleep. "I might be able to handle being nice. Not sure yet."

I softened my voice, dropping all pretense of the game. "Rough day or is this about last night?"

She stared into the mirror, tucking an errant hair behind her ear.

Would she think I was invading her privacy? "You know I can see you?"

Her face tilted up to the corner of the penthouse foyer, as though looking right at me. "Yeah, I noticed the cameras last night. When the elevator arrived for me, I figured it out."

"Do you need me to stop teasing?" I tapped the button to unlock my door for her, and she walked to it. The manual security locks had been undone for seven o'clock.

"No, I think a healthy dose of Antonio Ferr—" She opened the door. "Holy shit!"

My head fell back as the laughter erupted from me. "Is that good or bad?"

She hung up her phone, and the manual lock engaged. "What is all this?"

"What is what?" I called to her, as innocently as possible.

I tossed the tortellini into the water and turned it down to a low boil. Her boots dropped to the floor in the foyer and the closet opened and closed. My love was finally home, with only a wall and a long room standing between us. The butterflies took over my stomach. It was just as well I knew the sauce was perfect; my mouth had gone so dry my taste buds would be useless.

"And I thought that painting in the bedroom was a fire hazard! How many candles did you light?"

I stifled my continued laughter and retrieved a corkscrew

from a drawer next to the refrigerator. "Romance is never wasted on you, is it?"

"I think the word you were looking for is 'always.'" Her voice grew louder as she crossed through the living room to the kitchen.

"At least you'll keep my ego in check." I uncorked a bottle of red wine, keeping my back to the room. This would be a momentous evening, so I had to maintain control. Be light and flirtatious. No falling at her feet. "And I knew you'd say that, so most are battery-powered."

I turned to face her, bottle in hand, and my heart skipped at her smile. She still wore the white sweater from this morning, her hair in the braid. Beautiful, but underdressed. Perfect for my next surprise.

"You look..." She placed a hand on the back of a breakfast chair, eyes widening and mouth falling open. Her gaze traversed the length of me as I exited the kitchen. Perfetto. A tuxedo was precisely the right touch for the evening.

"I would say rendering you speechless is a first..." I placed the bottle on the table and gave her a quick peck on the cheek before returning to the kitchen. "But we both know that's far from the truth."

"Mouth watering," she chuckled.

I smoothed the front of the apron. "I have a hot date tonight. Do you think she'll like it?"

"Very much. Guess I should get out of your hair before she arrives."

"I think she's hiding in the bedroom. Would you mind letting her know il primo will be served soon?"

She winked and inclined her head to the hallway next to the kitchen. "You coming with me?"

"Not yet, bella, I'm cooking." I withdrew a colander and placed it in the sink. "Go by yourself."

She tilted her head, furrowing her brows. Perhaps romance was lost on her.

I waved her toward the bedroom. "You have ten minutes, so hurry."

Narrowing her eyes, she turned slowly toward the hallway.

"I said hurry, Samantha."

One more laugh, and she quickened her pace. Butterflies swirled in my stomach. Would she like this surprise? Would she be offended?

"What's this?" she hollered from the bedroom.

"My date!" I took the pasta off the burner and poured it into the colander. The plan had been to wait for her to come back, but I could hardly bear it and followed her.

"I can't wear this!" She stood in front of the tall mirror beside the door, holding her new floor-length dress against her work clothes. Cranberry-red, made of a silk jersey that would hug every subtle curve of her delicious body. It was a halter top with a plunging neckline, gathered at the waist, and a full skirt slit to mid-thigh. The shoe box on the bed remained untouched.

Folding my arms, I leaned against the door frame. "Sofia picked it out. She was sure it would fit you."

"Stop smirking at me!" Her eyes were wider than when she had first seen me, stuck on the neckline, which would fall to her navel. "It doesn't leave anything to the imagination!"

"Trust me, bella, my imagination is far more active than that. Put it on." I winked at her—which was met with a feigned scowl—and headed back to the kitchen. "The food will be on the table in five minutes."

As I began plating, she yelled from the bedroom again. "Antonio, I'm five-foot-nine! I can't wear three-inch stiletto heels! I'll be a giant!"

The heels clicked against the hall floor, and she appeared. I froze in place, hands covering my heart. She was awe-inspiring. "My date has finally arrived."

She rolled her eyes as she approached me. "Tell me you didn't buy me a dress and shoes for one dinner."

"Would you believe me if I said they were secondhand?"

She shook her head, stopping before she entered the kitchen.

I rounded the counter to scoop up her hand and kissed it gently. "We have tickets for the New Year's Eve Ball at the Convention Center."

A sparkle appeared behind her tired, pretending-to-be-irritated eyes, and she scanned the space I'd made in the room. "Dancing?"

"Sì, there will be dancing." Still holding her hand, I spun her slowly, and she finally smiled at me when she had made it all the way. "I thought you may want some practice in the shoes after dinner."

She pulled close to me, eyes almost level with mine, and slid her hand to the back of my neck. "You did not just set all this up for dance practice."

"Always so suspicious." I kissed her cheek and separated from her, returning to plating. "Go sit."

"It smells divine." As she crossed to the table, the dress swirled around her, accentuating every movement. Her long stride, playful sway of her hips, tall and confident posture. "Where did you order it from?"

I sucked in an exaggerated breath to feign offence. "I made it!"

She cocked a doubtful eyebrow as she settled into the chair.

"From scratch!" I finished my work and stripped off the apron, hanging it on the wall with the others.

"You never said you could cook."

"The morning we went to Russo's together..." I fixed my cuffs, did up the links, and buttoned my shirt. "You told me of the family you boarded with the summer you studied in Italia and how much you adore authentic Italian cuisine."

"Did I?"

I frowned at her as I shrugged the tuxedo jacket on and tied my bow tie. "I've been planning this meal since that day."

"Have not." She sat sideways in her chair, legs crossed, leaning against the back and watching as I picked up the plates. She hadn't looked at the glasses yet.

I approached the long, dark wood table, set formally with rows of cutlery and placed my pasta bowl first. I'd chosen the white plates with silver etching, matching the napkins, which were folded like swans. Lifting hers by the beak, I snapped it, and draped it across her lap as she squared to the table.

"Il primo, handmade tortellini with porcini mushrooms in truffle sauce." I placed the dish in front of her, kissing her neck before straightening, taking in her citrusy scent, which mingled with the aromas of the meal perfectly.

She turned her face toward mine, but I escaped before she could kiss me. Her brows knit together, so I ran my thumb across one, encouraging her to relax. The candlelight flickered across her face, and she smiled. "You're serious?"

"Of course, amore." I picked up the open bottle and poured her first glass. "And Chianti."

She ran her fingers over the cutlery as I poured my wine and sat. There it was, the staring and blinking. The not knowing how to respond, afraid of the feelings overwhelming her. Her jaw flexed, eyes on the food. "Looks like a lot of work."

"Sì, but you're worth every moment." I raised my glass, the motion catching her attention.

Without looking down, she picked up her glass to clink with mine. "To…" Her words hung in the air, mouth forming the start of many words, but none coming.

"Surprises."

A smile creased her beautiful face and she nodded. "To surprises. I guess they're not all that bad."

I kept my eyes on her as we drank. The Chianti was a lovely, dry, full-bodied red, which tasted faintly of cherries. After her sip, she looked to where she'd retrieved the glass from before putting it back down.

She saw the jewelry box.

What now?

My heart rate accelerated and the butterflies swirled. We'd spoken of gifts and my money in the past, and about how that contrasted with her minimalist ways. But if she accepted me for who I was, which she said she did, any gift was part of it, whether it was worth a fortune or not.

She froze, her free hand raising to her face for a moment, clenching, then drifting to her lap. Her eyes stayed on the box as she placed the glass down and picked up a fork.

"No?" I had another sip of my wine and winked at her.

She took her first bite, and her eyelids slid closed as she groaned. "This is delicious!"

And with that, we were ignoring the box. I took a bite myself, and she was right; I'd outdone myself. "Marone. This *is* quite good."

With a laugh, she swallowed the piece in her mouth. "It's not just the tortellini, is it?"

"Oh no. We have several courses."

"Is this all you did today?"

I took another bite, washing it down with the wine. A perfect pairing. "No, I visited the office, then went out to see Mamma and Nonna."

"And you still had enough time?"

I waved a hand while she continued her meal. "They were brief visits. I told them I had a woman to woo."

She laughed around the food in her mouth. "You don't need to woo me, you know."

I picked up my glass and held it out for another toast. She'd have to raise hers and see the box again. Was that cheating? "Here is to wooing you because I enjoy it. Not because it's needed."

"Fine." She clinked her glass with mine and we sipped before she returned to her pasta. Completely ignoring the jewelry box the entire time she ate. "Time to dance now?"

I stood, shaking my head at her. When I picked up the dishes, she removed her napkin from her lap and pushed her chair back.

"You sit, bella. You've had a long day and I'll take care of everything." After placing the dishes on the counter, I went about plating the steak. "But tell me about your day. I spent mine cooking and you'll see all of that."

She swiveled to sit sideways in the seat again, watching as I worked, enjoying more of her wine. "Office hours were boring. Got a few police reports in and updated some notes from my site visits from yesterday. I went out to Mason's Gallery with SIU." She paused, taking a deep gulp of her wine. "Then a kitchen flood and two water damage claims."

I withdrew a salad from the refrigerator and set it between our place settings. "Cortorno, arugula with figs and Grana Padano, in a peppercorn sauce."

She leaned closer, taking a deep whiff, then stealing a piece of the cheese.

After drizzling the balsamic glaze over the steak, I brought two more plates to the table. I set mine down, then hers, stopping to kiss her shoulder. "And il secondo, tagliata steak with balsamic glaze. This will pair beautifully with—" I uncorked a new bottle and poured each of us a fresh glass. "—Valpolicella."

When I sat, I raised my glass. "To Mason's Gallery."

With a laugh, she toasted with me, and we drank. "You trying to get me drunk?"

"Never!" I reached between the glasses, pushed aside the common plate, and held my hand out for hers. When her fingers slipped into my palm, a lightness surged through me. "I want you to relax. I want time to slow down so we can enjoy each other's company before I have to leave."

She squeezed my hand tight and raised her glass. "To relaxing and slowing down time."

I clinked my glass with hers and drank to that.

∼

AN HOUR AND A HALF LATER, we'd made it through the formaggio e frutta, grilled peaches with mascarpone and Moscato d'Asti; then though dolce, panna cotta with raspberries. She sipped her limoncello, rubbing her foot along my calf.

"Not yet," I'd said over and over. The more she drank, the more forward she became. But this was time for wooing. Making love would have to wait.

"Do you remember the limoncello we had in Capri? At the beach club?" She reached down to her side. Her shoe fell and she sank down in her chair, mischief in her eyes. The foot made its way up to my thigh and between my legs. I caught it before she arrived at her target and dug into it with my thumbs. Her lids slid closed, and she moaned. The sound vibrated inside me, through my belly, warm with wine and liqueur, doing more damage to my self control than anything else she'd tried.

I patted her foot and stood, lifting my chair and carrying it to her side of the table. I placed it next to her and sat, while she put her shoe back on and turned to face me. Pulling so close our knees intertwined, I took her hands in mine. Enough avoidance.

Bringing her hands to my lips, I kissed each of them tenderly, and stared into her glorious eyes. "I love you, Samantha Caine."

Her hands twitched, but I held fast. She would not be rubbing her face through this conversation.

I moved her wineglasses out of the way and retrieved the white jewelry box, placing it on the edge of the table next to her.

She shifted in her seat, as though the box were about to bite her. "What is it?"

"A token of my affection."

She stared at the box, clenching my hand. Her breathing was rough. How was this brave woman so scared of what I wanted from her? Did she still doubt me? Or was it herself she doubted?

"You know, bella, our relationship has progressed quickly."

"Understatement."

"I believe every great romance begins with a whirlwind. But it's the calm winds at the center that keep it together." I leaned closer to her, squeezing her hand, dropping my voice to a whisper. "You are my calm winds."

"You know—" She tore her gaze from the box to look at me again. "—we could just go have sex instead."

I spluttered a laugh. "Not yet, I said. Stop being so stubborn and open it already."

"Fine." She rolled her eyes and dropped my hand, retrieving the box.

Time slowed. So much depended on this. My trip home, my hopes for our future, my worries about being apart. I never hid my feelings from her, despite her occasional discomfort. Someone as closed off as her needed someone as open as me.

Her body tensed, and her fingers shifted this way and that, turning the box over. With a deep breath, she creaked it open. And her face fell. "What the—?"

"Keys!" I took the three keys on their ring out of the box and showed her I'd numbered them. "One for the exterior door, two for the elevator, and three for the condo."

Her brow was tight.

"I came home to spend time with you." I put the keys in her palm and closed her hand around them. "I understand you can't just take off work, but you were gone for twelve hours today, and that only leaves me with so much time with you. We have ten more nights together, and I don't want to miss a single moment with you. I want you to move in with me."

"Move in with you?" Her voice had raised a full octave.

I had to bring her back down to her comfort level. "Just for the nights I'm here."

"Is this because they're kicking me out of the hotel? Is this a pity move in?"

"Well, that's a very logical reason for you to say yes. But, no. I spoke with the concierge after you left this morning and had them made."

Her face hardened further. How was that the wrong response?

"Bella, you were alone for a long time before we met, and I understand changing that is hard for you."

Instead of rubbing her hands over her own face, she reached for my cheek, saying nothing, her face softening.

I'd attempted to stay light through the conversation, so she wouldn't be afraid of my feelings. But the serious look in her eye weighed on me.

Her smile broke slowly, reminding me of the way she looked at me when we were in Capri, when she first kissed me in that way I knew meant she loved me. No matter what words she would or would not say. "Yeah, I can do ten nights."

"Molto bene." My shoulders eased, and I wrapped my arms around her, feeling her relax as well. Kissing a cheek as I separated from her, I whispered in her ear, "When I'm home for good in April, we'll have another discussion."

She shoved me away playfully. "Time to get out of the dress yet?"

I stood, pulling her up with me. "Oh no, bella. Now, we dance."

"Or..." She snuck a hand under my jacket, around my waist, then slid it down to my ass. Pressing against me, she squeezed, and ran her tongue along her upper lip. "We could dance later?"

Her heart hammered against my chest, and mine echoed it, the two competing for which could beat the fastest. Sure I would win that contest, I took her face in my hands and our lips touched. Softly, briefly.

"No." I forced us apart with a wink. "I'm not finished wooing you."

CHAPTER 18

SAMANTHA

I PULLED into the side lot of a small brown office building early Thursday afternoon. "I'll be quick. Then we'll head over to the hotel to pack."

Antonio inspected the sign next to the sidewalk. "Are you here for the tax preparer, the designer, or the lawyer?"

After I'd put in a half-day of work, I'd swung by his place to pick him up. He'd argued about driving, I insisted my truck had more space for my things, and he'd rightly countered that I didn't own enough to need much space. Still, he grudgingly went along with it.

"The interior designer." I sucked in my bottom lip as his eyebrow cocked. It probably would have been wiser to come here before picking him up, so I wouldn't have to go into details about Saturday. "I told you I was at Mason's Gallery on Saturday?"

He nodded, hand traveling to grip mine.

"Rhonda spotted a painting in a real estate listing that she thought might be suspect. I thought I knew who owned the house, but Lucy texted me some new info this morning." I pointed to the sign. "Felicia White owns White Cedar Interior Design and inherited the house where this painting is a couple of months ago."

"And you intend to go in there and question her about it?"

"Rhonda went to their house, and apparently Felicia's boyfriend was a real jerk to her. I figured talking to Felicia herself, away from him, might yield different results. I know, it's not my job, but—"

"Stop. This is your passion, bella." He brought the back of my hand to his lips. "What's our cover story?"

"Our?"

"You don't think I'm going to remain out in the cold and miss you interrogating some poor art criminal, do you?" He acted like it was a tease, but from the way his gaze darted to the scar at my hairline, I knew better. "We're stronger as partners than as individuals."

Energy pinged around inside me. Partners. He'd used the word over and over since Naples. I tried to hold back the foolishly happy smile, like I was a kid receiving praise from my mom, but I couldn't help myself. His face mirrored mine and we leaned in for a brief kiss.

When we separated, he chuckled. "Married and looking to decorate our dining room, like when we were snooping at the gallery in Napoli?"

"Hold on." I snatched my hand back. "That wasn't our story."

"It was. I just didn't mention the married part." He winked and I shoved him playfully. "Bella, she would assume from the rings, anyway."

"I could take mine off."

"Mine has not come off since you put it on my finger."

"I take mine off every time I go climbing. It's a safety hazard."

He let out an overdramatic sigh. "Such the romantic."

"Seriously, though, I just booked a rush consult with her. I didn't give her any details. So almost anything goes."

"Bene. I'm planning to rent out a space I own as a furnished apartment. The tenant leaving it—"

"Tenant?"

"Sì. The prior one had their own furniture, but I'd like to redo the place before renting."

"Is this true?"

"Real estate is an excellent investment." He shrugged and got out, pointing a finger at me to stay put. "It's a simple cover."

I feigned a scowl as he walked around the front of the truck, continuing to point at me until he opened my door. "Would you believe I've been opening my own door for most of my life?"

He held out a hand for me, but I used the grab bar to hop down to the running board and the ground. "What if your target is watching out the window? Surely you want to sell our story?"

"You've got me there." I leaned my cheek toward him for a kiss as we walked through the building's front door and into the short main hallway. "I don't suppose we're planning to decorate *our* condo with minimalist beige, are we?"

"Certainly not!" He threw his free hand to his heart. "I was thinking more of a sage green for the bedrooms and citron in the kitchen."

"Isn't yellow kind of dated?" I asked, as he ushered me through the glass door to the designer's office.

The main room was open and airy, a large pale wood meeting table to the right, surrounded by shelves of hanging fabric samples. To the left, a desk with a computer and printer that didn't look like it was used for daily work—it was too neat and uncluttered. At the back, an open door passed into what was likely a private office.

"A sunny hue is very on-trend." A woman in her mid to late forties with short brown hair and dark-framed glasses came out from the back room. She wore a crisp white blouse with emerald pencil skirt and smiled broadly. "Citron is one of my favorites this year."

"You see?" said Antonio.

"You're not helping," I said with a conspiratorial grin. "He refuses to take any of my suggestions seriously."

"Then you've come to the right spot." She held out a hand for me to shake. "I can help design something you'll both be happy with. I'm Felicia. You're Samantha, I assume?"

"Yes, and this is Antonio."

"Her husband," he said, extending his hand to shake. "We're planning to rent out a furnished condo which is currently empty and are in need of a mediator."

She laughed politely and guided us to the table, with stacks of magazines, sample binders, and a photo album.

The longer we talked, the clearer it became that Antonio wasn't making this up as a cover. Not only did he have a floor plan and photos on his phone, but he spoke for over fifteen minutes about his ideas for the space, even doing a few sketches. I kept mostly quiet, frowning occasionally to convince her we'd disagreed about a point prior.

As he spoke, Felicia nodded, asked questions, and showed us—him, really—various samples of paints and fabrics. When she brought out some photos of artwork, it was finally my turn.

"I was thinking…" I shuffled through pictures as I spoke, keeping my words innocent. "For the living room, I'd like something with loose brushwork and soft visuals. Like an English countryside with a windmill or a wagon."

Felicia's hands paused over one of the magazines.

"Would that work with these colors?" I asked. "I know we're going a little modern, but I enjoy that sort of softness."

"That sounds lovely." She stood from her chair and approached the fabric sample shelves.

While her back was turned, Antonio winked at me. Going in together with a plan was working much better than the last time we'd tried investigating someone as a pair.

She returned with another fabric book and flipped to a soft blue and tan large-checked pattern. "If we switch the sofa to this, I think it would work well for what you're describing."

"Are you sure?" asked Antonio.

"Yes—I actually have a piece similar to that, and this is the fabric I used in my living room."

"You do?" I asked. "Any chance you have photos to show us?"

She blew out a sharp breath. "I should have, but we had to take it down."

Tread carefully, Sam. "Selling it?"

"It's being cleaned, then sold." She slid over her color swatches and pulled out a few next to the fabric. "My boyfriend found it at a pawnshop in Detroit and I put it up, but he said it needed work."

Antonio browsed the samples, flagging the ones he liked. "If it meets Samantha's requirements, perhaps we could buy it?"

"I wouldn't recommend it. For your own place, maybe, but it's worth quite a lot." She kept her eyes on the samples, pushing another fabric toward Antonio, this one in a velvety gray-green. "Between the three paintings he discovered, he estimates they'll bring in—"

Three paintings. The LA theft was of three paintings.

Felicia straightened, shaking her head. "I'm sorry. He told me they were supposed to be kept under wraps. He's worried about thefts."

"Understandable." I tried taking part in their swatch and chip matching game, but each time I did, one of them changed something which was clearly better. "Maybe we should check out this pawnshop, honey. They could have other pieces like what I'm looking for."

"Sì, this is an excellent idea. We'll go after Christmas. What was the name of the shop?"

Felicia pulled out her phone and snapped some pictures of the collection of open magazines and samples strewn across the table. "I don't know, but I can check with him. I'm not sure if they have other pieces as high-quality, though. He's an art restorer and has a remarkable eye."

Art restorer boyfriend? There weren't a lot of professional companies in the Lansing area, so this was interesting.

Felicia left the table to sit at the laptop and prepare our printouts.

Antonio's gaze snapped to mine as soon as her back was to us. He mouthed *Parker's?*

Of course! I nodded once. Parker's was the restoration

company that authenticated the stolen painting from the auction. The FBI had gotten involved, but if Parker's was still in business, that meant they hadn't found anything incriminating.

Or at least, not enough.

"Could you give us his contact information?" I asked. "I'd love to talk to him."

"I'll let him know you were looking." She hit a button and a printer on her desk began spitting out pages. "I'm sure he won't mind getting in touch."

"You should call Special Agent Skinner with this information," Antonio said as he settled in the passenger seat.

I tapped my fingers against my lips, staring at the squat brick building. Everything was still conjecture. We didn't have any proof. "Not yet."

He chuckled, pinching my thigh, memories of last night vying for my attention.

"Stop." I shoved the hand away, trying not to laugh. "I don't think the fuzzy pictures from the real estate listing, plus this tiny bit of information is enough for a search warrant, so it's not worth calling him. Lucy and I were going to request an invite for the showing on January third, so I'll check in with him after that."

"If the painting's not sold by then?"

Dammit. "Or at Parker's Restoration undergoing work."

"Either way, we don't have to figure it all out right now. And we have other priorities, bella."

It was only Thursday, but I had an appointment with

Elliot on Tuesday, anyway. To dig a hole even deeper and snoop on the amazing man sitting next to me, helping with this investigation. I could still swing by Felicia's house and look around, but she knew my face now, so I wouldn't be able to con my way past her.

And who was her boyfriend? Was it the owner of Parker's himself? Or one of his employees? I'd never found out from Elliot who—specifically—was behind the auction painting.

"Bella?"

"Hmm?"

"Priorities?"

"Right." I pressed the ignition. "Packing."

"And then..." He tipped his head, eyebrows easing up expectantly. "We go back to my place and..."

I flipped my sunglasses down from the holder and used them to cover my reaction as best as I could, my stomach tightening at the prospect. "Get ready for Christmas Eve dinner with your family."

"They're very excited to see you."

"I don't know why. I just saw Sofia, Lorenzo, and your father two days ago."

"I think Nonna started cooking yesterday and Mamma had a cleaning crew in when I was there."

The last time I'd visited Antonio's parents' house, I'd stumbled on his big secret—that he'd been hiding the authenticity of the Chagall for weeks—and I'd told him I never wanted to see him again.

Great first impression for his mother. How could I top that one?

I put up a finger and hit the call button on my steering wheel. "Call Lucy Chapman."

"We *are* still going tonight, sì?"

"Hey, Sam!" came Lucy's excited voice. "Did you get my text about White Cedar?"

"I did, and we just finished there."

"Is Antonio with you?"

"Y—"

"Hi, Antonio! Why am I always talking to you on the phone together, but never get to see you as a—"

"Lucy," I said on a long exhale. "Felicia gave us some information I'd like you to track down. She mentioned they had two other paintings that came from the same place we suspect the Constable did. Can you—"

"Want me to check that real estate listing and find some other mega-sus artwork?"

"Sort of. Send me the best shots you can of every piece of artwork or sculpture on the listing, including any that aren't on the public site anymore."

"On it, boss."

She clicked off and I sighed, "Not your boss, Luce."

Antonio eased my sunglasses down so there was no barrier between us. "I won't go without you, but I'd rather not have to cancel on my poor, old, frail grandmother."

I chuckled at his puppy-dog eyes, the way he batted his eyelashes at me. "Listen, I've met your grandmother. Poor, old, and frail are not the words I'd use."

"Then how about... she'll kick your very firm little ass if you don't come with me? She and my mother want to fawn over you. And more than that..." He kissed the tip of my nose. "My mother wants to make up for what happened."

My family was small. Me, my sister, her husband and kids, plus Nathan. Antonio's family was the opposite. The only saving grace was that his aunts and uncles and most of their kids were scattered across the country and Italy. Bringing him to Christmas dinner with my family meant a lot to me. It was a chance for them to meet him and hopefully for him to win Cass and Nathan over. He'd be going into the lion's den tomorrow night, so it was only fair if I went with him tonight.

"Of course I'll go with you."

A smile spread across his handsome face. "And I was hoping we could do our gift exchange there tonight? Mamma wants to see you open what I got for you."

"Just tell me it isn't more lingerie."

I expected a loud, Antonio-esque laugh.

Instead, he cupped my cheek, thumb brushing across my lips. "It's something special for my special woman."

A wave of the panic I'd felt last night jumped in my stomach. I'd foolishly thought that jewelry box had an engagement ring in it. And how quickly and easily he teased about us being married... he wouldn't propose at his parents' place.

Would he?

CHAPTER 19

SAMANTHA

ANTONIO LAY across the bed in my hotel room, flipping through a thick book chronicling my life. For a man who'd worn suits to most of our early meetings and dressed like a model while we were in Naples, his faded denim and t-shirt seemed out of place. He propped his head on his right hand, turning pages slowly, while I packed the last few items I owned. "You don't strike me as the scrapbooking type."

"Cass made it." I should have hidden the scrapbook at the bottom of a bin before he saw it.

"Before or after?" He looked up, hand paused on a page.

"After." I pulled the final shirt off its hanger. "It was maybe two days after her diagnosis, my first day back in Brenton, and she dragged me out to the craft store. She dropped about five hundred dollars that day alone, buying books, stickers, pages, tools, everything she could get her hands on. Then we took some online classes together, and she was off to the races."

"You took classes with her?"

"Yeah. You're definitely the only artist in this relationship." Folding the shirt, I dropped it into the bin with the rest of my casual clothes. "It ended up with her telling me what and where to stick or cut, and I obeyed."

He smiled up at me, that smile that had my heart fluttering from the first day we'd met. "You're a good soul."

"Thanks." I leaned over to give him a peck on the lips.

"This woman looks like you." He pointed to a photo near the front of the book with a man, woman, and two young children. "Is she your mother?"

"Yeah." I headed to the living room to double-check I'd gotten everything from the room. My step stuttered as I passed the balcony door, despite the shooter being in custody. They'd scrubbed the blood out of the carpet, leaving a brighter patch that was too clean. *Keep moving, Sam.*

"Is that all I get to hear?"

"That's Cass and me with my parents." I opened and closed each drawer in the side tables, desk, and kitchen, finding nothing left behind. "I'm taking the side table. They can bill me, I don't care."

He chuckled but kept flipping through a few pages as I got down on my hands and knees to check under the couches and chairs. "This is your father? I don't see him in any other photos."

"He left when I was five." I'd run away from home that day, intent on finding him and bringing him home. His face was nowhere in my memory, just like my feelings for him. It had started as sadness and guilt, transformed to anger, and now there was nothing left. He was a fact in my history, nothing more. "I don't know what my mom did with all the other photos, but she only kept two. The other is in one of Cass's books."

"Really?"

"Really." I ducked into the spare bedroom, the first room I'd cleared. My work clothes had been stored in here, plus the dresses I'd worn on my dates with Antonio.

He raised his voice, rather than following me. "Is this too sensitive a topic?"

I crawled across the floor to ensure I had everything. The closet was clear, nothing under the bed or in the drawers.

"Would you prefer to tell me about these photos of the gorgeous woman in the wedding dress?"

Closing the spare bedroom door behind me, I made my way to the bathroom. "Seriously? You want to go from my father to my wedding?"

"As beautiful as you were in that dress, you're even more stunning today."

I peeked through the door into the bedroom to frown at him. "You're incorrigible."

He winked in return. "Sì, this word suits me!"

"Cass made me add that page." She had said it was supposed to be therapeutic, like it would help me let go.

Antonio hummed quietly but didn't comment.

After confirming I'd cleared the bathroom, I returned to the bedroom and sat next to him. One suitcase to get me through the rest of the days I'd be staying with him. Everything else was ready to take to Cass's for when he left for Naples.

He began to reach for me, to touch my arm or back, but made the faintest grimace and resumed flipping pages. The stitches in his shoulder were bothering him more than he'd admit. Stubborn man.

I watched in silence as he stopped on a spread near the

middle. On the left, the end of high school, on the right, the start of college.

Tapping a finger on my prom photo, his voice less strained than I would have expected, he said, "Nathan Miller was your prom date?"

"Yeah, my original date got sick, so Nathan took me."

He pursed his lips and turned to a page with a pressed lily, a photo of my mom, and a group photo at Cass's house. "All in black. This was your mother's memorial? And he was there, as well?"

I nodded, and he slid a hand over mine.

"I didn't understand before, but I think I do now." He brought the hand to his lips, and I looked down at him. "He's everywhere in here, from when you were young."

"Twelve."

"He truly is your family." The way he smiled, I knew the jealousy was done. It had sunk in. Good thing I hadn't hidden the scrapbook.

Taking the hand back, I flipped to a different page with the heading 'Adventure Seeker.' Far less emotional. "This is me—"

"How many children do you want to have?"

A fluttering ran through my chest, replaced quickly by a fist clamping around my heart. My hand hovered over a picture of me after getting my skydiving C license. Where did that question come from?

"I grew up with two siblings, so always thought I wanted three. All boys, just like Sofia has." He flipped the pages to a family trip we took to the Grand Canyon when I was eleven. "But seeing these pictures of you and Cassandra has me thinking. Maybe two? Maybe girls?"

I slid to the edge of the bed. We were not having this

conversation; it was too early. But the image was in my head; our family at the Grand Canyon with our kids. He'd be wearing hiking gear, like when we went to the river together in August. I'd be teaching the kids how to climb rocks safely, while he taught them how to capture the light for painting.

The tightness gave way to a looseness, an ease. But it was ridiculous. Married and having kids with... Dr. Antonio Ferraro? Less than six months ago, I could barely string two words together when we were in the same room.

He shut the book and hauled me backwards on top of him. With a low grunt, he rolled me onto the bed, pinning me.

"What the—"

"How many?" He dug his fingers into my waist and I squealed. "Tell me!"

"Stop!" I laughed, while he continued, only encouraged by my weak attempts to get free, trying not to hurt his shoulder.

He smooched my neck, loud, goofy kisses, over and over while tickling me.

"No!" I howled, squirming loose, but he grabbed me again, eyes squeezing shut as he did.

"Tell me!" He snuck a hand into my armpit, and I yelped.

I sucked in one rapid gulp of air. "Broccoli!"

He stilled immediately. "Did you just safe word a tickle fight?"

I flagged against him, trying to catch my breath.

"Are you alright?" He rolled us so I was lying on the bed, and he hovered over me. "Did I hurt you?"

"Fine." I cleared the tears from my face, the laughter still coming in bursts. "I could barely breathe."

He smirked, the mischief resuming its near-constant state in his eyes, his hand sneaking down to the waistband of my pants. "No matter, I have other ways of making you talk—"

"Two!" I grabbed his hand with a giggle. Not a giggle. I didn't giggle. "Boy and a girl! Now stop! I can tell you're in pain, you fool."

"I'm fine." He winked—shooting back the words I used every time I was injured—and planted one more smooch on my neck. "That was not so hard, was it?"

"Jerk." I lay back, chuckling as he gripped my waist. He was about to try something else. Did I want to fend it off? If we got carried away here, maybe I could avoid visiting his family.

But he rolled off the bed, saying, "Now hurry up. We need to take this stuff to your truck and get ready for dinner with my parents."

CHAPTER 20

SAMANTHA

"Et la pièce de résistance, my studio." Antonio came up the last steps of the winding metal staircase from the foyer and wrapped his arms around my waist from behind, his head nestling on my shoulder.

With an hour to kill before we had to leave for his parents' house, I was finally getting the grand tour.

The studio was larger than the main room downstairs, with exposed wooden beams crossing the ceiling and off-white walls covered in paintings. The short wall at the far end was all windows, leading to an expansive patio, which likely held a few seating areas in the warmer months. Eight skylights dotted the ceiling, which would bring in a great deal of natural light when the sun was up. "Wow."

"This is where I paint." At least sixty canvases were stacked against each other, two on easels by the glass wall, and twenty hung up. The styles varied wildly, from Baroque and Rococo to Cubism and Abstract Expressionism. Two rolling tables like the ones at his office were pushed against one wall, next to a ventilation hood. "I sometimes do restorations here, so had a professional extractor installed. The more sensitive work remains at the office, of course."

"I love this." I squeezed his arms around me. Drop cloths under the easels, paint splatters on the floor, and half-finished paintings and sketches. This was my artist's home.

"This studio is why I bought the place. The glass wall faces south, so it gets a great deal of sunshine." He kissed my cheek and let go of me, crossing to a stunning canvas at the front of one of the stacks. Three feet by four, it was reminiscent of Monet's *Water Lilies*. There were over two hundred paintings in the *Water Lilies* series, but the palette reminded me of a particular one which hung at The Met in New York, all rich greens and blues with yellow lily pads and red flowers. It was a distinctly post-Impressionist twist. "I was thinking of giving this to Cassandra and Kevin for Christmas. As a thank you for having me for dinner."

"I don't know. They like to keep the price tag low on gifts."

He waved a dismissive hand. "My father bought it for next to nothing at an antique store."

I squatted beside it, taking in the brush strokes, the movement, the rich colors. "And you bought my dress and shoes secondhand?"

Laughing, he joined me in front of it. "He bought it when he was first training me. Someone had used polyurethane instead of varnish—" He shuddered theatrically. "—to coat it. It had caked and yellowed, ruining the painting. I worked on it for weeks, an hour or two at a time, scraping the polyurethane off, then filling and correcting the paint."

"Sounds like fun." I brushed my fingers along the raised impasto texture, over the ridges and into the valleys.

"It was a terrible job, but he was proud of me for working so long on it. After all that time, he used it as a lesson on how reversible our paints are. He had me go over the entire thing with the restoration paints, then remove them all to reveal the original painting again. Finally, he had me strip all the paint off it and prepare the canvas for fresh paint. At that point, he gave me the canvas to do as I wanted. So, this is what I painted on it."

The bright lights in the room flattened it somewhat, but if the sun was still up, it would have cast shadows, adding depth and beauty to it. I glanced at him out of the corner of my eye while he scanned the painting. My boyfriend. So talented.

"I want to make a good impression on them. This painting has a lot of my soul in it, and I thought that was important." His eyes fell to the floor, the shy smile making a rare appearance.

What a curveball my life had thrown me. On the road for six years, coming home for Cass's treatments, and full-on colliding with this amazing man. I'd wanted nothing to do with romance or anything that tied me down. But he'd started chipping away at my resolve, bit by bit. And here we were, four and a half months after meeting, staring at his artwork, talking about how he wanted to impress my sister for Christmas.

I took his hand, and we stood as one. I tucked my arms around his waist and lay my head against his shoulder. "They'll love it."

"Bene." He pressed his lips to my head and sighed.

We separated, and I scanned the paintings on the walls, until I saw one that stood out. Crimson at its center, radiating out to azure at its edges. Like a burning sun in the sky. I gasped and clapped a hand over my mouth. We'd seen it at a gallery in Naples.

"You've finally spotted it." He chuckled, nudging me with a hip. "You said it reminded you of our trip to the beach in August."

"I said I didn't want it!" I'd told him it reminded me of the sky, the first day we'd almost had sex, when he had me splayed out on a blanket in the middle of the woods.

"Sì, so I bought it for me." He took my hands when I tried to shield my eyes. "I had it shipped home after you left."

Heat crept up my cheeks, and no doubt even my neck was beet-red. "This is humiliating."

"And worth every penny." Antonio bit down on his lip, working hard to suppress his laugh. "Now, come see the rest."

He walked me to the end opposite the wall of windows, set up more like a laboratory. A tall bench extended the length of the shorter wall, shelves above, drawers underneath, with a deep metal sink and equipment I hadn't seen since college. Including a large table-mounted microscope, several plaster bricks, and stacks of glass bottles and petri dishes.

An eight-foot-long adjustable-height desk with one chair separated the studio from the lab space. It was topped with a laptop, two widescreen monitors, and a printer. "Quite the office."

He directed me to the lab bench and pulled out a clean petri dish. "I started on my postdoctoral research after I graduated. There are several strains of bacteria used in the conservation of frescoes, and I worked with a few for my doctorate."

"I remember from your dissertation."

He smiled. "I thought to continue that and identify new ones or new methods of applying the existing ones. Particularly, to make wall and ceiling work easier. But I enjoy working with my father so much I stopped."

"But you still have all this equipment here. Ever think about starting it again?"

"I had not until the project in Pompeii. Truly, my doctoral research was for frescoes which had endured far more environmental damage than the Casa has, given how recently it was excavated. But I've spoken a great deal with the other conservators, and we're planning to test some changes when working on the garden walls."

"Can you do both once you're done? Work with your father and do the research?"

He put the dish back in its stack and threaded his arm around my waist. "I could, but that would leave precious little time for making love to you."

I grinned, trying to hold back my laughter. "Well, when you put it that way..."

"I suppose..." He heaved a great sigh. "I'll just have to suffer and choose you."

My laughter escaped this time. "I appreciate your suffering."

"Speaking of suffering—" He tugged me against him suddenly. His hand trailed down to cup my ass. "We still have almost an hour before we have to leave."

I pushed against him, my weak attempt to separate a complete failure. "I have hair and makeup to do. That's not enough time to christen the studio."

"Not up here. I was thinking about the library." He moistened his lips and touched them to mine, sending a shiver through me. "Your eyes lit up in there."

I traced his lips with my thumb, feeling him harden,

answered by the tightening between my thighs. "I'm betting my eyes light up a lot around you."

"Again, I'm a lucky man." His powerful hands gripped the sides of my waist, holding me steady as he kissed me again, deeper this time.

I pulled back far enough our lips touched as I spoke. "If you don't mean to be late for your parents, we should—"

His hand dragged up one side, so the thumb brushed the slope of my breast and my leg instinctively wrapped around his. "Head to the library?"

With a groan, I nodded, letting my leg fall. "But a quickie only. I don't want to be late."

CHAPTER 21

SAMANTHA

Twenty minutes late.

"Come now, bella, it was worth it." Antonio opened the passenger-side door of his SUV for me, taking my gloved hand in his. He may have been slightly right, but I was not about to admit that to him. "And my sister is always at least half an hour late, so we're practically early."

He'd parked behind the only other car in the circular driveway, the others likely in the four-car garage off to the side. My eyes lingered on the large fountain the driveway curved around, remembering the last time I'd been to Antonio's parents' house.

Everything had seemed perfect that day—a new relationship, being introduced to his family, the warm welcomes from all the guests at their dinner party. But today, I couldn't walk slow enough.

In one hand, I clutched the small gift I planned to give him, and the other held tight to his.

We passed white lights strewn around the hedges, which climbed up the columns stretching to the second-floor balcony over the large double doors of the enormous house. Masses of electric candles flickered in every window.

"It's beautiful." I paused, taking in the massive two-part wreath. Each of the double doors held one half, four feet tall and wide in total, adorned with red and gold bows, foot-long ornaments, and twinkling lights.

"Sì, my father rarely does anything small, including his Christmas decorations." He kissed my temple as we climbed the few steps to the expansive porch.

I stopped on the top step and looked down at it, my heartbeat speeding up. "Is this travertine?"

Antonio nudged me forward, recognizing the stalling tactic. "There's no need to worry, bella."

"But the last time I was here—"

"Did I ever tell you what my mother said after that?"

After she brought me to her private art gallery, and I practically had a panic attack when I saw the real Chagall there? "No."

"She felt bad at first, like she ruined everything. But after that, she told me I got what I deserved. That lies and secrets never produce anything positive."

She was right about that.

"And the only warning I'll give you for tonight is that she's going to be overly nice. The word, I think, is smothering."

The doors swung open suddenly and Dominico appeared, his expression as joyous as always. He waved us inside. "Samantha, my love! Come in from the cold."

As my feet crossed the threshold, he snatched my face in his hands, coming in for enthusiastic kisses at each of my cheeks. The foyer of Antonio's parents' house soared up three floors, decorated with bright marble, and painted a warm off-white. A chandelier dropped from the ceiling high above us, while a wide spiral staircase went up to the second- and third-floor landings.

"Dr. Ferraro, it's good—"

"Dom! How many times do I have to say this?"

"Nothing for me, Papa?" said Antonio with a chuckle.

Dominico took my hand and placed it on the inside of his elbow. "I'm surprised you left the house when you had such a beautiful woman to distract you!"

Antonio's mother, Valentina, glided into the foyer, wearing a stunning red sweater and flowing black pants, her black and white hair upswept. She was almost as tall as me, taller than Dominico by an inch. Her side of the family must have been where Antonio and Lorenzo's height came from, let alone their cheekbones.

I smiled, overly conscious of the way my jaw clenched and hand shook on Dom's arm. Good thing the present was so solid, otherwise I would have crushed it.

She liberated my hand from Dominico and wrapped her arms around me. "It's so good to have you back."

"Good to be here."

"Has my boy been treating you well?"

I tried to withdraw from the embrace, but she held tight, longer than necessary. "Yes, very well."

"Good." With a final squeeze, she let go and shifted to Antonio. She cupped his cheeks in her hands, pulling him down to look her straight in the eyes. "And you. How are you doing? Not stressing that shoulder, are you?"

"No, Mamma," he sighed.

"My poor baby." She pouted, then kissed each of his cheeks, not letting go of his face.

"It's only a couple of stitches."

Her eyes widened and she jostled him. "You were shot!"

"My love..." Dom's voice softened, and he placed a hand on one of her arms.

"We were over this yesterday, Mamma." Antonio pulled his mother's hands away from his face and straightened. "It was glass. And I'm fine."

This seemed like a good time to flee out the front door.

"This sort of thing shouldn't be happening here." Her eyes narrowed and snapped to Dominico, her tone sharper than I would have expected from her. "Maybe around your brother, but not here. Not in *our* town."

That caught my attention. Dom's Brother? Was this the same one Nathan was referring to?

Before Valentina could continue, Antonio put a hand on her shoulder and said, "Is Samantha's gift ready?"

The cloud over her vanished in an instant, the same mischief sparkling in her dark eyes that Antonio frequently possessed. "It is."

We stripped off our jackets and switched our winter boots for indoor shoes. Why would Valentina be getting my gift *ready*? Antonio didn't strike me as the sort to have his mother wrap presents for him, but it was always possible.

Antonio snatched my hand and pulled me toward the stairs. As soon as we were halfway to the second floor, the pleasantries below us halted. Valentina and Dom exchanged heated whispers. I only caught snippets, including 'I don't want to talk about it' from Dom and 'dangerous' from Valentina, then 'about time' from her, and 'what will she say' from him.

Nerves churned in my stomach. When we were leaving the

interior designer's office, he'd said the gift was something special. And he wanted to exchange it here because his mother wanted to see my reaction. This was going to be significant.

But really, the gift I was going to give him was significant, too. Something so deeply personal, Cass was speechless when I first brought it up with her.

The open walkway looked down over the foyer and grand living area, with its tall paintings and two-story windows over-looking the terraced gardens in the back. A ten-foot Christmas tree twinkled with red and gold decorations and hundreds of lights.

The churning escalated as we hit the top of the stairs and he took a left.

"We're not going..."

He was taking me to the private gallery. To the scene of our breakup. The walls closed in on us as the walkway became a hallway.

"This is important, bella." He stopped and brought my hand to his lips, a gentle but confident smile lighting his face. "There's no going forward if the past is always in our way."

Forward was what I wanted. But this was going to be hard, and I was far better at running from moments like that than facing them.

Antonio began walking again, backward, that warm *I love you* look in his eyes. He was right—we had to go forward—so I walked with him, down the hall, to the last door.

Valentina's words that night came back to me, 'Dom says it's for family only, but I have a feeling you're close enough.' It had startled me four months ago, but wouldn't have surprised me now, given so many things Antonio had said and done since then.

The octagonal room was painted a rich burgundy, with heavy curtains to match, blocking out the light which could damage the amazing artwork in the room. In the center sat the circular white couch, which allowed you to sit and enjoy any of the carefully curated pieces the Ferraro family didn't share with the outside world.

Antonio walked me directly to where I'd instinctively known he would.

The Chagall. Vibrant blue background and a vase of red and yellow flowers, two floating heads in the top left, and the table with its bowl of fruit and violin.

Les amoureux dans le ciel.

Antonio's hand tightened as we stood in front of it, silent for a moment. He took the present from me and placed it on the couch so he could take both of my hands.

"The last time we were here…" His voice shook and he exhaled slowly. "My heart shattered. The apologies were easy to make because I knew I was a fool. I risked the greatest thing that's ever happened to me."

"We don't have to do this."

"We do." He swallowed hard and stared at me for a long moment. Once he spoke again, the shake was gone. "I want to apologize once more for what I did. I want to close the door on that piece of our past and move forward with as few obstacles as possible."

"I forgave you months ago, Antonio."

"I know, but…" His eyes drifted to the floor, then up to the painting. "I asked Papa to sell it."

"No!" Every muscle in my body tightened, and his gaze snapped back to me. I may have been louder than called for. "Do you have any idea what this painting means to me?"

"I would have assumed pain and betrayal, but your reaction makes me think not." Of course he didn't know, because I'd never told him.

God, I sucked at honesty.

"When I was ten, my mother took me to visit Bobby Scott. She was delivering some sort of paperwork to him, and I waited patiently in the living room for them to finish." I released one of Antonio's hands and turned to face *Les amoureux*. "This was hanging in that room all those years ago, and it captured my imagination."

"This was the painting that sparked your love of art?"

"It was." I took a step closer, my free hand gravitating toward it. "Can I touch it?"

"This is not a museum."

I ran my fingers over the brush strokes of the sky, traced the faces floating in the corner. "After we left, my mom bought me a book about Chagall and that was the first step that decided the rest of my life. At least..." My hand dropped. That path ended a long time ago.

"The life you were planning until your mother's death?" he whispered.

Pins and needles pricked at my fingers, and my heart searched for a slower rhythm. "Yeah."

He stepped behind me and wrapped his strong arms around my waist, kissing the side of my head. "This painting tore us apart."

"No." I turned around in his embrace, looking up into his soft eyes, the gallery lights playing against their flecks. "This painting—at least, the fake—brought us together. And as much as I hate to say it..."

He pressed his lips to my cheek and the pain shooting up

my hands faded, my heart rate slowing. What was this power he had over me?

"The truth tested how I felt for you. Everything was too easy before that and didn't make me challenge anything."

"Easy?" His eyebrows drew down. "Obviously, you were not paying attention to how hard I worked to convince you to go on a date with me."

I laughed and tugged at the hair at his nape. "You know what I mean."

"Our whirlwind."

"At least a hurricane."

He tilted his face down to mine, but I backed away from the impending kiss.

"No makeup transfers at your parents' house."

"No?" The corner of his lips rose into a smirk and the twinkle in his eye told me that distracting him with a kiss might have been a wiser idea. "Then I suppose..." He let go of me and reached to the flat top of the couch, where I hadn't seen a small white jewelry box. "We'll just have to exchange our gifts."

Oh no.

I picked up my wrapped gift and handed it to him. "You first."

"You can't avoid my gift all night, you know. This isn't like last night."

I glared at his ridiculous smiling face and pushed my present toward him, not reaching for the box he held. "It's nothing extravagant..."

He placed the jewelry box back on the couch, took my gift, and sat. "Is it from your heart?"

"It is." I sat next to him.

"That's what matters." He peeled back the wrapping and box lid, casting me a sidelong glance as he went through layer after layer of tissue paper. When he revealed the dark brown calf-skin cover of a book with a ribbed and cracked spine, the continual smirk slipped. He shook his head as he ran a hand over the weathered cover with its stamped surface.

I nudged his arm. "You going to open it?"

He blinked slowly and pulled it out of the box, cradling it in one hand, as though it was already precious to him. Using the red silk bookmark I'd placed inside, he slid it open to a page near the middle, his jaw falling slack. He touched the yellowed page, running fingers over the little stains and cramped writing.

Energy zipped around my chest while he, for once, was silent. "So? What do you think?"

He dragged his eyes away from it, up to me. "A copy of *The Merchant of Venice* from 1637? And you complain I spend too much on you?"

"It—" A lump lodged in my throat, so I flipped the pages to the inside cover. There were four inscriptions, and I pointed at the last one.

He read, "*To the man who hath music, May your spirit continue to shine like the sun and your affections remain as bright as Eros. All my heart, Samantha.*" He covered his mouth with a hand. "This a is play on Lorenzo's speech to Jessica?"

I nodded. "Read the inscription above it."

"*My dearest Deborah, I am so proud of you. Congratulations and well deserved. All my love, Charles.*" He shook his head and looked at me.

"My dad gave it to my mom when she graduated from law

school. Her will said we had to keep it, but it's just been collecting dust all these years up in Cass's attic. I thought it was appropriate, considering how—"

"How you love finishing my Shakespeare?"

"Yeah."

He turned several pages, running his fingers delicately across each thin sheet. I watched, visions of my mother reading and re-reading it coming back to me. After my father left, she never spoke of him. This book must have made her think of him, so how could she keep it after he abandoned her with two kids?

Maybe Antonio owning it could redeem it.

"This is..." He shook his head. "I'll send it to a friend in Boston for repairs. He's one of the best in the business."

"Do you like it?" Would my mother be happy I'd chosen him for her book? Cass wasn't, but she'd eventually come around.

"That you would give me something so precious to you..." He placed it and its box on the couch, and brought my left hand to his lips, kissing my promise ring. "Thank you. Thank you so—"

Whispered voices cut him off. A shushing noise. And the scramble of feet.

I looked toward the door, then back at him. "I think someone's there."

CHAPTER 22

ANTONIO

SAMANTHA CUT off at the familiar sound of my mother shushing someone. So much for my stealthy family.

She swiveled on the couch, craning her neck to look at the door.

I plucked the jewelry box from the top of the couch and raised my voice so they could hear. "I've not given it to her yet."

My mother, father, grandmother, and sister all poured into the room with ridiculous smiles on their faces. Samantha's entire body clenched. Fortunately, Sofia's husband and sons were not there—likely still removing their jackets while she'd charged upstairs—nor were my cousin Frank and his girlfriend.

Samantha turned back to me, doing her best imitation of a deer in headlights. "What's going on?"

"I told you I had a special gift for you." With a deep sigh, I took one of her hands and placed the box in it. "And apparently everyone wants to see the look on your face when you open it."

She remained frozen, only her eyes moving, flicking back and forth between me and the direction of my family.

I placed a hand on her knee, rubbing lightly with my thumb. "I wanted to bring you up here because I didn't want what happened in this room to hang around our necks for the rest of our lives. We needed a better memory."

Samantha blinked at me in a pattern I didn't recognize. There were many ways she stared, some to tell me I was being too much, some that she was confused, and a special one that told me she loved me. This one was likely the *There are people watching us* stare, as it was very similar to the one she gave me to avoid public displays of affection.

No matter. They were already there, not going anywhere, and I'd rehearsed what I wanted to say with my mother. "Samantha, you're the first woman I've ever dated who sees me for who I am. I could tell you post-Impressionism is the best style and—"

She opened her mouth to debate, but I put a finger to her lips.

"—and you could give me at least five reasons why Impressionism is better. I've rarely dated women who would know what either was. They all wanted my money or my reputation. They saw me as a thing, not a person."

A faint smile crept across her lips. "Sounds like you haven't picked your girlfriends well."

"No kidding," muttered Sofia, and Samantha chuckled. Perhaps having them there would help, rather than hinder.

"There is truth to that." I took a deep breath. "Until you. Everything is until you. There is my life before that night at Caruther's and then my life after. I know you want to take things slow, and I'm trying. But from the night we met, there was a voice in my head that told me I was done with other women."

A faint sigh escaped someone's lips. Samantha's free hand twitched, and I took it, stopping her before she could rub it across her face or put up a shield between us.

"I know your first reaction to this will be to say no, but have an open mind."

"You flying home to see me is all I want for Christmas. I don't need more stuff."

"This is not just stuff." I placed the hand I held on top of the box.

She was quiet.

The entire room was quiet.

Things were rolling about in her head, stories of losing her mother, her father's abandonment, her best friend in college, her first marriage. The man who promised to move from Italia to be with her. All those people who were there for her one day and then weren't the next.

I leaned close enough that only she would hear my quiet words. "I'm not going anywhere, bella."

One of the women said something, but my focus was so tight on Samantha that it was little more than a buzz in the background.

"Everything you said..." She rubbed her nervous fingers together, whispering in return. "As terrible as I am with words, I feel the same."

"So open the box." I placed a hand underneath the one that held the jewelry box, offering her my strength and belief in us. "It's something I *do* hope will hang around your neck for the rest of our lives."

With a slight tremble, she creaked it open, peeked inside,

and then snapped it immediately shut. She pushed it back to me. "No."

"What?" exclaimed my mother, who separated from the group and came to my side. "You don't like it?"

"Mamma—"

Samantha nudged my leg with hers. "That's not it. It's just —it's too expensive."

"Expensive?" said Mamma. "He didn't pay a cent for it!"

I'd told her Samantha would say no, but my mother had insisted. I accepted the box and opened it for her. A single round cut diamond on a gold chain, roughly a carat and a half. Under the multiple small lights of the gallery, its fire exploded.

Samantha's wide, insistent eyes bored into me. The insurance adjuster in her had likely already calculated its worth. "There's no way you didn't spend a small fortune on this."

"Then it's mine!" said Sofia, rounding the couch to stand next to Mamma. "I'm older, after all."

Samantha's brow furrowed, and her eyes darted over everyone in the conversation.

Papa joined the women and took the necklace from me, gazing at it with reverence. "I gave this to Valentina early in our courtship. She said something very similar to what you're saying, Samantha, but I promised her it was an heirloom to be passed down."

Mamma took the box from him and placed it back in my hand. "And I want you to have it, my dear."

"Much like you gave me something precious from your mother," I said, holding out the box. "We all want you to have this."

Cheater, mouthed Samantha.

I shrugged my shoulders, recognizing that she had surrendered. "May I put it on you?"

She nodded and turned, lifting her long hair out of the way for me to drape it around her neck and secure the clasp. When she faced me again, a blush had risen up her cheeks. My love was the most beautiful creature in the world, even under the harsh attention of my family.

A sudden loud clap startled us all, and we whipped around to Nonna, who was leaving. She called over her shoulder, "Back to the kitchen, Valentina!"

"Oddio." Sofia grabbed Samantha's hand and hauled her up. "You're coming with us." Without so much as a glance at me, Sofia pulled Samantha out of the room, stealing my moment the celebrate the gift with my girlfriend.

Mamma watched them leave. "Samantha needs to test everything we're going to serve tonight to be sure it's perfect."

My gaze went heavenward. "Don't scare her off."

She glared at me. "You're getting old—and heaven knows your brother's hopeless, but at least he's younger than you and has more time—so we need to put some meat on her bones."

"She has a very healthy appetite," I said.

"Nonna's outdone herself, although I think there are too many sprinkles on the struffoli." She gestured to the book. "This will be something wonderful to pass on to your own children." She gave me a lingering look, her meaning clear. *Give me more grandchildren and hurry up about it.*

I sighed as she left, leaving me alone with my father. "Time for you to harass me, too?"

"No." He sat next to me on the couch and leaned forward on his elbows. "Unfortunately, we need to talk. I got a call from Andrea earlier today."

"Is everything alright?"

"They found out who was behind the stolen painting at the Rome studio this past summer." He flexed his fingers and his jaw. "She was a short-term employee by the name of Eva Zabelle."

The breath caught in my throat. I was sure of the fact already, but my father and I hadn't had time to talk about everything that happened in Napoli in September. "So she started at Uncle Andrea's studio and then came to Pompeii to steal from me."

"I want to do something about this, Antonio. My *brother* —" He ground the word out, making it obvious he was speaking of Zio Giovanni. "—has been enough of a stain on our family. I moved here to get away from his influence, but just left Andrea open to it."

"What are you planning?"

"You've told me much about the good your Samantha's done, from catching stolen paintings to tracking down this Eva in Napoli. And it has me thinking..." He sat up straighter, resolve streaming off him. "We have contacts and resources at our disposal. Perhaps we should invest in a company that does that sort of thing. Maybe Samantha can help me choose where to spend that money or come up with some recommendations?"

Were she not destined to return to her position in the FBI Art Crimes Team—no matter how much she shrugged Elliot's pursuit off—I would have suggested he hire her. "I think she'd like that."

"I haven't decided, so don't say anything yet." He patted my knee and stood. "Now let's go rescue her from your mother before she pins her down and force-feeds her."

CHAPTER 23

SAMANTHA

I BOLTED UP from my pillow.

One. Observe.

Dark room. I was naked.

Two. Orient.

Where the fuck was I?

Heart racing. Why wasn't I in my hotel room?

Antonio had been shot. I needed to—

I gulped in air as my eyes adjusted to the darkness. It was Antonio's bedroom. No noise but his soft, rhythmic breathing. I rubbed my chest, clearing the sweat from between my breasts, breath coming too quickly.

Just a dream. Just a dream.

He lay on his back, one arm behind his head, the other outstretched, sheets at his waist. Christmas Eve with his family had been overwhelming, but wonderful, the entire evening full of laughs and amazing food. We were still together. He was safe.

I was safe.

There was space to snuggle against him, listen to his steady heartbeat, and relax. Go back to sleep. But that might wake him. It was only—I tapped my phone to wake the screen—two in the morning. He said jet lag didn't bother him, but he'd barely slept since he got home.

I eased out of the bed, shaking, and draped his silk robe around me, slipping my phone into the pocket. I held the collar up to inhale his lingering scent and tiptoed to the kitchen.

Every time I closed my eyes, we were at the hotel. Instead of running into the table, he'd kept walking, and the first bullet had been a direct hit. We'd fallen, the same as Tuesday evening, but he was dead. Half his head blown to pieces. Blood all over the floor.

I wandered toward the windows that lined the wall, staring out at the sleeping city, clutching the diamond at my neck. The shooter had been on the balcony, not in the trees at the edge of the parking lot. I'd seen him—the thug from Naples who'd slammed my face into the floor and somehow ended up unconscious next to me—lift the gun and fire. Paralyzed with fear, I hadn't warned Antonio.

I closed my eyes and leaned my head against the door, its smooth, cool surface calming me. No sounds came through the insulated glass, but in my head, the screaming continued. I'd run after the shooter, out onto the balcony, and found nothing but the bullet casing. The thug had vanished.

When I'd come back in, the police were there. I knelt by Antonio's lifeless body and cradled him next to me. The scene shifted, and we were all on the sidewalk in front of Mason's. Harry was there, examining the bullet casing I'd found, humming and hawing the way he did. 'That's interesting,' he'd said.

"Interesting?" My eye flashed open. What was interesting? Something about the casings.

My stomach flipped and I raced to the foyer, to my jacket. Both sets of bullets and casings were still in the interior pocket. Grabbing them, I tore up the steps to Antonio's studio two at a time. I took a piece of paper from the printer and slammed it down by the microscope. Drawing a line down the middle, I wrote *Mason's* to the left, *Hotel* to the right.

I placed the evidence on the sheet and swiveled the microscope into place, turning it on as I moved it. The bullets were easy to distinguish from each other, both misshapen from impacting the brick and the damage I'd done with the pliers.

But the casings were very similar. They'd both been ejected onto smooth surfaces and were pristine. Under low magnification, I could see them clearly, eyes flicking back and forth between them. Every marking—from the impact of the firing pin, the breech face, and the ejector—was identical.

A tingle ran up my spine, and I braced against the desk. They were identical. Either two different people had access to this gun or the same man who fired at Rhonda was firing at me and Antonio on Tuesday.

Bullet casings could be a match and be from different guns. Right? Was I drawing big conclusions from little coincidences? Did I suddenly believe in coincidences at all?

It was barely three in the morning. Who could I talk to about this?

Janelle. I whipped out my phone and dialed.

She answered before the first ring was done. "You okay, Sam?"

"Yeah, I'm fine. Sorry if I woke you."

"Got on an hour ago."

"Merry Christmas?"

"Right." She laughed. "Now, why are you calling me in the middle of the night?"

"Do you have the results back from NIBIN on the shooting at my hotel?"

"Why? What's going on?"

"Please, Janelle, do you?"

"Gimme a minute." I heard footsteps, the creak of a chair, and a few taps on a keyboard. A long minute passed. "Not yet."

"Shit, seriously?"

"Sometimes things get a little backed up around Christmas. Or paperwork gets misplaced. You know how it is."

"Janelle..." I rubbed my free hand over my face. "I found a bullet and casing at Mason's Gallery."

"When?"

"Two days ago. One bullet impacted the brickwork between the two panes of glass."

"You're kidding me." She muttered a few curses under her breath I didn't make out, and what could have been a name or two. "So, why didn't you turn it over to us?"

I shrugged, like she could see it. "Here's the thing..."

"Sam?"

"I found the same stuff at my hotel. One bullet wedged in the outside wall and the casing that went with it."

"And you're assuming those are from your shooting on Tuesday?"

"Well... the casing from Mason's and the casing from my hotel are a match."

"Fuck. The guy we have in custody for your hotel claims to have an alibi for the shooting at Mason's."

"Claims to?"

"They always do, and we're still chasing it down." She tapped a few more keys. "NIBIN tested the gun he had in his possession when we arrested him. Hits on a gas station robbery a couple of months ago. That's it. It wasn't a match for Mason's Gallery."

"You got that back before the results from my hotel?"

"Maybe Lansing's still processing your bullets. I'll check with them."

I peeked through the microscope again and took a deep breath. The guy who came after me in Naples was locked up, as were his accomplices. There could have been others working with them, but why wait three months to come after me? And what link could they possibly have to Mason's or Rhonda?

"What are you thinking, Sam?"

"You have one witness pointing to the guy in custody. What if that witness is wrong?" If the same gun meant the same shooter, only one thing made sense. "What if it's David and Olivia Scott?"

She was silent a moment, then the clacking of keys again. "Special Agent Skinner's out here every week to talk about that. There are no sightings of them anywhere near here. And if you think the two are related, what's the tie-in with Mason's Gallery?"

"A couple things. The artist who created the fake Chagall is the one whose painting was shot at Mason's."

"But the theory is Rhonda was the target, not the painting."

"I know." I straightened, hand on my face. "Rhonda's the one who told us there were offers made on the original Chagall when it was at the gallery. That led me to figure out Olivia had sold it after it was there." Although discovering the truth about Antonio's father buying it was the part that cemented that.

She clicked a pen a few times.

"Janelle, tell me I'm overreacting."

"I won't. You're too smart for that."

"Okay, tell me I'll be safe."

"I don't know if I can swing some officers to follow you. Maybe up the police presence in your area?"

"And near Cass's? She moved into Mom's old place."

"Yeah, I can do that. And I'll talk it over with Skinner."

"Thanks, Janelle."

"Be safe," she said, and hung up.

I put the phone down on the desk and stared at the microscope. It was a coincidence. They had the right guy in custody.

"What was that?"

I startled and spun to see Antonio standing at the top of the stairs, in his pajama pants. "Nothing."

"You were talking to your friend Janelle, the police officer. At three in the morning. You asked her to say you're overreacting and that you'd be safe." His eyes were wide as he walked to me and gripped me by the shoulders.

What could I say? He'd worry or get upset if I told him.

He glanced over my shoulder. Letting go, he passed me and pulled out the sheet under the microscope. "Marone, what's this?"

"Don't do that!" I launched at the paper, ensuring the bullets and casings didn't get mixed up.

"What's going on? Tell me!" He slammed a hand on the bench, causing the microscope to bounce. "No lies! That does *not* only apply to me!"

I flung my arms around his neck, the dream washing over me. "I had a nightmare."

He softened, pulling me close. "What does that have to do with this?"

"We were in the hotel Tuesday night." I held tighter, squeezing my eyes shut, focusing on his scent, his firm body, his soft skin. "You died."

"Shh now." He rubbed my back, his thick arms and big hands covering me like a protective blanket. I was safe in those arms. "It was only a dream, amore."

My heart beat against his, slowing to match his pace. He said nothing more, just continued to give me everything I needed.

We stayed like that for long minutes until he leaned away from me. "Now. Tell me what you're doing up here? I'm not a piece of porcelain. I can handle this."

I chuckled, playing with the hair at the nape of his neck. "Wednesday, when I was working with SIU, we went to Mason's and found a bullet and casing the police missed. When I stopped at my place, I found another."

He pursed his lips, waiting for more.

"Something in the dream—" I shuddered, but he held me steady against him. "—made me question whether there was a link between the shootings."

"Let me guess: It looks like there is?"

I nodded, slipping out of his grasp to retrieve the evidence. "The bullets are too damaged to analyze here and the formal forensics results are still pending, but the casings appear to be a match."

"And this means what?" He pulled out two Petri dishes and placed them on the sheet of paper.

"Same gun. So possibly the same gunman."

"You suspect the man the police arrested is behind both shootings?" He labeled the lids with a wax pencil to match the halves of the paper. In Naples, he'd tried to stop me from investigating the stolen fresco over and over. But tonight, there was no judgment, no complaint. He was simply helping without my needing to ask.

"I think—" I slid the labeled dishes onto a shelf, next to each other. "—the Scotts are out for revenge."

He took my hand and held tight. "That seems like a leap."

"The guy they arrested claims to have an alibi for Mason's and the gun he had on him wasn't the one used there. But if you think about that first shooting, both Rhonda and *Number Vee*'s artist were involved in the Chagall investigation, so either of them could have been the target and it still makes sense. Of course, then there's me, who they'd obviously come after."

"Alright. What do we do now?" He cocked an eyebrow and flashed a smirk. "Hunker down here and never leave the bedroom?"

"Janelle says I'm overreacting." It was a lie, but a small one. He may not be made of porcelain, but no need to worry him. "Says the FBI hasn't had any tips of the Scotts being anywhere near here. She's going to follow up with the forensics people on the bullets to see if I'm right about the match."

"What about Christmas dinner?"

I yawned, resting my head on his shoulder. "Said she'd up the patrols around Cass's neighborhood."

"There's a private security firm my family contracts with..."

"Private security?"

"Sì, for parties or when we have particularly high-value items at the office. I'll have them watch the house while we're there. Ensure everyone is safe." He ran a hand up and down my back. "Now, let's go to bed. I'm still tired."

"Good idea. All of it." I let him lead me to the bedroom and he snuggled in, keeping an arm around me. I rubbed the arm as his breathing slowed and his grip loosened.

But the blood was still there when I closed my eyes. The blood and the screams.

And Janelle's response when I asked her to tell me I was overreacting—*I won't.*

CHAPTER 24
ANTONIO

THAT NIGHT, we sat at a long dining room table. Samantha and I faced Lucy and Miller, Kevin at one end, and Cassandra at the other. Next to Cassandra, both of her children, the adorable little Emma, and the young man, Logan.

Lucy had stood from her seat, wandering to where they had already hung my painting in the room. "Sixteenth century Baroque?"

I squeezed Samantha's hand on her lap. The day she and Lucy had arrived to pick up my first repair of *Number Vee*, she identified a painting of that date and style. It had been such a turn-on, I'd thought of little other than how much I wanted to wrap her up in my arms and discuss art for hours on end.

Samantha laughed, and Lucy grinned at her. "Not even close, Luce! How do you remember that?"

Lucy tapped her forehead and sat in her chair at the dining room table. "It's got a number in it."

Miller sat sideways in his seat, inspecting it as well. "You seriously painted that, Ferraro?"

Samantha rubbed my ankle with her foot, which had been snaked around my leg all dinner. "He's quite talented."

He grunted in ascent, saying no more. I'd put on my best face the whole evening, focusing on each member of Samantha's family as needed. I won her three-year-old niece over by drawing coloring pages for her; with her ten-year-old nephew, it was showing him how to juggle a football outside in the cold; and Kevin called me his best friend when he accepted the bottle of Macallan I gave him.

Cassandra and Nathan Miller would require the long game, much like Samantha had.

"Speaking of paintings!" Lucy pointed her dessert fork at Samantha. "I searched around for other photos on that real estate listing."

Samantha made a quick cutting motion at her neck. Everyone's attention turned to her.

"There are a ton of paintings in that house, but I found—"

"Real estate listing?" asked Cassandra. "Giving up on the apartment hunt?"

Samantha shook her head sharply. "It's nothing. A friend of mine was looking to buy it and wanted my opinion."

Lucy continued. "—three other photos that had been taken down."

"Which friend?" asked Cassandra. "Someone from work?"

"Rhonda Wells," said Lucy. "The owner of Mason's Gallery."

Samantha's eyes narrowed at Lucy, who was not picking up a hint to be quiet.

Perhaps Lucy had enjoyed one or two glasses of wine too many. "Rhonda was checking out the house and saw a painting she thought was stolen. We were just looking. That's all."

Cassandra dropped her utensils on her plate. "Isn't that dangerous stuff to get involved in?"

"Nah, it's digital snooping only." Lucy's eyes lit up. "A few of them are really dark, so I'm going to sharpen them up before I send them."

"Could this be enough to pass over to Special Agent Skinner?" I asked.

Cassandra sucked in a breath. "Special Agent? Are you—"

"You know Elliot?" asked Miller.

While Samantha calmed her sister, who thought this meant Samantha was headed back to the FBI, I responded to Miller. "Sì, I met him in Napoli in September. You know him? He helped us track down the—"

Samantha kicked me. "He went to dinner with us while we were there."

What was she playing at?

She looked at me and scratched the scar at her hairline, using the hand to hide her bulging eyes from the rest of the table. *Be quiet*, that look said.

I did my best not to scrunch my face up in confusion.

"Lucy, email me the photos when you're done. Cass, I'm doing some legwork before reporting this to the FBI, so they can get a search warrant. Nathan, before you even bother to go there, I'm being careful. And Kevin, thank you for just sitting back and watching everything go on." Samantha gave a tremendous heave of her shoulders. "And can we get back to telling jokes or embarassing stories, because the kids are obviously bored?"

The children appeared fine. Logan had snuck his phone

out and chuckled over something playing at a low volume, while Emma shoved fistfuls of cake into her mouth.

Miller cleared his throat, cutting off the discussion. "When do you go back to Naples?"

"A week from tomorrow." The days were running away from me. It was my fourth night already. "Target completion for our project is April, but I'll try to be home sooner."

"That'll go by in the blink of an eye." He smiled that professional smile that made my stomach churn. *Don't hit him. Stay calm.*

Cassandra leaned her elbows on the table, steepling her fingers. "You planning on tearing off to Naples again without telling anyone, Sam?"

Samantha's foot stopped moving, and a tremor went through her hand.

"I mean, you have leave scheduled after New Year's, don't you?" Cassandra's face was pleasant, but tight, and Samantha's reaction indicated there was something much deeper.

"She won't leave until your treatments are complete." I brought my love's hand to my lips, and I locked eyes with her. *Thank you* was on her face. "Her priority is you right now, as it should be."

The edge of Cassandra's frost thawed slightly. That was my cue.

"And my priority—" I kissed Samantha's hand again and stood. "—is to clear these dishes."

Miller stood at the same time. "Trying to make me look bad?"

He was directly across the table from me, so I leaned forward slightly, holding my voice to a mock whisper. "Trying to make both of us look good."

~

ONCE THE KITCHEN and dining room were clean, I stood at the living room window. I raised a hand, and a car in front of the house flashed its lights.

Samantha appeared at my side, took my hand, and leaned close enough to whisper. "That the security guy you were talking about?"

I pressed my lips to her wondrous cheek. "One of them. He parks out front to be obvious. There are at least two or three elsewhere."

"Thanks for doing that." She hugged my arm tight.

I freed the arm and wrapped it around her shoulders, her arm finding its way around my waist. "Your sister cornered me in the kitchen."

She grimaced. "I warned you."

"She asked what my intentions were with you."

The grimace grew to an exaggerated one. "What did you say?"

"I told her the truth." I kissed her temple, her playful look softening. "That I intend to chain you to my bed—"

Her eyes narrowed, and she smacked my chest.

"—and keep you as my sex slave."

"You did not!"

"Seriously, though, bella. You didn't tell them what happened in Napoli, did you?"

She shook her head slightly and rested it on my shoulder. "I told them I got the stitches from the grotto where I sprained the ankle. That it was just an accident. It lowered the overall stress level when I got home."

There was no blaming her for that. I'd worried what they

would say when they found out the danger she'd been in. Not telling them was likely wise. I leaned my head against hers and held her tighter.

"That's enough, you two lovebirds!" Kevin appeared next to us, holding up the purple and gold box of the exquisite single malt I'd brought. "The wine was good, but it's time for us to head to the man-cave and watch some basketball."

I raised an eyebrow at Samantha, who rolled her eyes. "Yes, Dr. Ferraro, I'll be the responsible one and drive home."

With one more kiss, I descended into the biggest test of the evening.

The walls were covered in sports memorabilia, posters, pennants, and jerseys from baseball, American football, and hockey. A long couch, bracketed by two recliners, all in black leather, faced a large television, which was playing a sports commentary about the Christmas Day games. Behind the couch, next to the bottom of the stairs, was a well-stocked bar.

And Miller.

"I'll give you this much, Ferraro. You've got good taste in Scotch." He pulled two leather boxes from under the bar and opened one at a time, revealing two Glencairn Whiskey Glasses in each. "Really went all-out to impress the family?"

"I believe we got off on the wrong foot."

"Fist, you mean." He withdrew three glasses and poured into each.

"You have quite the right hook."

He picked up a glass by its squat stem and opened an ice drawer in the bar. "Ice?"

"I certainly hope that's a test." I accepted the glass from him, without ice, swirling gently to admire the light mahogany shade.

The corner of his mouth twitched. "Sam told me to give you a chance. But I'm a straight shooter, so let me be clear: If you hurt her again, my right hook will be the least of your worries."

Don't hit him.

"So Sam was right," said Kevin, appearing next to me.

Miller frowned, likely mirroring my own expression.

"She told me to make sure the two of you didn't get into a fight." Kevin held his glass aloft, smiling, but keeping a keen eye on Nathan. "To family."

We all raised our glasses and took measured sips.

"Mmm. Cloves, oranges, and oak." Kevin clapped an arm around my shoulders before taking another drink. "My door is definitely always open!"

"Family." Miller rolled his glass between his palms before sipping again. He at least had the decency to close his eyes and savor it. "Why don't you tell us about yours, Ferraro?"

"I seem to recall you telling me once you were familiar with my family already?" What had that meant? The night he and I first met, when he had Samantha out for dinner. That evening had nearly come to blows, as well.

"C'mon, you two. Either whip 'em out or shut the fuck up and sit down." Kevin crossed to the recliner while Miller and I continued our dance.

I threw back the contents of my glass—a poor fate for such a superb drink—and put the glass back on the bar. I cocked my head and an eyebrow. Miller downed his and poured us another round. We repeated our childish actions. There was no way this pretty, polished man, in his nice little checked dress shirt, could out-drink me.

Kevin flipped channels to a game in progress. "If you two insist on doing that, pick something cheaper."

Nathan glanced at his best friend, tapping his fingertips on the bar. He closed his eyes and took a deep breath, swaying slightly enough I could have missed it if I hadn't been watching for it. How many glasses of wine had he drank at dinner? He poured another round and looked at me. "What are Sam and Lucy up to?"

I hesitated before grabbing my drink. The abrupt change of topic was unexpected. "As they said, just following up on some questions Rhonda had."

"Keep a close eye on her. I've been out of my mind with worry since Tuesday night."

"As she likes to point out, she can take care of herself."

He huffed, raising his gaze heavenward. "Spare me the politically correct boyfriend bullshit. She's reckless and from what I read in the police report, you've seen it firsthand."

I nodded, sipping my scotch again. He was right. She was an adventure seeker who drove too fast, jumped out of too many planes, climbed too many mountains, and got herself in the way of bullets. "Why does she do that?"

"Because she's as stubborn as my wife!" Kevin was paying closer attention to us than I thought.

"I think—" Miller took another swig. He was past sipping. "—she's desperate to be in control. And somehow, by throwing herself into situations where she's completely out of control, she finds it. I mean, try and get her to do something small she doesn't want to do and you don't stand a chance. But throw her into the middle of danger, where she can't just walk away, and she grabs the reins to take charge."

That explained so much of her. Why she pushed away

from me so hard, despite obviously wanting to be with me. Her feelings for me put her out of control. She had tried and failed to push me out of her life, so instead she found control by denying those feelings.

Miller smiled, the look of a proud brother. "She would have kicked ass in the FBI if she'd gotten that in check."

"Or she would have ended up dead," Kevin said.

"True that." Miller raised his glass to drink again. He rounded the bar and grabbed me by the elbow, leading me to the couch. "Don't take this little chat to mean I like you, Ferraro."

"Not to worry, Miller. I hate you, too."

He laughed, not letting go of me, until he dropped onto the couch. Kevin turned up the sound on the television.

"But I'll keep an eye on Samantha and Lucy."

CHAPTER 25

SAMANTHA

Sunday morning, Antonio pulled up in front of Felicia's house. We'd driven by a few times Saturday, but she was home all day and I didn't want her to see us. No sign of the boyfriend, so we couldn't get a hint as to whether he was involved in Parker's Restoration.

But today? It was a glorious Michigan winter day. The sky was clear and the sun bright, temperature hovering around the freezing mark. And no Felicia. Nor any boyfriend.

Antonio put his SUV into park. "So, we're simply going to look into the windows and see if we can spot anything?"

I sat in the back seat with my binoculars. Between the darkened glass and all-black interior, I was well-hidden. "I want a layout of things. Where's the master bedroom? If I'm lucky, it's in the front on the main floor and we can peek inside."

It was a two-story house with a small third-floor gable window, likely a narrow attic space. All the curtains facing us were open, allowing me a clear view into a dining room on the right and a living room plus all-glass four season room to the left.

"Are you lucky?" asked Antonio, snaking a hand back to pinch my leg.

I jumped and knocked the binoculars into the window. "Not today, apparently."

"Do you want to take a stroll down the road? Maybe you can see something on the approach in either direction."

"Gimme a sec." I zoomed in closer through the living room window. "Lucy sent me a ton of photos of their artwork. But there was one painting where all you can see is part of the frame. It should be in the living room."

I couldn't see the correct wall and needed a different angle. Maybe that walk was the right idea. But was wandering down the street in broad daylight a wise plan?

Pivoting to look out the back, I trained the binoculars on the car parked three lengths behind us. It was only two days after I'd compared the bullet casings and the security team had been everywhere. "Are they going to be following me tomorrow?"

"Do you have results back from Janelle?"

"None."

"I'd prefer if you let me do this." He reached back to rub the side of my leg. "I respect you can handle yourself, but I was worried sick all day Wednesday until you told me they caught him. I'd prefer not going through that again."

"I know." How could I argue the point when I'd felt the same worry about his safety? "And maybe a walk is a good idea, but I'm not sure."

Antonio swore under his breath, the exact opposite reaction I'd expect to my being cautious.

My head snapped up to see a Mercedes SUV park across the street, in front of the house. A lovely woman in a long navy coat over suit pants walked toward the trunk. "Looks like we've got company."

"Do up your seatbelt. We'll come back later."

"They're not home. She'll knock and leave. Besides, we can go for that walk, regardless."

Antonio slid his seat back and turned to face me, grimacing. "That's not it."

A knock on his window caused us both to startle.

"Sorry," he whispered before turning around to roll down his window.

The Mercedes woman's face lit up. "Antonio! I thought it was you!"

"Buongiorno, Irene. Long time."

She either didn't notice me lurking in the back, mostly hidden behind Antonio, or was choosing to ignore that there was a woman in his car. "Are you here for a pre-check of the house? Doing a little drive-by?"

"Sì, that was the plan."

"Many people have been doing that." She lowered her voice to a whisper, with a little extra huskiness added in. "I'm the agent. I'm here to set up a few new photos and I could... ah... give you a private tour?"

The way she purred those last few words, she definitely hadn't seen me. I slid across the buttery-soft leather—polished so much I almost continued to the opposite side—and plastered on a smile as bright as hers. "We'd love that!"

Irene's face fell.

Antonio raised a hand to point back at me, but it was his left, ungloved hand.

Irene's eyes fell to his ring and bulged slightly.

"This is Samantha," he said.

"His wife," I added, my voice an auditory slap across her face. Hit on my man, will you?

Her real estate agent polish returned almost instantly. "Wonderful. I just need to grab a few things from my car."

Antonio hit the button to roll his window back up and turned to me. His pinched mouth and rare lack of words told me this wasn't some random acquaintance who thought she had a chance with the amazing Dr. Ferraro.

"Oh, shit." My stomach fell and I ran a hand over my face. "She's in the Calendar Club, isn't she?"

He shrugged and raised his hands like he was trying to grab an excuse out of the air. "We met at a friend's party and got along well—not as well as you and I, of—"

"Spare me the details." No wonder she was offering a *private tour*.

"One date, I swear. Then I found out she was engaged."

"Even better. She disqualified herself." I moved to the door and pulled on the handle to open it. "And she's a cheater."

He launched out of his door and hastily opened mine. "Have I told you yet today how beautiful you look?"

The petty pang of insecurity was ridiculous. He flew all this way for a week and a half with me. No one else. He closed the door behind me, and I leaned in to kiss him. It was a small peck on the mouth, but he grabbed the back of my head, holding it longer.

My brain and nether regions had a brief argument, but the brain won out and I eased away. "Don't kiss me for her sake."

"You're going back to work tomorrow, so I need to take all

the opportunities I can." He gripped my waist tight against him and lowered his voice. "We have little time to plan, so what's the goal now?"

"Full tour. Master bedroom for the Constable, living room for that frame, and... I don't know... anything that looks suspicious."

"Are you coming in, Antonio?" came Irene's voice from the walkway. She paused before adding, like an afterthought, "And Mrs. Ferraro?"

"Mrs. Ferraro," hummed Antonio. "That has a nice—"

I rolled my eyes at his ridiculous smirk and maneuvered myself out of his grip. But there was the image again. Us and our kids. A life together. "You know, I got top grades at the Academy for slipping into a fake identity."

"I'd accept a fake marriage with you." Antonio slid his hand into mine and we headed up the sloped walkway. He let go of me to hurry the last stretch to the door and take the plastic tote from Irene. "Are these staging materials?"

She smiled and nodded, opening the door. "The photographer should be here in fifteen or twenty minutes, so we'll have to be quick. We can start upstairs. The master ensuite is stunning."

After hanging up our jackets and placing boots to the side, she led us up the stairs, reviewing the highlights of the house.

"I'm surprised you're selling your place." Irene walked with Antonio into the master bedroom, and I became a long-distant memory. She stopped between the two of us. "You sounded so happy with it."

"We are, but Samantha—" He looked over her shoulder at me, and she turned around to do the same. Long enough for him to wave his hands, directing me to check around. "—

wants a yard. So, here we are. I like this tile in the bathroom. You said they installed it recently?"

I hovered in the doorway and casually closed the door over, inspecting the space. No painting, no nothing. Just a blank wall.

No, wait.

I leaned against the wall and scrutinized the surface. There was a slight indentation where I would have expected the hanger. With Antonio and Irene in the ensuite, I pulled out my phone to run its flashlight over the surface. It was hard to be sure, but the indentation and space around it was darker than the wall paint.

It was a patch job. If Felicia's boyfriend was actually a restorer, you'd think he would have done a better job matching paints. Then again, wall paints differed greatly from conservation paints.

I opened the door fully and meandered about the room, peeking behind the bedside tables and the dresser, keep an ear out for Irene leaving Antonio's side.

The Constable painting I was looking for was only about two feet high, making it easy to hide.

I scanned the bookcase to see if they could have stashed the painting behind it. Nothing. The walk-in closet was large, with plenty of space for hiding things. The entire house would be perfect for hiding something small. But where would they put it?

We were running out of time before her photographer arrived, so I shifted my focus. Reconnaissance only. No searching for the actual paintings.

I peeked around the door into the bathroom. "I'd like to see the living room."

"One minute," said Irene, putting up a vague hand but not turning to look at me. Considering she remembered how happy Antonio was with his condo, he could probably buy me more than enough time.

As I made my way out of the bedroom to the stairs, they laughed. Something about Dr. Steve, a dog, and Valentine's Day. Was she Miss February?

Keep moving, Sam. Ignore them.

One foot on the top of the staircase and Irene was right behind me.

"While we're up here, let's sneak up to the attic." She batted her ridiculously long fake eyelashes at Antonio. "It's also newly renovated and would make a perfect studio for an artist."

"Fantastico," said Antonio, caressing a hand down my arm as he passed me.

Irene continued talking as she led us through a door next to the bedroom and up a flight of stairs.

The attic space was narrow, with a slanted roof and ceiling low enough Antonio could touch it without effort. The space ran the length of the house, with finished surfaces and windows at either end. Despite the room being clean and obviously new, it was full of clutter. Upholstered wing chairs, a few old laptops, and a bookcase stacked with books so musty I could smell them as we walked past.

The walls and ceiling were matte white, reflecting light from the small windows and the one overhead light fixture.

"What do you think?" I asked Antonio as I paced the length of the room, searching for anything the right size, but finding nothing. "You can still hurry us through the rest of the house?"

"Certainly." Irene headed for the stairs, but Antonio remained stationary, staring the length of one long wall.

I approached him, touching his arm. I'd never seen him do this before. "Antonio?"

The doorbell rang and Irene said, "Shoot. That must be my photographer—he's early. I'll have to see you out."

"Too bad," said Antonio, tearing his gaze away from the wall. "I like what I've seen so far, but we'll have to tour the rest. When's the open house?"

Irene's eyes lit up, either at the promise of seeing him again or possibly at the wad of cash he could use to purchase the house outright. "I'm holding an invitation-only showing next weekend. I'll add you to the list. Same phone number?"

"Sì. And do you think you could provide a floor plan when we return?"

"I can." She saw us to the front door and let her photographer in, making small talk with Antonio the whole way.

I trailed a few steps behind, poking my head into the living room at the bottom of the stairs. The frame I'd been searching for wasn't there.

That made two paintings removed from the walls and hidden from the real estate listing. It was still all conjecture, but the odds were high that at least two of the paintings Felicia's boyfriend bought at the pawnshop were from the LA theft.

But where were they?

ANTONIO STARTED the SUV and turned on the seat heaters,

running a hand through his hair. "You realize this will make the rounds, sì? That I was secretly married in Napoli?"

"You used that line yesterday."

"With a stranger. But Irene? She knows many of the same people I do."

I put my hand on his arm. "Sorry, I hadn't thought about that."

"I suppose we'll simply have to carry through with it." He flung his hands up and smirked at me when I scowled. "Seriously, though. Did you get the information you were looking for?"

"Neither the bedroom nor the living room paintings are still up. It's possible they just moved them, but if an interior designer hung them in her own house for listing photos... odds are, they were in the best locations when the original pictures were taken."

"Good point."

"And what was up in the attic? You spaced right out."

He turned away from me to point at the house. "Look at the roof. There's a dormer on the left side, at the same height as the gable window of the attic."

I leaned forward, looking around him. "I was so focused on the rooms, I hadn't thought about it."

"And how much light came into the attic from the dormer window?" He turned back to me, his lip crawling up into a smirk.

"None!"

"Exactly. Irene said they recently renovated it, which explained the drywall dust I saw near roughly where that dormer should be, but—"

"They just covered it up and there are probably stolen paintings in there?"

"Possibile. Do we call Special Agent Skinner now? Or wait for the showing and take a closer look?"

The excitement bouncing around in me fell to the background. Elliot had told me more than once that Antonio and I made a good team. The auction painting, the fake Chagall, the stolen relics in Naples, and now today... we *were* a good team.

"Bella? What next?"

"Right." A smile started in my chest and spread outward. A good team. But teamwork meant business. I had to get back to business. "It's Sunday. I'll call him tomorrow and get his thoughts. I'll go through Lucy's photos again to compare against the paintings from the LA theft and—" My phone rang. Lucy. "—see if the third painting's in there somewhere."

He answered the phone through the stereo system. "Ciao, Lucy!"

"Antonio! Is Sam there?"

"I'm here Luce, what's up?"

She let out a high-pitched squeal that had Antonio turning down the volume. "I did it!"

"Did what?"

"The five-point-six top rope!"

"No way! That's amazing! You went to the climbing gym without me?"

"You told me if I didn't practice every week, I'd never be ready to go out for real with you. Paul was worried when you weren't there. First Sunday you've missed in eleven weeks."

Antonio cocked an eyebrow. "Paul?"

I nodded. "Owner of the rock-climbing gym. Good guy, but a bit of a stickler for the rules."

Lucy laughed. "Sam started climbing the top-rope wall last week without her harness, and he—"

"That's enough, Luce."

"I'm on my way out from the gym. But I've got other news!"

"On the Constable house?"

"Yeah! I did some canvassing yesterday. Non-digital snooping!" The sound of a door, a whoosh of air, and she cursed the cold. "The owner, Felicia, has two kids, a toddler and a teen, and she's rushing it to market. Two neighbors were saying they're pissed the price was set so low, because it'll drag down values. It's roughly fourteen percent below where it should be."

"Any theories on why?" I asked.

"You know, coming in your truck is way better than driving myself. Your truck's always warm by the time we get to it!"

Antonio said, "Mi dispiace, Lucy. I promise to leave soon enough for her to join you next Sunday."

One week? How would he be gone again in one week?

He smiled and ran a hand along my cheek, probably thinking the same thing I had. I held the hand there and nestled against it.

There was a hum on the other end of the phone call and the hairs on the back of my neck stood up. "Lucy? You're strangely quiet."

"There's a car circling the lot, but... I've been spending too much time with you. Seeing bad guys everywhere."

Lucy saw the best in everyone. An eternal optimist. If she was worried, something was wrong.

Goosebumps crawled up my arms. They *did* have the wrong guy locked up.

I punched the gym's address into Antonio's GPS and mouthed, *Drive!*

A quick shoulder-check and we were moving, fastening our seatbelts as he got underway.

Don't spook her. Keep the tone light. "Are you closer to your car or the gym?"

"The gym... uh, Sam?" Her voice quavered. "He's coming around again. His face is covered up..."

Antonio made a corner and sped up.

I braced a hand on the dash as we veered around another vehicle. "Get back inside the gym!"

We could hear her over the phone, her feet hitting the ground in rapid succession. My chest constricted. The gym was in a strip mall with an overhang and thick concrete posts. That would give her cover if she got there in time.

Please be wrong. Please be overreacting.

"Lucy! What's going on!"

I heard a clattering noise like her phone dropping, and the shots began.

She screamed.

Someone else screamed.

Panicked voices.

The goosebumps reached my legs.

Antonio tossed me his phone as he hit a dangerous speed on the frozen roads. "Call 9-1-1."

I made the call, while trying to make out any distinguishing sounds on the open line with Lucy. I wanted to grab hold of Antonio, but he had to focus on the road.

The sound of tires squealing.

"It'll be alright." A woman's voice, distant over the phone. Was that Lucy? I couldn't tell. "We need an ambulance!"

CHAPTER 26

ANTONIO

"Goddamnit, Janelle!" Samantha unlocked the front door of my condo and shoved it open. "What exactly is the Brenton PD doing about this?"

"Calm down, Sam." Janelle was hot on her heels, slamming a hand into the door. She was off duty but had arrived on-scene after Samantha called her. "At least the guy who was shooting at you and Dr. Ferraro is still behind bars."

"I'm telling you: You've got the wrong guy! There's no way we have two different shooters in this little town within the same week." They both tore off their boots. "I can't believe you wouldn't bring any of the evidence with us."

"Be serious, Sam. There are rules."

I held the door open as Lucy stepped in behind me. "You'll be safe here."

She was pale, the difference between Samantha and her best friend never as clear as at this moment. Samantha was on the warpath while Lucy retreated into a shell. My heart ached for her; she was normally so outgoing and full of life. But violence could do that to a person unaccustomed to it.

I put an arm around her, and she clutched onto me, shaking. "Shh, now. You did everything you could for him."

"I swear—" Samantha's jaw flexed. "If Lucy hadn't called us..."

"How many times do I have to say this? You don't even know Lucy was the target!" Janelle dragged her hands over her close-cropped hair, while Samantha did the same over her face. "It could have been Paul or any of the other people wandering around. Hell, you're normally there with her, aren't you? Maybe it was you again. Stop making all these assumptions!"

"Come upstairs, Janelle. I'll show you what I was talking about."

They marched off to the stairs. Seeing the two of them like this, it was clear they'd grown up together. Two peas in a pod.

"So much blood." Lucy shuddered, uttering the first words since we'd arrived at the gym.

I took Samantha's coat off her and lowered her onto the bench by the front door.

She slipped her boots off. "Your place is really nice."

"Grazie."

"Does Sam like it? She's hated every apartment she's checked out."

"She says it's too big."

A faint smile appeared on her lips. "Sounds like her. I think she should move in here. You two belong together."

"I've tried telling her that, but she won't listen to me." I offered her a hand, and she stood. "Perhaps I should have someone else try to convince her?"

She gave a weak laugh. "Do you think Paul's going to make it?"

"He was stable when the ambulance left. I expect you saved his life."

Lucy had run from her hiding spot the moment the gunman left, applying pressure on the wound in Paul's chest, using her own jacket to cover the injury. He'd also sustained gunshots to his leg and arm, but the chest was the worrisome one.

I led her out of the foyer. "Do you want anything to drink? Water?"

She shook her head.

"Let me show you to your—"

"What if the guy in jail *was* the one at your hotel—" Janelle came down the spiral staircase ahead of Samantha. "—but he'd stolen the gun he used from the guy at Mason's. Or the Mason's shooter offloaded it after that shooting and your guy picked it up?"

"Fuck!" Samantha's face was tense. "Possible. It's all fucking possible."

"Matching casings mean matching gun. Not matching shooter."

The two women stopped at the bottom of the stairs, jaws and fists tight. The energy vibrated off them.

"Could it be related to the Constable?" I asked.

"What, you think Irene's in on it?" Samantha huffed and rolled her eyes, the sarcasm dripping off her. "Maybe she's hired a hitman to take me out so she can have you."

Janelle rounded on Samantha. "Who's the Constable?"

"Thieves can be dangerous. Unpredictable," I said. "Just look at what happened—"

Lucy let out a small, strangled sob. "You mean Paul might die because I..."

I put my arm around her again. "It's not your fault. It's the fault of the man who did this."

Janelle's glower grew darker. "Someone tell me—"

"We're not discussing this right now. The Constable—" Samantha put up a hand and looked pointedly at each of us, then Lucy, whose face had fallen into her hands. "—has *nothing* to do with this."

Janelle frowned. She nodded at Samantha's not-so-subtle protection of Lucy and surveyed the room. "The entry and way up here are secure. What about the glass wall upstairs or the balconies? Those seem like obvious ingress points."

"Security glass," I said. "It's all attached to the alarm system. And my exterior space doesn't join with the other penthouse."

"Good." Janelle approached Lucy, her tone gentle. "You have everything you need?"

Samantha joined them, softening as she rubbed Lucy's arm. "Whatever she needs, we have or we'll have delivered. She's not going anywhere until this is sorted out."

"The same goes for you, bella."

"Not a chance. I've got work tomorrow. We agreed to the security guys following me."

"That was before all this!" I released Lucy so I could express myself better with my hands. Flinging them open at her. "Before Lucy was nearly shot and your friend Paul's in the hospital!"

She looked me up and down, a scowl forming.

"I'm putting my foot down on this!"

"That's not your choice!"

"Sam—" Janelle touched her arm, but Samantha jerked it away from her.

"I'm a grown woman!"

"So is Lucy," I snapped. "But you just told her she's not allowed to leave!"

"Have you all forgotten I trained for this?"

"I won't lose you!" I grabbed her hands, pulling her to look at me. She was reckless. In need of being in control, just as Miller said. I looked intentionally at the scar on her forehead so she knew what I meant when I said, "I can't do that again."

Samantha's eyes were frantic, the energy inside her raging to get out. She glanced at me, toward the door, Janelle, and back to Lucy. But she didn't break my grip.

"He's right, Sam." Janelle spoke calmly, as she had in the hotel room after the shooting.

"Sam?" Lucy peered up at her, the soft voice blanketing the room in quiet. "I'd feel safer if you were here with me. I could really use a friend."

Samantha's shoulders sagged as her gaze settled on Lucy. "What you need is some sleep."

I released Samantha, and she wrapped her arm around Lucy. They walked down the hallway to one of the bedrooms.

Janelle came to stand next to me. "Who's the Constable?"

"Not a who, a what. It's a painting we suspect was stolen and hidden in a house here in town."

"That sounds like something the police should be taking care of, not her."

"She only has suspicions, not proof." Although if someone wanted to hide them enough to attempt multiple murders, that strengthened the assumption they were stolen.

"You need to watch her. I'm worried about what she may do."

"Was she always like this?" In many ways, it felt as though Samantha had been in my life forever. Sometimes, the truth of it, the newness of our relationship, struck me. Despite the knowledge deep in my core that we were meant to spend our lives together, it hadn't even been five months yet.

She rested her hands on her hips, the two of us still staring down the hallway. "The stubbornness? The fierce loyalty? Keeping her circle small and tight? To a degree, yeah. But from what I hear, it's gotten a lot worse."

"From what you hear?"

Janelle exhaled slowly, pivoting to look at me. Her dark eyes held a simmering rage inside them. "How much has she told you about us?"

"Just that you two have been friends since you were young."

"We were *best* friends for a long time. Then some shit went down about ten years ago and we didn't speak until the Scott case." She tilted her head toward the hallway as the voices grew louder. When the other two didn't return, Janelle lowered her voice. "Suffice to say she's fucking brilliant, but sometimes she has the judgment of gnat."

A gnat?

"When she thinks she's doing the right thing, nothing gets in her way."

"Like Tuesday night at her hotel." And with the thieves in Napoli who nearly killed her.

Janelle put a hand to her head, rubbing it slowly, then looked me square in the eyes. "Don't let her out of your sight. However you do it—whether it's guilt, humor, use her sister or Lucy, keep her in fucking bed all day—I don't care. Let me do my job and figure out who's behind this."

I nodded, unsure how I'd keep Samantha in the apartment for even a day, let alone for how long it would take the police to solve this case. "I'm only in town until Saturday."

"Sam, I'm leaving!" Janelle hollered down the hall, then turned back to me. "Then I guess I have six days, don't I?"

Samantha and Lucy appeared in the hallway.

"My shift starts in an hour. I need to get home and clean up before I go in."

Janelle and I headed for the door, and the other two joined us.

"Thanks, Officer Williams," said Lucy, tucked tight against Samantha.

"I'm not in a uniform. Call me Janelle." She leaned down to Lucy's height, a gentle smile on her face. "I promise I'll find out who was behind this."

"Thanks."

"I'll check in on your friend at the hospital and let you know how he's doing." Janelle straightened, her jaw flexing as she put a hand on Samantha's shoulder. "And don't do anything stupid."

CHAPTER 27
SAMANTHA

THE NEXT DAY, Antonio shifted his SUV into park, across the street from the Ferraro's office. "This will only take a moment."

We'd argued that morning and barely spoke on the drive. He'd pressed his luck about me taking the rest of the week off. Maybe people could get away with that when they worked for their father, but not when their boss was counting on them. Let alone when he was their ex-husband.

Hiding inside the condo like a scared little bird was ridiculous. But I'd agreed to one day—for Lucy's sake—and rescheduled my appointments.

Once I undid my seatbelt, he rested a hand on my arm, stopping me before I grabbed the door handle.

"Bella, please." He dipped his head, forehead wrinkling.

A gray car moved slowly past us, and my gaze followed it. Claude, today's security guy, parked two spaces ahead. Someone else had watched the building overnight, then this guy tailed us to the office. Like we were in imminent danger.

Antonio thought he was doing this for me, but he didn't

get it. All he was doing was undermining me. Telling me he didn't think I was strong or competent. Like he knew better.

He was such a fucking *man* sometimes.

I blew out a long breath, scanning his face. The little crinkle at the bridge of his nose. The big, brown puppy dog eyes.

But he'd also taken Lucy in without my asking, drawn me a candlelit bath, and held me until I fell asleep. Made a wonderful breakfast. Was it really that bad he was worried? Christ, I refused to let Lucy come with us, and we were only picking up a single painting for him to work on while I was at the office tomorrow.

The cold began seeping through my pants. "We need to hurry up. Lucy'll worry if we take too long."

His face fell—he was hoping to make up from the fight—but he nodded. "Let me get your door."

My phone buzzed in my bag, and I pulled it out. I flashed Janelle's name to him before answering, and he turned the car back on to keep it warm, motioning for me to stay.

She cut me off before I could finish saying hello. "Sam, it's Janelle. How're you doing?"

"As well as can be expected when you're under house arrest." I kept my eyes on Antonio as he crossed the street to his office. Why couldn't I just let him care? Let him worry about me? Through the big front windows, I could see Sofia at her giant desk, talking with Frank and Dom. "Antonio and I stepped out for a moment to pick up some supplies and—"

"Fuck." At her word, the prickle crawled up my neck. "Head to the station or to his place, whichever's closer."

"Why?"

Antonio pulled open the glass door, and Dominico held his arms out for a hug.

"Before forensics sent the evidence from the gym to NIBIN, I took it for a detour."

Via Calabria was only two lanes wide, and it wasn't busy. A black car slowed next to Antonio's SUV and stopped. No space behind us, so he wasn't parallel parking. Maybe letting a passenger out?

"Based on what you showed me yesterday at Dr. Ferraro's, we did a visual comparison on the bullet casings from the gym—"

I stretched up in my seat to look into the car next to me. The blond passenger—slight stature, hair at shoulder length, likely male—was talking to the driver, but not exiting. Maybe they were lost or had broken down and needed help.

Or maybe... The moment at Mason's when I noticed the slowing car flashed through my brain. *No. Relax, Sam.* Black was a common vehicle color. People stopped all the time.

The security guy approached casually. He was tall, broad, with dark brown hair. Sunglasses and an unzipped gray ski jacket. Designed to blend in, but the tight smile on his lips likely wouldn't have reached his eyes, and the unassuming walk was well-cultivated.

Deep breaths. Claude's got this.

"—they were a match to the shooting at Mason's Gallery."

"Shit!" I fell back into my seat, eyes still on the car next to me. That made three shootings, aimed at people involved in the Scott case: Rhonda, me, and now Lucy, who'd been my right hand.

Or the people asking questions about the Constable, like Antonio suggested. Rhonda after she asked about the painting, Lucy after she canvassed the neighborhood, but Antonio and I hadn't gone there until yesterday.

"What about the evidence from my place?"

The security guy rapped on the driver's window.

"It's missing," she said. "NIBIN doesn't have your paperwork. We apparently didn't retain anything here, either."

"How can that happen?"

The driver and security guy exchanged some words, arms stretching down the road and moving like they were discussing directions. The security guy waved and headed back to his car.

"But if you were right..." Janelle hadn't slowed down the entire time, but now she paused. "That means the shootings at Mason's, your place, and the gym were all with the same gun. And I know I said same gun doesn't mean same shooter, but that's a big coincidence, and I—"

A deafening crack sounded from the car next to me, and I jumped in my seat.

Gunshot.

"Sam!" yelled Janelle over the phone.

Two more shots, so rapid I could barely keep track of what happened. The Ferraro's glass shattered. The passenger grabbed the driver. Claude spun, tossed his jacket open, hand diving for something at his belt. The driver knocked the passenger back.

Three more shots.

The security guy fired a Taser and hit the side mirror.

My eyes flew to Ferraro's. No one was standing and the shooter's car blocked my view of the floor.

Ice splintered in my veins, breath lodging in my throat.

His laugh.

His smile.

The look in his eyes when he told me he loved me.

I had to make sure he was alright.

The black car sped off, slamming into Claude, sending him stumbling into the oncoming lane. I had to check on him, but he recovered almost immediately.

In the end, there was only one thing I could do.

I threw my legs over the center console, dropped the phone on the passenger seat, and put the SUV into drive. I pulled out to follow, waving to the security guy to go into Ferraro's.

Antonio was alright. He had to be alright.

It was a thirty mile-an-hour road, but we quickly hit fifty. I slammed my hand on the horn to alert other drivers.

Janelle's voice was faint in the background.

I flicked my eyes down to the phone and hit the button to put her through the audio system. "Janelle, you still there?"

"What the fuck was that?"

"Shooting at Ferraro's! Holy shit!" I clenched the steering wheel, blinking rapidly to combat the stinging at the back of my eyes. Antonio was fine. They were all okay. I had to focus. "I'm in pursuit of the shooter."

"Sam! Back off!"

"We're heading east on Calabria, at the intersection with Walnut. Get someone to their office!"

"Sam! Stop!"

There were few vehicles on the road, and the car ahead of me veered back and forth from one lane to another to avoid anything in front of him. A foot of snow from Christmas clung to the yards and roofs, but the streets were clear, so traction was good.

"It's a black Honda Civic, Michigan license plate!" I read

the plate off to her and swerved around a car the shooter clipped. "That's the plate from the Mason's shooting!"

The car fishtailed, but they regained control quickly.

Janelle was hollering in the background, and she put me on speaker on her end as well. "Police and ambulance have been dispatched to Ferraro's. We've got cars near you."

"Taking a turn north onto Chestnut! Driver and one passenger visible in the car."

Chestnut was residential and had few cars moving on it, although many were parked along the sides. We hit sixty miles an hour quickly after making the turn.

"Sam! We've got three patrol cars closing in! Back off!"

"Not a fucking chance! I swear to God, if this asshole—" The dream flashed through my brain, Antonio laying in a pool of blood. *Please let him be alright. Please! I can't lose him!* "Chestnut and Auburn!"

Even if it wasn't Antonio, what if it was Sofia? Or Frank? Or Dominico? It would devastate Antonio. I slammed my foot down harder on the gas, gaining ground, prepared to ram him instead of giving him any chance of getting away.

I kept punching the horn, and the car ahead of the shooter suddenly pulled out of the way. The shooter's car over-corrected. It spun, crashing into a parked vehicle on the side of the road. I slammed on the brakes, and fortunately the SUV's wheels found traction where the other's hadn't.

"Ran into a parked car at Chestnut and Water! He's stopped! I'm going in!"

"Sam! Don't you—"

Her words faded away as the shooter's car door opened, and a man stumbled out. He stared at the ground, wobbling, clutching his head. He still had the gun, and the passenger remained in the car.

How long until the police arrived?

I eased my door open and stepped out. I was not letting him get away with this.

His head snapped in my direction. Glassy eyes, not fully focused. Either from the crash or maybe he was on something.

Calm, stay calm. "Are you alright, sir?"

He blinked at me several times, like he couldn't make out what was going on. His light brown hair was cropped short, eyes dark brown. Just shy of six feet, probably a hundred and eighty pounds. Long-sleeve black sweater and jeans, no jacket.

He reminded me of someone, but I couldn't put a finger on who.

"You?" He lifted the pistol toward me. Glock. Subcompact. "Why is it always you?"

"Listen, sir, I don't know you." I held my hands in front of me, emphasizing the distance between us, trying to hide the stutter in my voice. I only had to distract him long enough for the police to arrive. "But if you could put the gun down—"

His lip curled into a sneer. "I should have killed you when I had the chance."

It was him. The shooter from my hotel. They really did have the wrong guy in custody.

"Better late than never," he snarled.

The ear-splitting crack from the gun jolted through my muscles, but he shot wide, the hissing noise near enough to hear over the ringing in my ears. As close to my head as the one Tuesday night.

The puff of smoke from the barrel.

The slide locked back.

That was his last bullet.

I realized it before he did, but he hurled the gun at me after my first step—with less accuracy than the gunshot—and turned on his heel. I overtook him quickly, knocking into his back so we smashed onto the road together.

A spray of blood exploded across the pavement, and he threw an elbow into my side. The air rushed out of me, pain erupting from the ribs he connected with.

I spread my legs to brace myself on top of him and locked my arm around the elbow he'd rammed into me, twisting it up into an arm bar. "Police are on their way, asshole."

"You fucking bitch!" He spit out blood, trying in vain to pull out of my grip. "At least I got your fucking husband."

Husband? Antonio? The dream. The blood. I wrenched his arm harder and he wailed.

"I saw him fall when I hit him." His words shot a fresh wave of panic through me, and I tensed. It gave him enough time to grab the back of my neck with his free hand and throw my balance forward. He pushed up with his legs, and my hands flew forward to catch myself from falling face-first over his shoulder.

His elbow found my ribs again, harder this time, higher. I wasn't ready for it, the full force knocking me over. He scrambled on top of me, the stench of cigarettes and alcohol foul on his breath. It was a miracle he hadn't killed anyone with his driving.

He straddled me, a wicked grin spreading across his face as his hands landed on my throat. "That bitch was supposed to lie low. But oh no, you work your fucking magic and sic the police on me. Just like the auction. Now they're trying to recruit your husband, but I'm their man, not him!"

I tried rolling my legs up to wrap them around him or push him off, but his grip tightened.

"You should have left my girlfriend out of this." He leaned into the choke, sending an army of black spots swirling around my vision.

But it was the opening I needed.

With his body canted forward, I bucked up with my hips, throwing his balance to the side, and rolled us so I was on top of him again. One swift knee into his crotch, and the glassy, angry stare evaporated. He squeezed his eyes shut and cupped his balls.

"Who are you?" I yelled, considering a second blow to his groin.

The sirens broke through the haze surrounding me as a squad car pulled up and two officers jumped out.

I didn't recognize either of them, so stood and backed away from the driver. "He's the shooter from—"

"Ma'am, hands, please," said one of the officers, hand on her duty belt.

I raised my hands, ears still ringing from the gunshot, beads of sweat rolling down my spine. I had to get back to Antonio. He had to be alright.

"She attacked me!" The driver remained in the fetal position. "Tried running me off the road."

The female officer's partner—an average-height, but excessively muscled man—approached the driver. "Both of you on your knees."

"Please—" My voice broke as I lowered, and I blinked several times to get ahead of the tears welling in my eyes. "—do you have any news about the shooting at Ferraro's? Talk to Officer Williams. She'll vouch for me."

The female officer paused. "Name?"

"Samantha Caine."

The two officers shared a cursory glance. She nodded at me, and flicked her fingers to indicate I should stand, while her partner cuffed the driver and began reading him his rights. A few people had emerged from their houses to see what had gone on, and two more police cars arrived.

"Not sure of the total injuries, but one man is being removed from the scene."

I swallowed hard, my stomach twisting in knots. "Is he—"

"It sounds serious, but he's alive."

My knees buckled, and I balanced myself by grabbing her shoulder. "Oh, god! Who?"

She was so calm, I wanted to shake her. "A man in his mid-thirties."

My heart stuttered. "Name? Please?"

"No more details than th—"

"Am I free to leave?" I had a foot planted ready to spring.

She nodded. "Officer Williams said to let you go and we'd talk to you later."

I spun on my heel and tore off to Antonio's car. A glint of brass caught my eye near where he'd shot at me. Barely slowing, I scooped up the bullet casing. It would match the one from my apartment. It had to. But damned if I wouldn't check.

One of the newly arrived officers was speaking with people on the sidewalk, while another was helping the dazed passenger out of the car.

I scuffed my boot on the pavement as I ran, almost tripping when I saw his face. The passenger—I knew him.

~

THE PERIMETER WAS fifty feet from the Ferraro's office, squad cars and officers keeping people away.

An ambulance was leaving. Lights flashing and sirens screaming.

I slammed on the brakes when I got as close as I could and leaped out of the car, almost forgetting to turn it off. My stomach churned, flooding my mouth with the taste of bile.

He wasn't in the ambulance. He couldn't be.

I dashed through the small crowd, but a police officer got in my way, telling me to back up.

The Ferraro's reception area was full of strangers. Professionals. Plus Jimmy and the security guy. But no Antonio.

"Jimmy!" I yelled. "Jimmy Slater!"

"Ma'am, are you alright?" asked the officer who wouldn't let me closer.

"My family's in there!" One hand flew toward the studio, the other clenched at my stomach. A paramedic and officer inside moved, revealing Dominico holding Sofia at the reception desk. That left Antonio, Frank, and Zander. All fitting the officer's description of a male in his thirties. "Tell Officer Slater that Sam Caine's here. He'll clear me."

"I'm sorry, but this is a crime scene. I can't let you—"

"Slater!" I screamed.

Jimmy spun to see me, and his whole body seemed to relax. He signaled to the officer in front of me, who stepped out of my way, and I ran for the building. Zander came around the reception wall. That left two of them. As I bolted through the door, I saw legs on the floor, obscured by a paramedic.

Gray slacks, that's what he was wearing. My heart lurched one more time.

"Thank heavens," said Jimmy, holding open the door for me. "We gotta stop meeting like this."

"Is Antonio—"

"Samantha?" Antonio craned his neck around the paramedic who was kneeling over him.

My knees almost gave out under me. He was there, sitting up against Sofia's desk. He was alright.

But as I got closer, I saw the blood. Covering his white shirt.

He sucked in a deep breath, eyes wide. "Where were you?"

I crumpled to the ground next to him and latched my arms around his neck, ignoring the pain still streaking through my ribs. My lips pressed to his forehead, his cheek, his lips, and back to his cheek again.

"Where have you been?" He wrapped an arm around me, his voice stuttering. "They said no one was hit outside, but marone, I thought—"

"How bad is it?" I asked, withdrawing from the embrace and taking his hand in mine.

"Frank will be fine."

"No, you! All this blood!"

The paramedic was working on Antonio's hand, with no regard for the blood on his face, neck, or torso.

"Frank was shot. When he fell, I grabbed him and pulled him behind the desk. I tore some stitches in my shoulder, but most of this is his blood."

I flagged, leaning my head against him. "Is he alright?"

He kissed my temple. "They said he was stable."

"But there's so much blood."

"I've seen far worse and Mr. Ferraro is in excellent hands." The paramedic, a red-haired man in his forties, sat back on his haunches. "And your wrist looks like it'll be fine. Keep ice on it and the swelling should come down soon enough. I need to check you for any other injuries."

"Give me a moment," said Antonio, waving him away. He pulled my hand to his lips. "I was so worried, bella, when you didn't come in after the shooting. I was afraid—but then Claude rushed in and said you drove off—"

"I caught him." *Now he can't hurt you.*

He squeezed my hand suddenly, his breath catching and voice raising. "You did what?"

"I went after the shooter. Police have him."

"Cazzo! Samantha!" Heat flared in his eyes. "Why?"

"Instinct." Desperation. Panic.

Before he could say more, a hand touched my shoulder. "Sammy?"

With a deep breath, I stood and faced Jimmy, maintaining my firm grasp on Antonio's hand. "What do you have?"

He inclined his head toward the studio space.

I shook my head, clenching Antonio's hand harder. "I'm not leaving him."

Jimmy looked at Antonio, who pulled his hand out of my grip. "I'm not going anywhere until the paramedic is done with me."

This was the second time within a week I was leaving him behind for medical care. Jimmy and I made our way to the studio space, out of earshot of everyone else.

"What the hell happened?" he asked. "I heard you caught the guy?"

I rubbed my hands over my face, over my hair. "I saw a car

stop in front of the office. The driver fired, then drove away. I was right next to him, so I just went." The adrenaline was ebbing and a cold seeped into my bones. Partially from the open front of the office, partially from relief of finding Antonio alright.

"I should go down to the station and help process him. Who knows what was going through that maniac's head?" Jimmy fiddled with his cap, pushing it up and pulling it back down again. "I'll do that as soon as we're done here. But listen, Janelle's on her way over right now, so you better get your story straight. She's pissed."

CHAPTER 28

ANTONIO

JANELLE HAD BARELY GLANCED around the scene as she strode in, heading directly to my office with Samantha. The storm clouds followed behind them.

"If you ever pull such a stupid ass move again—" Janelle's voice carried through the closed door in the back. "—I will throw you in a goddamn cell and not let you out until you see some fucking sense!"

"I'm alright, sì?" I inclined my head past the reception wall, eying the paramedic who'd finished fixing the stitches in my shoulder. "Because I fear my girlfriend requires some backup."

He helped me up, and I stretched out my back from sitting on the floor for so long. I'd hit the ground when the first gunshot sounded, smashing my knees and wrist as I pulled Sofia down, then tearing my stitches when I hauled Frank behind the desk. My back was the worst of it, other than the panic.

After the first bullets shattered the front glass and we were all on the ground, the shooting paused. Samantha didn't come rushing in. The other bullets sounded, and it was Tuesday night all over again. But so much worse. I couldn't hold her, put myself between her and the shooter. All I could do was pray she was safe.

Like Napoli. When I'd run through the streets after talking to the man who'd threatened to hurt her.

Deep breath in. She was alright. *Deep breath out.* Frank would be fine.

I made my way toward the back; the voices quieting for a moment. With one hand on the doorknob, I waited. Perhaps a few more minutes of lecture were warranted. Janelle could say things to her I couldn't. Our relationship was still too fragile, not like theirs. A decade of silence between the two of them, but their bond remained strong.

"Jesus Christ, Sam, he could have killed you!"

Exactly, Janelle. Get it through her stubborn head.

"That asshole boyfriend of yours—" Un momento. That was not right. "—was supposed to keep you at his place! I told him you'd do something brainless!"

I knocked, put on the smile, and entered. "Mi scusi, but the *asshole* needs a fresh shirt from his office."

Janelle's narrowed eyes fell on me. "Don't you try and play cute, Ferraro."

"May as well tell him not to breathe," Samantha muttered from the chair she sat in.

"Fucking hell, Sam!" Janelle rounded on her, slamming her cap on the table, sending papers fluttering to the floor. "I was worried shitless. Don't you ever do something like that again!"

Samantha shrugged, nonchalant. "The guy's in custody now, so I don't have to."

I crossed to the rear of the office and opened a drawer where I kept clean clothes for days work became too dirty.

"Yeah, about that." Janelle paused, clearing her throat. "I talked to the officer who met you at the scene. Suspect's claiming you tried to kill him?"

"Did not," Samantha grumbled.

"What the hell are you doing back there?" Janelle's words were likely directed at me, as I was stripping off my blood-stained shirt.

"Changing." I turned as I finished hauling it over my head. Should I make a crack about trying not to be too cute? Tease about giving me some privacy? No. Jokes would work on Samantha, not Janelle. "I intend no disrespect, Officer Williams, but unless this conversation is confidential, I mean to be here to support Samantha. And to do that—" I grabbed the fresh shirt and tugged it on. "—I'd rather not remain covered in my cousin's blood."

Janelle's jaw clenched, and for a moment, I thought she was about to throw something at me. Instead, she ran her hands over her head and clasped them behind her neck. "The witnesses who actually saw anything said it was the other way around. So at least I don't have to arrest you. Yet."

I sank into the seat next to Samantha and rested a hand on her back. She was trembling. It was slight, but constant, and I hadn't noticed until I touched her. Moving my chair closer to hers, I wrapped an arm around her shoulder.

Her hands remained clasped in her lap, projecting an aura of calm despite the torrent raging inside. "Do you have a name yet?"

"Parker Johnson," said Janelle.

Samantha turned to me. "Well, that answers one question."

I cocked an eyebrow.

"He said we went after his girlfriend. Felicia's restorer boyfriend is clearly Parker."

"Went after?" asked Janelle.

Samantha shook her head. "Those are his words. We had a very personable consult with her."

I asked, "Did he say anything else? About the Constable?"

Her hands tightened their grip on each other. "He said someone was trying to recruit you."

"Scusi? Recruit me for what? For their company?" That made no... Another of Cristian's warnings echoed in my brain. Someone was moving in on Zio Giovanni's business, and Cristian said they might approach me for help.

"I don't know. But you won't believe the craziest part."

Janelle said, "I'm all ears."

"The passenger." Samantha straightened, brow furrowing. "It was Cam-ron Parker."

"The copyist who made the Chagall?" What was going on? Was there a link between the two men?

"Parker Johnson's his dad. He uses his father's name as his artist's pseudonym."

Janelle looked from Samantha to me, and back again. "What am I missing here?"

Samantha took in a rough breath, and I squeezed her shoulder. Her eyes remained locked with mine. Something was going through her brain. Something important. The blinking started, her eyes narrowing and flicking back and forth.

"What's your theory?" asked Janelle.

Samantha dragged a hand down her face, exhaling sharply. Her lips tightened, and she stared at me for a long moment, as though debating. One slow blink, signaling a decision, and she was on her feet. "We've got four shootings in Brenton in the last week. I expect that's a record around here."

Janelle nodded as Samantha rounded my desk and retrieved a blank sheet of paper and a pen.

She wrote the numbers one through four, adding words connected with lines. "NIBIN hasn't provided us with any useful results from their analysis of the bullets yet. However, your team identified that shootings one and three were the same gun and my review says the same about shootings one and two."

"If the evidence from your hotel shooting is really lost, you'll need to give me what you found there," Janelle added.

"Sure. But for now, let's say the shootings at Mason's, my place, and the gym—" She paused and looked at me.

No words passed between us, but her request was clear. As she continued, I pulled out my phone and texted Lucy that we'd been distracted, everything was alright, and we'd be back soon.

"—were all committed with the same gun. All three of us, Cam-ron, Lucy, and me, were involved in finding out what Olivia did. She thought she'd gotten away with a million-dollar crime. My theory was that she's out for revenge."

Samantha added Olivia and David to the diagram. "Until today, that theory makes sense. Lucy and I met with them, and they know Cam-ron provided the invoice we used to prove intent to defraud."

"I proved the painting was a forgery," I said. "So they come here. Everything still makes sense, except that it was Parker, not David or Olivia?"

"It doesn't, though." Samantha circled her hand to indicate the three of us. "*We* know you worked on the painting. I mentioned at the press conference that Ferraro's did the work, but I didn't use your name."

I took the pen and wrote *Press conference* under number four. "But this makes sense. He came here and shot up the studio."

"But this wasn't about Ferraro's as a company. He said…" Samantha bit down on her bottom lip, barely able to look at me. "Antonio was the target. So the theory still ends today."

"Alright." I maintained my calm, thinking to infuse her with it, and stood next to Janelle. "You said Cam-ron was in the car? If he were party to this, why would he or his father shoot up his painting?"

"Parker said he wanted 'the bitch' to lie low and that I sicced the police on him. That has to mean the shooting at Mason's." She took the pen back and tapped it on the paper a few times. "Although Cam-ron fought with Parker after the first few shots today, so maybe he was in the car for some other reason? Didn't know what was going to happen?"

"Back up." Janelle leaned her hands on the desk, twisting the sheet of paper to face us. "You saw the suspect in the car and chased him down, so we're certain the driver of that car is responsible for this shooting. That's the only thing we know for sure."

"True." Samantha deflated. "But I'm pretty sure he's the shooter from Tuesday night, too. He told me—" Samantha wrote *Parker* under headings four and two. "—he should have killed me when he had the chance."

My stomach fell. It hadn't been an accident or a one-off. He tried to take her. I placed my hand on top of the one she balanced on, leaning over the table.

I love you, bella. You're safe.

But she withdrew the hand, not looking at me. This was professional Samantha. No time for comfort.

"So, we've got at least three options." Samantha swallowed hard. "One: The Scotts are behind it all and hired Parker to do their dirty work. Two: Parker's out for revenge over the auction. Since his company approved the painting, the FBI was investigating them. But then we don't know why he'd go after Mason's, Lucy, or the gym. Or three—" She tossed the pen to me and gave a reluctant shrug. "—you were right."

I wrote *Constable* with arrows pointing to each number as I spoke. "Rhonda told you about the painting, you were there to save her, Lucy investigated, and so did I."

Janelle huffed out a long breath. "At a minimum, I'd bet we have the wrong guy locked up for your hotel shooting. We'll know more once we've talked to everyone involved and forensics is done."

Samantha and I nodded.

"And," continued Janelle, "I want you to come to the station tomorrow for a statement. Elliot's scheduled to be in town for an update on the search for the Scotts, so we should discuss your theories with him. Especially if there could be any link to another stolen painting."

A knock on the door, and Jimmy opened without waiting for a response. "Interviews are done. Forensics should be here soon. I gotta get back to the station."

Janelle retrieved her cap, reaching across the desk to squeeze Samantha's arm. "That was some stupid shit you pulled out there today and never do it again. But... thanks. Hopefully, we can put this whole thing to bed."

"No need for the house arrest anymore?" asked Samantha, circling the desk to stand next to me.

I touched her back gently, finding the tremble gone. "She insists on going to work."

"Can't say that surprises me." Janelle shook her head. "But I think you're fine. It sounds like Parker was the one after the two of you, and we have him in custody."

Jimmy leaned against the door frame, his earlier hurry to leave seemingly forgotten. "Big break in the case?"

"Big enough." I resisted slipping my arm around Samantha's waist, pulling her close, and telling her again how worried I'd been. She needed to display power and control in front of her friends. More than anything, I wanted to make up for our argument that morning. There were precious few days for me to spend with her this trip, and I couldn't waste it. "And just in time. I need to escort this vision of beauty to the New Year's Eve Gala on Thursday night."

Samantha rolled her eyes dramatically and nudged me with a hip. A good sign.

"You got tickets to that?" asked Jimmy. "Thought they sold out months ago."

"I pulled a few strings." It would be a perfect evening. I would dance the night away with the love of my life before I had to leave her for another season.

"Well, you two are in luck!" Jimmy folded his arms, puffing up his chest. "I volunteered for New Year's Eve duty, so if the break isn't big enough and anything happens, I'll have your backs!"

Samantha chuckled. "It's in Lansing, Jimmy."

"Might have to swing by to say hello. Bet you two'll be quite the sight." He pushed off the door frame when Janelle made the sign it was time to leave. "Been an exciting week in Brenton. Crime rate used to be so low, I barely recognize the place!"

CHAPTER 29
ANTONIO

WITHOUT OPENING MY EYES, I rolled over, draping my arm across... an empty space next to me. Her scent was on the pillow, but no Samantha. I cracked an eyelid, but the room was still dark. Likely in the bathroom. She'd return soon and nestle against me, falling back to sleep.

Wakefulness prodded at my brain, along with the stabbing pain in my shoulder. I needed more painkillers.

Her phone was not on her bedside table, and my robe remained on the chair where she'd draped it last night. I rolled to my side and checked my phone. Five thirty in the morning, plus a text from her at five: *Gone downstairs to the gym. Didn't want to wake you.*

With a yawn, I pulled back the covers and got up. She'd be down there another half hour at least, so I could join her if I hurried. Perhaps convince her to cut her workout short and enjoy an extra-long shower.

Today would be a better day, even though she insisted on going to work.

We hadn't spoken about the shooting after we left the

office. I'd tried, but she'd have none of it. Nothing about the danger she'd placed herself in, her theories on what it all meant, nor what would come next. But we did speak of Frank. Alice had called; he'd made it through surgery and would be discharged in only a couple of days. Truly a relief.

Bathroom routine, into my shorts and a gym shirt, and I was ready to go in ten minutes. Lucy was staying another night, so I walked quietly to the kitchen on my way to the door, planning to leave a note on the breakfast bar in case she came out wondering where we were.

But the light from the studio shone down into the common area.

I gripped the metal hand railing, unsure what I expected to find upstairs. Had I mistakenly left it on last night? Surely Lucy wouldn't have wandered up there at this hour? Considering the sleeping pills she took last night, it was unlikely I'd see her before Samantha left for work.

As soon as my eyes crested the floor, my heart took a leap. Samantha, in shorts and tank top, at the microscope. Obsessing. Not letting it go. And hiding it from me again. Sneaking up here while I was asleep.

We were supposed to be wrapped around each other and enjoying the time we had before I left. But she chose *this* over me, and a lie in a text to cover it up.

"Samantha!" The name came out so sharp, it startled even me.

She jumped back from the workbench, hand flying to her chest. "Jesus, Antonio! You scared me half to death!"

I hurried up the stairs and over to her, clenching my fists, as though I could clench the anger away. "I let it go yesterday. Didn't say a single word about how reckless—"

"Stop." She put up a hand, her voice and features softening. "I wasn't hiding anything from you. I was letting you sleep."

"Really?" I jabbed a finger at the sheet on the bench, with bullet casings in three quadrants now. "You texted me you were going to the gym. This is not the gym!"

She slid the sheet out from under the microscope, slowly, ensuring nothing moved. "I found the casing after he shot at me—"

"He what?" My stomach twisted and turned. I'd been good all day. Hadn't interrogated her, chastised her, or made any demands. I'd watched movies with her and Lucy, cooked a lovely dinner, made love to Samantha. I even refrained from telling her I loved her, at the risk of causing her stress. But this? Should she not have told me this? "What do I have to do to make you trust me?"

"Stop," she said again, more firmly. "I want to share this with you, but I can't if you're going to continue like that."

I backed off, running hands through my hair. *Deep breath.* "Alright."

"I'm sorry I didn't tell you about that, but I didn't want you to worry."

I folded my arms and leaned against the bench. "Sì. Heaven forbid."

She sighed but continued. "You've been acting all day like the shooting didn't affect you, but I was scared out of my mind that something happened to you. I forgot about grabbing it in all the chaos. I was more concerned about you than anything else, and just forgot."

Perhaps remaining quiet about it had been the wrong choice. A thickness gathered in my throat, as I remembered the panic before she arrived. Everything was a blur, except my worry for her safety, which remained crystal clear.

"I *was* heading down to the gym." She gestured to her gym shorts and tank. "And when I went for the keys in my jacket pocket, I found the casing."

She paused, waiting for me to say something, but all I managed was a nod.

"So, up I came, and did the comparison. Mason's, my hotel, and your office yesterday. Any guess about what I saw?" A hint of excitement twinkled in her bright eyes.

"They're a match. This shouldn't be news."

"Yeah." Her shoulders sagged, and she stared down at the sheet. "I was worried—maybe—I don't know. What if Parker wasn't talking about Tuesday? What if the police really do have the right guy locked up and maybe what Parker said about killing me when he had the chance was some other time? What if—"

"Stop with the 'what if' scenarios." I unfolded my arms and cupped her chin, forcing her attention to me. "I want to go back to bed. The police can handle this."

"What if they miss something?"

"Bella." I sighed and stepped closer, wrapping my arms around her waist. "You can't protect the world."

She slid her hands around my neck. "Not the world, just the people I love."

The disheartened laugh which escaped my lips was unintentional. "So, you were concerned about Sofia at the office yesterday?"

She frowned, ignoring my words, rubbing her nervous fingers behind my neck. "I know it sounds reckless, but catching him was the right choice. I couldn't let him try again."

I placed a light kiss on her forehead.

"I can't lose you," she whispered, eyes glistening. The real words remained difficult for her, locked deep inside.

"You will never—" I shifted a hand to the side of her face and leaned in to hold a kiss to her cheek. "—lose me, bella."

Her eyes slid closed, and I pulled her tighter against me, her rare vulnerability sparking through my body. Our lips met and she pushed her hips against me. I squeezed my eyes shut and thought the words into her brain, begging for the same in return. *I love you, Samantha.*

I lifted her, our tongues still intertwined, and carried her the few steps to the computer desk. With a swipe of my hand, I cleared space, set her down, and hit a button to raise it.

She broke from the kiss. "Lucy's still here. We should go to the bed—"

"She won't be up for hours." I sealed my mouth to hers again, using more teeth than usual. Frustrated. Afraid. Angry.

How dare Parker do this to her. To us. Make her doubt herself, make me worry about her. Make us fight.

As my hands dragged up her sides, to her breasts, I breathed, "If he took you from me—"

"He didn't." Her eyes locked with mine, and she shifted from hip to hip, removing her shorts and underwear. "I'm still here."

I pulled my shorts down only enough to free my cock and kissed her again, stepping between her legs. Pressed against her warmth, I cupped my hands under her ass and pulled her to me as I slid inside.

She curled her legs around my thighs and raked one hand

down my lower back, moaning as we moved together. Slow. Measured. Trying to quench the fire—the rage—in my belly.

I rolled my hips, moving in and out as we kissed, pulling her with my hands to magnify each thrust. There was a desperate need to the moment, like the first night I was home, yet so different. Loving. An apology. A commitment.

She was my world. My future. And he tried to take her from me. More than once.

"Antonio," she groaned, reaching for the far edge of the desk. She arched her back, inviting me in deeper, harder, and one of her legs eased up to my waist.

We moved as one, fighting against the memories. Making love last night had been fun and laughter, full of teasing. Pretending the shooting never happened. But this morning, we battled through it and finally made up from the arguments.

I need you.

I plunged into her and stopped. "If he took you from me, I would have chased him to the ends of the earth—"

She flexed her leg around me and I held my full length inside her, focusing on the way we fit together. Her other hand found the edge of the desk and her head fell back, hips squirming against me. The desk shook, pencils rolling off the edge and clattering onto the floor.

But I held her still with all my strength, just being one with her. "—and I would have killed him with my bare hands."

Her tiny inner muscles quivered, slight at first, growing as the pleasure built inside her. She shot up to sitting, latched an arm around my neck, and met her forehead to mine, whispering, "I know."

No one will ever hurt you.

I moved again, pumping furiously, her gasps stealing the air from my groans. Something smashed to the floor, but all I knew was her, and it was quickly forgotten. The connection was glorious. I drove into her, over and over, until her eyes snapped shut, the silent wail erupting from her chest.

My orgasm followed, ripping through me in an explosion of joy and relief. Joy that she was there with me. Relief that we were mostly unscathed. I slowed, easing in and out of her, and our breaths calmed.

"Antonio," she breathed, stroking her fingers against the back of my neck.

I love you with all my heart.

"That dream I had the other night... I saw it all again when the gunshots started and I..." She leaned backward enough to see me clearly, her hand coming to rest on my cheek. Staring and blinking, not talking. Withholding things from me. Things she was not ready for yet.

I pulled her tight against me, unable to watch her confused face. I had her love—I knew I did—whether or not she could say it. She put her life on the line to protect me. It was infuriating, but it was how she showed she loved me.

She buried her face against my neck, her words so quiet I barely heard them. "I can't imagine my life without you."

Warmth bloomed through my chest. "You don't have to, amore."

That wasn't it, but it was the closest she'd ever said. Words were not as important as actions to her. And it was about time I started behaving like I knew that.

CHAPTER 30
SAMANTHA

NINE O'CLOCK THE NEXT MORNING. My fingers hovered over the burnished brass door handle. There was still time to make a run for it. Maybe I could send an email explaining Cliff sent me out on another priority. He was the claims manager—he had the authority to cancel this meeting, right? Or I could just say I forgot.

I was looking forward to this about as much as I was looking forward to saying goodbye to Antonio at the airport.

A temporary name plate was affixed to the door, reading *Matt Foster*. My ex-husband had stepped in as interim president of the insurance company while his father awaited trial. Underneath Matt's name, Roger's would still be there until they locked him up for good, however long that took.

With a centering breath, I pushed down on the handle and opened the door.

Matt looked up from the other side of his father's desk and smiled. The mahogany monstrosity fit suits-and-ties Roger more than it did polos-and-jeans Matt. "Morning, Sam."

I closed the door behind me. Time to face the consequences of bringing my former father-in-law to justice. I plastered on a smile and crossed the room, taking the seat he gestured to.

"Long time." Matt was an attractive man with light brown crewcut hair, hazel eyes, and a short beard. His smile looked as forced as mine, his perpetually furrowed brow just as creased as always. It telegraphed how kind he was, how much he cared for everyone around him. He was so unlike his father.

I opened the notebook I'd brought for the meeting, pen at the ready. Business. I could always do business. "What do you need?"

He hadn't set an agenda, just emailed me to be there at nine. As much as I'd fought Antonio tooth and nail about coming in to work, that email made me want to call in sick. In the four months since Roger was arrested, I'd spoken to Matt exactly three times.

"First, an apology." He clasped his hands on the desk and leaned forward.

I was *not* about to apologize. Roger had been defrauding the company for years and when he finally went to trial, he'd get what he deserved.

"I'm sorry—" Hold on. *He* was apologizing? "—for avoiding you the last few months. A lot fell into my lap when we found out about Dad. It's no excuse, but I've been under some significant stress."

Anxious butterflies swirled around my stomach at the pained looking in his face. He was hurting. Good. Serves him right for... no, not good. "I can't imagine."

The tight smile reached his eyes, and he nodded. "And the company needs your help with something." He pulled a stapled sheaf of papers from his desk.

I glanced at the front page when he slid it toward me. The contract between Foster Mutual and my actual employer, Thompson Claims Services. The butterflies all dropped as one. "You're terminating my contract with Foster?"

He sucked in a quick breath and stiffened. "Heavens, no!" Scratching the hair on his chin, he added, "And yet, hopefully, yes."

This wasn't good. Before the assignment in Brenton, I lived on the road, working wherever Thompson deployed me around the country. Storm seasons through the Midwest, hurricanes in the east, wildfires in the west, winters in California and Texas. I went where they needed me and declined deployments I didn't want. It was good money. Traveling the country was freeing, and I had all the outdoor adventure time I wanted.

But I was trying to settle in Brenton with Antonio. *With Antonio?* If I didn't have this daily contract in Brenton, I wouldn't be able to stay. I'd have to find a new job or pack up the RV in spring and move on.

That had been my original plan. That's why I was living in a hotel. Come back to small-town Brenton, see Cass through all her treatments, then hit the road again.

And then Antonio happened.

Maybe this was a sign from the universe. *Cut your losses, Sam. Leave town and don't look back.* I didn't want to, though. For once in my life, I wanted to tough it out and really try something that was eating me from the inside out.

"As you can probably guess, our reinsurer wasn't happy about what Dad did. They threatened to cancel our contract. Finding a replacement after that whole ordeal would have been hard." Just like insurance companies provided coverage to individuals and businesses, reinsurers provided coverage for insurance companies, so they could afford to pay out their claims. Without a reinsurer, Foster wouldn't be allowed to operate. "So, we negotiated some conditions."

"What does that have to do with me?"

"You've only been here since June, and you've picked out more fraudulent claims than the rest of the team for the calendar year. Plus—" He patted the contract, staring down at it instead of at me. "—you're the one who caught what Dad was doing. It was under everyone's nose, but no one questioned him. Including me."

The energy in my stomach spread to my arms, tingles firing along my fingertips. He needed to get to the point.

"You're the best property adjuster we have, by a wide margin." His smile grew as he glanced up at me and back down again. "Quinn's been on me for months about offering you something full time."

My throat dried up. "Matt, can you just cut to the chase?"

The big leather chair rolled almost soundlessly across the short pile carpet as he stood and rounded to my side of the desk. He eased into the chair next to me. "The reinsurer's requirement was that we hire someone else in SIU. And the Board—not to mention Harry and Quinn—want that person to be you."

"I already work with them, though."

"Only a few hours a week. Like I said, we're hoping you'll take on the position permanently."

This was a very different sign from the universe. This was a 'Stay in Brenton' sign. That was what I wanted. Right? Cass, Antonio, Nathan, Lucy, Kevin, and the kids. They'd be so excited.

But I'd be stuck in Brenton, even if this whole thing with Antonio didn't work out.

"What about storm season? Don't you need me in adjusting?"

"Sam, at least for the short term, we need you with SIU if we're going to have a company."

Dammit. No pressure there.

"Give it a few days. Mull it over." He placed a gentle hand on my shoulder, just as my own was covering my face. "Even if you don't want a permanent position, but you want to work with SIU, I'll see what I can swing for a change to the contract with Thompson."

I stared at the notebook in front of me, as blank as when I'd arrived. "Yeah, I need to think about this."

"I had a feeling." His hand traveled to my upper arm, rubbing gently, attempting to calm my nerves. "I already talked this over with Cliff—he's pissed, by the way—but I asked him to reassign your appointments for the next few days. Take that time off, plus I know you're on leave for two weeks. But I'll need the answer when you get back."

CHAPTER 31

SAMANTHA

ELLIOT STOOD as I entered the meeting room at the Brenton Police Department, extending a hand. "Sam, good to see you."

He was a few inches taller than me and possessed a commanding aura. He'd always been clean-shaven with a buzz-cut, but he'd switched to a goatee and had let his hair grow into short sponge twists. His skin was a warm brown, dark, but still several shades lighter than Janelle's.

"Thanks for seeing me." I took a seat at the table opposite his laptop. "I have a lot of questions—"

"Slow down." He chuckled as he shrugged off his black suit jacket to hang it on the back of his chair. "You've had a rough week. How're you holding up?"

"Still standing." I leaned backward and crossed my legs, trying to contain the tremble shooting through my extremities.

My heart was beating too fast. I was a bad girlfriend. I hadn't called Antonio to tell him about Matt's offer—hadn't called anyone, because it was my choice to make, and I didn't want the pressure. Plus, I was about to ask an FBI agent about my boyfriend's family and their possible link to a smuggling ring.

I should have asked Antonio about it, but he'd hidden too many things from me in the past. He swore there'd be no more lies, but I needed to know for sure. "Pretty shitty, to be honest."

"That sounds more like the truth." He sat, waking his laptop and the wall-mounted screen at the end of the room. "Distracting yourself with work?"

"Certainly trying to."

"And Dr. Ferraro? I understand he was hurt yesterday?"

A shiver burst through my chest, icy cold in my veins. Seeing him with the blood covering him. The panic. "He's alright. Tore open some stitches. His cousin Frank was the one shot but should be out of the hospital by Thursday."

In my periphery, a change in the glass wall of the meeting room caught my attention. I swiveled to see the smart glass finish switching from clear to frosted opaque for complete privacy.

He hit a button on his laptop and a world map appeared on the television, with easily over a hundred circles of varying sizes across it. The largest ones were concentrated in the United States, but there were several across Europe and Asia, Canada, and a few in South America. The space around Brenton, Lansing, and Detroit was clear.

He stood and walked to the windows, closing the blinds as he spoke. "I know you wanted to talk about the smuggling ring, but I figured we could review the Scott case first, instead of sending you my weekly update by email."

"A warmup?"

"Exactly." He grinned as he settled back into his chair.

"We've had 215 sightings of Olivia and or David Scott since we put out the appeal to the public at the end of August. We've had local agents and intelligence sources investigating each one." He tapped a button and the map changed, showing less than twenty bubbles, the largest around Boston, with a smattering around New York and Montreal. "We've narrowed it to thirty-six credible sightings. Most of them are in the Boston area, so that's where we're focused."

Boston. Nathan's old stomping grounds and home to the Gardner Museum.

"Officer Williams told me you thought they were behind the four shootings in Brenton over the last week?"

"That was my theory until we caught Parker yesterday." I uncrossed my legs, leaning forward to inspect the map. "I want to believe they paid him off."

He chuckled. "Because you don't want to be wrong?"

"Maybe. Have you learned anything from him about the painting at the auction?"

"Not about that one, but he confessed to signing that Chagall copy."

"He what?"

"It was the only thing he said before asking for his lawyer, so I'm guessing it's about protecting Cameron, who created the copy." The corner of his lips twitched. "But I leveraged his company's role in the auction painting to get some information on the shootings."

"Did Janelle also tell you Antonio's theory?"

"She did. Something about another potentially stolen painting, but she knew little beyond that, except that it sounded credible."

I gave him a summary of our investigation, from meeting

with Rhonda to my research with Lucy, and visits to Felicia's office and the house with Antonio. He nodded while I spoke, following a link to the Interpol site describing the Constable I suspected was at the center of it all.

When I finished, he said, "What about the paintings that were stolen with this one?"

"There were two others." I sent him another link, to a newspaper article about the LA theft. "At least, I'm fairly confident that's the right theft. It fits with Parker's girlfriend saying he bought three paintings from a pawnshop in Detroit—"

Elliot put up a hand. "Stop. A pawnshop in Detroit?"

"Yeah?"

"Interesting." A sly grin spread across his face. "Let me share something with you I shouldn't. The auction painting apparently came from an anonymous donor who claimed to have purchased it from—"

"A pawnshop in Detroit?" I said with him.

"Exactly. We talked to the shop owner during the initial investigation, and he pointed us to the person who sold it to him, who says they picked it up at a weekend flea market a couple of years ago. They didn't remember the date and it was a huge weekly market. We interviewed everyone we could find and came up short." He leaned back in his chair. "But if you're right about these paintings, that pawnshop might be the key."

"Do you think all this is enough for a search warrant?"

He stared at the details on his laptop. "Let's say for a moment it isn't. What's your next step?"

"Before I knew about this link to the auction painting, I was going to attend a showing on the weekend. Antonio and I secured an invite and have a suspicion of where the painting's hidden—if it's still there."

"Will Dr. Ferraro be here for that?"

A lump rose in my throat, and I swallowed it down. He was leaving too soon. "No, I'll be taking Lucy, my data genius."

"Alright. Now let's say for a moment it *is* enough for a warrant. And that it was going to take me until... what shall we say... Monday?" He clasped his hands over his stomach, tapping his thumbs together. "Sure, Monday for a warrant. What would you do in that case?"

My inner detective did a cartwheel. He wasn't saying I should go back, but he wasn't saying not to either. "I would—"

He raised a hand to cut me off. "Actually, I don't want to hear it. Just keep it legal. Don't worry about the pawnshop— I'm already on that."

"Will do." Matt had told me to take the week off, so this would be a perfect distraction, especially after Antonio left on Saturday.

"And I hate to argue, but it sounds more reasonable that the shootings are related to this investigation, rather than the Scotts being involved." He gestured to the big screen television, displaying the top three candidates for sightings of David and Olivia. "Considering Olivia allegedly paid someone to kill her husband, I won't discount them, but let's hope they're not involved so the Brenton PD can wrap this up."

"I know." All the evidence pointed to Parker and the Constable, so it was just stubbornness that had me clinging to my original theory. We'd been talking about finding David and Olivia for so long that part of me wanted them to be risking their freedom to come here, because we might catch them finally. But if it was all Parker, at least we were safe. "I don't want to talk about them anymore. Can we move on?"

He opened his briefcase and withdrew a sheet of paper, pushing it toward me. He produced a pen, uncapped it, and handed it over. "You sure you're ready?"

CHAPTER 32
SAMANTHA

"What's this?" I ran my eyes over the simple letter, with space for my signature at the bottom.

"Formal request to re-apply to the FBI."

I first worked for Elliot the summer after I graduated with my Criminal Justice Master's degree, as an intern at the Detroit office, working for him in support of the Art Crimes Team. We'd stayed in touch over the years—his session at Quantico, art losses in Napa after a wildfire, an art loss fraud in Miami.

Then the auction in August and the thefts from Pompeii. And every time, it ended with the same question: *When are you coming to work for me?*

He tilted his head, surprised. "You weren't expecting this, were you?"

"This is a personal letter, not an application form..." I slowly took the pen from him, staring at the paperwork.

"And there's one from me that will accompany it. I'm not leaving it up to chance that someone may flag you for resigning the first time." When I didn't move to sign it, he continued, "You didn't actually think I'd share details about an ongoing FBI investigation you have no part in, just because you asked nicely?"

With a shrug, I said, "You've been feeding me information about the Scott case, and now this pawnshop."

"Trust me, there's more that you don't know than you do." He folded his arms, face tightening. "We've been dancing around this for seven years, Sam. I pulled strings to get you into the first class at Quantico after you met the qualifications because I thought you'd have a bright career with us."

So did I. My mom's face came back to me. Her words: *The next time I see you, I'll be calling you Special Agent Caine.*

"I had hoped that you texting me meant you were ready to come back."

I closed my eyes and took in a slow breath, trying to calm my racing heart. The shootings, fighting with Antonio, the future of Foster Mutual—all on my shoulders. Now this. Everyone wanted a piece of me, and all I wanted was to be left alone. Climb some rocks. Look down on the world from the top of a mountain or an airplane.

No responsibilities, except to myself. Not letting anyone down. No one leaving.

Mom's words echoed in my head. *Special Agent Caine.*
One deep breath. Swallow it all down. Calm.

I pushed the sheet back to Elliot. "Not yet. Sorry."

"Unfortunately, that's what I expected." When I offered the pen, he ignored it, swapping the sheet for another from his briefcase. "How much does Dr. Ferraro play into this decision?"

Dinner and dancing Wednesday. A candlelit bath Sunday night. The almost-disappointment of finding keys and a necklace in the jewelry boxes. My heart calmed just thinking about him and everything he'd done this visit.

I scanned the sheet, another letter with space for my signature. "Authorizing background check and security clearance?"

"I'll be damned if you wake up one day and realize you're ready to join my team, and we have to wait on all this red tape."

My eyes rose to meet Elliot's. He'd been a mentor of sorts, despite how short our formal working relationship had been. I looked up to him, trusted him. Had wanted to do what he did for a living. "Can I be completely honest?"

He nodded. "I wouldn't expect anything else."

"Antonio plays a large part in it, but so does my sister. She's sick and I can't leave town until that's over. And if she doesn't get better..." I put the pen down, swallowing the lump in my throat. "I promised I'd stay here to help my brother-in-law with the kids."

"So, you can't go back to Boston?"

"Even Detroit might be too far. And I can't tell you when I'll know either way."

He tapped the sheet in front of me. "For consulting, I might be able to work with you remotely, but that's not my call in the end. Between the auction, the Chagall, and your experience in Naples, you're building a reputation. That'll influence the decision when you're ready."

"But consulting wouldn't be full time, would it?" Could I do this *plus* Special Investigations at Foster?

He shrugged. "Also not my call. But for now, why don't you sign that, and we'll continue building that reputation together."

That I could do. "And in return?"

"If you're not here to join my team on the smuggling ring, what do you want?"

To be a shitty girlfriend and have my friend at the FBI spill Antonio's secrets. "Nathan Miller told me Antonio has a dangerous uncle and that if I wanted to know more, I needed to ask you about it. I suspect it's related to the smuggling ring."

The corner of his lips twitched. "That sounds an awful lot like asking about the smuggling ring itself."

It wasn't, but it confirmed the uncle was related to the case. "I know, but I'm asking anyway."

"Sign the consent and let me know what you find by *not* following any leads on that Constable," he said with a grin. "And I'll tell you what little I can."

I skimmed the letter. I was getting the better end of this bargain by a long shot.

"But be warned..." He turned back to his laptop while I read. "You can't unknow what you'll find out."

Nathan said Antonio wasn't involved. Was he wrong? Either way, I needed to know. I signed and he took the sheet from me, filing it away in his briefcase.

"Dr. Ferraro's likely going to throw a wrench into your background check, but from what I know of him, I should be able to clear anything up." He tapped a key on his keyboard, and a new image lit up on the wall-mounted screen.

A satellite map of a small town on the edge of a body of water zoomed in close enough I could see the Cypress trees and terracotta roofs. Streets labeled Via and Vicolo told me it was Italy.

"As you no doubt know, Dr. Dominico Ferraro has two brothers. One operates an art restoration company in Rome, while the other lives here." He pointed to a large estate on the edge of the town, near the water. "Since you signed the smaller letter, I'll only say this brother's well connected. He arranges for the sale and transfer of stolen art and cultural heritage items, using the Ferraro name to give him credibility within the art world."

Shit. That must have been what Valentina had been talking about on Christmas Eve.

"The Carabinieri have a revolving wire tap on the estate, so we pick up calls every now and again with the family members in the States."

That explained so much. The Carabinieri officer accusing Antonio of the theft in Naples. The call Nathan said they intercepted, which proved to him Antonio wasn't involved. And why he had a burner phone in Naples. But that also meant Antonio was in recent contact with these smugglers.

"How does this tie in with the Gardner heist?"

Elliot's face snapped back to me. "Did Miller tell you about that?"

"No, it was a guess. But you just confirmed it."

His face tightened for a moment. "The wire tap on this Ferraro estate and a few others started picking up chatter about the light and a piano over the summer."

"Light and a piano?" What did that... I sucked in a sharp breath when it dawned on me. "Light as in the 'master of light'? You're kidding me?"

He shook his head. "That's all you get, unless you want to sign the first letter."

"I'm tempted." I tapped my fingers against my lips. In the art world, the master of light was Johannes Vermeer. He completed four paintings of people playing harpsichords or virginals, both similar enough to a piano for it to work as an obvious code word. One belonged to Buckingham Palace, two to the National Gallery in London, and one—*The Concert*—had been stolen from the Isabella Stewart Gardner Museum in 1990. It was the most valuable stolen object in the world, worth up to five hundred million dollars, depending on who you asked.

"And if I tell you the chatter's been steadily increasing?"

"How the hell did you get on this one?" I asked. "Isn't Boston still in charge?"

"Lucky coincidence. I was on the smuggling case before this came up. Having a prosecutor from Boston helped smooth things over."

That's why Nathan was in on this. The Boston angle.

"That's all you get for now." He closed his laptop and started putting things away in his briefcase. "Once your paperwork is through, I'll see if I can swing something your way, but your relationship with Dr. Ferraro is a wild card. It might mean there's no chance, it might mean there's a good one."

It was a break in my dream case. The case I was supposed to be working on when I joined the FBI.

Matt's voice came back to me: *At least for the short term, we need you with SIU if we're going to have a company.*

How short term did Matt need me? And how much time until Elliot's team cracked this case? And why was I stuck in the middle?

"One other thing, Elliot. It'll be in my statement to Jimmy, but you should know, Parker said someone's trying to recruit Antonio. I don't know what that means, and he doesn't either." At least, he said he didn't. "But maybe it's related to all of this."

"Interesting." He pulled out his phone and tapped something into it. "I'll keep that in mind."

"Thanks. This has been... yeah."

Elliot shook my hand and opened the door, letting me go first. "Thanks for stopping in. I apologize if I kept you longer—"

"Samantha!" came an urgent voice as I stepped into the hallway, paired with a jangle of metal. A cuffed Cam-ron Parker was exiting a room two doors down from us, escorted by an officer and a woman in a suit. Dirty blond, shoulder length hair, goatee, and his ridiculous 'Stay calm and paint on' T-shirt under a zip-front sweater. "You're okay! How's your husband? They wouldn't tell me—"

"C'mon." The officer pulled at Cam-ron's elbow.

Husband again. Same thing his father said. That must have come from Felicia. "We're fine. Why did you—"

"We were going for lunch. He saw you two in your car and totally lost it! Turned the car around and followed you. I tried to stop him! I didn't know he had a gun! He said you two ruined his life! I couldn't—"

His lawyer shot him a look, shushing him, while the officer pulled more forcefully.

"I was so worried!" Cam-ron stumbled behind the officer, craning his neck to look back at me. "Thanks for everything you did! You turned my life around!"

All I did for Cam-ron was leave midway through the worst blind date of my life and threaten him with legal repercussions for forging the Chagall—even though it was a copy, not a forgery. Scared straight, maybe?

They disappeared around a corner at the same time Jimmy rounded it.

Jimmy watched in the direction Cam-ron headed, stifling a laugh. "I think you got more words out of the Johnsons than anyone here has. Let's go get your statement taken care of so you can get out of here."

The faster the better. I needed to talk to Antonio about this uncle of his. A smuggler? I was making life changes for this man. Wore his diamonds on my finger and around my neck. Planned on giving up my life on the road for him.

And his family was what I wanted to fight against most in this world?

CHAPTER 33

ANTONIO

WITH PARKER IN CUSTODY, I chose to work at the office instead of remaining at home. Soft stringed music floated from the speakers in the ceiling, just loud enough to cover the heavy metal pounding from Zander's headphones at the back of the studio. Alice had taken the day off to be with Frank while Papa was working on a design in his office. The store next to us was going up for sale, and he was already commissioning blueprints for expansion before his purchase was complete.

"Happy you came home?" Sofia leaned a hip on my worktable. "Not quite what you expected, is it?"

"Too many close calls, Frank in the hospital, Samantha off at work." I maintained focus on the painting in front of me, scraping the swollen layer of rabbit skin glue from the back of the canvas. The scalpel slid easily through it, my wrist and forearm working through muscle memory, fighting against the pain from the injury across my shoulder. The rhythmic whisper of a scalpel across the fabric was akin to a meditation, sadly not strong enough to distract me from what happened. "But if I hadn't been here?"

She rested a hand on my forearm. "Frank's fine. He's being released in a couple of days."

I paused, wiping the sticky curls of glue to the side.

She squeezed my arm. "And Samantha—"

"Could I be wrong about her?"

"About what?" She settled her hands on her hips, frowning at me. Sofia knew what I meant, but always made me say it out loud.

"I love being with her, but she's so... infuriating. Like I'm banging my head against a wall." I swiveled my high work stool to face her. "What if I'm wasting my time and she's not—"

"Oddio!" Her gaze shot heavenward. "Did you see the look in her eyes when she found you here yesterday? Or were you too busy being angry that she caught the shooter to notice?"

"Sofia!" called Papa from his office. "I need your help."

"You can't control a woman like her, little brother." She patted my arm before going to see Papa. "Don't bother trying."

She was right. Always right when it came to women, especially Samantha.

Before I could resume scraping, my phone buzzed. I pulled it out from the chest pocket of my apron, and my heart swelled, a smile creeping up my face. Doubts and worries aside, Samantha's name on the caller ID invariably did this to me.

"Ciao, bella." I stood and made my way to my office, next to Papa's. "How's your day going so far?"

"Good." Her voice was strained, serious. "You at home?"

"No, at the office." I closed the door behind me and took a

seat in the closest chair. "Alice is still off with Frank, so Papa needed some help. I'm finishing up some—"

"Good. I want to stop by." Something was not right. We'd argued early in the morning, from little more than stress, but had made up. "I need to talk to you."

Was I reading too much into the tone? "Fantastico! We can go to Russo's together, like our first date."

The mention of our first date should have elicited a laugh from her. But she grunted. "No, just a chat. In the office. I'll be there in five minutes."

She hung up without another word, leaving me staring at my phone. What was bothering her? And how could I make it better?

Not enough time to run to Russo's or even enough time to make her an espresso. Only enough time to tidy my office, fluff the decorative pillows on the leather couch, and ensure the paintings and my diplomas were straight. Pull the navy half-zip sweater back on—she loved me in blue almost as much as black. And brush my teeth.

Maybe a hint of cologne.

Five minutes later, the front door opened and closed, and the click of Sofia's stilettos came from Papa's office.

"I have it," I said, hurrying to the door. My heart leapt into my throat as I rounded the reception wall and saw her hanging her heavy winter jacket on the coat rack near the door. Beautiful. So beautiful. She'd worn a robin's egg blue blouse under a black suit with slim pants, her glorious hair cascading down her back.

Her smile was tight, so I crossed the lobby and scooped up her hand to kiss it gently.

I looked up from where my lips hovered over her hand.

"Have I told you yet today that you're the most stunning sight in all the world?"

The smile changed. From tight to sad. A devolution instead of an evolution. "Yeah, you said that this morning."

But I could thaw her frosty exterior. I'd always been an expert in that. "Apparently, I'm becoming too predictable for my clever girlfriend."

She inclined her head toward the huge front windows. "Those were fixed quickly."

"Papa has connections."

"Is your office free?"

"For you? Always." I leaned in to kiss her, but she presented a cheek. "You know, it's not a public display of affection if there's no public."

"Sorry." She gave me a peck on the lips and took my hand, her free one swiping along her jaw. "It's been a rough morning."

"Then my job is to smooth it over." I brought the hand to my lips again as we walked into the studio, passing Papa's office where he and Sofia were arguing in Italian.

Samantha didn't even look in.

Once we were both in my office, I closed the door behind me and wrapped my arms around her waist, pulling her back against my chest. Her body remained rigid.

I leaned in close, nudging the hair away from her ear with my nose, and lowered my voice. "What's the matter, bella?"

Her eyelids fell and her head dipped forward. There were words she needed to share.

My lips grazed her jaw. "You can tell me. I'm here for you."

"Stop," she whispered, a hand clasping one of mine. For a moment, she sank against me and relaxed. But she quickly straightened and slid out of my grasp, turning to face me. "I need to talk to you. With words."

One of her hands extended between us, making it clear she didn't want me to touch her. Creating an ocean of distance. The food in my stomach churned, and I swallowed hard, searching for moisture in my dry throat. The minty taste of the toothpaste taunted me. So much for my charm fixing her mood.

She rubbed the hand across her face, unable to speak or look at me.

Surely she was not breaking up with me? Telling me she would move out? Marone, had I been right about Nathan Miller all along? I flew all this way and—I shoved my fists into my pockets. I was being ridiculous.

"So talk, Samantha, and I'll listen."

"Samantha?" Her nose scrunched with the word, eyes flicking back and forth between mine, searching for something. Searching for *bella* or *amore*. Until realization spread across her face and she took a half-step toward me, but no more. "Antonio, no. Not cheating, no other man, not leaving you, none of that."

That was something, at least.

"Of course. Why would I think any of that?" I waved a dismissive hand and crossed to the couch, sitting lightly, resting an arm across the back. Perhaps I could convince her I was not worried and it would make whatever weighed on her easier. It was unlikely I could convince myself of it.

But she was not Faith, and I shouldn't act like she was. Nor was she one of the shallow women I dated in the past. Samantha had a depth to her which I'd longed for much of my adult life.

She swiveled one of the guest chairs at the desk and sank into it, staring at the leather armrest. Picking at lint, which was not there. "I need you to listen until I'm done."

"Sì, I can do that."

Her eyes met mine for an instant, but then fell to the armrest again. "I met with Elliot Skinner this morning. He gave me his regular Scott case debriefing in person. He's looped himself in with the shootings, too." The words tumbled out, coming faster and faster as she went, so unlike her. "I told him about the Constable while I was there, showed him the pictures, and he asked me to do some more digging. He wants me to work for him, so he's treating this like bait."

I nodded, the jumble of energy in my stomach becoming more frantic the longer she spoke. None of this felt like a problem or even a surprise yet. When I met Elliot in Napoli, he'd told me he wanted her to work for him. And based on what she did while she was there, it was hardly a shock.

"As part of it, he's doing a background check." She took in a deep breath and let it out slowly. This was it. "He said my relationship with you may pose a problem in obtaining security clearance."

"Scusi? How would I pose any problem to that?" Unless he meant... of course he did.

She looked up slowly, flexing her jaw. "What can you tell me about your uncle who lives in the big estate outside of Rome? I'm assuming that's the one you never talk about."

Heat exploded through every molecule of my body, and I launched off the couch. "Cazzo Madre di Dio!"

I stalked to the back of the room, looking for something to throw or break. Cristian and Gio. It always came back to them. No matter how many good choices I made, the poor ones continued to haunt me.

"So there's something to it?" Samantha's voice trembled.

I spun back to her. "That was for me to tell you, not Elliot Skinner."

"You were planning to?"

"Of course I was." I yanked a sheet of paper off the printer and crumpled it. "What did he say?"

"Not much more than I just said." Her eyes stayed on me, features difficult to read. Disappointed, most likely.

I threw the paper into the recycling bin, losing all its momentum as it dropped only as quickly as crumpled paper ever did. Paper was not the right choice.

Neither was anger.

I eased onto the edge of the desk, facing away from her, and dragged my fingers through my hair. "Is he involved with the Constable?"

"I didn't even think to ask."

I gripped the desk. Where to start? And how much to tell her?

"He's speaking of my Zio Giovanni. My father and he were close when I was growing up in Roma, and my middle name is after him. He worked as an accountant with the International Monetary Fund. At least, that's what I was told, true or not." I paused, scarcely able to remember myself as the innocent boy running through the hallways, the gardens, or through the vineyards. "His homes became larger and larger every few years, and I recall Sofia telling me she thought he was involved in criminal activities. I was still naïve enough that I just knew him as the uncle who gave me the best presents."

Samantha's hand slid over mine, and she gripped tight.

That was something. She may have been hurt, but she was still mine. For now. Once I finished, though, would be another matter entirely.

"My Nonno ran the office in Brenton back then, and Papa ran the main studio in Roma. He and Gio had a falling out after Nonno died, and Papa decided it was best for us to move here." All my friends, my cousins, my aunts and uncles. All that Italia offered, given up for small-town Brenton. Because those two couldn't get along. "I was furious."

Samantha squeezed my hand while I stared at the floor.

"As soon as I finished my undergraduate degree, I left the States and went back. I lived with Gio's son Cristian—"

"The guy from the nightclub in Sorrento?"

"Sì, one and the same." I'd met with him in private more than once while she visited me in September, hoping she would never meet that part of my family. "Papa was livid, but I was on my own and thought I could make the best decisions for myself. Cristian was the one who helped me lose the weight and become strong. He had a large place in Roma, with plenty of room for me, which was just the way of things in our family, so I thought nothing of it."

I shook my head slowly, eyes closing. "Until one night, Cristian arrived home drunk after being out with his friends. He made such a ruckus I came out to be sure he was alright. Marone, his shirt was stained with blood—not his, he'd said with a laugh. He was so proud of himself for beating some man who... I don't know why, but I know it was for his father."

She put her other hand on mine. It was a comfort. I could have stopped there and pretended that was the end of the story. Let her feel sympathy and never know the rest. But every time I failed to tell Samantha something, it came out, and hiding it from her would only make the discovery worse.

"You said this morning I was acting like the shootings didn't affect me. The truth is, I saw much violence after that night with Cristian and became numb to it. Except when I thought you could have been hurt."

"You never got involved, though?" She paused, but I didn't respond. "Right?"

"I had a great deal of education in Roma. Not all good. He taught me to defend myself, which I did when I needed to." I didn't want to go further, but I had to. "Until it became less about defense and more about pleasing my uncle."

She sucked in a breath, and her hands left mine, yanking my heart away with them. Law and order Samantha didn't want to hear I had a dark side. "That scar on your groin. That's—"

"I was shot. I got twisted into their world for the blink of an eye and almost died because of it." I pushed off the desk, pacing across the floor, my hands taking on a life of their own as I flailed for meaning. "But after I got out of the hospital, Mario arranged for the last year of my Masters to be spent in Pompeii, so I could stay with him. He saved my life by doing that."

My eyes finally found hers, but the emotion which had settled there—Contempt? Disappointment? Judgment? I turned away, unable to look at her.

"And despite it all, Gio offered me a job when I graduated, to authenticate works of art which *came into his possession*. Not that he bought or was thinking of selling." I grabbed another sheet of paper, crumpling it. I wouldn't dare to laugh in his face, no matter how preposterous the idea had been.

"After all that, I finally understood why my father moved to America and why he never speaks of Giovanni. And I normally don't either."

Until today. Until an FBI agent told my girlfriend things I was not ready to tell her. My worst secrets were out and there was no going back.

"You said you would have killed Parker with your bare hands." Her voice quavered. "Did you ever—"

"Samantha!" I snapped. "How could you even ask that?"

"I don't know." She cupped her hands over her mouth, tears welling in her eyes. "Your family…"

"My family what?" I gestured in the direction of the studio. "Are wonderful people who adore you? Who would never do those things?"

"That's why that Carabinieri officer accused you of stealing the fresco, isn't it? Because he knows *that* side of your family. And they were the ones who gave you that burner phone in Naples, weren't they?"

"My family in Brenton is the one you should judge me by. Not a blood relation who has nothing to do with me anymore." But I did have something to do with them. Cristian's man had saved Samantha's life in Napoli. For that, I let him leave with the fresco and never told her the truth about that, either. And this week, Cristian was the one I called to ask for help.

"Like how your father insisted you and Sofia lie to me about the Chagall?" She shook her head. "Your family's always going to come between us, aren't they?"

"No, bella." I took a step toward her, and she matched me by moving away.

How could I make this better? What was there I could say

to make her forget the images now floating in her head? "I suppose it's good timing. With me out of the way, you're free to rejoin the FBI, sì?"

The hands fell away from her mouth, dropping to her heart. "Antonio, you have no idea."

"Of course I don't. Because you never tell me anything." I folded my arms, attempting to soften my stance or my jaw or my voice. Failing at each one. "You just stare at me and expect me to figure everything out on my own. My smart woman— always thinking and never feeling."

Her hands curled in on themselves, rubbing to counteract whatever sensation she felt in her fingers when she was panicking inside.

Stop lashing out, Antonio. Fix this.

My office door swung open, and Papa appeared. "Antonio, I need your help with—oh, my love!" he said to Samantha. "You didn't stop in to say hello. I hope you don't mind, but I need my son to clear up his notes on some blueprints."

"Of course." She plastered a professional smile across her face and walked over to him, presenting her cheeks. "Family first, right?"

"Always," he said, as I would have expected him to.

I hurried after her. "I'll see you at home when I'm done?"

She sniffed and marched out to grab her jacket and leave, saying nothing more.

CHAPTER 34

SAMANTHA

I BRUSHED snow off the top of the gray granite stone, my boots crunching in the snow with each step. This was silly. I hadn't visited since Cass forced me when I moved home in June. My heart thundered in my chest as I stood there once she was cleaned off, staring at the dates carved into the front.

"Hey, Mom." A silver puff of breath hung in the air for a moment before floating away on the wind. "I needed to talk and wasn't sure where else to go."

The next time I see you, I'll be calling you Special Agent Caine.

But I hadn't seen her again. She left—like everyone else did—just not by choice.

"I met this really great guy. You would have liked him." I moved the snow around between my feet, dragging my boots to clear a space in front of her gravestone. "He's smart and funny, super-talented, and he..."

I blew into my gloved hands, cupping them over my nose to warm it up. The sky was thick with clouds, which held in a little warmth, but not nearly enough. The temperatures had plummeted that evening, falling well below freezing.

"He told me some stuff today that I'm not sure I can handle. Think you can give me some advice?" I chuckled at the ridiculous question, which slowly evolved into a quiet sob. I looked up to the branches of the leafless trees dotting the cemetery, blinking away tears.

Did his confession change anything for me? For us? Obviously, things were different, but how? How could I get past knowing what he'd done? Not knowing—guessing and assuming. Those strong hands being used to hurt and destroy, rather than to comfort and create.

"I guess I should catch you up first, shouldn't I?" I held up a hand and lifted a finger for each awful point of my life. "First, I left the FBI. Second, I married Matt. Third, I got a divorce. Fourth, I left town. Fifth, Cass got sick and I came home."

Seven years of my life, and all it took was a single hand to summarize it.

"But then—" I held up the other hand and started counting. "—I met Antonio, we started dating, broke up, and I flew to Naples to make up with him. He's been there since September, but came home for Christmas to surprise me."

I dropped the hands back into my pockets, clenching and releasing them to keep the blood flow going. Coming out here wasn't one of my smarter ideas. At least, not in work dress. I should have put on something warmer, but I'd torn out of the Ferraro's office and driven aimlessly for an hour before winding up with Mom.

"There's no way you would have thought I'd date this guy. *I* didn't even think I would. He's loud and charismatic, loves joking about everything. But, Mom—" I leaned closer to the stone and lowered my voice. "—he's an art conservator. Can you believe that? And he keeps telling me he's going to marry—"

My throat closed over, and the first tears spilled over, down my cheeks. I sniffled, bringing in a gush of cleansing, frigid air.

"But he's got a past, and I don't know what to do about it."

"Don't we all?" A deep voice sounded behind me and I spun around. Nathan's boots crunched in the snow as he approached. How hadn't I heard him?

"Fucking Christ, Nathan! What's your problem?" I kicked snow in his direction and quickly wiped at my eyes while he was distracted.

Surprisingly, he didn't throw any of it back. Instead, just brushed off his long navy jacket and stopped next to me. I hadn't heard his car, so he must have parked on the main road like I did. And those weren't boots. He was in dress shoes, so this stop must have been as spontaneous as mine. "How's Mrs. Caine doing this afternoon?"

"Not very chatty." I stared at the gravestone, sniffling again, turning away from him enough to clear my last tears.

He reached an arm around my shoulders and pulled me close. My head fell to his shoulder, then I turned into him, burying my face against his jacket. He wrapped me in his arms and held tight, pressing a kiss to the side of my head. "What did the Italian do this time?"

I pulled my hands out of my pockets to hug him back. His dislike of Antonio was probably what I needed at that moment. It would help me stay angry.

Nathan released me and took my face in his hands, the low sun glinting off his deep blue eyes as they flicked back and forth between mine. "Shit. You talked to Elliot, didn't you?"

I nodded, swallowing hard. "He gave me the tip of the iceberg, and Antonio gave me the rest."

"Now you're sinking." He leaned in to kiss my forehead and pulled me against him before I could come up with any response.

But yeah, I was sinking. The voice inside me that kept saying Antonio was too good to be true had been right all along. "How can I be with a man who's involved in something like that, Nathan? It goes against everything I believe in. What I wanted to devote my life to."

He rubbed my back and let out a long sigh. "You remember that jerk who stood you up on prom night?"

I stepped out of the hug to see him clearly. Strange question. But the memory filled my chest with warmth. "Yeah. You dropped everything and drove from Ann Arbor to take me."

"And the jackass who strung you along for months, telling you he was going to move to the States for you? Who didn't bother to tell you he'd landed a job in Italy until you flew over there to help him pack?"

"You tried getting him on the No Fly List," I chuckled.

"I could have, if you hadn't stopped me." The corner of his lip twitched, and he grabbed my hands. "And the asshole who divorced you for someone else?"

"You took me out drinking, and I passed out on your couch. Tina was pissed." His wife—now ex-wife—had still made me breakfast once my stomach was up for it.

"And the prick—" His face grew hard, lips and eyes tight.

"—who lied to you about that painting and broke your heart?"

I pulled my hands away, turning back to the gravestone. That memory pushed the warmth aside, still raw despite everything Antonio and I had been through since then. Or because of it. "You drove out to pick me up and sucker-punched him."

"Then you fly off to Naples on a whim to make up with him, not even a week later. Play this ridiculous long-distance game with him for months. Then he shows up out of the blue and you're miserable again." He stepped in front of me, leaning over so I couldn't avoid looking at him. "You ever think maybe he's no good for you?"

Nathan had been there for me through so much. And he'd been telling me from day one that Antonio was bad news. If I'd just listened to him in the first place, none of this would be happening. I'd be safely single, living in my hotel, counting down four more months until I was back on the road.

"Stop arguing with yourself." He nudged my shoulder and cracked a smile. "Answer me. First thing that comes to your mind when I say Antonio Ferraro is no good for you."

Waking up with him every morning. His arms around me. The way he always wanted to be in contact with me. My heart racing at every text, every call, every video chat while he was gone. How he admired my brain before anything else.

"I've known you since you were a knobby-kneed kid." He rubbed his hands together, letting out a long sigh, surrounding us in his frosty breath. "You've grown into a strong, capable, brilliant, and somewhat reckless woman."

I rolled my eyes. "Yeah, thanks."

"What you need is someone who respects that. Not just as a friend admiring all you do, but as a partner who'll stand next to you while you do it." He paused, stomping his feet. His toes must have been frozen in those shoes.

"But that's not who I'm dating. You saw Antonio after the shooting at my hotel. Then he got angry at me after the shooting yesterday."

"Angry? Or worried?"

"Ang—" I stopped before the word was all the way out. *Be honest, for once, Sam.* "Worried."

"I hate to say it, but I gave him the chance you asked me to, and I liked him. It wasn't just the fancy car or the wicked Scotch he totally bribed me with. It was the way you two looked at each other all evening. You and Matt never had that look. That's what I want for you. A man who'll look at you like that. And who'll put up with your shit."

This was not feeling as supportive as it had started out. "You said I'd run the other way if I knew who he really was. And now I do."

"Jesus, Sam, even I can admit I was wrong about him."

"I'm doing it again, aren't I?"

"Pushing him away before he has a chance to hurt you?"

I pulled the neck of my jacket closed, wanting to bury myself inside it. Not just from the cold air, but from the ice running through my soul. What if he left me? It would destroy me. At least for a bit. I'd eventually pull myself back together, but I'd basically been on the run from Matt's betrayal for six years. "Vincenzo and Matt told me they loved me. So did my dad. But it was nothing more than words; their actions proved different."

"Actions? Antonio put his very-big-deal project on hold and flew half-way across the world just because he missed you.

You don't owe him anything for that, but that *action* tells me that man is head over heels for you."

I shoved his shoulder, breaking the intense look in his eyes. "You're supposed to be the one telling me he's not good enough for me."

"No one is. But he's the closest thing I've ever met."

My heart lurched. Who was *I* ten years ago? It had only been seven since I graduated from Quantico, heading to Boston for my dream career. That wasn't me anymore. Why couldn't I trust Antonio to change?

Because I was running. Scared of getting attached to Brenton again and having it let me down.

Nathan bounced slightly, his breaths becoming ragged. "We should have held this conversation indoors."

"Why are you even here?"

He shrugged, ushering me toward the road, arm around my shoulder. "I was driving by, saw your behemoth parked on the side of the road, thought maybe you'd broken down."

"I have a cell phone." I wrapped an arm around his waist. "I would have called someone."

He chuckled. "Fair. Alright, I realized where you were parked meant you needed a friend and were too stubborn to call one."

I nudged him with a hip, but he held on tight enough we stumbled to the side.

"So, did he actually propose?" He stamped his feet when we got back to the shoveled path leading to the road.

"No, he just keeps threatening that he will." I clenched my hand inside my pocket instead of rubbing it over my face, the trinity ring on my ring finger digging into my flesh.

He grunted, obviously not fully in Antonio's camp yet. "For record—I'll deny every positive thing I've said about him if you tell anyone."

CHAPTER 35

ANTONIO

"DR. FERRARO?" said Alessa, as I marched through the lobby of my building. "There's a package for you."

Her voice pulled me out of my head, out of *With me out of the way*. Could I have said anything worse? Of course I could. I could have said she never felt anything. That was a brilliant move.

I huffed at myself and detoured to the concierge desk, where she produced a small, nondescript brown box, along with a few letters. "You understand you can call me Antonio, sì?"

She grimaced and shook her head, her short blond hair swishing gently. "Marcus's rules."

"And you can't call him grandfather, either?"

Alessa laughed, shaking her head again. "Not while I'm working."

I collected the box and letters, making my way to the elevator. There was no return address on the package, which I turned over a few times while riding to my floor, hearing a soft thud each time I did. I hadn't ordered anything to be delivered here, so it was a mystery. Except not. It had been a private delivery, which meant I knew not only who it was from, but what it was.

Lucy's broad smile greeted me as I entered my condo. She sat on the bench by the door, lacing up her boots with her jacket and bag next to her. "Janelle just called."

"Good news?" I hung up my jacket and removed my boots, at once grateful and regretful. When Samantha arrived —*if* she arrived—Lucy would have been an excellent buffer.

"You've been so nice, but she gave me the all-clear to head home. I talked to Paul's sister, and things are looking better for him. He stabilized last night, so that's really good." She chomped on a piece of gum so rapidly, it made her more diffi-cult to understand than normal. "I left a note on the breakfast bar that I was leaving—boy, am I going to miss eating here, you're an amazing cook—but I guess you can just ignore it now!"

"You're feeling better, as well? You don't need to stay another day or two?"

"Are you kidding me? I'd love to!" Her eyes shot wide and she stood from the bench. "But I think you and Sam need some private time."

A knot formed in my stomach. Did she know something? Had Samantha called her?

"I mean, if I was away from my boyfriend—if I had a boyfriend—did Sam tell you I met your brother?—anyway, three months is a long time, and you don't need me around here spoiling that." She threw on her jacket, wrapped her arms around me for a hug so quick I didn't have time to return it, and picked up the bag. Then she paused, looking at the floor, and the gum chewing stopped. With a deep breath, she said, "I can do this."

"Sì, you can. You're a resilient woman, and you have a place here if you need it." I kissed the air next to her cheeks and she headed out.

Once Lucy was in the elevator, I slunk through the great room and dropped the box onto the dining table. Before opening it, I pulled out a dozen of the battery-operated candles and set them out on the table. Maybe another dozen through the rest of the room. And another dozen in the bedroom. The sun was near to setting, so I turned off the lights and let the candles set the mood.

Samantha would come back. This was not the end, despite how my heart sat firmly in my throat.

And when she did, I needed to have the box taken care of and in the trash.

I grabbed a knife and sank into a chair, slicing the box open. Inside, I found exactly what I'd expected.

A cheap flip phone with a note—*Dial 1*—as though I could've forgotten. I hit the eighth speed dial, as I'd been trained.

It rang twice before Cristian's voice came from the other side. "Cugino! I hope I'm not interrupting anything."

"I'm preparing dinner for my girlfriend." A lie, but one I should make reality. I made my way to the pantry to make noise, if nothing else.

"Smart man! Have you made her the salmon yet?" Something thudded on his end, then a squeak, as though he'd slid into a car with leather seats.

"Not yet." I pulled out a bottle of Lambrusco, intending

to pair it with a caprese salad. It would wait as long as she took, and we could figure out the rest from there.

"I won't keep you." He became muffled for a moment, providing directions to someone. "I made some inquiries after your call and came up empty until the incident yesterday."

He'd already gotten the details. Not surprising, despite him being half a world away.

"And?" I uncorked the bottle and poured a glass for myself. The subtle frizzante danced over my tongue, highlighting the notes of black currants and blueberries. With the flame on high, I set balsamic vinegar and honey to boil.

"The man arrested yesterday was under consideration by some old associates of ours as a link in their shipping operation. As I hear it, they began cutting ties with him after the auction you and your girlfriend attended."

"That explains the forged provenance documents at the auction."

Parker wanted in bed with people he should have steered clear of. He was lucky for only parting ways with them, and not being punished further for that failure.

I said, "You told me in Napoli that you had an interest in that auction?"

He barked a laugh. "An interest in them failing, nothing more. Former associates, remember?"

Cristian had also told me the last time I saw him that Zio Gio was getting out of the business. From the sounds of it, that didn't extend to Cristian's network of whisperers.

I ran a finger around the rim of the wineglass, watching the tiny bubbles pop. "No link to Umberto, Eva, and her brother? Or their threat against Samantha in September?"

"I pursued that lead, but those three were independent."

"Your man who took the fresco told you that?" I shouldn't have called him out like that, since the man hadn't said it clearly, but my brain was exhausted from the day.

Cristian was quiet for a moment. "He did. And he's monitored them for me to ensure they won't become a problem again."

My head sagged forward and I closed my eyes. Thank all the saints in Heaven above. As panicked as I'd been about Samantha at the office yesterday, it was nothing compared to hearing Eva's brother's voice on Samantha's phone in Napoli, warning me that I had not heeded his threat. He would have killed her. "So Parker was the end of that?"

He made a humming noise. "I hope so."

"I do have something else you may not have heard from yesterday." I paused, watching the sauce undulate, a sign bubbles would form soon. "He told Samantha that someone wants to recruit me."

Another moment of silence on the other end.

"Exactly like you warned me might happen."

"Any clue how? Or who?"

"None. Only those words."

"This is concerning. Less so that it would happen, but more that someone like him would have heard. Let me know if anything comes of it."

"I will." I turned the balsamic down to reduce once it was boiling. It would have to cool before serving, so I pulled out some fresh mozzarella Nonna had given us when we visited on Christmas Eve. "Do you have anything else?"

"Just the standard." In the call's background, the sound of the door opening and closing again, followed by shoes crunching on stones. "You know, when are you coming to visit?"

I'd been avoiding them since I arrived in Napoli in August, but having received so much help from Cristian, I'd have to oblige. They were pulling me back in again. "Soon, I promise."

"I'll tell Papa you said that. You remember what to do with the phone?"

"Sì, I do."

"Antonio?" came Samantha's voice in the apartment, then the click of the front door.

I snapped the phone shut and placed it on the breakfast bar. What tone had she said that with? I was too focused on the call to catch it. I should have cracked the phone in half and thrown it out, but she'd hear that, and I'd only be digging a deeper hole.

It was time for complete honesty.

No more hiding.

CHAPTER 36

ANTONIO

"I'M IN THE KITCHEN, BELLA."

The screech of hangers scraping against the rod was a good sign. She was taking off her jacket and hanging it up, so she was not leaving right away. An agonizing moment later, she appeared, stopping at the dining table, hands on one of the chairs. She didn't come into the kitchen with me, though, which was not a good sign.

The knife slid easily through the mozzarella, my gaze shifting from it to her and back again. She stared, chewing her bottom lip. Occasionally glancing at the phone.

One of these phones had almost ended things for us in Napoli. It sent her running off across the city, putting her life at risk. I pointed at it with the knife. "Burner guy in Napoli was my cousin Cristian."

She nodded, maintaining the silence.

"I called him Wednesday morning, asking if he had any information. I was afraid..." My jaw quivered, and I swallowed hard, finding my center. "I was afraid the threat from Napoli had followed us here."

Her eyes widened, knuckles whitening from her grip on the chair. Something else I should have told her.

"He sent the phone so we could speak plainly. As it turns out, Parker was being courted by a group of smugglers, but the auction fallout put an end to it."

Still, she remained silent. Not surprising that her emotions were hiding behind those accursed walls of hers and that she'd say nothing of Cristian, Parker, or any of this debacle.

I set the knife down more forcefully than planned. This staring and not speaking was becoming tiresome. "What are we doing?"

"I don't know." Her gaze remained on the phone, no doubt replaying my confession from earlier. I was not about to apologize for my past choices. I'd beaten myself up over them enough over the years.

"Marone, Samantha, I'm trying so hard." I braced my hands on the edge of the counter and closed my eyes. *Just ask. Get the question out and deal with the consequences... if she even answers.* "Are we done? Are you leaving me now that you know the truth?"

But she continued to stare and blink, gaze traversing the room until it meandered back to me. The kitchen lights were the only ones on, save the candles, casting a soft glow on her hard face.

"I had an idea in my head of what it would be like to spend this time together." I turned from her and plucked some tomatoes from their bowl on the counter. "It's much harder."

"How do you feel when you're with me?" she whispered.

I placed the tomatoes on the cutting board. "Like pulling my hair out?"

She exhaled with a half-laugh. "Not right now. When it's good. Like Wednesday night or Christmas Eve? What do you feel? And don't call it love."

Love was the right word, no matter how frustrated I was at that moment. No matter how much she doubted me. I took a deep breath, running through all the things I'd said to her before, what I'd only thought, what might finally convince her.

But in the end, it was not my job to make her believe me. It was my job simply to offer her my heart, whether or not she would ever return the offering.

"I could give you flowery words or recite Shakespeare's sonnets." I turned to the stove behind me, moved the balsamic to the side to cool, then returned my focus to her. "I could prepare a feast for you every night. Give you diamonds and pearls, fly you around the world, and proclaim to everyone that you're the woman who owns my heart."

She didn't move, barely blinked, but her chest heaved with a deep breath.

"Remember when I repaired that first torn painting for you, and you told me it was fantastic work?" One hand rose to cover my heart, which beat marcato against my rib cage. "I carry that praise inside me every day, as I try to live up to your impression of me."

I rounded the end of the counter, keeping my eyes on hers. "When I look at you, I see my future. All the hope of what's to come."

She nodded slowly, continuing to clench the back of the chair. "I broke my promise to you."

I stopped five feet from her, and my heart fell to the floor. Which promise?

"When you gave me this ring—" She held up her left hand, the diamonds sparkling in the candlelight. "—I promised I'd stop running. It's tougher than I thought."

Was this an apology? An explanation? Were we still together? She hadn't removed the ring, so likely?

Before I could take another step, she hurried across the distance to me, taking my face in her hands. "Antonio, I don't want to live in the past anymore."

"Nor do I, Samantha." I pulled her hands down to my lips, kissing each one. "I'm none of the people who hurt you, save one stupid decision. And I'm not the man we spoke of earlier. I was a hot-headed child and turned away from that life a long time ago."

She wrapped her arms around my neck, and I did the same around her waist. Our bodies pressed together, relaxing as one, cheek nestled against cheek.

"Oh, bella," I sighed. "Holding you makes me feel like I've found my home."

"Antonio, I—" Her voice caught, and she tightened her hold on me. "Me, too."

And if I knew anything about Samantha Caine, it was that fact which scared her more than chasing down the man who nearly killed us twice.

I smoothed her hair as her head sank against my neck. "Is this what life with you would be like?"

"What do you mean?"

"This roller coaster. Arguing so much."

She tilted her head to look up at me. "You've been back for a week. So far, we've been shot at more than once, you got stitches, Paul and Frank are in the hospital..." Her face found my neck again, and she shuddered. "I hope I never have another week like this in my entire life."

"These are good points." I kissed the side of her head. "But at least we faced them together."

"Together," she whispered.

We remained like that for some time, and I curled a hand around hers as we began to sway to unheard music, the only sound our slow breaths. "Is this the part where we kiss and make up? Or should I get back to the food?"

She chuckled quietly and looked up at me, a twinkle in her eyes. "I'm pretty hungry, to be honest."

"As am I." I kissed her, a gentle sigh mingling between us. As we broke apart, I winked. "But which type of hunger?"

"Both."

I leaned down to kiss her, but she escaped my grasp.

"But the more immediate one wants to know what you had on the stove because it smells amazing." She wound up behind the chair, pulling it to shield herself from me.

"Not so fast." I planted a knee on the chair, securing it in place, and grabbed her, capturing her lips. She laughed in the kiss, and I released her, returning to the kitchen on my terms.

She gestured toward the bottle of wine, and I poured her a glass as she sat at the breakfast bar to watch me work. This was far better. This was something I'd imagined doing while I was home. Chatting over wine while I prepared a meal—her culinary skills were limited to the microwave—and simply enjoying each other's company.

"I'm not sure if I want to ask or not..." She tapped the phone, spinning it around once.

"It arrived by courier." I cut the last of the tomatoes and

began alternating it with cheese on a plate. "He only speaks of important things in person and this way. We can't provide details to your friends at the police department, but if they require a nudge, we can do that."

"I'm hoping Cam-ron's going to give them enough information. I ran into him at the police station. I can't put my finger on it, but there's something different about him. Like he's finally woken up." She took a sip of her wine. "Did your cousin find anything out about the fresco or the last pigment pot?"

I placed the knife in the sink, rolling words over in my head. Partners. Together. No more lies. Pulling some basil leaves off a plant next to the refrigerator, I placed them on the counter and steadied myself. "This goes no further than here. But Fiori has them."

Her reaction was not the shock I'd expected, but rather a triumphant, "Yes! I knew it!"

"No further than here. I'm deadly serious."

"I know." She took a gulp of her wine. "I wouldn't be surprised if the FBI already found out. There's a lot Elliot won't tell me."

Hours earlier, I would have said Elliot's information about my uncle was the worst possible thing he could share. But the truth truly was the way to her heart. The more she knew, the more she accepted an honesty which would have been impossible before our discussion at the studio.

She touched the phone again. "Can I break it?"

I laughed. "The shredder upstairs will take care of the SIM card, but go ahead, if you wish. A burner's not critical for me, but I wouldn't be surprised if someone has his lines tapped."

After removing the SIM card, she snapped the phone in

half and frowned. It was a strange sort of intimacy. After having fought over my past with Cristian and the burner in Napoli, she didn't avoid the phone, as I would have expected.

She frowned at the pieces. "Not as satisfying as I'd hoped."

I tore up the basil leaves and placed them over the salad. "I truly am sorry I didn't tell you about this."

She sighed, staring at the broken phone. "We've only known each other five months. It takes time for all the secrets to get out."

The sweetened balsamic reduction went on last, and I placed it in front of her with two forks. She took a bite and her eyes fluttered closed as she chewed.

"Not mentioning I could cook was an intentional surprise, not a secret, you know." I cleaned up after myself and rounded the counter to sit next to her. "Is this hunger sated yet?"

Her eyes snapped open, and she covered her mouth as she laughed. "Not yet, Ferraro. Besides—" She snaked one of her legs around mine. "—I passed Lucy on the way out, so I know we've got the place all to ourselves again. Plus, I'm off work the rest of the week."

My heart leapt. "You are?"

She nodded, leaning in as I pulled her face to kiss her cheeks. "Sort of. Elliot wants me to follow up on the Constable theft. I just need a private space to do some research."

"We already made space for you on the desk upstairs." I winked, and the blush was already climbing her lovely face. "I may have to order a new monitor after we broke the other one this morning."

Her face fell into her hands, the crimson shade all the way up her forehead. That desk was not built for romance.

"And I'll join you. I'm feeling inspired to paint."

"I'd like that." The hands dragged down her face as she looked up at me. "But I want to start tonight. Food, sex, then work."

"I would question the order of your priorities," I said with a wink. "But I suppose for one night, I can agree to this."

CHAPTER 37

ANTONIO

Three hours later, we were working. She sat at my computer desk while I stood in front of an easel. Alternative rock played through speakers in the ceiling. It was quiet enough we could chat, but loud enough I could sing along.

How could life get any better than this?

"You could paint a landscape." Samantha didn't have to lift her head from her paperwork for me to know she was rolling her eyes at me.

I hummed aloud, staring at her from around the side of my canvas. "No, I'm not in the mood for that."

But if she didn't look at me, how could I wink at her? Or smirk at her? She was stealing all the fun out of the room with her seriousness.

"And you should put your shirt back on," she said with a chuckle.

"I prefer to paint in lounge pants." I reoriented myself behind the easel so I could no longer see her at the long desk. Three blues and greens combined, and they were still not quite the right shade for her eyes. Some white, a yellow—I'd have it eventually. "Plus, I like the extra glint in your eye. I want to capture that."

"The glint of exasperation?"

"I'm fairly certain that's not the correct word." I leaned my head to the side, winking at her when she glanced up. "Now get back to your work before I do something else to put that look in your eye."

Another laugh as the printer next to her clicked a few times and spit out more papers. She took a sip from her wineglass and spun the chair to the high laboratory bench behind her, adding the sheets to her collection. Standing to study them, she leaned on her elbows, a stance which provided a breathtaking view of her long legs. She'd thrown on her tiny gray sleep shorts and one of my navy T-shirts after making love, knotting it at her waist just as she knotted her hair into a loose bun.

Her ass was stunning in those little shorts, not to mention the lean muscle of her legs. And the way she shimmied back and forth to the music made my blood stir. I could paint that long V-shape from her hips to her toes, but she likely wouldn't appreciate it.

I placed my brush aside, retrieving a palette knife. Abstract. That was the solution. If she realized what I'd painted, I could tell her it was her own interpretation and not my intention. "I worked on a Constable once."

"Hmm?" Her voice was distant, as engrossed in her task as she'd been for the last two hours.

"Under my father's very close eye, several years ago."

"I got to watch one of the in-house conservators working on one at the British Museum."

"The summer you worked with Thomas?" I knew

precious little about that time in her life. Thomas had been as tight-lipped about it as she was. They both claimed nothing romantic, but I had a feeling there was some history there, despite the nine-year age gap.

"Yeah." She chuckled. "You think I work a lot now? You should have seen me then. I spent most of my waking hours bouncing between there, the V&A, National Gallery, and the Tate. Lots of options in London."

"You've not mentioned ever going back?"

"No." She sighed, looking up from her paperwork for a moment, but not turning around. "Too busy working."

My love was an intense woman in so many ways who threw everything into her passions. It was one of the things I admired most about her, despite it occasionally frustrating me.

"If we could go anywhere in the world, where would you want to go first?"

She shifted along the bench, moving to a different set of papers. "We already took care of Pompeii, so that crossed off number one on my bucket list. Probably Paris? I've never been there, either."

I sucked in a deep breath, feigning my horror loud enough for her to hear it. "An art historian who's never been to Paris?"

At this, she finally turned around. "I'm a claims adjuster."

"Your talents are wasted." I put down the knife, which I'd not actually done anything with, as I'd been studying my muse. "I know I'm not the only one telling you this."

She shrugged. "But if I'm going to stay in Brenton, that's what I've got."

My soul wished to cheer. Rejoice in her choosing to stay to be with me. But her heart was not fully engaged with the plan.

I spoke slowly; the words fighting to remain inside. "So... don't stay in Brenton?"

She stilled, the staring and blinking resuming. Elliot Skinner had given her this research to remind her of where she belonged, which was not working as a claims adjuster. How strong was the lure of returning to the FBI?

"You don't belong in this small town. You're meant for more."

"I promised I'd stay until you got back." Her jaw flexed, and one hand ran over her cheek. "After that, I..."

Every muscle in my body urged me forward, to take her in my arms and tell her how I felt, yet again. Perhaps even mention Papa's thoughts about backing an investigative company. But she had decisions to make—ones I already had —and she had to make them of her own accord. "Samantha Caine, I would follow you anywhere in the world, if you would have me."

She blinked rapidly, chin dipping. This was either news to her, or she'd finally actually heard it. And apparently it was too much. She spun back to her research, moving pages about, rustling them together.

I had to release her from the panic, change the subject. "How about Venezia? Have you ever been there?"

She shook her head, saying nothing.

"Then I suggest we start with Paris and Venezia. How about once I'm done in Napoli? Or June for my birthday?" We would ride a gondola under the Bridge of Sighs and kiss at sunset as the bells of San Marco tolled. Perhaps that would be the time to propose to her? We would have been together almost a year and it would easily be the most romantic moment of either of our lives.

I sighed at her silence and pulled out my phone, switching the music streaming through the room. Something soft, relaxing, and romantic. A serenade. *Perfect Symphony*, the song we first danced to at the hospital gala in August.

She straightened, rolling her shoulders and neck, the tension easing.

This was my cue. I crossed the room to her. "Need a break?"

"No, I'm just a little sore." She stretched both arms up over her head, twisting side to side. "I'm not used to working a desk."

I dug my thumbs into her traps. When she winced, I immediately stopped. "Too hard?"

"No." She patted my hand and let her head roll forward. "It's perfect."

I snuck a quick kiss on her neck and resumed kneading the knots in her shoulders. "Have you figured anything out yet?"

"The FBI had this case for years. I'm hardly going to crack it in a couple of hours."

"Except you know where..." A photo in front of her caught my attention. A middle-aged man with the Constable behind him. I stood next to her. "Is this the owner?"

"Yeah."

I turned to her. "I know him."

"You what?"

"He owns a gallery in Los Angeles." I picked up the printed photo, scanning the others next to it. "I met with him and a few other brokers and gallery owners in New York last summer."

"Really?"

"Sì, this is an odd coincidence. We were negotiating

conservation and authentication work for some purchases they were making." I dropped the photo and resumed my place behind Samantha, pressing into her shoulders again. "What happened?"

"September 2013. He was living alone—divorced and the kids were with his ex-wife—but he was out of town at the time. Guess where he was?"

"Don't say New York."

"Exactly." She shuffled through the papers to show me a series of photos as she explained. "They came in through the front door, disabled the alarm, and grabbed three paintings from the study. The Constable we found at the house, a Delaroche, and a Gainsborough. Insured for almost two million, all told. The Constable was the most expensive and had a separate alarm triggered when they pulled it down. Police were there in seven minutes, but no leads off the bat. Clean crime scene. The door wasn't forced, and the house's security system wasn't tampered with, so they suspected the owner or the staff who had access."

"Suspected, but not charged?"

"Right." Her voice slowed and she groaned as I dug harder into the knots. "They all had air-tight alibis and no trace of the paintings."

When her head lolled to the side, exposing her neck for me, I closed in, brushing the soft skin with my lips. "I thought you wanted to put in more than two paltry hours of work tonight?"

"I did." She sighed and straightened. "But I'm gradually changing my mind. One more quick search and I'll call it a night."

"So long as it's quick." I stepped closer, blowing lightly

across her ear. "Because I can't bear to watch you in those shorts anymore."

She reached one hand back to grip the nape of my neck. "You like them?"

"Very much." I pressed my hardening cock against her, gave her a kiss on the cheek and separated from her, hopefully leaving her wanting more. "And I have plans for you."

"Plans?"

"Sì, important ones. We've not yet made love in the third bedroom. There are only so many days left and several rooms to go."

Her lips tightened, as they so often did when she was battling a smile. *Never let Ferraro know how much you like him,* she must have been saying to herself. *Keep your walls high and strong. Don't risk falling in love with this remarkable man.* Sì, that was it. Those were the words in her head.

"So anyway..." She riffled through sheets of paper and handed one to me. A real estate listing of Felicia's house, with a photo of the living room. One of the hidden photos Lucy found. "Along the right edge, you see that strip from a painting's frame?"

I nodded.

"That's the frame I mentioned. The one that we can't find a photo of the actual painting. But check this." She pointed to a photo of the stolen Gainsborough in a newspaper article. "Frame look familiar?"

They were a match. "Still a coincidence, though?"

"It is, but..." She took the sheet back, plans and schemes sparkling in her eyes. "Elliot told me—and this is definitely confidential—that the stolen painting at the auction also came from a pawnshop in Detroit. They have to be linked and if

Parker had both the Constable and the Gainsborough, I guarantee—"

"The Delaroche is there, as well?" These were the moments I was proudest of being with her. No matter how reckless and stubborn she was, she was truly brilliant.

"Can you call Irene and see if you can get the floor plan early? The dormer you pointed out is my top candidate for a hiding spot, but I'd like to get your thoughts on the rest of the layout."

"Since I won't be here to help?"

She shriveled her nose and nodded. I was leaving the day before the showing.

I pulled out my phone and before I had to face the uncomfortable moment of Samantha realizing I still had Irene's number from when we'd gone on a date, my phone rang.

"Speaking of coincidences..." I held it up for Samantha to see. "It's Irene."

CHAPTER 38
SAMANTHA

THE NEXT MORNING, we stepped into the small entryway of the Constable house, with its gleaming birch hardwood. The scent of chocolate chip cookies hit me before the multiple voices and footsteps registered.

Irene had called to let us know the invitation-only showing was being moved up to Wednesday, without providing a reason. The best guess? Felicia was hurrying the process because of Parker's arrest.

While Irene hadn't been able to send us the floor plan last night, at least Antonio was with me, which gave us two sets of eyes. And from the way she looked him up and down when we stepped in, it was clear he'd be just as successful a distraction as last time, in case the real estate agent got suspicious.

A dozen pairs of adult shoes sat by the door, so there would be plenty of cover for snooping. Maybe I wouldn't need Antonio to keep Irene's attention off us.

"As you requested—" Irene handed a long tube of papers to Antonio. "—the floor plan. It includes the four season room, which was added in 2017, so it's at least that recent. You have renovations in mind?"

"Sì, we do." He smiled at her, that ridiculously charming smile that left brain cells melting in its wake.

I leaned over as he unrolled the plans, immediately scouting hiding spots. "I'd like to take some measurements of that storage room in the basement."

Irene glanced at me and pointed to the schematic. "The dimensions are—"

"Often inaccurate, and as you said, potentially out-of-date." Antonio smiled at her again, eliciting a nod. It was like the man had a superpower. I'd been immobilized by that gaze only four months ago—and maybe a little last night—so knew its power well.

Footsteps sounded overhead as people moved from room to room. I caught glimpses of a couple in the living room and someone in the kitchen.

"Very busy today," Antonio said. "Do you mind if we take our own tour?"

Irene gestured toward the stairs. "Be my guest. I'll be doing some rounds once a few others arrive."

We had a game plan. Start from the bottom and work our way up, using the floor plan as a guide. The attic would come last. If they were hiding the paintings behind a fake wall, there had to be a way to open it, and I wanted to find out as much as I could before we revealed it.

Antonio walked with the sheets unfurled, nearly knocking into a couple coming up the stairs from the basement.

The man glowered at Antonio, down at the floor plan, then whispered something to the woman he was with. All I could make out was "unfair advantage" and they headed in Irene's direction to complain.

"Take that end," I said to Antonio, handing him the hook of my measuring tape. I backed through the storage room in the basement, down the clear path between boxes, bookcases, and a couple sets of golf clubs.

I scanned every nook and cranny, behind the books, and along the top of a shelf running the length of the room. But nothing stood out and most of the items were coated in a thin layer of dust, which quickly narrowed down anywhere the paintings could be.

"Sixteen feet." I nodded to Antonio, who released his end. "Do you think it's big enough?"

He consulted the floor plan, a woman in a bright blue jacket peering over his shoulder. "That's the outside wall, so there's nowhere to expand. Unless you wish to build an extension."

"The attic has storage space," said the woman, another prospective buyer. She inclined her head toward the man with her, also hovering behind Antonio. "We went up there first."

"Grazie. We're almost done down here." Antonio ushered her out of the cramped area, touching her back lightly to guide her, earning a glare from the man. There wasn't enough space in the house for how many people were inspecting it.

We headed for the main floor and toured around, paying particular attention to the width of the wall separating the four season room from the living room, the kitchen pantry, and the dimensions of a linen closet.

Nothing, nothing, and more nothing.

As we reached the top of the stairs to the second floor, Irene came out of the master bedroom. "Any questions?"

Six people moved through the space, coming in and out of the bedrooms, causing us to stand against the wall by the attic door to let them through. Irene—the cheater who didn't seem to care that Antonio was married, or at least said he was—plastered herself against him, gripping his arm.

A silly pang of jealousy struck me, like we hadn't discussed this in the car. He was the distraction. That was the plan. But there was no need for a distraction right now. There were too many damn people inside this house all at once. "It's a little crowded."

Antonio shifted subtly to release Irene's grip and took my hand. "Shall we go upstairs first, then come back for the bedrooms?"

"Yes." Snooping around the entire house was all well and good, but if those paintings were hidden anywhere, they were behind the walled-up dormer. We needed to get up there, expose at least one stolen painting, then I could call Elliot and get out of this house. And away from Irene.

Plus, calling him five days earlier than his deadline would look even better in the portfolio we were building.

Irene skulked behind us, reviewing more facts and figures about the neighborhood than she'd shared on our last visit. Pointing out that three of the viewers already confirmed they'd be putting in offers.

When we reached the top, we found four other people there. A man and a very pregnant woman at the rear window, a man in a wing chair staring at his phone, and a woman inspecting the musty bookcase. Another woman came up the stairs behind us.

How was Antonio going to distract all of them long enough for me to check his theory?

We stopped at the center of the room, Irene hanging off his every word. He had her entranced. But what about the rest of them?

"Honey," I said. "You were asking about natural gas lines?"

"Sì, I was." He winked at me and steered her toward the window at the back. "Do you know if the gas lines run through the backyard or the front? We were thinking about adding an in-ground pool."

I eyeballed the distance between the front and rear gable windows, estimating where the dormer was. Antonio had seen something, so I should be able to, as well. Running a hand along where the slope of the roof met the wall next to a book-case, I could almost make it out.

"What are you doing?" asked the man in the chair.

Shit. The woman near him turned to look at me as well. That meant I'd have Irene's attention soon, too.

"I was—" I groaned quietly and shifted from feeling the wall to leaning against it, like that's what I was doing all along. Eyes closed, I put one hand to my belly.

Antonio rushed to my side. "Samantha?"

"I need to sit down."

My accuser's face paled and he shot out of the wing chair when Antonio helped me to it.

I leaned forward, elbows on my knees.

Antonio knelt in front of me, taking my hand. "What's the matter?"

I squeezed his hand and looked him square in the eye. "Just a little morning sickness. I need to sit for a sec."

His eyes widened for less than a breath, then brows furrowed when he caught on. "Always at this hour. Every day."

"Every day." I kissed his hand, a hint of regret for the hope I'd seen flash across his face. Seriously, we'd been dating for less than five months. "I think the heat from all the bodies is making it worse."

The woman who'd come up behind us hurried for the stairs. "I'll get a damp cloth and some ice."

"I'm okay." I gave a weak smile to all the people in the room who gathered around me.

The couple who'd been by the rear window came closer and she took my free hand. She said to the man with her, "Go get my ginger chews from the car."

Irene's focus was on me, likely just praying I didn't vomit. The scent alone would scare buyers off.

I could work with that. "Irene, can you get me a bowl, just in case?"

"Yes!" She snapped into action and hurried down the stairs.

Wing chair man and musty bookcase woman snuck out of the attic behind her, leaving the ginger chew woman and Antonio up here with me.

"How far along are you?" she asked.

I slipped my hand out of Antonio's and placed it on my belly, groaning again. "Only a couple of months."

"That was the worst for me." She ran a hand over her full belly. "We've still got three months to go."

Antonio drifted away from us while I engaged her in light

conversation, trying to retrieve all the memories I had of Cass's pregnancies. She talked about salty chip cravings, we laughed over our panicking husbands, and she gave me multiple recommendations on where to find the best pregnancy clothes.

I pushed back the invading images of Antonio cradling a baby and focused on holding the woman's attention away from him. But a knock on the wall had us turning to look at him. He knelt where the ceiling stood only three feet high, knocking and listening.

"Renovations—he's checking for structural." I blurted, "What about daycare wait lists?"

"Don't even get me started!" she said, while I watched him in my periphery.

He ran his fingers along the seam where the roof met the wall, then toward the floor. Adjusted his position and repeated the action. He clenched a hand, pulled it back, and smacked the side of his fist against a spot on the wall.

It popped open. Not a hole, but a door. And light streamed in through it. Three feet high by five long, exposing a storage area and the dormer window.

"Please tell me it's in there," I said, launching from the seat and rushing to his side, all pretense vanishing.

"Look for yourself." He eased back, drawing to his full height.

Irene's voice came from the stairs. "What are you doing?"

I knelt in front of the opening, and a delicious jolt of adrenaline coursed through me. Not the risking my life kind like Monday. Not the boyfriend telling me stories I couldn't handle, like yesterday. No, this was the thrill of the hunt. Of finding a piece of the mystery. Hidden behind the door was a packing blanket folded underneath six frames.

The front one was the Constable.

Another was the frame we suspected was the Gainsborough. I pulled out my phone and snapped a picture. "Don't touch them. We need to—"

"I'm calling the police." Irene already had her phone at her ear, the bowl tucked under her arm.

"Don't," I said, standing with Antonio. Before she could protest, I continued. "I don't need you to trust me. Just look up the phone number for the FBI office in Detroit and ask for Special Agent Elliot Skinner."

She paused, mouth moving as though to speak several times, and finally did as I asked.

I could watch Antonio do just about anything with pleasure. But this—helping solve the case I was working on—was one of the sexiest things I'd ever seen him do. "You're so clever, Dr. Ferraro."

"I have to be, to keep up with my clever, pregnant wife." He leaned closer to whisper in my ear while Irene spoke on the phone. "Did it turn you on?"

Heavy footfalls ascended the steps, and the pregnant woman's husband returned. "I have the ginger chews!"

"And I have the ice chips!" came a woman's voice behind him.

"It's passed," said the pregnant woman, taking the candy from her husband and popping it in her mouth.

"I have him." Irene held out the phone between the three of us, with Elliot on speaker.

"Sam Caine here, Elliot."

Caine? mouthed Irene.

Elliot chuckled. "That was faster than expected."

"I'm at the house we discussed yesterday, with the Constable." There couldn't be much more he'd expect me to do on this case, so this would be the end. Sadly? Happily?

"Dr. Ferraro with you?" Had Irene told him that? Or was it a guess?

"Sì, Special Agent Skinner, I am."

"Have you touched the paintings?"

"No, Antonio found a secret compartment in the attic. There are six paintings lined up together, and we're fairly sure at least two of them are from the theft in LA."

"Are you inside the residence legally?" His tone was serious. The Art Crimes Team's primary goal was returning stolen cultural property. Prosecution came after that. But it was still there, and he didn't need us spoiling their case.

"We are. We're here with the real estate agent."

Elliot laughed. "Good job, you two."

All the color had drained from Irene's face as our conversation with Elliot progressed. Based on her reaction, it was unlikely she was involved, but she'd at least be questioned about her knowledge of the house and its occupants.

I said, "Now we just have to track down some more information about that pawn—"

"I will, Sam." Elliot's voice had dropped again. "That's my job, not yours."

CHAPTER 39
SAMANTHA

NEW YEAR'S EVE. I'd spent the last six by myself in my little RV or a hotel, depending on what town I was in at the time. Just me and a bottle of champagne. The way I liked it. At least, the way I used to like it. Antonio had blown into my life like a hurricane and changed everything. Part of me even thought it was a change for the better.

I'd left early in the morning for shopping and a spa day with my sister to prepare for the evening. My hair and makeup were a miracle and I couldn't wait for Antonio to see it.

The hotel was six floors and adjoined the Convention Center. The lobby was open to the second floor, where a walkway allowed guests to look down and people-watch. There were seating areas and a bar with many partygoers already milling about in their finery for the evening.

My phone buzzed with a text from Antonio. *Were you still planning to join me at the ball?*

A flutter burst in my chest. With a laugh, I sent a message back. *Coming up now. I'll knock three times, then you close your eyes. It's a surprise.*

He responded, *Looking forward to it.*

Then he added, *But not looking.*

We were on the sixth floor—no shock, knowing him—in a suite. I knocked three times and cracked the door open. "Eyes closed?"

"Sì, bella."

"Good!" I pushed the door open slowly, double-checking that he wasn't cheating.

The main room was large and open with two seating areas, while a kitchenette sat to the left, access to a bathroom beyond that, and double doors to a bedroom. A long set of track lights suspended from a metal bar stretched the length of the room, dimmed to pale light.

He sat in one of the over-sized chairs in front of the television, watching—

I stopped dead in my tracks. "Are you watching hockey?"

"Kevin and Nathan told me that watching the World Juniors over the Christmas and New Year's holiday is a tradition for hockey families. Can I open my eyes now? I missed you today."

"Keep 'em closed, Ferraro." I growled in his ear.

"I'm enjoying this." He smiled broadly and squeezed his eyes shut tighter.

I moistened my lips, the slight stickiness of the lipstick reminding me not to bite my lip or kiss him. It was hard not to.

His black tux, the shiny shoes, the little white pocket square. The jacket highlighted his broad shoulders, while the stark white shirt made his olive skin glow. "Dinner starts in an hour. Will you be ready?"

"Absolutely. You know me, I'm never late." I closed the

doors of the bedroom behind me, flicking the lock. "You can open your eyes now."

"You're hiding from me!" He rapped lightly on the door.

"Give me ten minutes."

I undressed, careful not to ruin the hair and makeup. Cass had forced me to buy a tiny piece of tissue that claimed to be underwear, plus garters and stockings. Not me at all.

Antonio will appreciate it, she'd said. *Try to woo him for once.*

Then she'd thrown a black silk teddy over my arm for after the ball. What was the point? I'd put it on, he'd take it off, and then it would sit in a crumpled heap on the floor.

Although doing that meant she was trying to support me in the relationship, which was a huge step for her.

Next came the double-sided tape to hold the dress to my chest, or he wouldn't be the only one getting a show. A quick glance in the floor-length mirror to make sure everything was in place. My hair was half-up, half-down, cascading over my shoulders, adding to the sweep of the halter neckline. Finished with his mother's—no, my—necklace and gold chandelier earrings.

And I was... beautiful. He was going to love this so much.

"One minute left." The hockey game was playing in the background and his voice was distant enough he must have sat back down.

"Eyes still closed?"

The television shut off. "They are now."

I eased the doors open. There was weight to the evening. Like it was bigger, more important than any other night we'd spent together. It was thick in the air and made my insides tingle to be part of it.

His perpetual smirk was there, hands casually resting on the chair arms, and his hair had that wave in it that begged to be touched. I didn't want to go anywhere other than the ten feet it would take me to get to him.

"You're so handsome."

"Does that mean I can open my eyes?"

I leaned against the bedroom door frame, hand on one hip. Heart hammering in my chest. This was all a crazy dream. "Yeah."

His sharp intake of breath and the anticipatory lick of his lips sent molten heat straight to my core. He scanned me up and down from his chair, possessing every inch of my body with his eyes.

"You like?" I asked hesitantly.

He stood, smoothed his jacket, and gave a slight tug to his shirt cuffs. He stalked toward me and scooped up one hand to kiss, eyes raking over me, full of all the innuendo he could manage. Which was quite a lot. "What are you wearing underneath?"

My lungs grew tighter as he looked at me like I was already naked. "It's a secret."

"Is it red? Mine's red. Always wear red underwear on New Year's Eve for luck."

I bit my lip to hold back a nervous giggle. "You'll have to wait until after midnight to find out."

He checked his watch and smirked. "It's after midnight in Napoli."

"Fortunately, you're here, not there." I withdrew my hand from his. "*Un*fortunately, that means you'll have to wait."

The smirk ratcheted up further. "You're wooing me now, sì?"

I inclined my head, batting my eyelashes. Looking foolish, for sure. "Why Dr. Ferraro, I believe I am."

"Consider me wooed." He traced one edge of the halter from my neck, along my cleavage, where he stopped and frowned. He'd found the tape. "What's this?"

"Insurance."

He laughed, a throaty sound, full of desire mixed with amusement. "You'll be the death of me, I think."

"Not likely."

"Samantha," he said, tumbling my name out slowly, staring into my eyes. The heat faded, replaced by a different intensity. By love. Absolutely pouring out of him. "I joke a lot."

I let out a little chuckle, mostly from nerves. His face was so serious.

"But I want you to know that you're everything I've ever wanted. I know you worry I'll grow tired of my boring claims adjuster from Brenton, Michigan—" He rolled his eyes, quoting my words back to me. "—but I hope last New Year's Day was the last one we spend apart."

"Watch yourself, Dr. Ferraro." I painted on the best smile I could to cover up the anxious energy swirling around my chest. "If you keep saying all that stuff to me, I might start believing it."

No sooner were the words out of my mouth than my stomach twisted into a knot.

Oh my god.

I *did* believe it.

"This is exactly what I'm trying to do." He winked and took my hand. "Shall we go downstairs now?"

My feet wouldn't budge. It was all real. I placed his hand over my heart. He *was* the one, wasn't he? "Thank you."

"For what?"

"For everything. For coming home to see me. For being so patient." I swallowed hard, the honesty catching in my throat. "For loving me."

He wrapped his free arm around me and must have felt me tremble. "There's nowhere else in the world I want to be."

Gone again in two days.

The skin on my arms and chest prickled. My breath picked up as the goosebumps spread to my legs. He loved me. Truly. Honestly.

Stop running, Sam.

Antonio Ferraro would do anything for me, including chase me down if I ran. He would have taken those bullets for me at the hotel. And all I could do for him was joke and deflect and keep my walls as high as possible.

I was making him work so hard, but he wasn't shying away.

"Take a breath." He eased me down to sit on the edge of the bed, hand rubbing my back.

What was wrong with me? Hell, I could jump out of a plane without a second thought. Dive into a shipwreck that could collapse at any minute. Cover him while bullets flew.

But this moment? With this man?

I squeezed my eyes shut. The goosebumps calmed and the instinct to run faded. He was my home. My anchor. And I could do this.

"Bella, are you alright?"

He was nothing I was looking for. But everything I needed.

Breath rushed in, burning my lungs. "You'll never leave me, will you?"

"Never, amore." He kissed my temple. For him, it was as simple as that. "I want to be your partner, Samantha. In all things. I think I've been clear about that, but if not, there it is."

I opened my eyes, tears welling against my lids, but I had to look at him. "I'm so sorry."

His brows furrowed. "This is not the response I expected to those words."

"Antonio, I—" I sucked in a deep breath, and let it all go. The pain, the regret, the loneliness. Dad. Janelle. Vincenzo. Mom. Matt. "I love you so much."

His smile faltered, and he blinked several times. "Mi scusi?"

I'd held it in so long, it was a surprising relief to let it out. I looked at the ceiling, blinking away the tears before they could ruin my makeup. Then brought my gaze back down and just kept going. "I love you. I love your stupid jokes, your damn smirk, your ridiculous hair."

His stunned silence was the most beautiful thing I'd ever seen.

"I love that look in your eyes that says how much I mean to you. You make me feel so safe and special, like I'm a treasure that's all yours." My tears faded as the knot in my stomach untwisted. For the first time in longer than I could remember, my feelings were right out there and it was alright. "A million times over, I love you."

"Oh, bella," he breathed, taking my face in his big, strong hands. His jaw flexed, and he smiled, shaking his head. "All the angels in heaven could never sing anything near as beautiful as those words.”

I laughed, leaning forward until my forehead touched his. “You are so cheesy.”

“I love you, too, Samantha.” He chuckled, inching closer to me on the bed, wrapping his arms around my waist while mine slid around his neck. “And can I just say how wonderful it is to say 'too' at the end of that?”

CHAPTER 40
ANTONIO

I PULLED Samantha close as the elevator descended. She'd withdraw from me and put on the public face the moment it rang to announce our arrival at the lobby. And I'd have to content myself with holding her on the dance floor. "Say it again, bella."

She pressed her cheek to mine and whispered, "I love you."

I squeezed her and chuckled. "Good."

The elevator stopped, the bell chimed, and she moved back. She threaded her arm around my offered elbow and nudged me with a hip. "Very funny, Ferraro."

We stepped into the hotel lobby with its cream-colored marble floors and plush seating areas. The room was crowded with dark suits, tuxedos, and evening gowns, the laughter and quiet conversations creating a buzz akin to privacy.

To the right, out of the elevator bank, the conference center's wide beige carpet stretched out before us, dotted with navy and persimmon swirls. Dimmed pot lights and caged chandeliers illuminated the space, while soft instrumental music floated out of the doors open into the ballroom.

I pressed my lips to Samantha's temple. That evening was the most remarkable thing in the world. She smiled and tightened her grip on my arm, giving me a private wink.

Samantha Caine loved me. I'd known this since our time together in Napoli, deep inside my heart. But to hear the words was a magic all its own. She loved me.

Everything would be perfect. Dinner, dancing, and some alcohol. I'd introduce her to my friends. There would be conversation and laughter. And after celebrating at midnight, we would go back up to our room and make love.

And then, finally, I'd fall to one knee and offer her the ring. She would stare and blink for a few moments, but she'd say yes. Truly, she'd say *not yet* or say I was losing my mind. But she loved me. Leaping over that hurdle meant the world for her, and tonight would be so wonderful that she'd see our future together, just as I glimpsed it the night we met.

She raised a hand to wave down the hallway, and I craned my head to see who she was waving at. There were easily over a hundred people milling about before dinner was served.

"Jimmy!" she shouted, and I caught sight of her friend in his police uniform.

He waved back and shook the hand of the man he was speaking with, who headed into the ballroom as we arrived. He nodded to us, a tight smile broadening. "Heya, Sammy! Dr. Ferraro. Don't you two look wonderful?"

"Didn't you say you were working tonight?" Samantha asked.

He hooked his thumbs into his duty belt and rocked back on his heels. "Shift starts in a half-hour. Told you I'd come by to say hello."

"How do Kim and the kids feel about you missing New Year's?"

His smile faltered, but it recovered quickly. "The kids are young. They can't stay up that late."

"I don't suppose you have any news on the Johnsons?"

"Bella." I clutched her hand to my body. "This is a night to celebrate, not to talk shop."

"Janelle didn't give you an update?" Jimmy tipped his hat up when Samantha and I shook our heads. "Prosecutor's office is going hard on them, especially the father. Defender's got a good case for the son to be released, but that ain't happening anytime soon."

A smile spread across her face. "Nathan Miller handling it?"

Miller again. Standing up for her in ways I could not. Inserting himself into her life. But he was a friend—a lifelong friend—and I'd accepted that.

"Right." Jimmy nodded, casting a glance at me, then back to her. "You and Miller are friends, aren't ya?"

She squeezed my arm, a subtle message that she knew tonight was about us. "We should let you go, Jimmy."

"Yeah, I'll see you two later." He gave us a casual salute and headed toward the main doors.

I sighed and kissed her cheek, inhaling the scent of her skin. "I'd like to have one day and one night with you, when there is no thought of danger or pursuing criminals. Just you and me."

"It's not exactly going to be just you and me in there," she said, gesturing into the ballroom.

"We could head back upstairs?"

She frowned and rolled her eyes at me, as was to be

expected. "Between the dress, the shoes, and the hair, I'm obligated."

The four ballrooms had been opened up to create a grand space for the event. Hundreds of mirror balls hung from the ceiling at different heights, while white spotlights shone across them, reflecting on every surface. Round tables were set for a dozen a piece, with black tablecloths and silver decorations. Each place setting included a noisemaker, New Year's celebration-wear, and bundles of white, gold, and silver balloons.

We were slow to get to our table as dozens of people stopped me along the way. It was good to see me back in Michigan, some said. Some voiced concerns about the shooting at the office. Others were surprised I was returning to Napoli.

And a few women gave Samantha an obvious glare. Her smile gradually faded into a frown, which wouldn't get me a *Yes* later that evening. So, I wrapped my arm around her waist as we moved through the crowd, pronounced with extra vigor that she was my girlfriend, and took her left hand with mine, ensuring our rings were on display when any of the so-called Calendar Club was nearby.

Not to mention the particularly handsome man whose pale gray eyes lingered on Samantha longer than they should have. For a moment, I considered having words with him, but I'd promised to get over the jealousy. She was with *me*. She loved *me*. I had nothing to fear.

All the same, I kissed her ring for the fifth time, at least.

"What are you doing?" she asked.

"Showing off the woman who loves me?"

Her lips tightened and she shook her head.

Only three people asked about our wedding. I told the first

it was a small affair in Napoli, as I'd told Irene. Samantha elbowed me for that, and whispered once we were out of earshot, "You're going to have to put an end to that, you know."

I pulled her closer and winked at her again. "Or we could head to Vegas?"

She frowned, somehow missing the point of my gentle nudge. "Why would we go to Vegas?"

"We could celebrate the start of our first full year together as newlyweds. Then we've not lied to anyone." I took her left hand to my lips. "Except Irene about the pregnancy, but we could at least practice—"

She nudged me with a hip. "You're ridiculous."

"I prefer..." I pulled her closer, nose brushing her ear as I breathed, "Relentless."

"Annoying." But she grinned and didn't say no, which was always a positive with her.

At our table, I held Samantha's chair out for her and introduced myself to the group. Last-minute tickets meant I hadn't been able to arrange sitting with those I knew.

The woman next to Samantha asked about her dress, and the two began speaking. I draped an arm over her chair back, stroking a thumb across her shoulder, and waved to another friend at the table beyond ours.

A group of servers approached and plates of field greens with goat cheese, pears, and pecans arrived in front of us. As did two men to occupy the seats next to me.

The closest was heavyset, in an impeccably cut tuxedo and dark blond hair in a low pompadour. His hazel eyes flashed up and down me as he put out his hand. "Tyler Nelson. And you are?"

"Antonio Ferraro. It's a pleasure." I shook his hand, then extended mine to the man who'd arrived with him.

The other man was slender, with light brown crewcut hair and a short beard. His eyes were deep set under a furrowed brow. And he was staring at Samantha.

"Matthew honey," Tyler said in a voice which was half singsong, half commandment. "This is Antonio Ferraro."

"What?" Matthew startled and looked down at my offered hand, taking it immediately. "Sorry. Ferraro, you say?"

"Sì. And you are?"

"Matt Foster."

I held his hand a moment longer than I should have. "*The* Matt Foster?"

"Shit," came Samantha's whisper behind me, likely meaning to have used her inside voice. But it did answer my question. This was her ex-husband.

"Sam!" exclaimed Tyler, who shot out of his chair and pulled hers out.

She stood, accepting his embrace, following suit with Matthew.

The gentlemen sat, and Samantha squared to the table. She took a gulp of the red wine in front of her and picked at her salad.

I leaned close to her. "Will this be too awkward? Should we trade seats with someone or—"

She shook her head and put her fork down. "If I weren't so stubborn, I'd say we should go back upstairs."

"Admitting it is half the battle." With a laugh, I kissed her temple and her tense face eased.

"I'll be fine." Her hand found my cheek, the soft look in

her eyes sending warmth through my chest. She mouthed, *Love you.*

Tyler touched my arm. "You're the one who took Sam to the hospital gala in the summer, aren't you?"

I turned to face the men. "It was more that we were not on speaking terms, my sister conspired for us to run into each other here, and we agreed to make a date out of it."

Samantha nudged my shoulder. "Stop that."

"That sounds like a good story," said Tyler.

"Sì, it's an excellent story, but telling it would likely require that Samantha not be sitting next to me."

Tyler laughed. "She's always been so serious."

Samantha dropped her fork onto her empty plate and held her wineglass toward a server. She had told me her ex-husband had left her for another man, whom he'd married. Obviously, this was Tyler, but she had not told me she knew him separately from Matthew.

"Have you known her long?" I asked.

He put his hand on my arm. "Good heavens, yes."

"This will be an entertaining dinner. I have not met many of Samantha's friends outside of her family." Picking up my fork, I dug into my salad. "I want to know everything there is to know about her."

Matt leaned forward and raised his voice enough for Samantha to hear him over the hum of voices and background music. "How goes the thinking, Sam?"

"Trying to enjoy the food right now, Matt." She speared a piece of cheese from my salad.

"Thinking?" I asked.

Matt looked from her to me and back again, his brow creasing. "Just a work thing."

"Work thing?" There was an unspoken conversation between them, but I'd no idea what it was.

A server arrived to refill her wineglass and she took another swallow. "Matt's trying to get me to sign on with Foster permanently."

Every molecule of my body wished to rejoice. Throw down the fork, leap from my seat, and swing her around. A permanent job in Brenton was an even bigger step than finding her own apartment. But the way her shoulders sagged and Matt shifted uncomfortably in his seat. She didn't wish to speak of it, and he realized he'd stepped over a line.

Her FBI dream pulled her away from Brenton. Foster pulled her to it. And I made it clear I'd follow her regardless of which decision she made.

"I apologize, Matt." I patted Samantha's thigh. "She's not had much time to think, as I'm keeping her busy while I'm in town. After I leave, her brain will be free."

"You don't live here?" asked Matt.

We continued to speak through the meal, discussing travel, wine, and food. Matt and I shared a passion for cooking, so spent quite a lot of time trading favorite recipes. They told me stories of adventures the three of them had taken, avoiding anything which might cause too much discomfort for the divorced half of the conversation.

After her second glass of wine, Samantha grew more social, laughing and teasing the men over inside jokes going back a decade.

Once the meal was done, the dance floor opened and the music switched from the background to the foreground.

"If you'll excuse me, gentlemen." I stood and straightened

my jacket. "This is what I've been looking forward to since I got home."

I pulled out Samantha's chair and bowed, presenting a hand to her. She slid her fingers into my palm, her smile broadening with every passing second.

"Me, too," she said.

We wove between tables, between people pushing out their chairs and standing. It was time to dance, to mingle, to explore the dessert buffet. But all I wanted in the world was to hold my lovely girlfriend next to me and forget everything else existed.

We arrived on the dance floor—after several interruptions along the way—to a romantic song, sweet and lovely. I spun her slowly one time and brought her to me.

"How long until midnight?" she asked.

"Two more hours." I guided us around the floor, careful with her in the heels she called excessive. "Brazil and Greenland are ringing in the New Year now. We could join them."

"No," she said playfully. "You brought me here to dance, so that's what we're going to do."

The music shifted from slow to fast. Romantic to energetic. She held tight to me, a wicked grin creasing her face. "This makes me think of the music at La Fiamma. Probably shouldn't dance like we did there."

I bit down on my lip, swaying my hips against hers. "Probably not. We might get kicked out."

The glint in her eye told me one more glass of wine and she'd likely do it anyway. I pulled away from her, maintaining a hold on her hands, and we switched to an easy hustle with a few turns and separations, so I didn't stress my shoulder or her balance.

"Spoil sport," she said with a laugh when I pulled her close before pushing her away again.

The crowd grew thicker the longer the music played, and several people interrupted our dance to say hello. Men I worked with, women I volunteered with, attendees at my parties. They came and went, hugs and cheek kisses. Everyone was gracious, and a few even remembered meeting Samantha at the charity gala.

After an hour, Samantha leaned to my ear. "My feet are sore and I want dessert."

I nodded and led her from the dance floor, heading toward the buffet.

On our way, a server with bright green eyes and thick glasses crossed our path. He balanced a large silver tray on one hand with a single glass of champagne he offered to Samantha. She took it while I grabbed one from another server with a full tray.

She shriveled her nose at the first sip. "It's kind of bitter."

More likely, she'd had too much wine and her taste buds needed help. I gestured to the dessert buffet, with its display of chocolate-covered strawberries. "I know exactly what can fix that."

"Good idea!"

I offered her a small plate with one strawberry to test.

She bit into it, then took her champagne. "Yeah, much better."

CHAPTER 41
SAMANTHA

I DRAINED the last of my champagne flute. That, plus the two—or three?—glasses of wine were hitting me hard. It had been a long week and a half with Antonio. Stress, joy, love, and nowhere near enough sleep.

Good thing I had a couple weeks of leave scheduled. There would be some serious recovery time needed once he left.

Antonio laughed at something Ty said, and I turned to look at them. Too fast. The room kept turning, although I was sure I'd stopped moving. I should have paid more attention to what I was drinking, rather than using it to avoid any conversation between my boyfriend and my ex-husband.

My stomach churned before the room settled.

I tapped Antonio's arm and he leaned his ear to me. "I'm going to the ladies' room."

He kissed my cheek and smiled.

I collected my clutch and stood slowly, bracing my hands on the back of my chair. The heels of my shoes were way too high.

"You're cut off, bella," chuckled Antonio.

"No kidding." I covered my mouth to hold a giggle inside, then leaned closer to keep my voice down. "Any more and you may have to wait until tomorrow."

He whispered, "Are there any private bathrooms?"

"We have a room upstairs." The giggle erupted. Heat would have flushed up my cheeks, but they were already warm from the alcohol. "I'm not having sex with you in a bathroom again."

"Your loss." He winked and I just shook my head, making my way through the party.

My reflexes were slow, and I nearly collided with a few people as I walked. The reflection of the mirror balls had been beautiful when we arrived, but they were too bright now. Too many colors and they moved too fast. The music was too loud. There were too many people.

An itch started at the back of my neck. I had to get out of the space. My heart was screaming, beating fast from a casual walk. This wasn't right. I needed a cool washcloth on my forehead or something.

I exited the wide double-doors from the ballroom, everything spinning faster until I leaned against the doorframe. With my eyes shut, I took soothing breaths until it stopped. Where were the bathrooms? I'd been here before but couldn't remember. To the left, maybe?

One careful step after another and I found the sign pointing me forward. Almost there. A trickle of sweat ran down my chest. It was so hot in there.

An older woman passed me, head down to her phone. She wore a white pantsuit with a clutch under her arm and a long flowered scarf in pinks and blues. "These washrooms are closed. You need to use the ones down the hall." She gestured vaguely behind her, not taking her eyes off her phone. "Hang a right just before the hotel doors."

"Thanks." I blinked rapidly, trying to force the hallway into focus. Bracing a hand on the wall to maintain my balance, I continued toward the entry to the hotel. My lungs couldn't grab enough air and I had to stare at the floor as I walked, otherwise I'd fall over.

I turned into the side corridor she must have meant. No washroom signs, but everything was so hazy I wouldn't have been able to see it anyway. Just had to splash water on my face. Then I'd be fine.

Ten feet or fifty feet down the hallway—I couldn't tell—I stopped and leaned my back against the wall. The stupid shoes were hard to walk in. I slipped one off and my toes rejoiced.

Soft footfalls approached from the end of the corridor. Why weren't there more women down here if the other bathroom was closed? My head snapped up to see who it was, sending the entire world into a spin.

I was falling.

Or not.

The wall was still at my back.

Or was that the floor?

"Had a bit too much to drink?" came a voice from the direction of the footsteps.

"I hate these shoes." I clamped my eyes shut and pressed my head back. It was definitely the wall. I was still vertical. "Can you help me get to the bathroom? I think I need to throw up."

Yeah, that would make me feel better.

"I'll help." It was a male voice, something familiar in it. An accent, a clipped tone, a something.

I cracked one eye open.

He was almost next to me. His eyes were so bright. So green. I knew those eyes. But from where?

"Do I...?" My mouth felt like it was stuffed with cotton.

He lifted my arm and wrapped it around his shoulder. "Walk with me. I got you."

Say thanks, Sam.

Spots appeared at the edge of my vision and a wave of heat flashed through my entire body, just before all my food came up in a rush, pouring out over the carpet.

The man groaned and threaded his arm around my waist, holding me up when my knees buckled.

Then the darkness pulled me under.

Eyes glued shut.

Vomit on my tongue.

My head throbbed.

Relax, Sam. One. Observe.

Scent: Vanilla and amber.

Sound: Voices bickering.

Touch: Nothing. Couldn't move my body.

Two. What was two? Where was I?

"How long will she be like this?" Angry woman. Refined speech.

"You think I've done this before? He said it would last an hour." Angry man. Petulant. Argumentative. "But I don't know if that's from when she took it or when she passed out."

"Did she take the whole thing?"

"I don't know!" he shot back. "I hurried out to the

corridor as soon as I gave it to her. You were close to the ball-room. You should have watched."

Two glasses of wine and a glass of champagne, my ass.

I tried opening my eyes, but the lids refused to move. My head weighed at least fifty pounds. *Don't move it, anyway. Don't give yourself away.*

"You'll need to carry her downstairs when the car arrives." The woman was still angry but wouldn't take the actions herself. She was in charge.

"Carry her? I told you we should have gotten a room on the first floor."

"You fool. We can't book a room around here. Even if there were any left on New Year's Eve, we'd be caught."

"We should have used a maintenance closet."

She made a noise of disgust.

I surveyed my body, checking for sensations out of place. The headache. Sore neck from my head lolled forward. Something holding my mouth shut.

Something else was wrapped around my forearms. Wide, flat, and tight around the tops and sides, a narrow bar underneath. Duct tape holding me to a chair? Then it must have been duct tape over my mouth.

Oh shit.

My heart rate picked up and I held my breaths as long and slow as I could.

My stomach had settled with no food left in it, but energy jostled inside.

Relax, Sam. Observe.

One leg was covered, likely with my dress, the other cooler, so just covered by the stockings. Lower legs taped to the chair, too.

"When's he going to arrive?" she said. "We've only got so much time to deal with this and get to the house for the safe."

"And to pick up the paintings." The sound of clattering nearby, then water running.

"I told you that wasn't happening anymore. *This* will get us the real money and we won't be indebted to those lunatics."

Feet. Only one shoe on. Was the other still in that corridor? Would someone find it and figure this out?

I managed to crack an eye open, only enough for a blurry view of my lap and the floor. With my head down, that wouldn't give me away. The carpet—it was the same pattern as inside the hotel. Antonio's cologne in the air. He wasn't in the room; it was lingering from when we'd been there earlier.

What was two? Right. Orient.

I was in our hotel room. Duct taped to a chair. The man or the woman had put something in my drink and he'd brought me up here.

My phone buzzed somewhere in the room, in the distinctive pattern that indicated a text from Antonio. My clutch was here. Of course it was. They'd used my key card to get in. If I could get out of the chair and find the phone, I could call for help.

The tap stopped and the man must have grabbed the phone, as he said, "She just got a text from the boyfriend. He wants to know where she's gone."

The woman said, "Text him back. Say she's got a migraine or something."

"Phone's locked." He hummed. "It's facial recognition."

"Try water."

The tap sounded again, then stopped. Footsteps approached. I braced myself.

Cold water streamed over my head and I tried to gasp, but my mouth was taped shut. My head shot up, eyes flying wide. I pulled in as much air as I could through my nose, burning as some water came with the air.

The phone was directly in front of my face, held by a woman all in white. The one from downstairs who'd told me the bathrooms were closed?

She handed the phone to the man.

Oh god. It was Olivia Scott.

And the man was the waiter with the green eyes. No, wait. I recognized him. David Scott, in a disguise I'd been too distracted to notice.

I'd been right all along. They were back. For me.

The duct tape muffled my scream, and I tried pulling at the tape holding my arms and legs down but couldn't break through.

"Have a migraine. Sleeping it off," he said in a stilted voice, typing on my phone. A gun sat on the kitchenette counter next to him.

Olivia leaned in front of me. I threw my head forward to headbutt her, but she was too far away. The room spun again, bile rising in my throat.

She grinned. "Good to see you, too, Ms. Caine."

CHAPTER 42
ANTONIO

THE ROMANTIC EVENING with Samantha had taken a slight turn. She'd left for the bathroom over an hour ago and hadn't come back. It was a spectacular opportunity to speak with Matt and Tyler, though. I learned so much more from them than constantly-frowning-at-me Cassandra.

"Did she make you watch Die Hard?" chuckled Matt.

"Of course!" I waved a hand. "It's the best Christmas movie of all time, is it not?"

Tyler's gaze went heavenward. "You are perfect for her."

My phone buzzed in my pocket, and I pulled it out. She'd likely been cornered by someone she knew, electing to sit and chat with them instead of being embarrassed by my discussion with these men. I'd done two circuits around the room looking for her but had resigned to use a text when she was nowhere to be found.

Surely she wouldn't leave without telling me.

An odd knot twisted in my stomach. The text *was* from Samantha, but the words didn't feel right.

"Something wrong?" Tyler put his hand on my arm.

"She says she has a migraine."

Matt's brow furrowed deeper than it had been all evening. "Really?"

You're overreacting. "I don't recall her mentioning suffering from them. Is this common?"

"She'd deny just about any injury," said Matt. "But no, I don't remember her ever having one."

Tyler nodded. "Me, either."

I began typing a response. *Come down anyway*—no, not that. Maybe playful. *Do you need me to come up and*—no, not that either. The knot tightened. Had I pushed her too far? Did the Vegas teasing scare her off? She'd finally admitted she loved me. She wouldn't run after that.

"Excuse me, gentlemen." I slid the phone back into my pocket and smiled politely.

"I hope she's alright," said Matt.

"Sì, I'm sure she is." I hurried through the ballroom, nodding to people who tried to stop me for conversation. Waving instead of clasping hands and avoiding open arms for hugs.

Was she even upstairs? Was it all a ruse? Had she already left the building?

Perhaps it was news about the Johnsons or the Constable? She hated being late, but sometimes those things captured every brain cell and she lost herself.

Marone, she said she loved me. Was that the last straw for her? Did it terrify her so much she had to leave?

I hit the stairwell, taking the steps two at a time. *Stop doubting her.* She'd be up in our room, nursing the migraine. She'd be alone.

Or could it be Miller?

I stumbled as I hit the sixth floor landing and put a hand out to catch myself.

She wouldn't do that. Miller might, but she wouldn't.

Or that man with the gray eyes who'd been staring at her when we arrived.

She'd had far too much to drink. I'd only seen two glasses of wine and the champagne, but she must have had more when my attention was elsewhere. Had someone taken advantage of that?

I leaned against the wall and sucked in deep breaths. Arriving at the room in such a state wouldn't help anything.

No jealousy. She was not Faith, she wouldn't cheat on me.

Be yourself, Antonio. Light footsteps the rest of the way. Light voice. Teasing manner.

"Samantha?" I knocked gently on our door, but there was no response, so I pulled out my keycard and unlocked it. The security bar prevented it from opening more than a crack. At least that meant she was inside.

The lights were on. Shouldn't they be off if she had a migraine?

I called through the opening, "Bella, is everything alright?"

"I'm here." Her voice was strained. "Just waiting for my migraine meds to kick in."

"Unlatch the door so I can come in."

"No," she snapped, a sound sending a shock wave through me. "I need quiet right now and to not move. I'll be out in a few."

I swallowed hard, trying to keep my tone playful. Another man was not in there. "You've been up here an hour already. The countdown is in forty-five minutes. You'll miss it."

"Medication should take about fifteen more minutes. But

you know me." She paused, her speech slowing. "I'm always fifteen minutes late for everything. So make it thirty."

My stomach dropped. She was never late. And certainly not fifteen minutes late for everything. It was a code. Something was terribly wrong in there and she needed fifteen minutes.

"Sì," I said, trying to keep the panic at bay, repeating it back to her to acknowledge I'd understood. "You're always fifteen minutes late for everything. I'll see you downstairs in thirty."

I closed the door and set a fifteen minute timer on my watch. My brain fought to remain in control. I had to stroll to the stairwell in case someone was in the room with her, listening for me. I pulled out my phone once the door shut behind me. My fingers shook as I searched in my phone for the number she'd given me after the shooting at her hotel.

When he answered, I blurted, "Jimmy, this is Antonio Ferraro! Samantha's in trouble!"

CHAPTER 43
SAMANTHA

THE DOOR CLOSED, and Antonio's footfalls faded. David watched through the peephole, gun still pressed against where he'd aimed it at Antonio's head. David had changed a lot in the last four months. Once he'd stripped off the blond wig, I noticed his hair had thinned and he'd lost at least twenty pounds. His eyes weren't as sharp as they'd been in August. The man looked beaten down, which didn't bode well for me.

"Good job, Ms. Caine." Olivia smiled. "Your boyfriend gets to live."

"Why thirty minutes?" I pushed against the duct tape with my lower legs, attempting to twist at an angle—the only way I could rip through the tape.

Olivia sniffed, just as smug and condescending as the last time I'd seen her. "Because by then, we'll be long gone."

When Antonio first knocked, David sprang to the door with his gun and Olivia gave me the rushed instructions before ripping the tape off my mouth. I'd deviated only enough to pass the message to Antonio. Thank god, he'd understood and they hadn't.

The clock near the door read 11:17 p.m. I had thirteen minutes before Antonio came back.

But David still had the gun. If Antonio barged through that door in fifteen minutes, David would kill him. If I screamed, David would kill me.

I had to get the gun out of the equation. "Alright. What did you have planned for the next thirty minutes? Want to write up a confession about the forgery, blackmail, and murder? Maybe tell me how you kept ahead of the police so long?"

David spun from the door, pointing the gun at my head. "Those are lies. Kathy's framing my mother."

That was another change in David. I couldn't have imagined him attempting to kill someone, but the way he waved the gun around told me he could.

"And I bet you'd never drug and kidnap anyone, either, would you?" I surged forward, telegraphing how I couldn't get out of the chair while trying to weaken the tape. If I could get one arm free, or even a leg, I could do something.

"David." Olivia placed a hand on his arm, encouraging him to lower the weapon. "Don't let her provoke you. We're better than that."

"I know." He dropped the gun onto a writing desk along the wall by the door, massaging his fingers into his temples.

A slight popping sensation against my left shin as the duct tape tore a fraction of an inch. That was a start. "What's your plan? Why come back to Brenton when you got away with everything?"

"We're here to pick up—" David started, but a glare from his mother silenced him.

"You," she purred. "I'm accustomed to a certain lifestyle, and I have a feeling you can help provide that for me."

The room swam again and I tipped my head down, breathing through it. What was she talking about?

A buzzing noise sounded, but not from the direction of my phone. David said, "He's almost here. We need to get her downstairs."

"Load up the syringe."

I groaned, eyes still clamped shut, trying to free my leg. "You're not a murderer, David. Don't do this."

"Murderer?" chuckled Olivia, as she fisted a hand in my hair and yanked my head up, spiraling the room out of control. "What use are you dead? Alive, I'm sure your boyfriend would spend at least a couple million to get you back."

I sucked in a breath to scream, but David slapped the duct tape over my mouth again and Olivia let me go.

I glanced at the clock. Maybe it was 11:28 p.m. I couldn't be sure. But if I was right, I had two minutes until Antonio arrived. Two minutes to get the gun out of reach.

But if the room didn't stop moving, I wouldn't be able to do anything.

11:29 p.m.

A shiver wracked my body. I didn't hear Antonio coming. All I could do was hope I hadn't misread things. Trust him and assume he was going to be there on time.

I leaned forward in the chair, and the tape on my left leg snapped. With the chair still attached to my arms and one leg, I lurched as best as I could at David and the writing desk, knocking the desk over, sending the gun clattering to the ground. I landed on the floor on my side, and the tape on my other leg snapped.

David scrambled after the gun while Olivia charged after me.

"Little bitch!" Olivia yanked the scarf from her neck and wrapped it around my throat, pulling tight.

With my arms still secured to the chair, I couldn't get enough leverage to roll us or get her off me. She pulled hard, preventing any air from reaching my lungs. It loosened for a moment, then tightened, a hard knot in the fabric at the back of my neck.

The door exploded inward, Antonio's shoulder leading the way. "Samantha!" He rushed in and threw Olivia off me.

Jimmy came in next, service weapon drawn. He smiled when he saw Olivia. "Well, what do we have here? Where's Dav—"

I yelled behind the duct tape, trying to warn Jimmy, but David launched himself from his spot behind the door and tackled Jimmy to the ground.

Jimmy was down, not moving, and David grabbed Olivia, pulling her out of the room and down the hall. Antonio fumbled with the knotted scarf around my neck.

"Call the police!" David hollered as they ran. "Room 605! She's being attacked!"

I gulped in air once the scarf and duct tape were free. Antonio righted my chair and ripped the tape off my arms. Before he could say or do anything else, I scrambled to my feet, grabbed my phone and clutch, and sprinted out the door.

CHAPTER 44

ANTONIO

"Stop!" I charged down the hallway after Samantha. Her hair was wet, neck red, and she was far slower than usual.

When I'd seen her on the floor with Olivia on top of her—Marone. Thank heavens. This time, I was there to save her.

"Samantha!" I caught her arm and stopped, spinning her back to me.

She hauled on my grip, attempting to free herself, but stumbled. "I have to go after them!"

"Leave that to the police!"

"Fuck's sake, Antonio! I've left that to the police for the last four months and what's it gotten me? Almost dead!"

Her eyes flew past me and I turned to see Jimmy stumbling out of the room.

She yanked again and I switched to a two-handed grip.

"Cazzo, Samantha! What do you think you're going to do?"

"Catch them, just like I caught Parker." Her face was a mask of barely restrained fury. "So they can't do this again."

I squeezed her arms so tight she winced, and I backed off. "You're not even wearing shoes, woman!"

She looked down, as though she hadn't realized it. Her breaths came fast and ragged, and she closed her eyes, wavering side to side.

"What—what happened?" Jimmy reached us, one hand to the side of his head.

"David Scott hit you from behind." Samantha pulled against my grip again. "Let me go."

"Never," I growled.

"I need to get changed." She yanked one more time and freed herself. Three quick blinks, and she tore back to our room, with its damaged door.

I ran after her, no question in my mind that she was about to do something reckless. In the bedroom, she was already ripping her clothes off, changing into what she'd likely worn to the hotel.

So I did the same.

"What are you doing?" she snapped.

"Partners, remember?" I threw the expensive clothes on the floor, pulling on my jeans and sweater. "If I can't talk you out of doing something stupid, then I'm going with you."

Jimmy came in. "Leave this to the police, you two."

"You see, bella?" I gestured to him. "You should listen to your friend. He's a smart man."

"They said they're going to their house for a safe. Probably money and assets to sell. If we're fast enough, we can catch them. They thought I was unconscious when they were talking about it, so they don't know that I know." She focused on lacing her boots up, missing the bow on the first attempt.

"Call in backup or not, I don't care, but I'm not letting them get away this time."

She threw on her jacket as she sped out of the room, shoving her clutch and phone into her pockets. We charged down the hallway together to the stairs, knowing it would be faster than waiting for an elevator.

"Stop running!" Jimmy called from behind us, but we were already in the stairwell.

"Call backup," I yelled to him. The door swung shut. "My SUV is parked—"

"Don't care," she said, taking the bottom steps two at a time, stumbling into the wall at the third floor. "I'm taking my truck."

"Mine's faster."

"Mine's tougher."

We burst out of the door at the bottom of the stairwell, startling several partygoers in their finery. The hallway to the rear parking lot was between the Convention Center and hotel. A cheer went up from the ballroom on the other side of the wall and "Auld Lang Syne" began.

Flying through the exit, she asked, "Where's Jimmy?"

"No idea." I ran next to her, wanting to guide us to my car, but knowing she was right.

She pulled out her phone without missing a beat and hit the app, which started the engine. "There it is!"

I overtook her and grabbed the driver's door handle.

"I don't think so." She shoved an elbow into my ribs, but I didn't concede.

"You're slow, Samantha. And I saw something upstairs— you're dizzy, too. They drugged you, didn't they?"

Her nostrils flared and she punched the side of the truck,

racing around to the passenger door. Once inside, she pointed out the unfamiliar controls, plugged the address into the GPS system, and we were off.

We drove in silence for a few moments and the urgency, the anger and panic, diminished.

"Samantha, I don't know what—"

She made a cutting motion with her hand and started a phone call to Janelle. "We can talk about it later. Right now, we have work to do."

This was not her job, not her work to be done. But I would help, no matter what. She was my future and I wouldn't let her do this alone again.

The call went to voicemail. She left a brief message, instructing Janelle to call her as soon as possible. Next, she called Elliot. Also no answer, and she left the same message. Finally, she called Jimmy.

"Sammy! Where'd you go?"

"I told you." She clenched her fists. "They're going to their house, so we are, too."

"Right. That David's a tougher guy than I expected. Jostled a few brain cells loose. I'll call this in, send a couple patrol cars, and I'll meet you there."

I let the vehicle slow to near the speed limit. "We should wait for the police."

"I swear—" She ground the words out through clenched teeth. "—if you stop this vehicle, I will push you out and not look back."

When I didn't speed up, she smacked my arm. "What happened to you threatening to kill Parker with your bare hands if he took me from you?"

I hit the gas. "I meant if you were already dead, not if you were charging into danger like a careless fool!"

She flipped up the center console, where there was a safe. A safe? She dialed a combination and pulled out a handgun. "I have two. Do you want one?"

"Che cazzo, no!"

She unzipped her jacket and attached a holster to her belt on the right. Then withdrew a smaller gun and placed it in the inner breast pocket of her jacket. Two magazines went into her pockets.

"You think you're Rambo or something?"

"They had a gun, Antonio. If they hadn't, this would already be over with."

"But they didn't use it."

"Because I knocked it to the floor just before you got there." She leaned a hand on the dash and covered her mouth as though about to be sick. "When you came up to the room that first time, he had that gun pointed at your head."

I swallowed and pressed harder on the gas, maintaining focus on the road. There was ice, but her truck handled perfectly on it. "And at you?"

"Don't go there, Ferraro." She sat up, fingers rubbing at her throat. "We can't afford to get all weepy over what *almost* happened."

We rounded a corner onto Oak Street and she gestured to the Scotts' driveway. "Turn off the lights and park over here. I just hope we're not too late."

CHAPTER 45
SAMANTHA

Antonio turned off the lights and pulled to the side of the road before Kathy Becker's house. Beyond that was the Scotts'.

I put my hand on his atop the steering wheel. "I want you to stay in the truck."

He frowned. "Not a chance."

"I'll be too worried about you to function properly."

"And I'll be too worried about you to stay behind." He brought the hand to his lips, kissing hard.

"I can handle myself."

"Marone, do you remember where I found you? The noise you were making as she tried choking the life out of you?" He clenched the hand tight. "We're stronger together."

I folded a leg underneath me to raise myself up and over the center console, grabbing his head and pulling his lips to mine. When we separated, I whispered, "Just don't get hurt."

"Same goes for you."

This was why it was best to keep your circle of important people small. Fewer people to lose. But I would not lose him. I was putting an end to this. Not just for me or our future, but for Bobby—for the man who'd inspired me to go into the art field. He deserved better than what Olivia did to him.

I startled when my phone rang. Janelle. I put her on speaker. "Sam and Antonio here."

"Sam! Elliot's with me. We just got three credible sightings of David and Olivia in town tonight. Are you at the penthouse? Are you safe?"

"Safe?" I laughed. "They've already had me taped to a chair with a gun in Antonio's face. So no, I wouldn't call that safe."

"What?" There was a hint of surprise in her voice, but mostly anger. In her heart, she was still my protector.

"They said they were going to their house and so are we."

"Dammit, Ferraro," growled Janelle. "I thought you were smarter than this! Restrain her before she gets you both killed!"

"Have you ever tried that?" He tightened his grip on my hand, jaw set.

"Jimmy's going to be here with backup any minute." I looked at Antonio, at his big hand circling mine. He was all the strength I needed. "We're taking them down, Janelle."

I clicked off and ignored when she called back. It was dark down the road, no lights coming from the Scott house. "I don't think the police are here yet. If they were, we'd see their cars."

"We should wait for Jimmy."

I shook my head and opened the glove box, withdrawing a large, heavy flashlight plus a smaller one. "Let's go look around. Officers will be here soon, whether it's Jimmy, Janelle, or someone else. If you won't take a gun, take this."

He accepted the heavy flashlight.

We slid out into the dark night. It was a day past the full moon, and it reflected off the layer of snow which had fallen earlier in the week. We walked out on the road, clinging to whatever shadows we could find between the streetlights, avoiding the snow, where we'd be even more obvious to the eye and the ear.

In the summer, when the fire had happened, the trees and bushes were all full of life, and you couldn't see the house from the road. In the dead of winter, though, you could easily spot the sprawling ranch-style home, with its red-brick facade and two-car garage. The large stone planters, which had been knocked over five months ago by the firefighters, were still on their sides.

At the base of the driveway, I tapped Antonio and pointed to a few evergreens along the edge of the property. He nodded and we stayed low, watching the house for movement as we went.

We settled behind a tree, and my phone buzzed. I almost ignored it, in case it was Janelle and her warnings again. But it was Jimmy.

"Where are you?" I whispered when I answered.

"Sorry, Sammy, but it's New Year's Eve. It's a crazy night for us. It's gonna take longer than usual for anyone to react. I had to stop a guy stunting. Thought maybe he was drunk, but just an idiot."

A light passed by one of the windows in the house. "Shit. Jimmy, someone's in the house."

"Gimme five minutes," he said and hung up.

The front door and living room windows were still boarded up, just like when David and Olivia skipped town.

The back window to the living room likely was as well. If they were in there, one of the other doors would be open.

"Do you see any footprints?" I asked, peeking around the tall bush.

Antonio stretched up on his tiptoes, a hand on my shoulder for balance. "Sì, at the far end of the house."

I took a step in the direction he'd indicated, but he held me back.

"We know they're inside. We could wait out here and be sure they don't get away. Give Jimmy a chance to get here."

"They're too slippery. They could sneak out the back, head to the road on the far side of their property or use the gate in Kathy Becker's fence." I led him to the dark wood fence up the property line until we spotted the door where the footprints led.

Antonio reached the door first and peered through the edge of the glass. "No lights."

I pulled the gun out of my holster. "Let me go in first. No arguments. This really is what I've been trained for."

The muscles in his jaw flexed several times, a war no doubt going on in that brain of his. "Are you fully recovered?"

Probably not. Adrenaline would counteract some of what they'd given me. Hopefully. "Yes."

He nodded and I eased the door open. Turning on the small flashlight made me a target but leaving it off removed any chance of seeing them, so I flicked it on. We stepped gingerly through the mudroom. From there, around a corner, into the living room. I swept the flashlight from left to right.

And there she was. Olivia Scott. Standing over the spot at the back of the room where Bobby had died.

She froze in the light.

"Gotcha," I said, lifting my gun to point at her.

A wicked smile curved across her face. "You'd like to think so, wouldn't you?"

"Samantha," said Antonio behind me. He turned the big flashlight on and stepped forward, veering far enough away from me I couldn't reach him.

The flashlight lit the entire room so I could see David walking behind him.

Gun in the small of Antonio's back.

No, no, no, no, no.

"Drop your gun," ordered Olivia.

She was not getting the jump on me again. Not again.

But it was Antonio.

Was David capable of pulling the trigger? Only he knew for sure, and it wasn't a risk I was willing to take.

I put my hands up and slowly sank to the floor, placing my gun down. "You aren't a killer, David. Don't do this."

David gestured with the gun, directing me to the far side of the room. The space had once been a big, lemon-scented, wood-paneled room. Lots of white furniture, a grand piano, and breath-taking artwork. All that was left was a mass of charred sofas and love seats, a stain on the memories this room held for me.

He nudged Antonio, instructing him to join me in the dim light.

I leaned my head against his back. I should have waited. Whatever they gave me was still impacting my judgment, and I wasn't thinking clearly. "I'm sorry."

"Shoot him," said Olivia, her voice flat. "In the knee or something, and we'll take her."

David blanched. "That wasn't part of the plan. No one was supposed to get seriously hurt."

"David." I stepped out from behind Antonio, who tried to tuck me back, but I resisted. "Your mother paid Kathy Becker fifty thousand dollars to kill your father. Do you really think she'd stop at demanding you shoot someone?"

"Lies." David's eyes flicked to Olivia, as though searching for instructions.

"You little whore," she whispered. "Plan be damned—shoot her!"

"I kept telling myself it was all lies, that you wouldn't hurt anyone, but..." David continued pointing his gun at us, but his focus was on his mother, pain etching his face. "It's all true, isn't it?"

The side door opened and closed. No voices, just footsteps and a bright flashlight. The police wouldn't come in like that, so it wasn't them.

Olivia saw the person coming in before we could. "It's about time you got here. You were supposed to drive us from the hotel."

CHAPTER 46
SAMANTHA

"Fix this." Olivia's hand shot up to point at Antonio and me. Her eyes were on the newcomer, still in shadow. "Shoot him."

"That ain't gonna happen."

My heart fell. I knew that voice.

Jimmy stepped into the room, sweeping his flashlight around the space.

"Come back on New Year's Eve, you said." Olivia glowered at Jimmy, her chin raised like she was in charge. "Easiest night to avoid the busy police."

"That's enough, Olivia." Jimmy's unnatural calm, plus how familiar he seemed to be with Olivia, sent shivers along my spine. He placed his flashlight on the sofa in front of him, lighting the room. "You don't wanna be confessing all that without your lawyer present."

"Lawyer? Are you trying to play innocent here? Useless. Both of you." She huffed and rolled her eyes, then held out her hand to David. "Give me the gun, David. I'll take care of this."

David's gaze wandered back and forth, unable to land on a

single person. "You said kidnap her, mother. The gun was just to scare them."

Jimmy's hand went to his duty belt and the pop of his holster practically echoed through the room. "Quiet, you two."

Not dropping her hand, Olivia said, "Really, *Officer* Slater? You had no problem getting the drugs to spike her drink—"

He what? No wonder it tasted so bitter. Antonio's hand flew to mine and he took another half-step in front of me, blocking part of my right arm from Jimmy's view.

"—or planning to pick us up and deliver her to whoever your contact is—"

Jimmy drew.

A deafening crack.

A flash of light and puff of smoke.

Ringing in my ears.

Antonio startled and took another half-step in front of me.

Olivia collapsed—a dot of red marring her forehead—in the same spot Bobby had died. David let out a wail and ran to her body.

Jimmy shook his head. "Nope, I haven't been alright with this for a while."

I sucked in a quick breath, pulse pounding in my ears. "Jimmy! What did you do?"

"That probably wasn't the right choice, was it, Sammy?"

"No," I breathed out. It didn't make sense. Jimmy had a deal with Olivia? He was involved with them avoiding the police. Tonight's kidnapping. Smuggling artwork. How far back did it go? What else had he done?

"Stand up, David." Jimmy gestured at David with his pistol. "I got a feeling my old friend Sammy ain't gonna listen to me anymore, so I need you to tell her the truth about Parker."

His head was just visible over the burned furniture, tears streaking his face. "She was guilty, wasn't she?"

Jimmy said, "Yeah, she was."

"I should have known." David wiped at his tears with his sleeve, ignoring Jimmy's orders. "I tried to convince her to come back and mount a legal defense, but she refused. Then the plan to transport those paintings to Boston, kidnap her... Doesn't sound like a law-abiding woman, does it?"

Antonio squeezed my hand. "What about Parker?"

David finally looked up, but it was at Jimmy, not us. "We went through the insurance money fast and were coming back for more. That and we were going to take some paintings to Boston for Parker, but his girlfriend screwed up and someone found one of them. He said he was taking care of it."

That must have been the Constable and the other two paintings from the LA theft. Or maybe all of the ones in his hiding hole in the house. If I'd waited for the original showing date, they would have been gone. At least I had that as my legacy.

"Who were you delivering them to?" I could help break Elliot's case, if we survived.

"You two..." David's gaze traveled back to me and Antonio, and the sharpness that had been in his eyes in the summer returned for a moment. He began rising, gun in hand. "Just like Parker and my mother said, you ruin everything."

The room swam. It was cold but sweat dripped down my back. The flashlights, the sound of the winter wind against the boarded-up windows, the remaining scent of ash in the air. I tightened my grip on Antonio's hand. What else was there to do?

"Put that down," said Jimmy, sights trained on David. "I'm going to take you in now and you can find yourself a lawyer."

"No. I've been following your orders for long enough." David closed his eyes and swung the gun in Jimmy's direction. "He's behind all of—"

Another crack, a flash of light, and David fell dead next to his mother.

CHAPTER 47
ANTONIO

IT WAS quiet in the ruined husk of the Scotts' house. Were my ears not ringing, I would've heard nothing more than Samantha's breath next to me.

A pile of burned furniture crowded the middle of the room, creating too many obstacles between us and Jimmy. He drew and aimed too fast. We wouldn't be able to stop him from where we were. As David and Olivia had spoken, I'd taken small steps to maneuver myself into a better position.

But now, they both lay dead. And Jimmy's attention would be solely on us.

There was no sneaking left.

All the windows to the room were boarded up. No escape there. Jimmy was between us and the door we'd come in. We could make a dash down the hallway behind us, but it was too long to avoid gunshots.

I could shut off my flashlight, but Jimmy had strategically placed his to light the entire room. And even if we ducked behind the furniture, his bullets would penetrate that.

Add to all that, Samantha had wavered once more. Whatever they put in her drink was still affecting her.

How was I going to get her out of this?

"Goddamnit!" Jimmy stomped a foot and pressed his wrists against his eyes, not letting go of the gun.

I took another step forward.

His eyes snapped open, focused on the place at the back of the room where the Scotts had fallen. "You could have just come peacefully!"

A buzzing sounded behind me. Someone was calling Samantha.

"Alright." Her voice was surprisingly steady throughout the entire ordeal. "Now that they're all taken care of, let's—"

Jimmy waved the gun in our direction, using it as a pointer. "This wasn't how it was supposed to go tonight."

"That's okay, Jimmy," she said. "It was obviously self-defense."

"She was right," he said, staring up at the burned ceiling.

Another step. I let go of Samantha's hand but saw her in my periphery. She moved with me, staying to my side, where part of my body still blocked hers. For once, not trying to be the reckless protector. Letting me do *my* job.

"Olivia wasn't right about anything," she said. "You're not useless. Look at how much good you've done for Brenton. You were there for me when Parker came after us. There for both of us after he attacked the Ferraro's studio."

How long until Janelle and the backup arrived? Did we have enough time? Keep him talking, distracted. That was her play.

Jimmy shook his head. "No, Sammy, I mean Kim. You asked how she felt about me volunteering for New Year's Eve?

Truth is, she left me two months ago. Took the kids and just left. I never was good enough for her."

I inclined my head, maintaining the same calm as she did. "I feel the same way about Samantha."

He pulled back an inch. "Seriously? Rich, handsome guy like you?"

"Sì, of course. We all feel like that at times."

"Nah, this ain't just *at times*, doc." His gaze fell to the floor, and he gestured behind the burned couch where the Scotts lay.

Another step.

"Kim hadn't been happy for years. Said I wasn't home enough, but I mean, I'd always planned on being a cop. She knew that." His gaze rose again. "You gotta let someone be who they are, you know?"

The buzzing came from behind me again. Jimmy's head tilted to look at Samantha, but before he got too suspicious, I brought his attention back to me, where it belonged.

"So, who are you, Jimmy?"

His focus returned to me, eyes crinkling around the edges, like he didn't understand the question. "I don't know why I started—maybe it was bitterness—but I let a few people get away with things. Shoplifter here, graffiti there. Problem is, you start doing stuff like that and certain people take notice. They expect you to keep doing it."

I gestured to the back of the room. "And that's how you got involved with the Scotts?"

"It went from some bogus contractor to Roger to his girl-friend, there, and her painting. They started paying me to do more and I thought maybe the money could help change Kim's mind." He flailed a hand in the direction of the bodies.

"But then I got in with Parker and that's where things got bad. His buddies at that pawnshop in Detroit had me—"

"Which one?" blurted Samantha, but Jimmy didn't seem to register it.

"—sneaking items into buildings before fires. Planting evidence." He tapped his forehead with the butt of his gun, walking closer to us until he stood next to the remains of a grand piano. He was maybe twenty feet away, which might be close enough to get to him before he could aim. "You wanna know who I am? I'm nothing more than a dirty cop."

"No, Jimmy." I put up my hands and gave him a rueful smile, my calm exterior in dramatic contrast to the terrified energy zipping around inside me. "You're a man who was pushed to the edge."

Samantha came closer to me. With Jimmy's change in position, she was half-hidden by the left side of my body. She touched my back with her right hand, out of his view. Five fingers making very deliberate contact. "Let us help."

Jimmy spoke right over Samantha. "I'm stuck, doc. Once I did one thing for those guys, they had me covering for their golden boy, Parker. Geez-o-Pete, but am I glad that guy's locked up. He lost it after you two ruined the auction for him. They were gonna cut him loose, but he talked them into giving him a second chance with those paintings, which you two spoiled yet again."

"Who are they, Jimmy?" asked Samantha.

Marone, woman. I was focused on saving our lives and she still insisted on solving every crime on the planet.

"Thing is, I didn't wanna hurt anyone. I told Parker I was throwing his ass in jail after he went to your hotel, but he threatened to tell everyone what I've been doing, so I found someone else. And then this kidnapping idea was the only thing I could think of to keep you safe. But you two ruined that plan, too." Jimmy's gaze fell toward the bodies, and Samantha and I took a small step in unison. "Then David and Olivia, they told you too much. What am I supposed to do now?"

Samantha shifted further behind me, withdrew her fingers, coughed, and put her hand back. "Just let us go, Jimmy. We won't tell anyone you killed David and Olivia."

"But I did, Sammy. Nothing's going to change that." His body sagged as he looked up at me. "I thought I was in too deep an hour ago but look at me now. I've got nothing left."

"Jimmy, you're a hero," whispered Samantha. "You saved my life. You caught the Scotts after the FBI couldn't for months."

His brows knit together in confusion, and he took a half-step toward us. "You don't get it. I tried leaving these people before this fire, but they threatened my family!" He flung his arms wide, and I tensed each time the gun swerved in our direction. "I got deeper and deeper, hoping to save my family, and Kim left me anyway!"

I'd seen this desperation too many times when I worked for my uncle Giovanni. Every decision drove people further and further away from who they genuinely were. One terrible choice after another, leading them down the path to hell. The path I'd almost taken.

Time to use that experience. "You didn't answer Samantha's questions. Do you know the men behind Parker?"

Jimmy shook his head. "Just the middlemen."

"Samantha didn't know this, but you've forced my hand. My uncle Giovanni owns the pawnshop."

An almost imperceptible hiss of air from behind me, and Samantha's fingers faltered.

"Of course!" Jimmy's mouth fell open. "I overhead Special Agent Skinner talking to Nathan Miller about his involvement in some—aw, geez—so your family's behind the smuggling ring they're investigating?"

This explained so much to me. Why Special Agent Skinner told Samantha about my Zio Giovanni being a complication in her background check. Why Miller claimed to know my family.

All the better for this lie.

I nodded to Jimmy, deepening my voice to add weight to my words. "Now that you're in my world, you know you need to put that gun down, sì?"

For the first time since he'd switched positions, he looked over my shoulder at Samantha.

"Because I guarantee, if you hurt me or my *pregnant wife* —" I gave her the clue she needed to understand what I was doing, growling out my words through clenched teeth. "—you and you family, no matter where they are, will pay. You will be last, and you will watch your children beg for their lives."

He tensed, eyes flicking back and forth. "But that only happens if they know I did it, right?"

"Trust me, the only way your family continues to breathe for another week is if you let us go."

Samantha let out a long exhale. "You don't want to cross the Ferraro family, Jimmy."

His head tilted and face scrunched up. "You can't be involved with this. I thought you were Miss Straight and Narrow?"

"He's the father of my child." She took a slow step to the

left and the fingers pressed harder into my back. "I'd do anything for him."

Every cell in my body demanded I move with her, block her off. But her words were an explicit recognition of my ruse and a signal she had a plan.

If only I knew what the plan was and could trust whatever they drugged her with was out of her system.

Sirens sounded in the distance, approaching quickly.

The five fingers switched to four.

Was I supposed to move out of the way? Duck? Run? Hit him?

Jimmy's gaze flew to the boarded-up front window.

Three fingers.

"What's this?" The sound grew louder, and Jimmy leaned toward the window, as though it were open to the outside. "Because I know I sure as hell didn't call in any backup."

Two fingers.

"Absolutely anything," she said.

One.

CHAPTER 48
SAMANTHA

My hand left Antonio's back and dug into the breast pocket I'd opened when I'd coughed behind him.

Jimmy's wide arms swung to point the gun at us.

Antonio's flashlight beam hit Jimmy in the face, and he faltered. Then the flashlight was spinning through the air, with Antonio right behind.

I whipped my gun out.

The room lit from a gunshot.

Antonio yelled.

Then another shot.

Jimmy yelled.

Only one was mine, but it happened so fast, I didn't know which man I'd hit.

The sirens blared outside. Janelle was here. Thank god.

Antonio landed on Jimmy, the two of them crashing against the wall where the Chagall had once hung. Antonio's flashlight dropped, and the collision knocked Jimmy's off the couch. Beams of light whipped through the room as the flashlights came to rest.

"Antonio!" I screamed.

They grunted as they rolled on the floor.

I threw my gun into my pocket and launched myself over the remains of the piano to grab a light.

Pounding on the front door. "Police! Open up!"

The unmistakable sound of fist meeting flesh sounded and Jimmy let out a cry of pain.

"Cazzo." Another thud. "Madre." Another.

My fingers wrapped around a flashlight, and I shone it on them. Antonio was on top of Jimmy, whose feet kicked and his hands dug at Antonio's arm. But Jimmy's face was already a bloody mess.

Antonio's fist flew and Jimmy's arms fell to his face.

The pounding came on the door again. "We're coming in!"

"Please," Jimmy groaned, blood trickling from his mouth, nose, and the corner of an eye.

Antonio's arm cocked back again, but I grabbed it.

"Stop."

He gave a weak yank, then flagged forward, catching himself with the other hand on Jimmy's chest.

"Where's his gun?" I let go of Antonio's arm, intending to search for the service revolver, coming away with blood. So much blood. "Antonio?"

His head rolled up, turning, turning, until he inclined it toward the back door. "It's over there."

I had to stop the bleed—had to neutralize the threat. The floor was still covered in a thick layer of dried sludge from the fire. Frantically, I ran the flashlight back and forth until I found them. Two guns. Jimmy's and the one I'd dropped when we arrived. Jimmy wouldn't be able to move that far with Antonio on top of him.

The front door blew open, more light sweeping the room. A man and a woman yelled, "Police! Hands up!"

"You should have killed me," moaned Jimmy. "I won't last in prison."

My hands flew up, shaking uncontrollably. "He's been shot!"

The flashlights—and likely guns—trained on Antonio. "Get the fuck off him! Now!"

He slumped further down, nodding his head. Slower and slower. Until he slipped onto the floor.

"No!" I screamed and fell to my knees next to him, but one of the officers hauled me back—into the waiting grip of another who cuffed me—and took my place at Antonio's side. "I think it's his arm. Put pressure on it."

New voices entered the house. Someone asked for the ambulance ETA. Someone else talked about getting me out of there.

"They tried to fucking kill me." Jimmy rolled to his side, rubbing at his chest, likely thanking his vest for saving his life.

"Don't you say another word, Slater." Janelle's voice rang clear through the room. She stalked past two officers setting up lights for the scene, stepped over the piano, and jabbed a finger at the one who'd cuffed me. "Take those off her and put them on Slater."

"What?" asked the officer holding me.

"Do it," said Elliot, flashing his credentials as he walked behind her.

"Did you hear it all?" While I was behind Antonio, I'd also

finally answered her repeated calls. And had her muted on speaker phone for the last of it.

"We heard enough." Elliot stopped in front of me while Janelle checked on Antonio. His eyebrow cocked. "Heard about the Ferraro family, too."

"You know it's not true, Elliot." I shook my head, unable to stop. "We're not married and I'm not pregnant. His family isn't behind this. It was all to convince him not to—" I choked back the sob. "David and Olivia are behind the couch over there. He just... Jimmy shot them to cover up what he was doing."

Janelle stood and came over to me, wrapping me up in her arms. "You should have answered my first text. When I found out Jimmy hadn't called in backup, everything started making sense. All the way back to the Scott fire case closing too fast."

"No more silent treatment. I promise." I leaned into her, the tremors becoming stronger, watching the two officers now tending to Antonio.

She stroked the back of my head. "He's going to be fine, Sam. Ambulance will be here soon."

CHAPTER 49
ANTONIO

THE BED WAS COMFORTABLE. Everything was comfortable. I was warm and cozy. But the scent was all wrong. It was clean, but no hint of vanilla anywhere.

Voices floated through the room, soft. One of them was Samantha. Why was she so far away? Was she sitting in the chaise? By the fireplace? Why were there multiple voices in my bedroom?

I cracked an eye open to find her. Pale yellow walls. A blue curtain hanging from the ceiling. This was not my bedroom. My head rolled toward the voices.

So many people over there. Samantha. Miller with his arm around her shoulders—which didn't actually bother me. Janelle in uniform. A man in a long white coat with his back to me. Heads nodded, Samantha brought a tissue to her eyes. They all looked tired.

"Samantha?" My throat was sore.

"Oh my god!" came her voice and she dashed across the room, twining her fingers in my left hand. She was so fast, this one. "How do you feel?"

I blinked at her, eyes fluttering closed for a moment. "Very tired."

The man in the white coat came to the other side. "Good morning, Tony."

"Steve?" I chuckled, the room coming into greater focus. The doctor had been one of my best friends in college, a friendship we'd rekindled once I moved back to town.

It was a hospital room. The curtains behind Steve were drawn, a sliver of light peeking around their edges.

"What time is it?"

Steve smiled and pushed back his sandy-blond hair. "It's morning. You came through surgery just fine."

"Surgery?" Flashes of memory came back to me. The Scott house. Samantha's fingers in my back. Two gunshots, but I'd only seen one muzzle flare. "Is Jimmy in custody?"

"He is." Janelle joined them at the edge of my bed. "And he's not going anywhere else anytime soon."

"Or ever." Miller rounded to the end of the bed. "We've got a recording from Sam's phone of your discussion about David and Olivia's murders. Video feed from the hotel of him, providing something to David to spike Sam's drink."

Janelle added, "We're waiting on a tox screen to find out what they gave her, but the top guesses only last a couple days, max. We're also working on bank and phone records. I have a feeling we're going to find a string of connections between him, the Scotts, and Parker Johnson. Sam suspects Jimmy was the one tipping them off about every solid lead we had."

Samantha's thumb rubbed circles on my hand, and she kept her speech soft. "I'm also guessing he's behind the missing ballistics from my hotel."

"Alright all of you," said Steve, in his doctor's voice. "Tony needs some sleep."

"When will I be discharged?" I asked.

"Probably this afternoon. Once we got you into surgery, we found the damage wasn't nearly as bad as feared. You got damn lucky, man. The bullet nicked your brachial artery, but it's mostly muscle damage to your right biceps. We'll go over it in more detail when you're more awake." He frowned at me. "I'm told you're planning on flying to Italy tomorrow, but I need to nix that. Give it an extra day or two and I'll get in touch with a hospital over there for the rest of your care."

I nodded. More time with Samantha and an excellent excuse for delaying work.

Steve patted my shin and walked to the door with Janelle.

Miller's face was tight. "Sam, can I have a minute?"

She looked at me, and I nodded.

"I'm not going anywhere, bella. For real."

Once she was out of earshot, Miller came to my side. "I told you to look after my girl, and it looks like you did a damn good job of that."

"She's all that matters."

"But let me be clear with you." He lowered his voice, nostrils flaring. "She's my little sister in every way but blood. And if she comes away from one more visit with you with more scars, we're going to have a problem, you and I."

"I understand." I was too tired to threaten him back, but he was right anyway. Tonight started with the Scotts thinking I'd pay money for her ransom, and ended with them dead, and us almost as well.

"Good." He gave a slight nod and left the room.

The door closed behind him and Samantha turned off the

light, leaving the glow of the machines as our only illumination. Her brows pinched together as she neared the bed and kicked off her boots. Clenching her jaw, she waved at me to make space. I inched over, breathing through the pain in my right bicep with each movement. The original stitches felt pleasant compared to this.

I extended my left arm, and she crawled into the bed, nestling against me. She trembled as her hand eased onto my chest, avoiding the bandages and sling.

Hot breath hit my neck as she rattled out, "Don't you ever do something like that again."

"Shh, Samantha." I held her as best I could, while her shaking deepened.

"When you went down—" Her breath hitched and she gripped so tight, a pulse ran through my injured upper arm. "Oh my god, I was so scared."

This was Samantha, the woman I loved. So strong, so brave, so stubborn. In complete control in a high-stakes moment but overwhelmed when the emotions flooded out afterward. And now chastising me, in a desperate attempt not to let me see her break down.

"Do you remember when we were strolling along the Lungomare in Napoli, and you stopped that purse snatcher?"

She chuckled, the slight bounce piercing through my injury. "Don't go there, Ferraro. It was hardly *chased*. He was within crutch distance."

"I told you never to do that again and you told me—"

"'Next time, you'll have to be faster.'" She leaned her face to look up at me, those stunning eyes red-rimmed and bloodshot. I must have been a far worse sight than her.

"Well, bella, I was faster this time."

"You just needed to be the hero?"

"Did it work? Did it turn you on?"

Her laughter spluttered out, rapidly evolving into a full laugh we shared. "You are ridiculous, Antonio Ferraro!"

"And yet still you love me, sì?" I began to raise my right arm to brush the hair behind her ear, by instinct, but a stabbing pain overcame me and black spots crowded my vision. My eyes slid shut as I breathed deeply to center myself. I'd need stronger drugs if I was to make it through two more days together.

"I was afraid I'd lost you for good." Her hand left my chest and brushed along my cheek, to the hair above my ear. She pushed up from her position to take my lips with hers, and we kissed gently. "I love you, and you're not allowed to leave me."

"So, you're willing to discuss the trip to Vegas?" My wink caused her face to flush and her eyes to roll.

"Stop! I'm being serious!"

More than anything, I wanted to tell her I was being serious as well. The ring was at the hotel though, and she wouldn't believe me without it. This was the delicate dance required to win Samantha's heart, and the music would have to continue until we found ourselves another perfect moment.

"You were amazing tonight, bella."

"If he hadn't been wearing that vest..." She sucked in a ragged breath, unable to say the obvious—that she would have killed her old friend to save us.

"But he was. And you and I made it out of there."

Samantha sniffled. "Stronger together, right?"

"We are." Squeezing her with my good arm, I said, "We'll be here some time longer. How about we get some sleep?"

She kissed my cheek and wrapped around me, settling her

head on my chest. "Maybe we could convince them you need to stay another night and we could just rest?"

I inhaled her fresh citrus scent, letting it wash over me, letting it replace the antiseptic smell of the hospital room. My hand stroked her back, soothing her. "No, bella, we've not yet made love in the wine cellar. I need to get you home."

"You don't have a wine cellar." Her face was hidden from me, but I could hear the frown in her words.

"I have a nook where the wine is kept."

"Oh my god." She yawned, her head becoming heavier. "You forget you were just shot?"

"I've had worse."

"I know." Her breathing slowed and I gave up on the teasing. Instead, I rubbed her back and hummed a gentle melody until she was asleep.

Protect everyone she cared about—that was her motto—and worry about herself later. That would become my job; being the one who looked out for her while she looked out for everyone else. And right now, that meant rest, so she would have at least the hours until they discharged me.

For all the adventure of my visit, the highs and the lows, our relationship was stronger and we were safe. I could return to Napoli, knowing she would be alright, confident in her love for me, and with the knowledge Nathan Miller was no threat to us.

As I kissed her head one more time, the door inched open slowly. Light spilled through the crack, and Cassandra poked her head in. Before she could disappear, I waved her over. She paused, staring into the room, not moving. It was likely too dark for her to see.

"Cassandra, come in," I whispered.

She walked softly, making no noise, stopping at the side of the bed. "I got here as soon as I got the message. Nathan let me in."

As she raised a hand to place it on Samantha, I said, "She's sleeping."

"Is she alright?" Her voice trembled the same way her sister's did. "Nathan said they—"

"She's strong. She'll be alright. The drug they used will be out of her system in a few days, and the skin around her neck will heal quickly."

"And he said you were shot?" She touched my hand on Samantha's back. "Protecting her? I—I can't thank you—"

"I'll be fine." I squeezed Cassandra's hand and her eyes lifted to mine. "But I have a big favor to ask of you."

CHAPTER 50

SAMANTHA

Two days later, Antonio and I sat in my truck at the Departures door. His right arm was bound in a sling and he'd rearranged his flights to depart from Detroit instead of Lansing, so we had more time together before he left again.

"Life is never boring with you around, bella," he said.

"Me?" I laughed. "My life was plenty boring before you came around. Just the way I like it."

He kissed my hand and reached over to brush his knuckles along my cheek. "I'll miss this face. So much."

"Just four more months. We've already done it once."

"I have a small parting gift for you." He dug into his breast pocket and retrieved a few folded pieces of paper and handed them to me. "I know you said no more stuff, so it's... not *stuff*."

Taking the papers, I opened them, and my heart did a cartwheel. Airline tickets to Naples.

"You can come with me." He winked. "You're on leave anyway and when you get home, it will only be three and a half more months!"

I closed my eyes and sighed. "You know I can't. I promised Cass."

"This is your only defense?" He waved a dismissive hand and dug into the pocket again, producing a passport. "Who do you think gave me this?"

My hand shook as I reached for it. My passport, which had been safely tucked away at Cass's house with all of my other belongings. "How did you get this?"

"Your sister's exact words to me were: 'You had better not fuck this up.'"

I stared at the passport and the tickets and just laughed.

"Your suitcase is already in the truck. Just bring that with you."

Could it really be that simple? "Are you serious?"

He put his hand on mine and dipped his head, fluttering his eyelashes. "What was it you said when you showed up on my doorstep in August? 'I only want to be with you.' That was it, sì?"

It was. The butterflies hit me, and my heart started pounding.

"I don't want to say goodbye so soon. Come with me." Grinning, he added, "My arm hurts a great deal and I need a nurse."

I clutched the passport and tickets to my chest. "There is nothing on Earth I'd rather do." I reached over the center console and grabbed his neck, kissing him. I would not cry. "But I have a condition. We have to spend at least one night in that hotel in Naples with the amazing bed."

He separated from me only far enough to rest his forehead against mine. "Anything for the woman who loves me."

~

I STOOD AT OUR GATE, waiting for Antonio. They'd called first class, so it was time to board. I felt eyes on me from behind and turned around to see Elliot approach.

"Hi, Sam. Heading to New York?" he asked, nodding at the departure sign.

I shook my head. "Just one stop on the way. New York, Rome, then Naples."

He looked at the leather duffel bag on the floor next to me. "Going with Dr. Ferraro?"

"Yeah. He's buying a book." I gestured to the store he'd disappeared into. "You're not heading to Rome already? What about the Scotts and the Constable?"

"It's just a quick check-in with the team. I'll be back to wrap up my involvement with the Scott case and hand it over to the local police, then deal with the paintings."

"Art Crimes work is never done, is it?"

"Very true. By the way, we recovered the Constable painting and the other two from the Los Angeles theft—you were right about where they came from—plus a few from a different theft. All told, the reward for information leading to their return totals $50,000."

"Really?"

"Once they verify the paintings, the checks will be in the mail." He grinned at me.

Before he could say it, I held up a hand. "Not ready to sign the other letter yet. But this helps with the portfolio we discussed, I hope?"

"Very much. I'll make sure the right people hear about this."

"Do you think it's linked to your smuggling case?" I looked in the direction Antonio had disappeared.

"I can say this much: It looks like Parker's girlfriend, Camron, and the real estate agent were in the dark about everything. We found cameras inside that captured your visits to the house, which is likely how he identified you."

Antonio appeared out of a store and waved a book at me. My insides went all liquidy at the sight of him.

"And just a little more than I should share…" Elliot waved to Antonio but kept talking to me. "We raided the pawnshop in Detroit and are going through items and records to see if we can track any more information about who was supplying them. We're working on further warrants for the people who allegedly sold the stolen paintings to them, but that's proving more difficult than we expected."

Before Antonio was in earshot, I whispered, "Is the Ferraro family involved?"

"I've already made you the offer. I'll just keep baiting the hook until you bite." He patted me on the back and went to wait for his row to be called.

Antonio kissed me on the cheek when he arrived. "Any news from Special Agent Skinner?"

"Same old same old."

He smirked. "Trying to steal my girlfriend away from me?"

"Pretty much. He's heading to Rome for some meetings."

"We should day trip up and have a visit. I can show him around the city."

I leaned over to pick up his duffel, but he waved me away. "I don't think he'll be there that long."

"Just as well." He hefted the bag over his left shoulder, wincing. "Sharing you with Mario will be bad enough."

As we walked down the gangway to the plane, I put my hand on his back and leaned over to kiss his cheek. "I love you, Antonio."

"I love you, too, bella."

THE END OF BOOK 3

BOOK 4: Sam and Antonio are intercepted on their way to Naples and whisked off to his Uncle Giovanni's estate. Eyes and ears are everywhere, but it's an undercover Carabinieri officer who poses the greatest threat.

Continue the story with *Enduring Caine* at
https://janetoppedisano.com/EnduringCaine

BONUSES: Did you notice all the red flags about Jimmy? Each Caine & Ferraro book has a bonus page available to my newsletter subscribers, including a list of every hint I dropped in this book and in *Burning Caine*. Also available are the short story *Admiring Caine*, the free novella *The Phoenix Heist*, and a host of behind-the-scenes specials.

Join Janet's author newsletter and get all these bonuses only at
https://janetoppedisano.com/newsletter_caine

ACKNOWLEDGMENTS

Here we are at the end of an era. Well, sort of an end. *Disarming Caine* marks the third book in the Caine & Ferraro series, and the last one I had fully drafted before I decided to publish them. There are still two (or more!?) coming, but this is a landmark for me. I'll never forgot sitting in the Miami airport in November 2019, watching the rain pelt down outside, and hearing my flight home had been delayed. That turned into a missed connection, then an overnight at an airport hotel, and a five-hour layover in the smallest airport I've ever been in.

I'd just sent *Burning Caine* off to its very first reader, so I used the delay for something productive... I churned out the first 20,000 words of this novel before I got home! *Chasing Caine* wasn't even a blip in my brain at that point, I hadn't paired up with my amazing editor yet, and didn't even know how the publishing world worked.

Such an innocent time!!

There have been so many changes since those days—to me, the world, and definitely to my plans for the over-arching Caine & Ferraro story. I feel truly humbled by all that's happened and can't wait for the next chapter (or the next book, I guess you could say!).

As for this book... First, I have to say thanks again to my husband and son for their support. And I should apologize (again) to my son that I write books he's not allowed to read. Maybe I'll let him read this page and then snatch the book away from him?

Next, I'd like to thank my beta readers: Paula and Pat (my evergreen alpha readers turned beta readers), Colin, Missy, and Kari. Their feedback and encouragement are absolutely critical in ensuring I put out the best product possible.

Then on to my editor, Miranda Darrow. I'm so blessed to have found someone I gel so well with , despite her original edit letter for this book including a few "Oh hell no!" comments, mostly around the house for sale. She keeps me (and my characters) in line (mostly), and I truly appreciate it!

And finally, I'd like to thank you, my reader. Without you, I'd just be typing in my basement (or at my dining room table or in a hockey rink or in the car) for nothing. Knowing someone out there is going to read my words and find a little bit of enjoyment or an escape for a few hours means the world to me.

So yeah, thanks again.

- Janet

ABOUT JANET

Janet Oppedisano delivers award-winning romantic suspense with smart, driven women and sexy, protective men that will keep you on the edge of your seat. Her heroines excel in their fields and aren't looking for love—until they meet the charismatic heroes who fall hard and fast for them. Throw in gripping mysteries, heart-pounding danger, and a touch of history or legend, and you've got stories that keep you hooked.

With a Mountie father and a Navy diver husband, Janet's life has been steeped in adventure, inspiring her high-stakes stories. She's lived all over Canada, from the Maritimes to the Prairies, and her books reflect the authenticity and depth of her journey.

When she's not plotting her next twist, Janet is baking, hiking, traveling, or cheering for her hockey goalie son.

And if you're wondering about her last name, it's pronounced oh-ped-ih-SAH-no—just like it looks. Honest!

You can find Janet and all her social media links at:
https://janetoppedisano.com

* 9 7 8 1 7 7 7 8 8 5 6 5 6 *